PRAISE FOR *MACHINE OF DEATH*

"*Machine of Death* is a marvelous collection, riddled with intelligence, creative reach, and a frankness that makes the best use of the central gimmick." —*Onion A.V. Club*

"Existentialism was never so fun. Makes me wish I could die, too!" —Cory Doctorow

"Recalls the best writings of Harlan Ellison and Charles Beaumont...easily one of the most engaging slices of short stories I've had the pleasure to read in quite a long while... *Machine of Death* brought me laughs, terror, and tears...Highly recommended." —*Paradox*

"*Machine of Death* is a collection of stories the whole family can enjoy, especially the Addams Family...[As] a group, they [do] a remarkable job of exploring the cultural changes such a machine could bring." —*Milwaukee Journal-Sentinel*

"*Machine of Death* hooks you from page one...As editors, Malki !, North, and Bennardo should be commended. If it's cheap, sadistic thrills you crave you'd do better to let *Machine of Death* alone and catch up on your *Jersey Shore*—but if you'd like to think as well as be mightily entertained, you're in the right place." —*Strange Horizons*

"For an anthology that deals with the inevitability of death, *Machine of Death* is a lot of fun. The editors knew not to start off heavy, nor does the tone of the anthology lean too long in any direction, providing a lot of singular entertainment for the reader...Highly engaging, interestingly crowdsourced, and crafted with a great deal of care. You'll be thinking about it long after you're through reading." —Tor.com

THIS IS HOW
YOU DIE

THIS IS HOW YOU DIE

Stories of the Inscrutable, Infallible, Inescapable Machine of Death

EDITED BY

RYAN NORTH,
MATTHEW BENNARDO,
AND DAVID MALKI !

GRAND CENTRAL
PUBLISHING

NEW YORK   BOSTON

Copyright © 2013 by Machines of Death, LLC

Grand Central Publishing Hachette Book Group 237 Park Avenue New York, NY 10017

hachettebookgroup.com I machineofdeath.net

Printed in the United States of America

RRD-C

First Edition: July 2013   10 9 8 7 6 5 4 3 2

Grand Central Publishing is a division of Hachette Book Group, Inc. The Grand Central Publishing name and logo is a trademark of Hachette Book Group, Inc. "Machine of Death" is a trademark of Machines of Death, LLC.

"Band-Aid" is a trademark of Johnson & Johnson. "Dumpster" is a trademark of Dempster Brothers, Inc.—the generic term is *front loader waste container*. Good luck defending *that*, Dempster. "Bubble Wrap"† is a trademark of Sealed Air Corporation. Did you know that? I did not know that. The generic term is *inflated cushioning*. "Hacky Sack"† is a trademark of Wham-O (for *footbag*). "Jet Ski"† is a trademark of Kawasaki (for *stand-up personal watercraft*). "Sea-Doo,"† on the other hand, is a trademark of Bombardier Recreational Products, for the generic *sit-down personal watercraft*. At press time there has been no trademark filed for *a lie-down personal watercraft*. Some clever entrepreneur should JUMP ON THAT. "Onesie"† is a trademark of Gerber Products Company (for *infant bodysuit*). "Ping Pong"† is a trademark of Parker Brothers (for *table tennis*). "Wite-Out"† is a trademark of BIC Corporation (for *correction fluid*).

†Term does not appear in this book.

Library of Congress Cataloging-in-Publication Data
This is how you die : stories of the inscrutable, infallible, inescapable machine of death / edited by Ryan North, Matthew Bennardo, and David Malki !.—First edition.
    pages cm
    ISBN 978-1-4555-2939-1 (trade pbk.)—ISBN 978-1-61969-839-0 (audiobook)—
ISBN 978-1-4555-2940-7 (ebook) 1. Short stories, American. 2. American fiction—21st century. 3. Death—Fiction. 4. Forecasting—Fiction. I. North, Ryan, editor of compilation. II. Bennardo, Matthew, editor of compilation. III. Malki !, David, editor of compilation.
    PS648.S5T48 2013
    813'.010806—dc23
                                    2012051311

CONTENTS

viii   Contents

Contents   ix

LIST OF COMIC STRIPS

PREFACE

Prophecies or predictions of death are not new in literature. Consider King Laius, the father of Oedipus. Or Shakespeare's Macbeth, erstwhile Thane of Glamis. Or J.R.R. Tolkien's Witch-king of Angmar.

Each of these characters is remembered in part because of prophecies detailing how they would or would not die—and in all three cases, the prophecies prove true. (More or less, anyway. Traditionally, the oracles who write such prophecies don't seem overly concerned with literal interpretations.)

This book is something of a continuation of that literary tradition, but it's also something more. You won't find many kings or thanes in its pages. Instead, you'll find lots of ordinary people (and some extraordinary ones) who find themselves confronted with the same kind of knowledge that Laius and Macbeth sought.

But this book is not full of doom and destruction. Neither is it full of ironic comeuppances. In fact, many of the heroes and heroines in this anthology exit their stories alive and well—but having learned something about themselves or having faced their fears or having overcome a challenge.

In short, these stories are a lot like the kinds of stories you might find anywhere else. The only difference is that we've asked our writers to add one new and fantastic piece of technology to the world—the Machine of Death, which can predict anybody's ultimate fate based on a simple blood test.

Beyond that, our writers were free to write about whatever and whomever they liked. In these pages you'll find science fiction, fantasy, mystery, romance, philosophy, and humor. You'll tag along with police officers, scientists, rock stars, middle school kids, aliens, and French aristocrats. Some of the stories are literary in style, while others are red-blooded pulp, and a few are something else entirely.

Above everything else, what we wanted from this book was for readers to be constantly surprised. Because that's the lesson that Laius and Macbeth learned centuries ago—even when you think you already know the ending, you still don't know it all.

Happy reading!

—Ryan, Matt, and David !

INTRODUCTION

The machine had been invented a few years ago: a machine that could tell, from just a sample of your blood, how you were going to die. It didn't give you the date and it didn't give you specifics. It just spat out a sliver of paper upon which were printed, in careful block letters, the words "DROWNED" or "CANCER" or "OLD AGE" or "CHOKED ON A HANDFUL OF POPCORN." It let people know how they were going to die.

And it was frustratingly vague in its predictions: dark, and seemingly delighting in the ambiguities of language. "OLD AGE," it turned out, could mean either dying of natural causes or being shot by a bedridden man in a botched home invasion. The machine captured that old-world sense of irony in death: you can know how it's going to happen, but you'll still be surprised when it does.

We tested it before announcing it to the world, but testing took time—too much, since we had to wait for people to die. After four years had gone by and three people had died as the machine predicted, we shipped it out the door. There were now machines in every doctor's office and in booths at the mall. You could pay someone or you could probably get it done for free, but the result was the same no matter what machine you went to. They were, at least, consistent.

THIS IS HOW
YOU DIE

OLD AGE, SURROUNDED BY LOVED ONES

THE "COMING SOON" SIGN WAS GONE, and in its place stood a shining silver booth. Leah stopped, fascinated, looking at the machine.

For a brief moment, she waffled over the decision, but it wasn't in her nature to be indecisive. Leah got things done. Every performance appraisal she had ever received had said so—though sometimes there was a gentle hint that she didn't always have to act immediately, that she could allow herself to think things over a little more.

But even that slight criticism had never been partnered with any real examples of when she'd made the wrong decision.

Leah had instinct.

Had anyone who'd known her been nearby when Leah Cole stepped into the small booth, they wouldn't have been surprised. She read the instructions, swiped her credit card, agreed to the terms and conditions without really reading them, and then watched as the machine ran through its cleaning cycle and presented her with a single sharp needle.

She pressed her thumb against it, feeling the slight sting of the needle. The machine beeped, and she pulled her thumb away. The needle retracted.

A moment later, there was a slight hum and a small piece of paper clicked with finality into the tray. Leah reached down and picked it up with her other hand, tucking her pricked thumb into her mouth. Just as she pulled the small white piece of paper free, there was another hum and a second piece of paper clicked into the tray.

Leah blinked, then took the second piece of paper as well. She read them both.

After work, Leah dialed the 800 number on the back of the slips of paper and waited.

"Alexandria Corporation," a gentle-voiced man answered the phone. "This is Nicolas. How may I direct your call?"

"I took the test this morning at the new booth in the Byward Market," Leah said. "But I think your machine is defective."

Nicolas didn't sound bored exactly, but he certainly didn't sound worried about the state of the machine. "In what way do you think there's a defect?"

"It gave me two contradictory results, on separate papers."

Nicolas paused. When he spoke next, he sounded interested. "Two results?"

"Yes," Leah said. "And it wasn't someone else leaving a copy behind in the machine—they both printed out after I gave my blood sample. I checked your website—the ID codes printed at the bottom of the paper are identical. It generated two results for me."

"I'm going to transfer you," Nicolas said.

Leah waited.

Nicolas transferred her to a woman named Alia, who then transferred her to a Dr. Lindsay Brine. Leah was growing impatient—not an unusual state—but she forced herself to take a breath and explained everything to the doctor.

Again.

The response sent a shiver up her spine.

"Are you a twin?" she asked.

Leah swallowed. Her throat felt tight. "Yes."

"Identical, I'd assume?" Dr. Brine pressed.

"We're mirror twins, if you know what that means."

"I do," Dr. Brine replied. "This has happened once or twice

before. If you ask your twin to take the test and you get the same results, I'm afraid that's the only answer we can give you. I'll have my assistant, Audrey, refund your activation fee."

Leah said nothing. Her mind spun.

"Miss Cole?"

"Yes," Leah said. "Thank you."

"You're welcome." Dr. Brine seemed anxious to end the call.

Leah obliged.

Then she called Julia.

"Not on your life," Julia said.

Leah sipped her latte, looking at her sister with the same mix of feelings she always had: love, protectiveness, and total frustration.

Julia had kept her hair long once the twins had been old enough to make their own decisions. Their mother had always dressed them in matching outfits and given them the same short haircut, and while that hadn't bothered Leah, it had driven Julia crazy. Now that they were adults, Julia's chestnut hair fell just past her shoulders, unlike Leah's chic Hepburn style. Julia wore soft pastels where Leah favored rich jewel tones. Julia wore no jewelry aside from her wedding band. Leah decorated her ears, throat, wrists, and fingers with simple silver pieces she'd had made personally for herself.

And still the waitress had exclaimed, "You two are twins, right?"

"No," Leah had said. "This is my girlfriend." The waitress had flushed and stammered and taken their order.

Julia had given Leah a rare smile of conspiracy. "You're terrible."

Leah had shrugged and then launched into her reason for calling. "So. Here's what happened."

Julia had listened, frowning with distaste when Leah had begun the tale and then glaring by the end of the description of what had happened.

"And that's the problem," Leah said. "I've got two results, and they're mutually exclusive, so the doctor asked if I was an identical twin, which would mean that one of them is for me, and one is for you."

"I don't want to know what either of them says," Julia snapped, holding up a hand.

Leah sighed. "You don't?"

"Don't sigh at me. And no, I don't." Julia put her coffee down with finality. "I don't know why anyone would want to know. It's... morbid. What if it said something like 'childbirth'? Tristan and I are trying for a child—you know that. It would change everything."

"Well." Leah had frowned, thinking that Julia was missing the point entirely—you couldn't avoid death, she felt. Knowing ahead of time at least meant you could live accordingly. "It helps you plan ahead."

"Some of us like surprises."

Leah crossed her arms. "The doctor said that if you took the test and it gave the same two answers, then I'd know that this was the reason for the two results."

Julia hadn't taken any time to ponder the question. As she shut Leah down, Leah couldn't help but think that this was one instance where they were indeed identical.

Left with no way to confirm a flaw in the machine—or to confirm that she'd have to be happy with two options for her life's ultimate end—Leah had gone back to work, tucking the two slips of paper into her purse and pulling them out every now and then to look at them.

Just in case, she decided to stop drinking alcohol, though the rational part of her mind reminded her that so far, no one had ever managed to avoid what was printed on the little pieces of paper the booths handed out. They were always right. But if that particular result was hers, there was no way to know if she could at least delay things. She decided to try.

Life went on. Her sister and Tristan had her over for dinner for the big announcement and then e-mailed her pictures of Julia's ever-expanding belly over the weeks that followed. Leah immediately bought expensive clothes that Julia insisted were too much and too stylish for a baby to wear—especially since the baby would grow out of them so quickly.

Leah helped her sister decorate the nursery once they'd learned they were having a little boy and tried not to comment too strongly on the stereotypical blue color or the cowboy theme. After they'd finished putting up the borders, the two sisters had moved to the kitchen and sat down at Julia's table.

"Being pregnant suits you," Leah said with a smile.

Julia burst into tears.

Leah jumped up, embracing her sister out of habit, but lost as to the cause.

"What's wrong?" she asked, squeezing Julia's shoulders tightly.

"I took the stupid test!" Julia wailed. "I kept thinking about what we talked about, and then I started wondering, what if there was something horrible that was going to happen to me before our baby grew up? And then I thought about how our dad died when we were little, and how horrible that was…and I couldn't help it…" Julia sniffled, wiping her nose. "But I can't do it." She sighed. "I just…I just can't do it."

"I don't understand," Leah said.

Julia pulled out her purse and opened it. She dug inside, pulling out an envelope that she'd obviously gotten from an ATM.

"I didn't look at them; I just put them in here," Julia said. She took a shaky breath. "It gave me two. All I want to know…" She swallowed and handed the envelope to Leah. "All I want to know is that it has nothing to do with being pregnant. And that it doesn't say I'll die before I get to see my baby grow up."

Leah opened the envelope and pulled out the two slips of paper.

"They're the same as mine," she said, then looked up at her sister. "And don't worry. Neither of them is about pregnancy, and they don't say anything about dying young. In fact—"

"Stop!" Julia raised a hand. "I don't want to know."

Leah bit her lip, considering. Then she nodded and put the slips back into the envelope.

"If you call the company and tell them what happened, they'll refund your test payment," she said.

"I never want to think about that again," Julia said.

Graham was born, and Leah found out that she did have a mothering gene after all—though she truly enjoyed handing Graham back to her sister when she was ready to go home and have a long hot bath. Tristan was a natural at being a dad, and Julia had never seemed happier.

"I'm a mother," Julia kept repeating whenever Graham was sleeping in her arms. "I'm a mother." From her sister's lips, Leah thought this sounded like the highest accomplishment of humankind. Leah felt a surge of fierce love for her sister, and the two were closer than they'd been in years, spending more time together than they had since they were teens.

When Julia bobbed her hair short, Leah began growing hers out. Julia must have noticed, but she didn't say anything.

Leah babysat on Saturday nights, so her sister and Tristan could enjoy an evening out—usually just dinner and a movie. It wasn't a chore, even when Graham was grumpy and refused to sleep. Leah generally read a book, the baby monitor tucked on the table beside her, and found herself feeling oddly content.

The phone rang harshly on one of those nights, and she scooped it up, annoyed at herself for forgetting to turn off the ringer and hoping that it hadn't woken Graham.

"Hello?" she asked, ready to tear out the throat of a telemarketer.

"Leah?" Leah barely recognized the voice, it was so ragged and raw.

"Tristan?" Her heart began to pound. "What's wrong? Where are you?"

"We're at the hospital."

A truck had run a red light and slammed into the passenger side of their car. Tristan's head was wrapped with bandages, two cracked ribs were bundled tight, and he was covered in small scrapes and cuts.

Julia had been in surgery for nearly three hours.

Tristan lay in his hospital bed, staring out the window of his room into the night.

Leah sat beside him, waiting for the doctor to return. Graham was bundled in a carrier and fast asleep despite the background noises of the hospital.

When the doctor came in, his face said it all.

"No," Tristan said, and his eyes grew wet.

Leah rose. "Tell me."

The doctor regarded her a moment, then spoke. "There are some major internal injuries. She lost a lot of blood. We had to remove her spleen and one of her kidneys. And the other kidney…" He took a breath. "We had to stop surgery. But her remaining kidney has also been damaged. Once she's well enough for surgery again, we can go in and we might be able to correct the damage, but—"

Leah's eyes blurred. She gripped the arms of the chair and tried to hold on to consciousness. This couldn't be happening.

"—would be the preferred option."

Leah frowned, coming back. "What did you say?"

Beside her, Tristan was crying quietly.

"Oh, thank God," he said.

The doctor repeated himself.

Leah made a decision.

At Graham's first birthday, Julia watched him frown at the candle and laughed when Tristan tried to get him to blow it out. None of the children really seemed to understand what the party was about, but the parents had fun, and the cleanup wasn't so bad. None of the kids had much cake, and Julia knew she'd probably end up throwing most of it out—assuming her husband didn't eat it all in the next two days.

The presents had all been opened—an excruciatingly slow process given Graham's preoccupation with the shiny red paper on the first gift, which he would have been happy to play with for the entire afternoon. There was only one thing left, and Julia was dreading it with her entire being.

But Tristan took Graham for his nap, and she was alone.

Now or never, she thought.

She pulled the sealed envelope from her purse and looked at the handwriting. Her sister's perfect penmanship had always annoyed her as a child. Leah's impulsiveness seemed at odds with her perfectly crafted letters, and Julia's own handwriting was terrible. Tristan said she should have been a doctor.

Open Me at Graham's First Birthday, the envelope said.

For a long moment, she wondered if she should just throw it out, but she knew she wouldn't. Finally, she slid open the envelope and pulled out the letter. It was a single page alongside two small pieces of paper, which were folded in half. Julia swallowed when she recognized them.

The letter wasn't long, which both relieved and saddened her.

Julia,

The difference between certainty and a chance is love. I never thought I'd wish with all my heart to be the one getting the second result, but right now I do. I hope you will understand why I'm doing this, and I hope that you'll read this someday. The doctor said he could operate on your kidney and he might be able to save it. Or I could give you one of mine. I'm going to give you one of mine. I know what that might mean for me, but I know what it might mean for you, too. I promise you that I thought this decision through.

> *Kiss Graham for me.*
>
> *Love,*
>
> *Leah*

Julia swallowed a lump and then fished out the two pieces of paper. She sighed, closing her eyes for a moment, and then opened the first.

Kidney operation, it said.

Julia felt her eyes brim with tears and allowed herself to cry. She opened the second.

It said, *Old age, surrounded by loved ones.*

"Thank you," Julia whispered, and then went to kiss her son.

Story by 'Nathan Burgoine

Illustration by Danica Novgorodoff

ROCK AND ROLL

"OKAY, KIDS, IT'LL BE JUST another five minutes or so. You just sit tight, now." The man flashed a hurried smile to the three young teens before disappearing once again. His unnaturally dyed hair portrayed an almost pitiful desire to look much younger than he was, to fit in with these kids who were easily thirty years his junior. His hair was matched by his shiny leather vest and spastically accessorized pants.

The man's words made Amanda suddenly aware that the three of them had been sitting in complete silence the entire time. She had been gazing at the laminated badge she had been given, attached to a green fabric neck strap. "Backstage Pass," it read in bold letters at the top, with the logo of the tour printed beneath it. The colors of the logo didn't quite line up, making the graphic appear as though it had purple shading on the left side and bottom.

The girl next to Amanda seemed to have the same realization and turned quickly to Amanda. "I'm Julie," she said, sticking out her hand.

"Amanda," she replied, clasping Julie's hand. Amanda blushed a little as she realized that her hand was sweaty because she was so nervous, especially compared to Julie's oddly cold palm. She let go perhaps a little early, embarrassed, and was flustered when Julie held on for another awkward second. Amanda thought she saw the hint of a smirk in Julie's face.

"I'm Austin," said the boy on the other side of Amanda. He was in a wheelchair and wore thick-framed, yellowish-tinted glasses. As Amanda turned to shake his hand, she was thrown off a little by his eyes, one of which seemed to focus on a point a little behind her. His hand was a little warmer than Amanda's, which felt a little weird—but she held on this time, determined not to have the same problem she had with Julie. She looked back at Julie, expecting her to reach over and shake hands with Austin, but she didn't; Julie just looked at him as if to acknowledge his presence while still holding on to the faint smile from before.

"I like your purse," Amanda offered, turning again toward Julie and trying to regain some of the power that the handshake faux pas had taken from her. She didn't really feel strongly one way or the other about the purse, but it did seem to be an expensive designer bag, or at least a knock-off. Either way it struck Amanda as being something Julie must be proud of.

"Thank you," Julie said politely, although without the glow of appreciation that Amanda was hoping for. Julie regarded the flawless black leather of the bag in her own lap as if it were the first time she had really noticed it and then opened her mouth as if to respond in kind. As she glanced over to Amanda's slightly worn cream-colored purse, though, she seemed to think better of it and instead looked up at Amanda with the same hint of a smile.

"So how many of Stephen's concerts have you been to, Amanda?" Julie had a devious sparkle in her eye. Amanda felt a knot form in her stomach, realizing that she couldn't answer the question honestly and still maintain any pretense of holding the upper hand. She resigned herself to her place, knowing at least that Stephen would not want her to lie about it.

"This is my first," she replied, mustering her confidence. "But I've been a huge fan since *Death by Rock and Roll*." She made sure to name-check Stephen's first album, if only to prove her devotion.

Austin chimed in, leaning forward to try to stake a claim in the conversation. "Did you know the slip on the album cover was his *actual slip* from his *first reading* in Portland?" He seemed to overemphasize the words to be more dramatic, but Amanda wondered if it was just the way he normally talked.

Julie rolled her eyes. "From Tim's Broken Cup coffeehouse, yes. And he played his first concert there one year later." She turned back to Amanda. "So you have all his albums?" It was phrased less as a question and more like a statement of obvious fact.

"Yes!" Finally, a chance to prove herself.

"And the bootlegs?"

Amanda wished she could go back to the silent sitting from before. "Um—"

"My dad got me bootleg recordings of all the concerts from the Fate tour." Julie sat back in her seat. "They're very high-quality recordings."

"Wow... that's great," Amanda replied, fighting to keep a smile on her face, looking down at her purse.

"When did you win your ticket?" Austin spoke to Amanda in a quieter tone, as if to form a united front with her against Julie.

Amanda turned to Austin with a smile. "Just yesterday. My friend Mimi and I had been calling the radio station since the contest started! Two times, we were caller number four, and then one time we were number seven. We figured we had missed our chance, and then the deejay said they had one more ticket and backstage pass available!"

"Wow, no kidding?" Austin seemed genuinely interested. Amanda smiled in appreciation, finding his lazy eye less creepy now.

"Mimi said we should go for it, and if we were caller number nine, she would let me have them." Amanda felt a lump in her throat. "I couldn't ask for a better friend. She loves Stephen too, but she knows how much he means to me."

"That's awesome! And so you won! That's so great!" Amanda's eyes were just starting to tear up, and she nodded. She didn't want to speak for fear of breaking down, both out of love for Mimi and out of the anticipation of meeting him.

Stephen. Stephen Conrad. She had seen him onstage from the

fourth row and it seemed like a dream—it all went by so quickly. She sang along with every word of every song, soaking up every bit of the experience. She had stretched out her hands to the stage to be nearer to him but knew that she needed only to wait: fate had arranged for them to meet, and that meeting was only minutes away.

She wanted to tell Austin. She wanted him to know that she was special. The arena had been full of thousands of screaming fans tonight, but Amanda was different. She wanted to tell him that, but how would it sound? Every teenage girl felt that way...but tonight she and Stephen would meet, and everything would change.

She sat back in her seat and opened her bag to get a tissue. As she rifled through the contents with her right hand she carefully laid her left hand over the top of the purse to keep the others from seeing inside, and when she found the small plastic pouch she pulled a tissue out quickly, deftly pulling the strap to cinch the opening with a single smooth motion. As she blotted the corners of her eyes, she noticed Julie looking in her own purse, and Amanda caught a glimpse of a strange-looking device inside, occupying most of the bag's small volume.

Amanda looked up at Julie with a quizzical look on her face, but Julie was already starting to talk. "*I* don't listen to the *radio*," she said condescendingly, without turning to look at either of them. She grasped her badge and held it up. "My dad bought me this for my fifteenth birthday, which is next week."

Austin leaned forward to look at the badge, which was identical to his and Amanda's. "I didn't know you could just buy them."

The smirk returned to Julie's face, much more obvious now than before. "Anything is for sale when you have enough money."

"What does your dad do?" Amanda asked, realizing now that the purse was probably not a knock-off. Knowing that she had bought her way in somehow made Julie seem so much less of a true fan. For Amanda, it was destiny. For Julie, it was just another soulless purchase.

"He's the CEO of Mortech, the leading manufacturer of death predictors," she replied with a mixture of condescension and pride.

"You know, it was a Mortech machine that Stephen used at Tim's Broken Cup."

Amanda's eyes widened and she could feel her pulse speed up a little. She wasn't sure what to say and was relieved when Austin spoke instead.

"Whoa...so what do *you* think will happen to him? Do you think he'll die onstage sometime? I mean, his slip says ROCK AND ROLL, right? How else could it happen?"

Julie sneered a little. "Or drugs. That's how most rockers die, you know."

Austin looked confused. "But his slip doesn't say DRUGS..."

"Drugs and rock and roll are practically the same thing. It's the rock-and-roll lifestyle."

Amanda felt insulted. Stephen didn't *do* drugs...She had read in a magazine interview that Stephen *hated* drugs and alcohol. He didn't need them to be happy, the article had said, because playing his music gave him all the happiness he needed.

Austin seemed to have been following some other train of thought. "Do you think he'll have his prediction slip with him? You think he'll *show* it to us?"

Julie looked over at Austin with her smirk and directed her answer instead toward Amanda. "It won't matter if he has it or not, because *I'm* going to get my *own*." With a grand gesture, she opened her purse and pulled out the device, which looked similar to one of those electronic ear thermometers that Amanda had seen at her doctor's office, but a bit larger.

"What is that?" Amanda asked.

"This is a *portable* death predictor. Battery operated, and works just like the larger units."

Austin was keenly interested and wheeled forward a few inches to get a closer look. "Whoa...I didn't know they made them like that!"

"They don't—at least, not yet. This is a prototype." She looked around and quickly tucked it back into her purse. She seemed a little worried about passersby seeing it; Amanda guessed that she had probably taken it without her father's permission.

As Amanda thought about Julie's apparent plan, she clutched her own purse a little more tightly, feeling flushed with nervousness. "Wh-what are you going to do?"

Julie looked at Amanda with a fire in her eyes. "I'm going to get the ultimate souvenir—my own slip that reads ROCK AND ROLL." She put her hands up as if the words were on a marquee in front of her. "Maybe he'll autograph it for me. Either way it'll be one of a kind—I have a blank slip loaded in that already has his picture embossed on it."

Amanda was mortified, partly out of jealousy, but mostly because it threatened to overshadow her fated meeting with Stephen. Why did there even have to be other winners? She had heard the deejay give away another backstage pass but daydreamed that somehow this moment would be just her and Stephen—no managers, no stagehands, no other winners.

"What if he doesn't want to?" Austin asked. Amanda nodded and gazed back at Julie. It wasn't Stephen's style! Even Austin knew.

"I already told you—anything is for sale when you're rich."

Amanda's concern was turning to anger. *Julie shouldn't get to be here*, she thought. *Stephen wouldn't approve of this.* She was mustering the courage to speak up, to put Julie in her place, when she was interrupted by the man from before, suddenly poking his head through the doorway into the small waiting area.

"All right, kids! Stephen's waiting for you. Follow me!"

"Stephen." The man looked at the paper he held in his hand and read each name carefully, pointing at each of the teens in turn. "This is Austin Chavez, Julie Morhardt, and...Amanda Thiessen. The contest winners!" Amanda gave an awkward wave when her name was called. She was relieved that the man had introduced them, since she had offered to push Austin's wheelchair and became worried halfway down the corridor that Stephen might think that she was just Austin's aide or something.

Stephen Conrad was there in the room, sitting backward on a

rolling swivel chair and looking every bit as beautiful as he did in the magazine pictures and on the album covers. His brown, tousled tresses glistened with the sweat from the stage lights, and he still had on the tight-fitting white T-shirt and black jeans that he wore onstage. His acoustic guitar leaned up against the wall to his left, and a few people sat chattering on cell phones behind the three visitors. Stephen sucked on a white plastic water bottle as they walked in, then pulled it out with a smack and let the air hiss back into it.

Amanda's knees felt weak and her mouth felt dry as Stephen motioned for the girls to sit down in two of three folding chairs that had been placed in an arc a few feet away from the musician. As Austin wheeled himself closer, Stephen put his foot out and sharply kicked away one of the chairs, glancing up at the man who had brought them in, smiling and rolling his eyes. Austin chuckled as the folding chair went skittering across the tiled floor.

"I'm so glad you could come to my show tonight," he told the three eager fans. "It really means a lot to me." He extended his hand to each of them: first Julie, who seemed less confident than she had in the waiting room. Then Austin, and finally Amanda. Shaking his hand took her breath away; it felt so strong, so comfortable. He felt just as she had always imagined he would feel. It was as though the sincerity she heard in his music was there in his touch. She smiled at him, melting inside as he smiled back.

Does he know? she wondered. *Can he feel the connection?*

Julie spoke, either trying to interrupt the moment or just blind to anyone else's matters but her own. "Stephen, I loved 'Breakaway' tonight... It reminded me of the way you played it in your show in Indianapolis a few years ago."

The rocker was taken aback a little but kept a warm smile on his face. "Oh, were you at that show?"

Julie stammered a little. "Ah, no, but I heard, uh, I have a recording of it. It's one of my favorite versions."

"Oh, I see." Stephen looked down and chuckled. "To be honest, they start to blur together after a while." He looked back up at Julie.

"But I'm glad you enjoyed it. It's a special tune, I think. You know, it's about trying to escape your fate. Something our generation has had to confront more than anyone else, I think."

Austin piped up, much in the same way he had in the waiting room. "Stephen, do you have your slip with you? Can we see it?" Amanda was a little disappointed in Austin. Why was he here: to see Stephen or his card?

"Oh, ha-ha...no," Stephen responded, in a way that was simultaneously considerate and well rehearsed. "The road is a pretty dangerous place, so I have it framed back home in my studio. It helps me remember that rock and roll is my life; it's what I was put here to do." He reached around to grab his guitar. "How about a song, huh? I think I've got one more encore in me for my superfans here."

The teens nodded expectantly. Amanda's heart raced as Stephen strummed a quick chord and then tuned one of the strings as he spoke. "This is a new song...something I've been working on in the tour bus. You know, all the extra time on the bus gives me a lot of opportunity to do songwriting."

Julie opened her mouth as if to speak, but Stephen continued. Amanda wasn't sure if Stephen knew he was cutting her off but found a wicked pleasure in it regardless.

"This one is about finding your soul mate. It's inspired by a dream I had a few nights ago." He played a few bars as an introduction, his fingers intricately combining melody and strummed chords, and then began singing.

Amanda felt dizzy as he sang of wandering through lonely days and then having his companion appear to him, first in a dream, and then in real life. As he played, he looked down at his guitar and only occasionally looked up, often closing his eyes to deliver the high notes. His enraptured audience drank up every note, not moving even to keep time with the impassioned performance.

After an expertly played and melodic bridge, Stephen launched into a third verse with a much thinner accompaniment, ratcheting up the emotion in his voice but singing more softly, more intimately. As he did so, his eyes locked with Amanda's.

She felt as though she were being transfigured by his words. She could feel his gaze and expected at any moment for him to turn away, to look down at the fingerboard of his guitar to change chords, to turn instead to Julie or Austin or anyone else in the room. But he did not, even as he moved into the final chorus.

She was in the clouds and knew that he had suddenly felt the connection. The connection that she had felt so long ago, that she *knew* he would feel when they finally met. He was acknowledging it, caught up in it, as if she had taken his hand and was gently guiding him toward his unforeseen future. He was no longer a face on a poster or a voice coming through iPod earbuds. He was her peer, her friend, her—she was afraid to say it, even in her mind, for fear of jinxing the heaven she had finally found.

He had barely strummed the final chord when Julie, who must have noticed the connection between the two, let out a gasp of angry frustration. Amanda turned just in time to see Julie swing the device that she had already gotten out of her purse, causing the now uncovered needle to pierce through Stephen's jeans and into his thigh. Stephen's face turned to surprise and to horror, and he let out a yelp as he instinctively swatted it away with his left hand, nearly dropping his guitar in the process. The device went sliding across the tiled floor behind the three teens, stopping in a corner where one of the cell phone people had been but which was now empty.

There was a sudden pause in the room as everyone absorbed what had just happened. After a second, the apparently still-functional device began beeping, and Julie dove toward it just as a small slip of paper emerged from the slot on the end. Stephen's face changed to a look of horror. The man who had brought the youths into the room, realizing now what the device was, rushed over to Julie, who was squatting next to her device and had already flipped the card over. Her expression changed to one of disgust as she turned back to look at Stephen.

"THYROID CANCER!?"

*   *   *

Amanda sat in silence in the backseat, her mind keeping time to the pulse of the streetlights going by out the window. The concert had gone by so quickly, but all that happened after the meeting with Stephen went so painfully slowly: the phone calls, the meetings with agents or lawyers or whoever they were. The parents coming in, signing papers, talking to men in silk shirts and ties. People talking about nondisclosure agreements and lawsuits. It had been a little satisfying to see Julie's father come in and find out about her taking the device without asking—Amanda thought she heard the words "grounded for a month" as they left the room—but to be honest, she didn't really care.

She was grateful that the people had explained everything to her own father, so he wasn't pestering her with questions during the car ride. He knew how much she loved Stephen and how much Amanda wanted to be left alone right now.

THYROID CANCER? She had always told herself that Stephen's death prediction didn't define him, that it could be something else and she would love him just as much. She loved his music, his attitudes, his ways. The whole death-prediction thing was something that the media latched on to. The paparazzi. Not her; she was so much more than a fan.

But it *did* matter, and she was having a hard time confronting herself with that fact. Not that there was anything intrinsically wrong with a prediction of thyroid cancer; it probably meant that he would live a long life. But the deception? The lie? It went against everything she thought he stood for.

She was reminded of the lyrics to a song she knew: "When our heroes turn and fall / We have no one to turn to but ourselves." It wasn't one of Stephen's songs.

She opened her purse, took out her wallet, and pulled out her own prediction. The one that she had gotten at the mall with Mimi when they were both thirteen, with the money her parents thought they were using for ice cream. She read the large block lettering in the light cast rhythmically by the passing streetlights.

ROCK AND ROLL.

She tucked the slip back into her wallet, leaned her head against the cool window, and fell asleep watching the city lights roll by.

Story by Toby W. Rush
Illustration by Meredith Gran

NATURAL CAUSES

THE MACHINE APPEARED ON A Friday morning. Lucy Swett said that she saw men in black unloading it from the back of a Mack truck, but no one had listened to Lucy Swett since she'd claimed to have been chosen to go to a special convention for young scientists, which was definitely a lie.

The contraption was a bit of a spectacle, mostly because we didn't have much in the way of modern conveniences. We didn't have much in the way of anything, truth be told. Almond Hill was the kind of town that you could drive through and not realize it. The kind of town where everyone knew everyone else and people liked it the way it was, thank you very much.

A crowd of people had gathered round on the corner across from the Jiffy Lube at about nine in the morning, when the sun was still rolling out of bed. I was bringing back a carton of milk for Mama and stopped to gawk with the others. The hulking red-and-black box looked almost like a vending machine, but there were no chips or soda behind the glass. Nothing except the ominous title MACHINE OF DEATH printed in crooked circus letters at the top.

"Machine of Death!" Lucy Swett gasped from the front of the crowd. "I've heard of those. They tell you how you're gonna die."

"Oh, posh," drawled Dr. Hudson, who had delivered most everyone in town. His wisp of a wife hung on his arm and looked up into his clear blue eyes, prodding him to tell Lucy off. "That's ridiculous. Who ever heard of such a thing?"

"No! It's true!" cried Lucy Swett, sandy blond ponytail bobbing up and down. "They're in all the cities. It was in one of my magazines. I heard of a girl who—"

"Now, Lucy—" The crowd was starting to get excited. People chattered, jostling for a better look at the machine.

"She's telling the truth," Helen Calloway said quietly, her face still and her eyes wide open under heavy, straight bangs. Everyone turned to look at her. Mrs. Calloway's late husband had owned the hardware store and gave it to her when he died. She didn't lie. "My sister lives in Charleston. Says everyone has 'em done, at shopping malls same as hospitals. Doing it to babies before they're christened now."

"My God," said Mrs. Hudson feebly, putting a shaking hand to her mouth. Dr. Hudson just shook his head. It was quiet for a long while.

"Well, I'm gonna do it," said Lucy, always one to try out the latest hairstyle or facial cream from one of her glossies. After glancing at the machine, she noisily pulled out her purse and fished around. A pout wrinkled her brow and pursed her lips. "Anyone got a twenty?"

"Twenty dollars?" asked Mrs. Hudson.

"That's what it says on the machine." She indicated the marking and gleefully pulled out a wrinkled bill she found at the bottom of her purse. "It's a medical procedure, Mrs. Hudson." Lucy fed the twenty into the machine, which sucked up the money like a little kid sucks up ice cream. She waited. "Come on!" She banged the side. "I paid my twenty—"

Then the machine rattled, a sound like a copper kettle would make if it fell off the highest shelf in the garage. It clattered and clanged until we all thought it would break, and then it spit out a slip of paper smaller than my palm. It fluttered to the ground as people craned to see. Lucy snatched it up and cupped her hands around it to read her prediction.

"Tell us what you got, Lucy!" Joe Schafer and his gang called, greasy duck-tailed heads wagging. There was a murmur of agreement among the crowd. I think Joe had had a bit of a crush on me for a while, but Mama wouldn't let me go out with boys yet, especially not boys like Joe. He was a good guy, but he wore a leather jacket and pierced his own ear behind the Jiffy Lube the summer before eighth grade. The symbol of rebellion had shocked Almond Hill; Principal Skinner made Joe take it out for school, saying that "ridiculous ornamentation for men was unheard of" in *his* day.

"She ought to tell us her prediction, seeing as she's the first one and all. There's no point to it if you don't tell us. It's part of the fun," said lanky Mr. Paganini, who owned the R&R diner.

"Fun, Hank?" asked Dr. Hudson.

"Shhh . . . It's not decent," Mrs. Hudson whispered loudly. "To tell other people."

The crowd looked to Mrs. Calloway, now the expert on this sort of thing.

"I never heard my sister tell of keeping them secret. She says she's gonna die of old age. Very matter-of-fact. Everyone knows, in the city."

We all turned back to Lucy Swett, who was shaking a little in front of the Machine of Death, staring at her sliver of paper. She looked up and was met with silence.

"Well," she said with her nose in the air, pausing for effect. "I got 'shot.'" There were a few gasps. Her voice was falsely brave, her face pale. "Must mean I'm going to be famous. Only famous people get shot."

"Stupid people get shot, Lucy," said Joe Schafer. "Let me at it. I bet I get hit by a car."

By now, people were leaving. I stood there for a moment, unnerved by the whole idea, then turned to go. Someone grabbed my shoulder.

"Hey, Tess," Joe Schafer said with a strange, earnest look about him. His hair was slicked back like always. Up this close, I could see his scar, a little line on his cheek where he said he'd been cut in a knife fight with some guys from Seeley.

"Hey, Joe." I got shy around him and his glinting green eyes.

"Will you get yours done, then?"

"I dunno." There was an awkward pause. "What'd you get, Joe?"

He took a deep breath. I'd never seen him shaken; he seemed almost concerned, faced with his own death.

"Motorcycle accident," he said, his voice strangely quiet and husky. There was a moment of silence.

"I'm sorry, Joe," I whispered, unsure of how to respond. He shook his head.

"Oh, 's'okay. I always said I'd ride till the day I die." He narrowed his eyes, dragging them over me. "You should get yours done, Tess. Live a little on the edge. It'd be good for you. I mean..." He looked over his shoulder at his gang. "Some people say you're a stick-in-the-mud. I know you're not. But you gotta show 'em."

"Joe!" Caleb, his right-hand man, motioned for their leader to join them. Joe nodded, then turned his head back to me.

"I gotta go, Tess. Don't let anyone tell you what to do. But think about what I said." I nodded, not meeting his eyes. "See ya later." I scurried out of there.

Did people really think I was a stick-in-the-mud? I tried to stay out of trouble. I just went to school and helped my parents out and went to the R&R for milk shakes. I generally liked Almond Hill. But most kids agreed that meant I was doomed. If you didn't rebel or have dramatic plans to leave, you could never get out.

My parents invited the Hudsons over for lunch. Talk quickly and unceremoniously turned from gossip about Marge Flicker and Toby Dale's upcoming wedding to discussion of the machine.

"What do you think, Hudson?" my father boomed, mouth full of potato salad. He hadn't been in the morning congregation across from the Jiffy Lube. "I mean, you're a doctor."

"It's a hell of a thing," muttered Dr. Hudson. "A hell of a thing."

My father nodded in agreement and swallowed. "The postman said he heard of a guy who got his done. Said it was gonna be kidney failure, and he died the next day of a kidney failure." He smacked his hand on the table. "Just like that."

"Well, it's a medical machine," drawled Dr. Hudson. "I guess there could be practical uses for it."

"We've got on fine without them for centuries, Doc—we don't need 'em now. It's just gonna make people crazy. Thinking about death all the time."

"It's not natural," Mrs. Hudson intoned. "Prob'ly the devil in it."

Everyone sat in silence.

"Well, I think that we had better just ignore it," said my mama, ever practical, as she gathered the plates. "Folks who want it should get it. Folks who don't, shouldn't. No need to rally one way or another. I wouldn't get mine done if you paid me, but I'm not going to tell anyone else what's best for them. It's nobody's business but the person gettin' it done."

But of course, the book-club ladies, who fancied themselves proper gentlewomen, started a campaign against the machine. Led by frail Mrs. Hudson, they marched around the machine's street corner, pausing only to read Scripture at those who decided to get their death predictions. At their strongest, they called a town meeting that got pretty rowdy but decided nothing. Their campaign quickly deteriorated into snide comments at dinner parties and disapproving glares in the supermarket. They took every opportunity to tell those who had gotten predictions that they were damned. That no one ought to know but God himself.

I don't know about God, but all the kids at the high school were getting theirs done. After Lucy Swett's bold decision to get her prediction, it became a test of character. "Do you have your slip?" The kids with younger, more liberal parents got their slips right away. But most of the older folks had "sensibilities." Some kids had to sneak out in the middle of the night to get theirs done. And even after they'd done it, they had to pass another test. "How's it going to happen?" Separating the wheat from the chaff. The more fantastic the death, the more respect earned. Crashes and firearms trumped natural causes and drowning. Those who didn't know were at the bottom.

"Tess, we have to do it," whined Debbie Hayes as we walked home from school, just as we had since we were five. She had been my best friend for as long as I could remember. "Everyone else is getting theirs done."

"Everyone else doesn't have parents like mine."

"But everyone does, Tess!" Debbie stopped and put her hands on her hips. "We all have parents like yours. Old farts. They're not gonna let us get our slips in a million years." I started walking again. "But we *have* to go get them."

"Go behind our parents' backs, you mean."

"Well, yeah."

I shook my head.

"Deb, I don't think—"

"Oh, come on, Tess—you've never done anything exciting in your whole life."

"Yes, I have!"

"Tell me one thing."

"I drank some champagne at your sister's wedding," I snapped.

"My five-year-old cousin Bobby drank some champagne at my sister's wedding." Debbie stopped again and wheeled to face me, eyes wide. "We're gonna die someday, Tess. You know that?"

"Yeah." I crossed my arms. Debbie was good at convincing me; I had to put up a defense.

"These little slips—they just say how it's gonna happen. They don't tell you when. We could die tomorrow. And we'd die boring little girls who lived in Almond Hill all their lives and never did anything, just like our parents. We have to be different from them." She sighed. "Maybe knowing how we die is the first step."

"I don't know, Deb...I don't have any money."

"I know for a fact you have exactly twenty dollars saved up."

"That was for the pink dress at Dillingham's!"

"Think about it, Tess. A dress?" She raised her eyebrow. "Or knowing how it's all going to end." She knew she'd hooked me.

"Oh, come on." She grinned conspiratorially, like she used to when she'd push me to steal a cookie from her parents' cookie jar (I had always been taller than her). "Sneak out with me. Get your slip." She bumped my hip with hers. "Show Joe Schafer that you're really worth talking to." I felt my face flush red.

"Joe Schafer already talks to me," I retorted quietly.

She ignored that comment and whispered the plan to me. When we got to her house, she skipped down her front walk, twirling around to give me a little wave at her door. I shook my head and trudged home, muttering to myself.

I was supposed to meet Deb in her treehouse at midnight. It wasn't hard to sneak out of my house; I had never done anything like that before, so there was no security. My parents slept soundly. We didn't have a dog.

Deb had a dog, but Cooper was an old, mostly deaf hound who'd known me all his life. He let me shimmy up to the treehouse after I slipped him a treat and sat quiet while I waited.

I had almost fallen asleep with my head propped up in my hand when I saw a flashing light coming from Deb's window. She was turning a flashlight on and off to get my attention. I squinted. She held up a piece of paper with a message written in her loopy handwriting. *Can't go. Daddy's watching TV.* Deb's father worked the late shift at the police station and sometimes had problems sleeping. I sighed and started to climb down, fully intending to go back home and slip into bed like I'd never left. Deb flashed the light frantically. I looked up.

You still have to go.

Crickets chirped. I shouldn't do it. But I'd come this far. But Deb couldn't go. But I had saved the money. But I could just get the dress and be done with it. But this was my chance to do something. But I didn't want to die.

Some people say you're a stick-in-the-mud. I know you're not. But you gotta show 'em.

I looked up at Deb's window. I nodded.

The machine was more terrifying at night. In the daylight, it looked almost comical, out of place on the sunny sidewalk. But in the dark, it lurked like a monster on the street corner, waiting for a victim.

I shivered as I fed it my savings. I thought I might wet myself when the machine came to life, clanking and whirring as gears turned and metal grated. It would wake the whole town. When I was absolutely sure that no one was around, I stooped to get my slip. It fluttered out of my hand in the night breeze, and I had to snatch it out of the chilly night air. I held it facedown for what seemed like an eternity, then took a deep breath and turned it over.

on the john.

I read the prediction again. Again. Again. Over and over. Memorized it. Lowercase black letters. How I would die. *on the john.* My face burned with shame; I felt nauseous. The world seemed to be spinning.

I couldn't die on the john. How could I ever tell that to anyone? How could I be respectable with that prediction? I could never admit that to Joe.

It had to be wrong. I had to save up for another prediction. Tell Debbie I'd chickened out. The kids at school were wrong. Getting *on the john* would be even worse than not getting my slip.

I'd only managed to scrape seven dollars and forty-three cents together when the machine disappeared the next Friday, exactly two weeks after it had arrived. It didn't make a fuss. Everyone just woke up on Friday and it wasn't there. Mr. Malloy at the Jiffy Lube said he was happy to see it go. "Gloomin' up the place," he said. "Bad for business."

There was absolutely nothing I could do. My parents wouldn't let me go to the city to get another slip. Dejected, I used the money to take Debbie to the R&R for milk shakes (vanilla for me, chocolate for her). Mr. Paganini served them up with a smile, then bustled back through the swinging door into the kitchen. I couldn't help feeling that maybe Mr. Paganini would be a good person to talk to about my death slip. He was nice and gave good advice. He was attentive. He noticed that we'd stayed long after our milk shakes were slurped down.

"What are you two lovely ladies still doing at my counter?" Mr. Paganini asked, long arms folded, pointy elbows sticking out as he leaned on the Formica.

"Thinking about dying." I sighed, swaying back and forth on my seat cushion while I looked at the black-and-white linoleum. Debbie tapped her fingers on the counter.

"Happens to everyone, one time or another," he said. There was a tired pause.

"How are you going to die, Mr. Paganini?" Debbie asked brightly. I elbowed her.

He chuckled. "That's fine, Tess. I'm not ashamed." More chuckling as his face turned pinkish. "Says I'm going to die on the john, myself." I couldn't help it; I gasped, then covered my mouth. "Not very dignified, is it? But I'm sure it happens to lots of people. That's probably why Mrs. Hudson and those ladies are so uptight about the whole thing—they probably got *underwear* or *false teeth* or something." He smiled and winked.

That had to be a sign. I had to tell someone what I'd done.

"I'm sorry, Mr. Paganini," I breathed, dragging Debbie from the counter and leading her outside the R&R.

"What are you doing, Tess?" she squealed, squirming.

"Stop it!" I hissed, looking around. "Debbie, you're my dearest friend in the whole world, so I know you can keep a secret." She nodded earnestly. "You have to swear that you'll never breathe a word of what I'm gonna tell you to anyone ever." She nodded again. "Okay." I took a deep breath. "I lied to you about how I'm gonna die." She got a strange look on her face. I rushed to explain. "I got *on the john*, same as Mr. Paganini, only I was so ashamed I didn't wanna tell anybody. So I lied. And told you I didn't get my slip at all. Then I started saving up for another prediction." She was staring at me. "I'm sorry." Still staring. "Deb?"

"Tess?" She had a weird look about her.

"Yeah?" I asked, red faced, staring at my shoes.

"I got the same thing."

My head snapped back up. "What?"

Talking fast like she does when she's anxious, Debbie told me she'd gotten so mad at me for not getting my slip that she'd snuck out by herself and gotten her prediction. Only she'd gotten *on the john* too and threw the slip in the fireplace when she got home. She said she nearly died of shame.

It wasn't long before the gossip spread. Debbie told Joe and Joe told his gang and someone in his gang told Lucy, and then everybody knew. Everybody had heard.

And everybody had done the same.

Even Mrs. Hudson, who had apparently been too curious to resist the devil's temptation, tearfully admitted that she had gotten the same slip as everyone else—all lowercase, *on the john*. Her book-club ladies shunned her for a day but quickly broke down to admit that they had done the same. One by one, people confessed. Joe Schafer scratched his head, embarrassed, and hooked his thumbs in his jeans when he told me, then asked me if I wanted to go to lunch at the R&R sometime. Lucy Swett went into hysterics and wouldn't leave her house, shrieking that her reputation was ruined. Marge Flicker and Toby Dale called off their wedding. Mayor Leetch called for a town meeting.

"Residents of Almond Hill, don't be alarmed." He cleared his throat. His hands were shaky and covered with liver spots. He spoke very slowly. "The so-called Machine of Death present in our community these past two weeks was a hoax, meant to swindle us out of our hard-earned money. I have contacted the FBI and they have informed me that they have identified a string of incidences similar to this one, perpetrated by the same suspect." He cleared his throat again. "They call him Johnny."

There were some nervous titters at that.

"We are cautioned to only use approved machines that employ proper medical and legal procedures. Trusted brands include DeathScope, Nex, Future-Care—" Coughs racked Mayor Leetch's frail body, and we half expected him to die right there. "Justice will be served," he wheezed. Dr. Hudson rushed to help him.

We quickly figured out that there was nothing else for Mayor Leetch to say. Everyone shuffled home, murmuring embarrassedly among themselves. I heard Mrs. Hudson sidle up to Mrs. Calloway.

"Helen, did you know?" Mrs. Hudson asked, trying to be tactful. "Did you know that it was a fake?"

"I didn't look closely. I've already had mine done."

"Could you tell, though? If you had looked closer?"

Mrs. Calloway made a sound halfway between a chuckle and a sniff.

"Didn't have you sign no forms, did it?"

"No," said Mrs. Hudson ashamedly.

"Didn't take your blood or nothing, did it?" asked Mrs. Calloway.

"No."

Mrs. Calloway shook her head.

"You all deserved it," she said. "Bunch of goddamn lying fools."

Story by Rhiannon Kelly
Illustration by Leela Wagner

BEAR

KC GREEN

SHIV SENA RIOT

Tuesday

"THANK YOU FOR CALLING MACHINE of Death Analysis. My name is Manisha; may I know your cause of death?"

"The card just says 'train.'"

Manisha's upbeat voice hid the fact that it was the last call of a very long night. She could barely keep her eyes open. Her mother simply did not consider an all-night shift to be an excuse to spend the day in bed, so it had been a while since she'd had anything resembling real sleep.

"Thank you for providing me with that information, sir. Let me see what data we have on people with the same reading, so we can find the most likely circumstances of your death," she continued, as friendly as ever. She typed the word into her computer and waited for the stat sheet to appear. "I see that there are twenty-three entries in the database who also got 'train,'" she continued dutifully. "That includes eight already deceased. I'm showing that five were passengers in a train that derailed, two were struck by trains while driving across the tracks, and the last one appears to be a suicide, since it shows he laid down on the tracks the day he got the reading."

"So you're pretty sure it's going to be a train crash?" the customer asked.

"Most likely, sir," Manisha replied. She muted the line so the customer couldn't hear her yawn. It was too bad they didn't allow coffee in the calling bay. "There is an average of three thousand train accidents per year, six percent of which are fatal, leading to an average of one thousand deaths annually. Statistically, it looks like you will join those numbers."

"So there's no chance of a...a what would you call it, a joke answer?" the customer asked.

"A joke answer?" Manisha knew what he was asking, but she was urged to never cast the machine in a malicious light.

"You know, like the guy on the news who got 'drug deal,' then had an allergic reaction to discount aspirin," the customer clarified.

"While overall the percentage of ironic readings is forty-nine percent," Manisha answered, "with your reading in particular it's been pretty straightforward. One hundred percent of those we've gathered data on have in fact been killed by locomotives."

"Well, the reason I'm asking is because I just started a new job, and I begin training tomorrow," the customer interjected nervously.

"No need to be concerned, sir." Manisha knew what he was getting at. "If training were your cause of death, the card would certainly say 'training' or 'trainer.' Not simply 'train.' While unexpected synonyms are often the cause of ironic readings, the machine always gets the grammar right."

Training might be the death of me, though, Manisha thought, remembering she had to be in three hours early for her next shift. For the third time in a month she was going to have to trade sleep for a mandatory training session.

"That's a relief." The customer sighed.

"Are you located in the city of Houston, Texas, sir?" Manisha asked suddenly.

"How did you know that?" the customer asked, proving her guess to be correct.

"As I mentioned, we have fifteen live listings in the database for death by train," Manisha responded, proud of her catch, "and all of them are in Houston, Texas. Given the close proximity, the likelihood of all of you dying in the same train accident is sixty percent, and in cases such as this, when all of the participants of a potential large-scale disaster are in the same place at the same time, the accident is likely to occur within seven to fourteen months. Most likely this winter, since accidents are more likely when there is ice or snow present."

"Oh God." The customer sounded terrified.

"Is there anything else I can assist you with today, sir?" Manisha asked pleasantly. She was sure she would get a good score on this call.

"I have a new baby on the way in March," the customer added.

"Congratulations, sir," Manisha replied.

"Are—are you sure that's what's going to happen?" the customer stuttered.

"Please be advised," Manisha quoted from her training manual, "that Machine of Death Analysis does not claim or provide advanced knowledge of the eventual details of your demise. We merely provide facts and statistics that may help you gain a better understanding of the likeliest possibilities."

The customer went silent for few moments. He began stammering as if trying to come up with something to say. Finally, he asked, "What is your cause of death?"

Manisha froze. No one had ever asked her that. "I'm sorry, sir, I cannot provide you with that information."

"I just need someone to talk to, you know?" the customer pleaded. "I can't tell my wife about any of this; this pregnancy's giving her enough to worry about."

"I cannot provide you with any personal information," she responded.

"What's the difference?" he asked. "I'm paying by the minute here, aren't I?"

Manisha knew he was right.

"I've never gotten a reading," she admitted.

"Never?" the customer asked. "Don't you want to? How can you spend all day answering questions about a machine you've never used?"

Do I? she wondered. Manisha had never really thought about it. After all, she spent six months answering calls for a GPS service without feeling like she was missing out on anything, and she didn't even own a car. "I'm located in Mumbai, India. We don't have the machine here."

"Are they banned?" The customer seemed relieved to have something to talk about other than his imminent death by train.

"Not officially," she explained, "but we have a group here called the Shiv Sena, who've appointed themselves the moral watchdogs of the city. And their leader doesn't approve of it."

"One guy gets to decide what is and isn't allowed?" the customer asked.

"Not officially," Manisha explained, since the customer was, after all, paying by the minute. "But if anyone ignores him, there end up being riots, so most everyone listens to him just to avoid the hassle. It's gotten to the point where all of the movie studios arrange private screenings for him to censor their movies before they come out because they know if he doesn't like them, people will end up setting movie theaters on fire. He doesn't like Valentine's Day, so if any stationery stores stock 'I Love You' cards, they get bricks thrown through their windows."

"What's his problem with Valentine's Day?"

"It's a Western holiday that he feels contradicts Hindu culture, just like he feels the Machine of Death contradicts local things like numerologists."

"Numerologists?"

"They use birth dates and times to predict marriages, deaths, and such. My mother has one, and she lets him control every decision my family makes. When I was baby he predicted that I would die in water. I mean, most people don't believe in it, but the Shiv Sena don't like Western technology telling them what to think." Saying this, Manisha realized that if she *had* taken the test, she could finally prove her mother wrong. It also reminded her how much grief her water-weary mother had given her for her entire childhood and she immediately felt guilty for having put this man so on edge.

"Look, this isn't the psychic hotline," she said, much calmer than before. "I don't know what's going to happen to you. The fact that you got 'train' probably means you're safer than most people. A train can't exactly sneak up on you. You're probably not going to run out and buy a ticket a couple of months before your baby's born, and you're clearly concerned enough that you know to steer clear of tracks. It will take a lot of long, happy years for it to slip your mind enough to happen."

"Thanks," the man said. She could hear in his voice that he meant it.

"Is there anything else I can assist you with?"

"Yeah, that villains-tying-people-to-the-railroad-tracks thing. That just happens in cartoons, right?" The customer laughed. Manisha was glad to hear him joking.

"Certainly," she replied, "but be wary of anyone with a handlebar mustache."

Wednesday

"Please excuse me," the trainer began. "I don't speak Indian, so I'll have to conduct this training in English."

Manisha was on her fifth cup of coffee. All of her fellow agents sat groggily around a large conference table while a jet-lagged but grinning middle-aged woman gestured wildly. Manisha had spent years trying to convince her mother (who had loudly protested the idea of her daughter spending her nights in an office, especially without consulting the family numerologist) that she actually liked being a call center agent. These training sessions were the one exception.

"But don't worry," the trainer continued. "This isn't going to be just any boring old training session. This is going to be fun!"

Manisha had never been to one of these 'boring old' sessions that every trainer she'd ever met was certain to distance themselves from. Every one she'd ever attended was conducted by some fresh-off-the-plane American who was convinced she had cracked the code to making learning fun because she had bought a book on team-building exercises or come up with an acronym. And they all thought that "Indian" was a language.

"What's the number one complaint you hear from customers?" the trainer asked.

Everyone was quiet. They knew she was reaching out for a certain answer and that it was more related to what she wanted to talk about than what the actual answer was.

"Come on," the trainer urged, "there are no wrong answers."

Keya raised her hand from across the table. "Hold time?"

"No, that's not it," the trainer replied.

Everyone remained silent.

"I want to talk to an American!" the woman exclaimed, and looked at the group expectantly. "How many times have you heard that from a caller?"

Everyone nodded their heads.

"Now, just what does the customer mean when they say that?" the trainer asked.

No one responded.

The woman walked over to the whiteboard and wrote the letters A-M-E-R-I-C-A-N across it. *Here comes the acronym*, Manisha thought.

"Agent Managing Empathetic Responses Instead of Canned Answers," the trainer said aloud as she wrote it across the board, then paused a moment, looking back over her own words with pride. "When the customer says they want to talk to an A.M.E.R.I.C.A.N., it just means that they feel you aren't showing them enough empathy. No offense," she continued, "but most Americans consider your accent to sound a little robotic and inhuman."

Why would I ever take offense at that? Manisha thought.

"So you really need to make up for that with a lot of empathy," the trainer said as she underlined the word on the board. "Can anyone tell me what empathy is?"

"Putting yourself in the customer's shoes," Vivek responded from the far side of the room, in a voice Manisha found to be quite human, despite the trainer's insinuation.

"Exactly," the trainer shouted, thrilled that someone had answered according to her script. "Death is one of the most uncomfortable things for Americans to talk about. Getting a reading and having it analyzed are very stressful experiences, as anyone who has done so will know. How many of you have gotten a reading?"

No one raised their hands.

"No one?" she responded. "Has anyone ever seen a Machine of Death?"

Everyone looked at one another anxiously but remained quiet. There were posters of the machine all over the calling bay, and diagrams in the training manual, but none of them had ever seen one in person.

"Well, how can you put yourselves in the customer's shoes if you've never even been in a shoe store?" The trainer chuckled. From beneath the table, she pulled out a large brown duffel bag.

Here comes the team-building exercise, Manisha thought.

But rather than rustle through the bag to find a rubber-banded bunch of dollar-store markers for some communal art project, or Lincoln Logs to make team towers out of, the trainer just turned the bag upside down so that a single object would thud dramatically onto the table.

A noticeable hush fell across the already quiet room. It was smaller than they'd all imagined it would be. The smooth white finish was scuffed as though it had seen its share of use.

It was a Machine of Death.

The silence was broken by a bit of nervous giggling as the two people closest to the machine reached across the table to touch it.

"Who wants to give it a try?" the trainer asked. Finally, she had their full attention.

Reno went first. He nervously placed his finger inside and jumped back in surprise as it was pricked by the needle. After a few seconds, a small card popped out.

"Choking," he announced, and immediately stopped reaching for the snacks in the center of the table.

He slid the machine over to Neha. She stuck her finger in without a moment of hesitation and seemed excited to read her card.

"Landslide," she told the group, then pumped her fist in the air victoriously, knowing what a cool way to go that would be. The machine continued to make its way around the table.

"Shellfish allergy," began Vivek nervously, "but I'm veg!"

"Sounds like you better stay that way," said Savio, who kept laughing until he read his own card. "Autorickshaw."

Manisha heard all of this happening, but her mind was elsewhere. She was picturing the look on her mother's face if she came home with one of those cards. She was picturing all of those summers she wasn't allowed to go to the beach. The days she had to stay home alone because she wasn't allowed out in the rain. The showers she wasn't allowed to take without her mother's supervision. The jobs she'd been fired from because her mother made her skip work during the floods. All because an old man in orange pajamas did some math problems and decided water would kill her. She was picturing the smile on her own face when she finally proved her mother wrong.

"Go on, do it," said Savio.

Manisha was startled by the interruption. She hadn't even noticed that the machine was now in front of her. How long had she been staring right at it? How long had everyone in the room been staring at her, waiting for her to do something?

"Oh, I didn't—," Manisha began.

"She doesn't have to do it if she doesn't want to," the trainer interjected, grabbing the machine away just as Manisha finally started to reach for it. The trainer quickly slid the machine along to the next person. "They told me some of you might have religious objections. I don't want to start an international incident."

Before Manisha could open her mouth to respond, Roohie was already thrusting her finger into the slot to get her prediction. It was a bad one, and the whole room paused to comfort her. Manisha hadn't meant to give up her turn, but it wasn't the right time to speak up.

Why did I hesitate? Manisha wondered.

After the last card was handed out, the trainer jumped right into empathy training without missing a beat and left little time for discussion. The next time Manisha had the chance to speak, it was to answer a question about customer satisfaction. Before she knew it, the training was over. The woman had packed her machine back up in the brown duffel bag and disappeared, never to be heard from again. Back to the phones.

"Thank you for calling Machine of Death Analysis. My name is Manisha; may I know your cause of death?"

Thank God, this customer was a talker. The 'cancers' usually were. Sometimes Manisha's job was more about listening than talking, and her head was swimming with thoughts too much to concentrate on holding up her end of the conversation. That seemed to be the case throughout the bay. She overheard Savio say "Thank you for calling autorickshaw."

"I wish I had called sooner," the customer said. "I mean, I wish I hadn't been so afraid of talking about this stuff. My wife and I, we made a pact not to tell one another how we would go. I didn't want to worry her with, you know, with that."

Why did I hesitate? Manisha asked herself again. Now that she thought about it, that card was exactly what she needed. Hard evidence once and for all that her mother was wrong. And if she was wrong about the water thing, what else was she wrong about?

"I knew she was acting weird," the customer continued. "I thought she was just being stubborn. We were trying to get to her sister's house, and I was sick of the weird little shortcut she always made me take that seemed to take us an hour out of the way. She insisted, but I told her that I was driving and I would take whatever route I damn well pleased."

That trainer was long gone now, probably on a plane back to America, where she would regale her friends with tales of her trip as though they took place in an adventure novel rather than on the highway between the Hotel Intercontinental Grand and a Goregaon office park. Manisha would probably never see one of those machines again.

"She didn't tell me," reiterated the customer. "God bless her, no matter how much I screamed at her and called her a stubborn old nag and an annoying backseat driver, she kept that promise and she didn't tell me."

It had been Manisha's one shot. Now she would be stuck living her life based on the whims of that orange-pajamaed old man until the day she finally got married and moved out. And she couldn't even do that without his say-so.

"Her card said I-94. That's why she'd been avoiding that road. God bless her, she kept that promise. And I told her...no, I don't even want to think about the last thing I said to her before the truck hit."

Manisha suddenly snapped back to reality and felt guilty for ignoring her customer. *Maybe I should have paid attention to that empathy training after all,* she thought.

Thursday

A mere five hours after getting home from work, Manisha was already awake and dressed, not to mention two buses and a train into the day's errands. All because it was time to cash her check, and her mother had chosen a bank with both a single location on the other side of the city and a two p.m. closing time.

Getting off at Grant Road meant a stroll through the Chor Bazaar and a chorus of shady shopkeeps in nameless and ever-changing stalls hawking everything from bootleg DVDs to the stolen DVD players you could play them on.

She had learned to ignore the salesmen, but there was something she enjoyed about the endless parade of nameless stalls draped in AV cables to devices that might or might not exist anymore. The piles of paperbacks that someone had meticulously photocopied page by page then tried to sell for more than a used original would cost. The way the man sitting on a pile of boosted car radios smiled like he was the most honest businessman in the world.

"Nokia, Motorola, Sony!" one man yelled out as Manisha approached. She focused her gaze on the bank just ahead of her and didn't acknowledge him. "Nokia, Motorola, Sony!" he repeated loudly. Just as she passed, he quietly added, "Machine of Death."

Manisha froze. She took a few steps forward, then stopped at a nearby stall and pretended to skim DVDs as she tried to figure out if he'd just said what she thought he'd said. The man caught on to her hesitation and strolled over.

"Machine of Death?" he asked her directly. The owner of the DVD stall caught the man trying to poach his customer and the two salesmen had a loud, angry argument in Gujarati. When the shoving started, Manisha slipped out and ran into the bank.

A few minutes later, she was back. The man sat on the ground quietly grinning, with his wares delicately laid out across a blue piece of tarp. Out-of-date cell phones. Faux-leather cases. Universal remotes. An orphaned Super Nintendo controller. He didn't say a word. He knew the fact that she'd come back meant he had her, and at double the price she would have gotten five minutes earlier.

"Machine of Death?" she quietly asked.

The man looked to his left, looked to his right, then silently folded the four corners of his tarp together and slung the whole thing over his shoulder. He stood up and started to walk through the crowd. He motioned for her to follow.

Between two stalls was a rusted old metal pull-down gate. The man raised it and walked into a dark, dirty stairwell. Manisha followed and waited for him to turn on the light, until she looked up and saw the broken pieces of fluorescent tubing dangling from the ceiling. Instead, he pulled the gate back down so that the only light coming into the room was that creeping in from under the gate. The only thing illuminated was the path of the rats scurrying across the floor. From deep under the stairs, the man pulled an old sack and plopped it, half-opened, out in front of her.

"One reading, nine hundred rupees," the man barked.

It was steep, but Manisha had just cashed her check. She started to reach into her bag before realizing what a vulnerable position she was in. Suddenly she was filled with dread. This man could just pull out a knife at any moment. It was too noisy outside for anyone to hear, and no one in the world knew where she was. She was terrified. It was exhilarating.

She had experienced a similar mixture of fear and excitement the weekend prior, when she had snuck out of the house after her mother floated the idea of an arranged marriage. She met up with the office's trekking team. This was nothing new. She'd been on mountain climbs with them before, always telling her mother she was on some made-up weekend training session at work (the one time her office's love of poorly timed training came in handy). Only this time, it was a white-water-rafting trip.

The feeling she had flying over the rapids, through the spray, after twenty-two years of not being allowed to so much as step in a puddle, was matched only by the feeling of stepping back onto dry land, safe and sound. There had been a moment when she closed her eyes and felt the mist splashing against her face, the bright sunlight streaming through her eyelids. It was the best feeling she'd ever had. She had felt free.

After that, this little man was nothing to be afraid of. She put the money back into her purse and barked back at the man, "Show it to me."

He opened the sack, and Manisha leaned in to get a look. It was dark, but she could tell right off that it wasn't even the right shape. It looked more like a broken kitchen mixer sitting on top of an old cassette deck. *He figures most Indians don't know what one looks like,* she thought. *He's right.*

"What is this?" Manisha demanded. She pulled open the cassette tray and found a stack of white cards that surely had deaths prewritten on them. "This is fake! Are you trying to cheat me?"

Manisha smacked the man across the back of the head and demanded he open the gate. She certainly wasn't going to touch that rusted old thing. The man dutifully obeyed, and she was on her way.

She stopped in the middle of the busy market and closed her eyes. The sun wasn't as bright as it had been on the river. She could almost still feel the mist. She wanted to feel that freedom again. *I've got to find one of those machines,* she thought.

"Thank you for calling Machine of Death Analysis. My name is Manisha; may I know your cause of death?" Back to work. Back on the phones. Manisha rubbed her eyes to keep from collapsing. She tried to figure out the last time she had gotten a good night's sleep. She'd been in meetings and on errands every day of the week. She had been too excited to sleep after the rafting trip. Even when she had the chance to sleep, she couldn't. The last time she remembered really being rested was before she and her ex had split up. Could it really have been a month?

Her customer sounded terrified.

"Hi, um...I was just on a plane. AL413 out of Detroit," the woman began. "I just—I had to get off. I've always been afraid of flying, but this was just...different, you know? They had already closed the doors, but I just...I just had to get off."

First timer, Manisha thought. *The ink on the card is probably still wet. They never answer the question right off. They're still trying to make sense of it in their heads. They feel the need to tell you the whole story before the dramatic reveal, as though it was a tale she'd never heard before.*

"So I'm sitting there in the terminal for over an hour," the customer continued. "My flight's left without me, I'm thinking about how fired I'm going to be for bailing on this meeting, and then I see they got one of these Machine of Death things over by the pay phones."

So you decide to use it, hoping it will prove your death isn't air travel related, and you can merrily catch the next flight and be on your way, Manisha guessed.

"So I think, here we go: I get my card, prove there's nothing to worry about, and get on the next flight."

Manisha tried to guess what air-related reading the woman had gotten. *Engine failure. Improperly stowed tray table. Single-serving salted peanuts. No, wait, they don't serve those anymore.*

"The card said AL413. The flight I'd just gotten off of. I don't know what...My heart just jumped out of my chest. There was a sticker on the side of the machine that said to call this number. Did I just...Did I just beat death? Is that possible? Was I supposed to die on that plane?"

Manisha laughed out loud.

"Ma'am, the machine is never wrong," she explained. "Just because you don't get on Flight AL413 today doesn't mean it won't fly again tomorrow. Or Monday. The airline's website says it runs five times a week. Maybe you'll never set foot on it again, but that doesn't mean that it won't drop an engine one day onto your car. Or crash into your house. Hell, maybe someone will invent a variation of the AK-47 named AL-413 and you'll get shot with it. The most likely scenario, though, is that the flight number itself has spooked you, leading you to get off the plane that would have taken you to safety, sending you into a dangerous situation you wouldn't otherwise be in, and you'll die this very afternoon."

"Oh, um. Okay," the woman responded.

"Flight tracker says AL413 landed twelve minutes ago safe and sound," Manisha added happily. "Is there anything else I can assist you with today?"

"Uh, no, that's it," the woman replied.

"Thank you for calling Machine of Death Analysis," Manisha said. "You have a great day."

Friday

Manisha stared at the patterns in the peeling section of wallpaper next to her bed that she had come to know well during her many sleepless days. The effort it took to hold her eyes closed in the hopes of falling asleep took more energy than she had. Her whole body ached. Her teeth clattered involuntary as if they had someplace more important to be.

She tried once again to close her eyes, hoping to feel the mist, but all she could see was the lingering pattern of the wallpaper. It had been burned into her retinas. This was wallpaper that her mother had chosen, not her. But it had become part of her through sheer repetition.

These missed opportunities with the machine had gotten her brain working overtime. She couldn't shake the feeling that she was stuck in a life that wasn't hers. One that had a beginning, a middle, and an end before she opened her eyes for the first time. Her name had been chosen before she was conceived because the seven letters in it were a numerologically pleasing combination. The second she was born, the date and time of her birth decided how she would die. Everything in between was paint by number. It wasn't her life. And without that card, she didn't know how else she could prove it.

As always, her mother had passive-aggressively turned the television up far too loud, to show that no respectable person should be sleeping at ten in the morning. Manisha could usually tune it out, but there was a lot of screaming and shouting on the news. She peered over the blanket to see what was happening.

"Malad West," her mother said. "They got one of those Death Machines at the big mall out there."

Manisha sat up quickly and saw for herself. It was one of the larger models, like they must have had at that airport her customer was calling from. Someone had risked the wrath of the moral watchdogs by importing one. The news quickly cut to the scene outside, where a mob of Shiv Sainiks were predictably throwing chairs through windows and employing their favorite move, setting a bus on fire. This machine wasn't going to be there for long, and if this was how people reacted, it really would be her last chance. Manisha started putting on her clothes.

"Where are you going?" her mother asked.

"I'm going over there," Manisha responded. She was too exhausted to make up an excuse.

Her mother was shocked into silence until a whisper creaked out. "I don't want you going out there!"

"It's selfish to think you can always get what you want," Manisha snapped back.

This time the words shot directly from her brain to her mouth, before Manisha even had the chance to think about it. It may not have been a conscious thought, but Manisha knew exactly where it came from.

It was the same line her mother had used on her a month earlier, upon meeting Ritesh. He and Manisha had been secretly dating for two years. She had finally worked up the guts to introduce him to her parents, because they were planning to get married.

They met for lunch. Manisha and her mother on one side of the table, Ritesh and her father on the other. And at the head of the table—surprise, surprise—a special guest who 'just happened' to drop by. The numerologist.

Mom and Dad didn't ask Ritesh where he came from. How he'd met Manisha. Where he worked. They didn't ask a single question. The only one speaking was that orange-pajamaed old man. He had one thing to ask.

"Do you choose three, five, or seven?"

Ritesh paused and waited for some sort of follow-up or context. Manisha knew it wasn't coming. Mom and Dad glanced at one another, taking his silence to be indecisiveness, not a good trait at all in a son-in-law. Manisha mentally pleaded for him just to pick one.

"Th-three," he finally squeaked out.

The numerologist was stone-faced. He didn't say anything. That one word was enough to seal Ritesh's fate. The old man politely washed up with the finger bowl and excused himself. Manisha's parents followed him out. Manisha and Ritesh sat silently at the table, pretending as though they couldn't hear the discussion on the other side of the door.

Manisha's parents were adamant. "That boy is not a good match for you." Ritesh was adamant. "I won't come between you and your parents." She never saw him again. She left the call center they both worked at soon after and started working for Machine of Death Analysis.

She hadn't slept since.

"It's selfish to think you can always get what you want."

It took all morning to get to the mall. No taxis would go any-where near the place, even if they could find a clear path. Not even the ambulances could find a way in. The violence was all over the street, and the unfortunate vehicles that were stuck in the result-ing citywide traffic jam were being rewarded for their patience with broken windshields and slashed tires. She'd had to fight her way to work before through situations like this. Many businesses closed down when it got bad, but the American companies who hired her were unmoved by Indian politics. In those cases, it was always about finding a way around the chaos. This time, she was heading right into the eye of the storm.

No one bothered Manisha on her way in. They must have figured that anyone with a look of determination like that must be on their side. She took no notice of the hundreds of people spouting party catchphrases, the bricks flying past her head, or the broken shards of glass she had to step over.

The rioters had certainly taken control of the city, but as soon as she reached the doors of the mall, it was like entering a sovereign nation. The Embassy of the Great Kingdom of Capitalism. The line to get past the lobby was like airport security, if the airport employees carried assault rifles to keep undesirables from even getting in line. They noted that Manisha was not one of the rioters and let her through to the scanners. She was herded through a metal detector and patted down, the contents of her purse emptied out on a table, and then politely handed a coupon for buy-one-get-one-free fruit smoothies.

Manisha looked around at the mall's palace-like interior. You could barely hear the commotion outside. Just the faintest hum of the unending symphony of car alarms and police sirens carried over the echoing Muzak. It was like a shrine, specifically designed to help people ignore the world just outside. This was where people came to buy overpriced foreign goods, double their already marked-up price, since they were imported. It was where people came to see the latest Bollywood movies while sitting in leather love seats. Where they tried on dresses that cost more than Manisha's apartment.

The machine sat deep inside an otherwise empty storefront. There wasn't even a sign above the door. This guy knew he wasn't going to be around for long and just wanted to make as much money off the machine as he could before the rioters forced him to shut it down. A guard sat sleepily on an overturned bucket next to the door leaning on his rifle, blissfully unaware that the guards outside were having a much rougher day than he. A line of about ten people led up to the machine.

Manisha joined the queue, standing behind a girl who couldn't have been more than twelve. Slowly but surely, they both inched closer to the machine. A parade of faces passed by, with expressions ranging from sullen to dazed, their eyes leading down to a pair of trembling hands clutching their forbidden fruit, those small white cards that sealed their fate.

The young girl soon reached the front of the line. She dug into her tiny pocketbook and pulled out the necessary twenty-five hundred rupees. Silently, she placed her finger into the front of the machine. The machine whirred and grinded, then spat out yet another card.

The girl's face scrunched up as she read the card a few times to herself. She then read it aloud, to no one in particular.

"Water." The girl's face started to turn red. Tears began to well up. "What does that mean?" she demanded. The attendant tried to shoo her away, but Manisha couldn't help but feel for the girl. She jumped between the two of them and went right into work mode.

"I don't have the numbers on me," Manisha explained, "but 'water' leans heavily toward drowning with a bit of slipping. It's notoriously hard to predict, though; it does end up being water poisoning and water intoxication sometimes."

She looked up at the attendant, who was trying to move the line along. He clearly wanted to get through as many customers as he could while he was still in business. "I work for the company that analyzes these things," she explained. The attendant didn't seem to care.

"I'm supposed to go to Goa with my grandma next week," the little girl told her.

"No!" Manisha snapped at the frightened girl as she grabbed her by the shoulders. Manisha stopped in her tracks as the little girl ran away crying.

Stay away from the beach, she had been about to say. *Avoid the lake. Stay out of the rain. Don't go into the shower alone.* The material she was about to cover didn't come from her training manual. It came from her mother.

"Next up," the attendant hollered.

This is what this knowledge does to people, Manisha thought. *I haven't even taken the test yet, and I've already become my mother.*

The impatient attendant demanded she either pay for her turn or step out of line. The guard had found his way off the bucket, slung the rifle over his shoulder, and started to lazily wander over to the front of the line to see what the commotion was. Manisha rustled through her purse and handed over almost everything she had. She put her finger in the slot. The machine did its humming and whirring.

It was bad enough waiting for her own card. Manisha wondered how much worse this would feel if the life of someone she loved were in the balance. *If this is what's been running through my mother's head for twenty-two years, it's no wonder she's gone crazy.*

She felt the prick of the needle on her skin. It was like a mosquito bite.

The fear and uncertainty were as real in Manisha's mind as they surely were in her mother's. *Is hinging your fate on what a piece of card stock tells you really any less silly than trusting a system that's thousands of years old?*

With its final whir and click, the machine deposited the small white card into the tray.

It stayed there.

Manisha closed her eyes. She felt it. Not the mist from her whitewater-rafting trip; that was just a memory. She felt what she really wanted to feel. She felt free. She was already living her own life. Not the one her mother had chosen, and not the one this white card was about to present to her.

"I don't need to know," Manisha announced to no one in particular. She walked away from the machine without ever touching the card.

The sound of the car alarms and sirens came back into focus as she wandered out the door, back into the sunlight, and back into the fray.

I'm going to go home and get some sleep, Manisha thought. *No, sleep can wait. I'm going to have lunch with my mom.*

Story by Ryan Estrada
Illustration by Ben McSweeney

ZEPHYR

"COME ON, YOU APES! You wanna live forever?!" yelled Company Sergeant Hurley [HEART ATTACK 28-Apr-2179 04:45.hrs ^.13] above the sudden roar of our navy troop transport dropping into atmo above the enemy's planet.

His exuberance was answered with amused silence. Tough to tell through armor, but I think Hurley became a little embarrassed. Choosing to "live forever" or not might have been motivating back in the Invincibles Battalion, but not so much here in the Ephemerals. If he didn't outrank me, and if there weren't fifty other soldiers watching, I would have told him to shut his trap.

The skids of the Rhino hit dirt, and a shudder went through the bulkheads to our seats. Our thick powered armor rattled against one another, our bodies tightly encapsulated, only our organs jostling inside. Sergeant Hurley jumped to his feet and smacked the release pad. The hatch slammed down, and the bay filled with the zips and crackle of incoming fire.

The Rhino's top cannon answered with a roar. Hurley pointed at me. "Platoon Sergeant Barrows, get your troops up and follow me!" He sprinted through the hatch and stood tall in the open, returning fire while waving us forward.

Flipping a switch on my armor's forearm activated the Platoon Communication link. "By squads, disembark," I ordered over the PlatCom. "Defensive perimeter up fast!"

My platoon bundled out quickly and spread out. I was last. The hatch closed behind me and the Rhino lifted off, rumbling along our flank to light up the enemy with its cannons. I headed for a nice thick wall, but halfway there I spotted Sergeant Hurley standing on the edge of a culvert, calmly shooting.

With a curse, I veered from my wall, waited for an opening, and crossed twenty meters in a terrifying dash, tackling Hurley into the ditch.

From underneath, Hurley clanged a fist on my shoulderplate. "Get the hell off me," he barked.

"Yes, Sergeant." I rolled over while keeping as low as possible.

Hurley sat up. "You want to explain your—"

I slammed him back on the ground as bullets whizzed where his head had been. "Don't give them a target!"

Hurley struggled under my arm. "Sergeant Barrows, we've got to destroy that anti-spacecraft battery so the cruisers can enter orbit and—"

I cut him off. "You can't destroy anything if you're dead." I released him when I felt him quit resisting. "You crossed the zero threshold, and now you're on your curve. You're not an Invincible anymore."

The Vanguard Regiment had just the two battalions. Hurley was a new company sergeant in our Ephemerals, freshly transferred from the Invincibles the day before. It was his first drop mission since his curve start date, and he had to learn that the bravado of an Invincible could—if left unchecked—get us all killed before our predicted times of death. Only Corporal Moeller [GUNFIRE 15-May-2177 16:33.hrs ^.87] was scheduled to die on this mission.

I've developed a knack for reading body language through powered armor, and I could basically see Hurley roll his eyes. "My time of death is four years from now."

"No. A TOD in four years just means that's when your percentage curve hits a hundred percent."

"But it just started. So my odds of dying are tiny—"

"Your *baseline* odds are tiny. But you're in the middle of a firefight. Your chances are spiking high."

Now I read exasperation as Hurley sat up again. "Chances of

what? The Death Machine said 'heart attack' for me, not a bullet. I just had a physical, so—"

I smacked him back down. "Everyone knows DM predictions are screwy. If the enemy shoots at your chest, wouldn't that count as an *attack* on your heart?"

For a moment, he just stared at me. "Right," he said gruffly.

The PlatCom chimed before I could drive home the point further. My squad leaders reported that they were in position. Hurley slowly lifted his head dangerously high out of the culvert to view the battle.

I couldn't imagine what he was going through. He'd done four tours in Vanguard Regiment, the navy's elite and unique special ops unit, and all of it in the First Invincibles Battalion. That's forty years of going into battle knowing you'd stay alive.

All humanity could learn *how* they were going to die, but the navy had secretly developed a way to derive a time frame of sorts, using a powerful quantum computer array. It wasn't definitive; they could only accurately predict the first moment in someone's life when the odds of dying were greater than zero. But from that point, they could also calculate the rate at which those odds of dying would increase. It formed a parabolic curve over time, rising steeply at the end. The date the odds hit one hundred percent was the TOD.

Hurley, myself, and the other ten thousand people in the Vanguard Regiment were the only humans who knew when our death could possibly first occur—and the date we had *no* chance of passing. Those off their curves, still at zero percent, were put in the Invincibles.

The men in the Ephemerals had crossed that threshold. Their curves had begun. Steadily, their lives would become increasingly likely to end.

Possibly *incredibly* likely in Hurley's case if I didn't do something. I yanked him over so we were viewplate to viewplate, low in the ditch. "Comprehend fast, Company Sergeant, that it's now possible for you to die at any moment, and act accordingly. Because I will not let your stupidity take anyone with you." I hit the PlatCom. "Execute as planned."

Squads on each flank opened fire simultaneously, and I glanced over the edge of the culvert. "Pull your head out. Follow me!"

The heads-up display in my helmet showed the blue blips of my men sliding across the terrain. Hurley and I joined the platoon pushing up the middle. We traded speed for safety, and just as the shooting began again, we took cover behind a berm. On the other side was a flat, bare field about two hundred meters wide: a daunting kill zone between us and the enemy's compound of trenches, bunkers, and steel palisades.

This was the breakaway colonies' staging area for attacks against the Confederation of Terran Systems and our busiest shipping lanes. Naval Command wanted to retake the planet, but before they could bring in the heavy cruisers, the anti-spacecraft batteries had to go. The giant gun emplacement over the next hill—past all those pissed-off colonist soldiers—was our responsibility.

From the berm, we threw suppression fire across the field to buy time for the flanking squads to move up into position. Hurley had apparently listened, finally, and was shooting from cover instead of standing upright like a jackass. He mimicked me when I hunkered down for the enemy's return volley. As bullets and plasma flew overhead, I tried to shake how surreal our moment in the culvert had been. How could I expect him to quickly shake a lifetime of confidence and invulnerability or calmly face his impending mortality?

The minimized map began blinking in the corner of my helmet screen. I expanded it to full view to watch my platoon's blue blips spread out in a semicircle around a sea of enemy red. The blips of my five squad leaders displayed "READY" icons. The time was 1630 hours.

"Alternating fire," I called out over the PlatCom. "Fourth Squad, begin your feint."

On the left flank, the ten members of Fourth Squad bounded out of cover. The enemy's fire shifted, focusing in on the squad. Fourth Squad scattered, diving behind anything or scrambling back over the berm, appearing to be pinned down, giving the impression of being routed.

A beeping sounded in my earbuds and I glanced at the time. It was 1631. On the right flank, a blue blip began blinking yellow.

"My turn," a voice said over the PlatCom. It was Corporal Moeller [GUNFIRE 15-May-2177 16:33.hrs ^.87]. It was time for Phase 3 of the tactical plan: Moeller and his last minute.

"Platoon Sergeant," said Moeller's squad leader, Sergeant Thompson [SUPERHEATED AIR 04-May-2178 19:38.hrs ^.54]. "Ready here."

"Copy that," I replied, then, "Covering fire for Moeller in ten seconds." I grimaced as the platoon filled the channel with "good luck," "thank you," and "we'll miss ya." I was silent.

I never knew what to say.

Seconds later, we popped over the top to send a wall of metal and fire tearing into the enemy camp. Moeller broke ranks and ran straight through the open. The enemy was still suppressing Fourth Squad, so Moeller made it halfway across before any of them noticed. We did all we could to ruin their aim, and Moeller reached the first trench with only a few grazing hits. Without a pause, he hopped a low wall and emptied his rifle into all around him. Then he drew his knife and viciously attacked anyone left standing. His flashing yellow blip turned black at 1633.

The instant Moeller leapt into the trench, the platoon charged. We caught them off-guard and blew through their defenses. During the brief minute of violence, Sergeant Zweig [PROJECTILE 04-May-2178 19:38.hrs ^.54] of Third Squad was shot and killed. And then it was over.

I opened a channel to Company Command. "Bravo Platoon, mission success. One scheduled casualty...and one unscheduled." Announcing the early death of Zweig was tough. It was a year before his TOD; his baseline death percentage couldn't have been higher than seventeen percent.

"Bravo Platoon, Charlie Command, acknowledged. Mission success across the board. Prepare for extraction."

I dispatched a demolition team to the anti-spacecraft battery, supervised the bagging of Zweig, and went to look for Moeller. I found him where GUNFIRE had finally got him: crumpled on top of a pile of defeated foes. It was a beautiful way to go.

I was Platoon Sergeant Barrows [ZEPHYR 04-May-2178 19:39. hrs ^.54], Ephemerals Battalion of the Vanguard Regiment, and I would one hundred percent cease to exist in a year.

In true navy tradition, the food on the NSS *Korsigan* battalion carrier was excellent, but today I was just picking at my chow. It had been months since we lost Zweig, and while there had been a steady stream of successful missions and lost Ephemerals, he kept returning to my thoughts. But my tablemates seemed in high spirits; you couldn't survive in the Ephemerals dwelling on the continuous death.

I was listening to PFC Norris [DISINTEGRATION 04-May-2178 19:38.hrs ^.54] tell a joke when, one by one, the mood of my messmates shifted to neutral. Following their looks, I spotted an officer casually walking toward us through the tables, and my demeanor went cool as well.

"Platoon Sergeant Barrows," the officer greeted me when he arrived. "Men," he added with a nod down the table.

"Lieutenant Dallas." I nodded politely to the short young man with the Naval Intelligence Command insignia on his lapels. "What a . . . pleasant surprise."

His smile was half-genuine, half-sly. "I just dropped by to say hello."

With a snort, I put down my fork and crossed my arms. This wasn't his first time visiting us; the lieutenant was here for a reason.

Dallas noticed my disbelief. "I also brought gifts." He beckoned across the hall to two men standing near the doors.

Lieutenant Dallas [SEX 20-June-2216 23:12.hrs ^.78] was a planner in Naval Intelligence Command. The NIC had smart, serious officers stationed throughout the navy who collected, analyzed, and utilized information on the tactical and strategic levels. The Vanguard Regiment was special, though, with its secret and highly valuable data on when and how we would die, so only the brightest and brainiest NIC officers were assigned to us. Of course, this kept the NIC especially busy planning our campaigns and missions. They had to anticipate years ahead, think fast in real time, all while making sure each mission matched the TODs of the thousands of men who could die anytime...the Ephemerals.

Our NIC detachment was a serious and humorless bunch, but that was where Lieutenant Dallas was unique. His demeanor was casual, even playful, and he never seemed to notice the crushing responsibilities he carried. I wasn't sure if that was a good or bad trait.

The two enlisted men reached the table and stood at attention. "At ease," Dallas said to them and waved them to sit. "Here are two transfers to your platoon, Sergeant Barrows."

"Uh, Lieutenant," I began, "this isn't how you process new troops. Besides, enlisted men sit elsewhere; this is a noncom table."

"No, it's not," Lieutenant Dallas said cheerfully. "This is the May Day table."

Stony silence descended, broken only by the clatter of a few forks. "Is that why...," began Sergeant Yarden [TIMING 04-May-2178 19:37.hrs ^.54]. "I mean, we noticed, of course, but we didn't..."

His voice trailed away. One of the transfers spoke up. "What does he mean? Do you all have a TOD fourth of May too?" We were silent. "Point-five-four curve rate?"

Our expressions must have answered his questions, because he stared mutely at the table.

"What is this, Lieutenant?" I eventually asked. "Putting all your eggs in one basket?"

The lieutenant shrugged. "Yes? No? Maybe? Honestly, we don't know yet. It might be coincidental; one big battle with the platoon spread across the front. Or, yes, you could all be together. We don't have any definitive plans or objectives for May, but signs are pointing toward something big happening around that time. The fourth in particular is vital. To me, at least."

"Just you?" I asked, reading between his lines. "What does the rest of our NIC detachment believe?"

Dallas shrugged. "The admiral is letting me pursue my hunch."

"Your *hunch*?" exclaimed PFC Winders [FLAMING CHAIR 04-May-2178 19:38.hrs ^.54]. "We're risking our lives—"

Dallas raised his hand to interrupt. "That was the wrong word.

I can't explain much of what I do or how I do it, but..." He looked up in thought for a moment. "I look at the big picture of the war, the small skirmishes, the percentages and TODs for sure, but also the causes. I grab as much info as possible that's even remotely connected with this platoon, and then pore through it, rearrange it, and study it all until something makes sense. It's like putting together a huge jigsaw puzzle that has no corners, straight edges, or box art. And it's a picture of a polar bear in a blizzard." He leaned forward. Unconsciously, the entire table leaned in and waited. "I'll admit the final hours before a mission are a bit hectic, but at some point the fog burns off and I see a clear path. The plan solidifies, and you guys make it happen. We've done pretty good so far, right?"

"Yeah, so far," said Sergeant Higgins [SHARD OF GLASS 04-May-2178 19:38.hrs ^.54] from two seats down.

"My favorite is still what was arranged for Moeller," said Sergeant Zhang [CONCRETE 04-May-2178 19:38.hrs ^.54], sitting next to me. "I hope my death has that much honor."

"Ah, you liked that, did you?" Dallas asked. "That was one of mine. It was a good plan to get past the large kill zone around the anti-spacecraft guns."

Specialist Collins [STYLUS THROUGH EYE 04-May-2178 19:38. hrs ^.54] snorted derisively. "It was just luck, not planning."

Lieutenant Dallas cocked his head. "Not by a long shot, but I guess you'll just have to trust I know what I'm doing." He stood, threw us a casual salute, and left the mess hall. "Take care, men."

We stared at each other, motionless and silent. Collins spoke up first. "What a crock. We're just toys for the regiment to play with," he said, getting mad. "We're expendable. Our TODs just give them an excuse to do what they want."

"It's not like that," I replied. "You heard the lieutenant. There's a lot of planning—"

"Yeah, right," Collins interrupted. "That's just what they say. Remember Zweig? It's all a coincidence. It's all crap!" He slammed his palm on the table. "If they'd told me before I applied that they'd tell me how long I had left—"

"What, you would have said no?" I countered. "And of course it has to be a secret. You want to tell the galaxy that the navy can get a TOD off the Death Machine? That wouldn't cause mass panic and destruction, oh no." His idiocy was getting me upset, and I tried to calm down. "Remember your history classes? Remember all the chaos and wars when we first discovered the Death Machine?"

"That's...that's different!" Collins blustered. "That was over a hundred years ago! People wouldn't be like that now."

I sat back in my chair and sighed. "Really? And why are we at war right now? Why did the colonists break away? Mandatory DM tests. Yeah, humans are completely different now."

"Maybe the lieutenant should join us on one of his perfectly planned missions, then. See if that changes his tune. Or just send all Invincibles, all the time!"

One of the new PFCs, Specialist Rocher [COMPRESSION 04-May-2178 19:38.hrs ^.54], raised a hesitant hand. "Platoon Sergeant? Um, why *don't* we just send Invincibles on all the missions? Why use Ephemerals at all?"

"Good question, Private." Holding up a hand, I counted off a finger. "Missions using only Invincibles have a thirty-five percent success rate. Sometimes the only way to complete an objective is to trade lives for it. Ephemerals succeed ninety-five percent of the time.

"Two, it never worked in the past to mix Invincible and Ephemerals below company strength, and it wouldn't work now.

"Three, the lieutenant won't have a glorious, honorable death like we will. He, I hate to say, is a Lucky Bastard."

Collins crossed his arms in disgruntled silence.

"Why is the lieutenant lucky?" asked Corporal Tildon [4TH DEGREE BURNS 04-May-2178 19:38.hrs ^.54].

A grin spread across my face. "Because Lieutenant Dallas's lucky Death Machine prediction is sex."

"Bastard," said Corporal Smythe [BROKEN ARMOR 04-May-2178 19:38.hrs ^.54].

"If you don't mind, Sergeant," continued Corporal Tildon, "what's your Death Machine prediction?"

I snorted. "The slip of paper said 'ZEPHYR.' Apparently, a gentle breeze is gonna take me out." I waved a hand at the sniggering. "Sure, laugh. Just wait till I break that wind."

The table erupted in laughter. I let it go for a bit, then stood up to address the table. "All right, listen up. We've got, at most, six months left in this universe. If we keep our heads clear and focused, we all might make it to our May Day. A TOD cluster is exceptionally rare, and I truly believe our NIC pals are going to seize the opportunity with both hands. Whatever is coming, it's going to be big." Determination began to replace their grim looks. "Or would you rather be like the rest of mankind, clueless and doomed to die with no purpose, no meaning?"

"No!" they cried in unison.

"We don't know how it'll end," I continued, "but our mission now is to make sure we get to the party."

I left the table and the mess hall, but I didn't go to my bunk. Instead, I headed aft to officer country. Just outside of a wardroom I found Lieutenant Dallas talking with Captain Aerols [ZIPSEAL 11-Sep-2227 14:03.hrs ^.09]. I caught his attention, then stood at parade rest until the lieutenant excused himself.

"What's up, Sergeant?" Dallas asked.

"Sir, the May Day mission—is there really no plan?"

"Sergeant, of course I would tell you if I knew anything concrete, but—"

"Stow it, John," I whispered. "What's going on?"

His eyes darted around to make sure we were alone. "I'm telling you, we don't know. But"—he leaned close—"trends really are pointing to an early end to the war. We have the initiative and momentum now, and I personally believe that a few key victories will carry the day."

"And you think May Day will be one of those?"

"I'm certain of it."

I gave him a disgruntled look. "You said 'hunch' at a table full of Ephemerals."

"I know, I know," he replied, pinching the bridge of his nose. "I had just come from a briefing with Command."

"John, these guys are—"

"Thank you, Sergeant," Dallas said loudly as a group of officers rounded a corner of the corridor.

"Sir!" I saluted and marched away.

Through heroic efforts, the navy pushed the breakaway colonies back to their home planets. Once contained, each colony in turn dropped its arms through force or surrender, until only the Torvo-ros colony on Solstice stood alone. It was the colony farthest from Earth, but it was also the largest, with the biggest army the break-aways had yet amassed. And they weren't going to quit unless they were stopped.

Hundreds of ships, most of the fleet, circled Solstice. Across the planet, Naval Command had gained beachheads for the bulk of our forces and was pouring troops in. The Vanguard Regiment, for the first time ever, put all five of its battalion carriers in orbit around the same planet and was dropping us in all over the place, wherever we were most needed.

Lieutenant Dallas had continued to transfer men in and out of the May Day platoon until all our percentage curves were identical and our TODs were within minutes of each other. All through April we dropped, extracted, and dropped again into the most intense fighting I'd ever seen. We kept our cool and took precautions, but we lost one May Day Ephemeral anyway: Sergeant Bolivar [HEM-ORRHAGE 04-May-2178 19:36.hrs ^.54].

Finally, the fourth of May arrived, and I'll admit I was glad for it: the worry was exhausting. Under cover of night, we were to drop from orbit deep behind enemy lines, far from any support, with no chance of being extracted. Our target was their central defense headquarters, where the bulk of their intelligence officers and upper leadership ran the war, a giant complex in the basement of a nuclear-hardened fortress that the navy couldn't destroy from orbit.

The evening of the fourth found me and the rest of the May Day platoon strapped into seats and jostling around in a Rhino as it broke through the stratosphere above Solstice. We were dropping onto the planet's night side, engines off, gliding ballistic. Decoy debris fired from cruisers in deep orbit screamed by all around us, making it difficult for anyone to target and shoot us down.

At eight hundred meters altitude, the Rhino flared into level flight, banking to dodge the decoy debris still plummeting down, lighting engines to skim us over the terrain below.

Exactly at 1929 hours, a red light came on near the hatch. "Squads to the door," I called out over the PlatCom. The men unstrapped and shuffled to the hatch, bracing themselves against the Rhino's bucking. As the transport roared into a hover mere meters off the ground, I hit the release pad.

We jumped out, hit the ground rolling, and popped up firing. We'd landed inside a large courtyard next to the main computer building. The Rhino had dropped us perfectly, right in the middle of the Defense Network compound, with all of the enemy's big guns pointed outside.

But we didn't have long. A few potshots were already coming from nearby buildings. We returned fire. An alarm dinged in my helmet as a platoon member's blue blip went black. We had already lost PFC Travers [STANDING 04-May-2178 19:36.hrs ^.54]. We had to move.

"Make me a hole!" I shouted, and Second Squad sent a rocket, blowing an entrance in the wall of the main building. "Get inside!" I yelled. "Fifth Squad, covering fire!"

The platoon swarmed the hole. Bringing up the rear, I heard a loud metallic *pok*. My feet were suddenly swimming in empty air, and I slammed into the ground. Lifting my head, I saw a jagged hole in my right leg armor. Then came a wave of excruciating pain.

Two soldiers darted back to pick me up and carry me toward the hole. "Put me down and get in there!" I ordered. They propped me up next to the entrance, shielding me behind a large pile of rubble. I waved them off as shots ricocheted off plasteel and concrete all around, chasing them into the building.

I now had four squads through the hole. Fifth Squad was fighting their way into the surrounding structures. I was immobile and alone.

Gritting my teeth against the pain, I sat up, scooted my back against the wall, and propped my rifle on a chunk of debris. After a few deep breaths, I expanded the map screen in my helmet to see what was happening.

The first thing I saw was a dozen black blips all around my position, where platoon members had died either securing the courtyard or assaulting the hole. An explosion and heavy gunfire corresponded with seven blips turning black, three inside and four in the outer defenses. Most of the remaining blips were blinking yellow.

The clock turned 1937. All my remaining blue blips turned yellow. Fifth Squad, still on the surface, dwindled down to one as the enemy got over their surprise and organized themselves.

Inside, the rest of the platoon had made it to the basement, but according to the floor plan now unfolding on my map, it was a convoluted nightmare of intersecting corridors. A mass of red blips appeared, and the five leading blues went black instantly. After a few seconds, the red blips disappeared, killed where they stood, and the blue blips continued forward. Over and over, they were picked off at intersections, but the main body surged on. The PlatCom was an overlapping torrent of curses and commands.

An explosion rumbled deep underground. Half my blinking lights went dark. Still the rest pushed through.

The clock turned 1938 as the remaining blips finally reached the deepest bunker. Gunfire and static filled the PlatCom. I couldn't tell what was happening.

I jerked my head up as a squad of enemy soldiers scrambled across the courtyard. I could have easily shot three or four, but they hadn't yet noticed me propped up behind the rubble. So I kept still and waited. A torrent of gunfire from their direction turned the last blip of Fifth Squad black.

Then all was silent. Through the hiss of static, a faint voice from the PlatCom whispered in my ear. It was Collins.

"Charges set. It's been an honor."

This was it.

The last eight blinking yellow blips had found the bottom of the basement maze. Up top, the enemy squad were massing around the hole, their backs to me.

I minimized the map and picked up my rifle. As I took aim, my mind flashed to the memory of sitting in the mess hall with the May Day platoon and a grinning Lieutenant Dallas.

I held down the trigger as the enemy headquarters erupted in fire. What had been darkness became brilliant yellow light as I was engulfed in heat and pain, flying through the air, everybody gone in that instant of glory.

My last thought before I sank into the black was about my zephyr. *Gentle breeze, my ass!*

It was quiet when I awoke in the predawn light, covered in rubble, in agony, and with my armor's power cell burst. I wasn't going anywhere.

Twisting my arm, I reached the emergency eject switch to pop the armor's joints. I drew my arms into the chest cavity and heaved against the breastplate until it unseated itself and dropped off to the side. Gasping from the exertion, I was able to sit up out of the torso, but I couldn't slide my legs out. The pain was too intense.

A few moments passed while I considered my options, and then a beautiful sound swelled my heart. It was the thin, slicing whine of a Rhino troopship shooting overhead to touch down nearby. I lay back and waited.

Crunching footsteps brought Lieutenant Dallas wearing light armor into view. He stopped and gazed down at me.

"Hey, John," I said as casually as I could.

"Sergeant Barrows," he said in an odd tone, "you're supposed to be dead." He searched the skies. "What, no zephyrs around?"

Before I could think of a witty reply, he crouched, drew a small pistol, put it against my chest, and pulled the trigger.

When I woke, I wasn't dirtside but in the familiar surroundings of a navy vessel. I tried to move, but there were tubes in me. A life-support machine made a comfortingly steady beep. I looked over to see Lieutenant John Dallas sitting next to my bed.

"Look at that," he said with a relieved smile. "My big brother is awake."

"You *shot* me," I said. I tried to glare, but my grin ruined it.

John rolled his eyes. "With a sedative, you baby. Made it easier to smuggle you out in a body bag."

"And you smuggled me to where?"

"This is the NSS *Hopkins*. Hospital ship. The records show Platoon Sergeant Barrows as KIA, and your Ephemerals rotation is officially over." He threw his arms wide. "Congratulations, you are once again Captain William Dallas, Invincibles Battalion of the Vanguard Regiment."

I exhaled deeply. It felt good knowing I could stop acting, but then I thought about my former audience. "And my platoon?"

"Took out nearly the entire high command *and* the planetary defense system. With our ships in total control over their airspace, the remaining leadership capitulated almost immediately. The war is over, Will. The May Day platoon saved a lot of lives."

"All of them?"

"All of them had their Turn in the noblest tradition."

I nodded, trying to be happy that their deaths had meant something, but all I could think about was my map screen filled with flashing yellow blips turning black one by one.

John eyed me carefully. "How are you doing?" he asked after a few minutes of silence.

"I'll be all right," I answered. "These undercover stints in the Ephemerals get harder each time."

John would never fully understand, but we had talked enough about my three previous tours that he could empathize. "It's the only way to have the effectiveness of a mixed unit," he said softly. "So many troubles in the beginning, when Ephemerals knew there was an Invincible in their midst; the jealousy, the rock-bottom morale, the—"

"Yeah, I know," I interrupted. "And it caused a lot of early Ephemeral deaths. It's just...I became close with them. I've lost four or five men on a mission before, but never all my men at once." I took a deep breath. "It's just hard, all right?"

John nodded. "It's brutal. But it's worth it. Ephemeral platoons have an overwhelmingly high success rate only because of the secret Invincible soldier to guide them, push them, and keep them alive. *And*"—he held out a hand to stop me from interrupting—"this gives us the best chance to make each Ephemeral death mean something. A sacred use of their precious lives." John relaxed into his chair. "Like I've always said, Will, everyone at the Vanguard NIC takes this very, very seriously."

I nodded, too weary to do anything else. The loss of my friends was tough, but my eyes welled up thinking how wrong Collins was about the regiment. It truly cared for its own, all of them, and considered each of their lives valuable. Not, as he thought, trash to be thrown away.

"What's my next posting?" I asked when I had blinked away the tears.

"The NSS *Parker*," John said with a grin. "The largest and most comfortable battalion carrier in the regiment." He sat back and propped his feet on my bed. "And your two-bedroom officer suite— did I mention it has a huge common room? With a galley, even! And a little brother for a roommate!"

His smile was infectious, and I shook my head. "Johnny, just how long are you going to follow me around the fleet?"

"Thirty-four years, four months, eighteen days, and change," John said with determination. "Then when a zephyr finally blows you gently away, I'll muster out of the navy, get a condo on Mars, and be sad. But don't you worry about me. I'll be celebrating your life for up to three years after that."

"At the finest nightclubs and casinos," I deadpanned.

"At the finest nightclubs and casinos!" John agreed without missing a beat. "Every night until, well…you know." He tried to look ashamed, but he was smiling.

I had to just roll my eyes. "You damn Lucky Bastard."

Story by George Page III
Illustration by c.billadeau

RYAN PEQUIN

EXECUTION BY BEHEADING

THE THUNDERSTORM MOVED IN WITH breathtaking speed. In a matter of seconds, or so it felt to ten-year-old Bradley Little, the sky went from clear and blue to bubbly and green like some foul witch's brew coming to boil. Lightning arced behind the willow trees whipping in the fierce wind. The drone of the tornado siren drove day campers and counselors in from the woods and fields.

Matthew will be scared, Bradley thought. He searched for his younger brother among the horde scrambling toward the community center.

The downpour held off until they made it indoors. Then the storm struck full force. Rain lashed the building in sheets and the lightning strobe was constant through the high gymnasium windows.

In the pandemonium, Bradley found his group, number seven, gathered along the wall near the drinking fountains. He got his backpack from the big wooden group box.

"I gotta go find my brother," he told his counselor, Jen.

"Please stay with the group," she said.

"He'll be scared."

He choked on the last word. To his horror, he felt his eyes well up with tears.

Stop acting like such a baby!

But he couldn't help it. Day camp had always been tough. Bradley was a shy kid—a "homebody" was Mom's word for it—and making friends didn't come easily. Much as his little brother needed Bradley—and Bradley was sure the storm had shaken Matthew up pretty badly by now, wherever he was—Bradley needed Matthew, too.

Jen relented. Her expression softened.

"Go find your brother," she said. "But don't leave the gym, okay?"

Bradley wandered through the maze of group boxes until he spotted Audrey, Matthew's counselor. Sure enough, she was crouched in front of Matthew, wiping his face with a tissue.

"Thank God," she said when Bradley walked up. She gratefully turned Matthew over to him.

The other kids stared as Bradley led Matthew away from his group. They sat together against the cinder-block wall.

"Come on, now," Bradley said. "Stop crying. It's going to be fine." It was easier to be brave when you had to be brave for someone else.

"Tor-tor-tor—"

"There's not going to be a tornado," Bradley said. "Have you ever *seen* a tornado in real life?" He pointed at the windows. "Look, see? It's lighter already."

Matthew immediately began to calm down. All around them, kids were starting to eat lunch. Bradley took Matthew's lunch bag out of his backpack. He emptied it, then ripped the brown paper sack apart along the seams, spreading it between them like a tablecloth.

"Eat your peanut butter," he said, taking his own lunch out of his backpack.

Matthew unwrapped his sandwich.

A bulging blue newspaper bag *thunked* on the polished floor beside Bradley.

"Mind if I eat with you guys?"

The girl, Izzy Severs, plopped down and crossed her legs.

"I *was* eating with Christina and Bri," Izzy said. She turned and yelled, so the other girls could hear her: "But they're acting like a couple of *douches*!"

Izzy's voice echoed and the groups around them got silent. Mike, the counselor for group sixteen, shot Izzy an angry look but didn't come over. The ruckus picked up again.

Bradley's cheeks burned, not just because Izzy had made everyone look. He could smell her body spray—something flowery, just barely detectable beneath her sunblock and sweat.

Izzy dumped out her sack. Her lunch was all junk food—Fritos, Twinkies, Ding Dongs, a strawberry pop.

"You all right, Matt?" she asked Matthew.

Matthew nodded. His cheeks were blotchy.

"You sure?" she asked.

"Yeah," he said in a small voice.

"There's a big man, Big Mateo, not even scared of a twister," she said, punching him lightly on the arm. Matthew smiled. "Here, let me do your juice box for you."

Holding a Ding Dong in her teeth, Izzy unwrapped the straw from Matthew's juice box and jabbed it through the foil. Juice squirted out the straw. Matthew laughed. Even for a six-year-old, Bradley thought, Matthew still seemed like such a little kid sometimes.

"Hey!" Izzy said to Bradley, eyes wide, mouth full of cake. "Wasn't it your birthday yesterday?"

"Yeah," Bradley said, shrugging.

"The big one-oh," Izzy said. "Double digits. Exciting." She chugged her pop and grinned. The spaces between her teeth were lined bright red.

"I guess," Bradley said.

"Or not?"

"I don't know," Bradley said. "It feels weird to have the *one* in front of my age. Like, I don't want it there."

"Aw, you'll get used to it," Izzy said, waving her hand. "The first couple weeks are the weirdest. Then it seems normal." She slid her second Ding Dong out of the package and held it out to Bradley. "Here, I bought you a birthday cake."

Bradley was so surprised he didn't even reach for it.

"You gonna wait till it starts growing mold?" Izzy asked.

She shoved the Ding Dong at Bradley's face and he opened his mouth in time to save his chin from getting smeared.

"Thanks," he said around the cake. He took it out of his mouth and placed it reverently on the paper sack. He picked up his bag of Famous Amos and held them out to Izzy. "Here."

"No way," Izzy said.

"We'll trade for—"

"Will you stop it? It's your birthday cake."

"Well, thanks."

"Well, happy birthday."

Bradley saved the Ding Dong till last and took a long time eating it, savoring every crumb—thinking, with each bite, that *she* had given it to him, that it had been *hers*.

Izzy guzzled the rest of her pop.

"Watch this," she said.

She crushed the can against her forehead. Matthew laughed, clapping wildly.

"Do it again!" he said.

"You got another can for me?"

Matthew looked dejectedly at his juice box. Izzy wrapped up her trash.

"So," she said to Bradley, slapping the crumbs off her hands, "did you get anything good?"

"Huh?"

"For your birthday. Any good presents?"

"Oh. Yeah, actually."

Bradley unzipped his backpack and dug through it. He'd been looking forward to this moment—he just hadn't expected it to come so soon. He and Izzy lived in the same apartment complex—in the same building—but they were in different groups at camp, and they usually only got to hang out on weekends, at the pool.

"He got cod cards!" Matthew blurted. He had his hands under his butt and was excitedly bouncing up and down on them.

"What the crap, Matthew!" Bradley snapped. "Will you shut up, please? They're *my* present."

"I got some too!" Matthew said, and started digging through his own backpack.

"So you're finally joining this century," Izzy said. She slapped Bradley's shoulder and he relished the sting.

He drew a thick black binder from his backpack. The vinyl was new, so smooth and shiny it reflected their faces. There was a crimson skull etched on the front. Above the skull were the words "C.O.D. CARDS," and underneath, in smaller type, "STARTER SET #3."

"Fancy," Izzy said. "Number three's a good place to start. You get a Cirrhosis with this one."

Bradley opened the album. There were plastic sheets with pockets for cod cards inside. The first several pages were full. Izzy took the album and began flipping through it.

"I forget," she said, "do they give you a Hypertension?"

"Yep."

"Diabetes?"

"Type 2," Bradley said. "But not type 1."

"I'll have to bring some of my albums by after camp so we can compare."

Bradley felt tingly.

"Yeah," he said, "that'd be great."

Izzy stopped on the second-to-last page.

"No way! You have a Homicide by Strangulation! That does *not* come with this set."

"Nah," Bradley said, feeling a surge of pride. "My dad's a cop, remember? He's certified to test blood. He brought the Homicide from work. It used to be part of a training kit or something."

"Mind if I take it out?"

Bradley shook his head.

Izzy carefully slid the card out of its protective pocket. She held it by the edges and examined it. It was visibly more battered than the cards that had come in the starter set, but at that moment, Bradley loved it twice as much as the rest of them combined.

"Man, this is an old one," Izzy said. "This is from, like, before we were born."

Matthew found his own tiny bundle of cod cards, wrapped in a rubber band, and thrust them at Izzy.

"I have some too! See?"

Bradley cringed. On Bradley's birthday, his parents always gave Matthew duplicates of most of Bradley's presents so he wouldn't feel left out. "Matthew's littler than you," his mother always said. "He looks up to you. He wants to be just like you. Try to understand."

Izzy took the cards from Matthew and admired them.

"They're just dupes of some of the throwaways," Bradley said.

"These are really cool!" Izzy told Matthew, flipping through them.

"Better than Bradley's?" Matthew asked.

"They're *just* as cool as Bradley's," Izzy said.

Matthew beamed.

At that moment, a kid walking behind Izzy stopped, crouched, and belched in her ear. Even where he sat, Bradley got a nasty whiff of bologna and Cheetos.

Izzy cried out in disgust and threw an elbow over her shoulder. The kid dodged it.

She whirled around, still seated, and looked up.

"Fuck off, you freak," she said, loud enough so the kid—Kip Steinmiller—could hear her, but not the counselors.

Matthew clapped both hands over his mouth, his eyes wide.

"Swearing," he mouthed at Bradley.

"Whoa, whoa!" Kip said, laughing and holding his hands up. "That wasn't a comment on your looks, Izzy. Just that pile of crap you call a cod collection."

Kip's collection of cod cards was legendary at camp. His parents were rich and could buy him almost any card he wanted. On top of which, Kip had been collecting cod cards longer than anyone Bradley knew.

"They're not mine," Izzy said. "They're Bradley's."

Bradley's face burned. Izzy sounded embarrassed that Kip might think Bradley's collection was hers.

"They're Bradley's," Kip mimicked in a screechy falsetto.

"You're such an asshole," Izzy said.

"At least I'm not poor white trash with a pill-popping mother."

Izzy shot to her feet. She snatched Matthew's juice box off the floor, aimed it at Kip, and squeezed. Purple Kool-Aid shot through the straw and spattered the front of Kip's pristine white camp shirt.

Kip lunged at her. Mike, group sixteen's counselor, caught him from behind while Audrey rushed over and held Izzy back.

"That's enough!" Audrey shrieked at Izzy. "Into the office! Now!"

"He started it!"

"Yeah, well, who sprayed the juice box?"

"You're just scared to get him in trouble 'cause you're scared of his dad!"

"Into the office!"

Izzy stormed toward the glass-enclosed office in the corner of the gym.

Kip took a parting shot: "It's not Audrey's problem your dad's such a drunk he wouldn't stick up for you if somebody took a dump on your head."

Izzy stopped dead but Audrey was right behind her.

"Don't even *think* about it," Audrey said over Izzy's shoulder. "Now, *march*."

After the near fight, all Bradley could think about was the expression on his dad's face as Dad watched him unwrap the cod cards on his birthday. Dad had been so excited—almost more than Bradley. Cod starter sets weren't cheap, and Bradley had been asking for one every occasion since he'd turned nine.

Now he slid the album back into his backpack like a cheap embarrassment.

Matthew balled up his lunch wrappers. He picked up his own little bundle of cod cards, looked at them for a moment, and wadded them up with the trash.

"Your cards," Bradley said.

Matthew looked up.

"You're throwing your cod cards out?"

Matthew shrugged.

"I don't want them anymore," he said. "You can have them if you want."

Bradley looked at the sad, crumpled cards in their tatty rubber band.

"Give them to me," he said gruffly.

Matthew picked the cards out of the ball of trash and handed them over. Bradley threw them into his backpack and zipped it up. Matthew's forehead wrinkled.

"Are you mad, Bradley?"

"No."

Bradley thought again of Dad's face. Of Izzy, sitting in the glass office, probably suspended from camp and definitely in huge trouble at home after this.

He hated Kip Steinmiller.

Thursday morning, Bradley was bent over the water fountain, lapping at the icy stream, when he felt a hand on his shoulder.

He stood up and wiped his mouth with the back of his hand. Izzy grinned at him, eyes sparkling with excitement.

"Hey, welcome back," Bradley said. "What's going on?"

"I got something to tell you."

The gym doors opened and Izzy's counselor, Bethany, stuck her head out.

"Ms. Severs," Bethany said, "what did I say? Straight to the restroom, then straight back. You need a babysitter?"

"Coming!" Izzy called over her shoulder. Then, to Bradley, "You walking home after camp?"

"Yeah."

"Wait up for me."

She disappeared into the gym, and Bradley headed back outside, where his own group was playing capture the flag.

A date, he thought, grinning.

"Damn it, Matthew, can't you just go here?"

Matthew's eyes got wide, and for a second, Bradley was afraid he was going to cry.

"Nooo," Matthew whined. "I really *gotta.*"

He reached behind himself and squeezed his butt.

"Damn it," Bradley said again.

He looked up and down the hallway, searching for Izzy. Half the campers had spent the afternoon at the pool; the other half had stayed in the gym.

I should have gone to the pool.

"Bradleeey!"

"Fine, fine, just...fine. Let's go."

Bradley swung his backpack over his shoulder and Matthew danced behind him down the corridor.

"You really have to get over this *thing* you've got against sitting on public toilets," Bradley said.

"They're gross."

"That's stupid. That's babyish."

"*You're* babyish!"

They bickered all the way back to their apartment building. Inside, Matthew rushed for the bathroom.

Bradley poured himself a glass of Kool-Aid and had just taken a seat at the kitchen counter when there was a knock on the door.

As soon as Bradley answered it, Izzy shoved past him.

"I told you to wait up," she said.

"I tried," Bradley said. "My stupid brother had to..."

He trailed off. Izzy slung her backpack on the counter. She turned around and stared, waiting for him to continue.

"Had to what?" she asked.

"You know. *Go.*"

"So?"

"So he won't use a public toilet. He always has to go number two at home."

Izzy snorted.

"That kid's a daisy," she said.

"Tell me about it."

She pulled a barstool around to the other side of the counter and sat facing Bradley.

"Drink?" he asked.

She shook her head.

He glanced at the clock over the stove. Though Bradley could have happily spent the rest of forever with Izzy, he needed her gone by the time Mom got home from work. Once, Mom saw Izzy and another girl trying a cigarette behind the pool clubhouse, and ever since then she didn't like Bradley hanging out with Izzy unsupervised.

Izzy noticed him looking at the clock and rolled her eyes.

"Oh, don't worry, precious little altar boy," she said. "The evil hussy will be long gone by the time Mommy gets home."

Matthew appeared in the kitchen doorway.

"What's a hussy?" he asked, hitching up his shorts.

Both Bradley and Izzy collapsed in giggles.

"What?" Matthew demanded. "What does it mean?"

They laughed harder. Though, if Bradley were being honest, he only had the vaguest idea himself.

"Go play video games," he said.

"I want a snack."

"Tell you what," Izzy said. "I got Fudgsicles in my freezer at home. You go play video games for a few minutes, and I'll bring you one." Matthew's eyes lit up. "But you gotta go play *now* so there's time for me to get one and come back."

Matthew tore out of the room. As soon as he was gone, Izzy leaned over the counter and grinned. She spoke very slowly.

"Want to beat the *shit* out of Kip Steinmiller's cod collection?"

Bradley smiled.

"How?" he asked.

"You know Mr. Al-Zahrani on my floor?" she said.

Bradley nodded.

"Well, my dad had a poker game last night," Izzy said, "and I heard him and his friends talking about how they *know* Mr. Al-Zahrani is a terrorist."

Bradley frowned.

"No, I'm serious," Izzy said, lowering her voice. "I mean, he's a towelhead, right?"

"I don't think that's nice," Bradley said automatically.

Izzy waved her hand like she was shooing away a fly.

"Like Osama, right? Brown? So if he's supposed to be Arab, then how come his face is all *white* like that?"

Bradley shrugged.

"Because he's always wearing *makeup*, trying to make himself look like the rest of us."

"Your dad and his friends must have been—" Bradley was about to say drunk, but Izzy was sensitive about that, and he stopped himself. "Wrong," he finished.

"No way," Izzy said. "And I'll tell you what else. Some guy has to *bring* Mr. Al-Zahrani his groceries. I've *seen* it. Mr. Al-Zahrani never leaves his apartment. Because he's in hiding."

"How come your dad thinks he's in hiding?"

"Because one of the guys at the card game," Izzy said, "his kid was selling cookies, and he was taking her around door to door. Well, towelheads love chocolate, you know, because they don't have it where they come from. Not like ours. It's all bitter over there. So Mr. Al-Zahrani bought some chocolate cookies, and when he took out his wallet to pay, the guy got a look at Mr. Al-Zahrani's cod card. And you know what it said?"

Bradley leaned farther over the counter and shook his head.

"It said Execution by Beheading."

Bradley exhaled, long and slow.

"No way," he whispered.

Izzy nodded.

"Mr. Al-Zahrani's real name isn't Al-Zahrani," she said. "It's... let me think...it's Mohammed...Mufarrij, I think. Something like that. He's on, like, the FBI's most wanted list and everything. Hiding out in this country. Though I guess it's not gonna do him any good, right? Because in the end—I mean, just look at his card. At some point they're obviously gonna drag him back to his own country, Afghanistan or wherever, and..."

Izzy slowly traced a fingernail across her neck.

"They say he's got a fatwa on him." The way she said the word made it sound like *fat-wad* without the *d*.

"What's that?" Bradley asked.

"It's, like, when their priests or whoever don't like you anymore, they make a law that anyone can cut off your head and they won't get in trouble."

"Why don't they like him anymore?" Bradley asked.

"Who knows," Izzy said. "All those towelheads are always fighting about everything. It doesn't matter. What matters is his cod card. Think about it. Execution by Beheading. I've never even *seen* a real Execution card before. Not even in pictures."

The awesome possibility that such a card was so close began to spill over Bradley like a brilliant sunrise. He actually felt warmer, thinking about it. An authentic Execution card would be amazing enough. But Execution by Beheading—those practically didn't exist, especially in the developed world. That was a serious, serious card.

"So you want to steal his card?" Bradley asked.

Izzy shook her head. She was grinning again and her eyes twinkled with the light spilling through the balcony door behind Bradley. She tucked her hair behind her ears with a gesture that made Bradley's insides feel like gooey warm batter and leaned close enough that he was breathing her flowery smell.

"I want his blood."

Bradley wasn't sure he'd heard correctly.

"You what?"

"His blood," Izzy said. "Three syringes of it. Your dad's a cop. He tests blood, right?"

"Right."

"He's got a machine here in the apartment? Vials?"

"Sure."

"Three syringes of Mr. Al-Zahrani's blood will make three cards," Izzy said. "One for your collection, one for mine. And we'll sell one to Kip Steinmiller for a small fortune. After we let him squirm for a couple days."

Bradley was so shocked he actually pulled away from her.

"That's sick!" he said. "That's gruesome."

"Thank you."

"No, I mean ... what are you, a vampire?"

"If we just steal his cod card," Izzy said, "what have we got? One card. You want to cut that in half and share it?"

"But taking his *blood*?" Bradley said. "Making a bunch of cod cards for the same guy? That's worse than counterfeiting *money*. That's *so* illegal—"

"You want to *get* Kip?" Izzy said. "Or do you want to let him walk all over us all the time? If we each have a cod card and then we let him stew for a while and *then* we tell him we can get *him* one too— we've got him by the balls, Bradley. He'll pay anything we want. He'll *do* anything we want. He'll probably let me squirt him with another juice box." She laughed.

Bradley thought about it. Izzy was right about the money, at least—Kip would pay big time for an Execution by Beheading card. And considering the fact that Bradley and Izzy had barely been able to pool enough cash between them to buy lunch on the last camp field trip, they could use it.

There might be other benefits, too, Bradley thought. If Izzy thought Bradley was brave enough to go through with something like stealing a guy's blood to make new cod cards...

"How would we get the blood?" he asked.

Izzy rubbed her hands together like a cartoon villain.

"Cookies," she said.

"I don't get it."

"Like I told you," Izzy said, "chocolate is catnip for those people. We dress your little brother up like a scout and take him to Mr. Al-Zahrani's door and say we're selling cookies—"

"Boy Scouts don't sell cookies," Bradley said. "They sell popcorn."

"You think Mr. Al-Zahrani's gonna know the difference?" Izzy said. "So anyway, my mom's got these pills that help her sleep. They really knock you out. I figure we crush a bunch of those into the middle of some Oreos, give Mr. Al-Zahrani some freebies, like *samples*, and wait till he conks out. Then we take his blood and get out of there."

"Where do we get the needles?"

"The syringes? My mom's a nursing assistant, remember? She's got cases of them."

"You know how to use them?"

"Only since I was two years old."

Bradley sat thinking, sipping his Kool-Aid.

"Wait," he said suddenly. "Mr. Al-Zahrani will remember we were there."

"So?" Izzy said. "He won't know what happened. He'll think he nodded off and we got bored and left."

"But what if he suspects something? Like, what if he finds a needle mark or a bruise or something?"

"What's he gonna do?" Izzy said. "Call the cops? He's a terrorist, remember? We should be calling the cops on *him*. My dad and his friends say there's like a million-dollar reward out for the guy. They're talking about turning him in."

Bradley stared into his cup.

"Three syringes," he said, as though tasting the words.

"Yep," Izzy said. "We feed the blood to your dad's machine, it spits out our cards, and we join the ranks of the rich and enviable."

Bradley laughed. Sometimes Izzy had such a funny way of saying things.

"So what do you think?" she asked.

Bradley met her eyes.

"I think I want to be rich and enviable."

She grinned.

"Beauuutiful. And your little bro? You think you can get him on board?"

"Do you think we need him?"

"We better include him," she said. "We'll be doing this before your folks get home from work tomorrow. We can't just leave him alone."

Bradley nodded.

"We can keep him on . . . what do they call it?" Izzy said. "Keep him on a *need-to-know* basis."

"Right," Bradley said. "Need-to-know basis."

"Which reminds me," Izzy said. "I better go get him that Fudgsicle before your mom gets home. We want to keep him happy."

* * *

"You ready to go?"

"Matthew's still getting dressed," Bradley said.

He stood aside so Izzy could come in. Then he shut the door behind her.

"You got everything?" he asked.

Izzy took the plastic Mickey Mouse bag off her shoulder. She dug out two packages of Double Stuf Oreos, set them on the counter, and pulled back the plastic flaps.

"See if you can tell which ones have the pills," she said.

Bradley studied the cookies for a long moment.

"They look the same," he said finally.

Izzy tapped the cookies on the left.

"Really?" Bradley said.

Izzy nodded.

"How can you tell?"

"Mothers can always tell their twin babies apart, can't they?"

Izzy stuck her hand into her bag again and pulled out three thin syringes.

Bradley's stomach knotted and flipped.

"Empty vials are with the machine," he said. "I checked. But you're doing all the blood stuff."

"Of course. I'm the vampire, right? Just keep Matthew occupied so Nurse Feratu can do her thing."

Bradley laughed. Izzy stuffed the syringes back into her bag as Matthew came in, adjusting his khaki shorts.

"I hate these shorts," he said. "They don't fit anymore."

"Have some cookies," Izzy said.

She took three Double Stuf Oreos from the package of untainted cookies and gave them to Matthew. He munched them happily.

"I like playing Cub Scouts," he said.

"Here are your order forms," Izzy said.

She removed a sheaf of papers from her bag and spread them on the counter. Matthew stood on tiptoes, peering at them, licking the filling off half an Oreo cookie.

"These are great," Bradley said. "Where did you get them?"

"Online," she said, shrugging. Then, to Matthew, "Now, when the customer opens the door, who are you and what are you doing there?"

Matthew squinted. His eyes rolled up.

"I am with Cub Scout Pack 5589, and we are selling...cookies..." He licked the rest of the filling off the Oreo, still thinking. "We are selling cookies to benefit the troop! Can I offer you some free samples and also how many boxes can I put down for you?"

"How many boxes can I *put you down for*," Izzy corrected. "Other than that, letter perfect."

She clapped Matthew on the shoulder and handed him the package of cookies with the pills in them.

"Now, you offer him a sample from *these* cookies, and *these* cookies are for customers only, okay?"

Matthew nodded.

"You are *not allowed* to eat these, understand? No sneaking any. If you want any cookies, you just ask me. I have special ones set aside just for you."

Matthew nodded again.

They left the apartment and took the stairwell down to the second floor. Bradley felt more nervous than he could remember ever feeling about anything. His heart was thundering, his stomach performing acrobatics.

You don't even have to do anything, he told himself. *Matthew will do the talking, Izzy will take the blood. All you have to do is keep Matthew busy after the old man falls asleep and you'll be rich.*

The thought of that rare cod card and the money they'd make from Kip kept Bradley putting one foot in front of the other until— long before he was really ready—the three of them stood before Mr. Al-Zahrani's door.

"Okay, Big Mateo," Izzy whispered. "Do your thing."

Matthew boldly stepped forward and knocked. Bradley felt a pang of guilt. He met Izzy's eyes over Matthew's head. She kept her expression controlled and masklike, but he could tell she was keyed up.

This is fun for her, he realized. Bradley himself had barely slept the night before.

Shuffling noises came from behind the door. It creaked open.

Mr. Al-Zahrani wore a billowy white tracksuit and a red turban. His brown skin was blotchy white in places. His feet were bare. His glasses were very thick and visibly dusty.

He peered at them, running his fingers through his long black beard. Then he spotted Matthew grinning up at him and smiled.

"How can I help you?" he asked. His accent was mild, his English excellent.

Matthew delivered his spiel flawlessly while Mr. Al-Zahrani listened, his smile growing wider.

"Yes, yes, yes," Mr. Al-Zahrani said, when Matthew had finished. "Please come inside. Come in. We will discuss business."

He opened the door widely enough for them to pass through. Bradley's heart was pounding so hard he could feel it in his throat.

The apartment smelled sweet and smoky. The furniture was ornate, clearly foreign, and richly upholstered. In one corner, an old, muted television was tuned to CNN; balls of aluminum foil covered the ends of the antennas.

"Please sit down and be comfortable," Mr. Al-Zahrani said.

"Here's the samples I'm supposed to give you," Matthew said.

He set the Oreos and the order forms on Mr. Al-Zahrani's coffee table.

"These are for *customers only*," Matthew said, peeling back the flap on the package of cookies. "I'm not supposed to eat these."

"It is very important to have discipline in your business, young man," Mr. Al-Zahrani said seriously, nodding at Matthew. "Very difficult as well. You must have a strong will."

"I do," Matthew said solemnly.

Mr. Al-Zahrani took four Oreos and pulled the stack of order forms closer to him.

"Do you have a pen?" he asked.

Izzy dug in her Mickey Mouse bag and found one.

"Here," she said. "I have others if it doesn't work."

Mr. Al-Zahrani ate all four Oreos as he filled out the form.

I hope four isn't too many, Bradley thought. He wondered how many pills Izzy had crushed into each cookie.

"I think, perhaps, some water," Mr. Al-Zahrani said. "Can I offer you children a drink?"

"No, thank you," Izzy said. Bradley shook his head.

"Do you have chocolate milk?" Matthew asked.

Mr. Al-Zahrani laughed.

"I have what you call Yoo-hoo," he said. "Do you like Yoo-hoo?"

Matthew nodded.

"Come with me to the kitchen," Mr. Al-Zahrani said, "and I shall get your money and we will also get your Yoo-hoo."

Mr. Al-Zahrani stood. He stepped around the coffee table, then stumbled and began to lose his balance. He caught himself and touched a hand to his forehead.

"Excuse me," he said. "I must have stood too fast."

The pills are starting to work, Bradley thought.

He glanced at Izzy. She was watching Mr. Al-Zahrani intently.

"Come along, then," Mr. Al-Zahrani said.

He led them down the hall to the kitchen.

Bradley noticed that Mr. Al-Zahrani kept stumbling as he walked. When Bradley's grandmother was dying of cancer, she'd been taking lots of painkillers. The way Mr. Al-Zahrani moved reminded Bradley of her.

In the kitchen, Mr. Al-Zahrani went to a row of cabinets and opened one. He peered into it, looking confused.

"What was I..."

He closed the cabinet and moved on to the next. He opened the door, gazed inside. Again, he looked mystified, as though he were solving a difficult puzzle.

"Are you all right, Mr. Al-Zahrani?" Bradley asked.

The old man tried to nod. But the second time he lowered his head, it cost him his balance. He began to tip forward like a falling tree.

Alarmed, Bradley started toward him. But before he reached him, Mr. Al-Zahrani's forehead struck the edge of the cabinet door.

His head snapped up and he was immediately sober. His eyes were wide. He looked terrified. Bradley felt sick with guilt.

"It's all right, Mr. Al-Zahrani," he said. "Here, why don't you sit down?"

The old man touched his head where he'd hit it. He pulled his fingers away and stared at them, mouth hanging open. Judging by his expression, Bradley expected them to be covered in blood. But they were clean.

"Come and sit down a sec," Bradley said.

He gingerly took hold of the man's sleeve and guided him to the kitchen table. He pulled a chair out and eased Mr. Al-Zahrani into it.

The man was mumbling.

"What's he saying?" Izzy whispered.

Bradley shook his head. "I have no idea. It's some other language."

Mr. Al-Zahrani abruptly stopped speaking. That same shocked expression returned to his face—like a child seeing fireworks for the very first time. Moving slowly, he crossed his arms on the table in front of him, lay his head down, and closed his eyes.

Matthew glanced anxiously at Bradley. "Is he sick?"

Bradley looked at Izzy. She was biting her lip.

"Well," she said, "we know it won't kill him, right?"

She met Bradley's eyes and traced her fingernail across her neck.

"Of course," Bradley said, relieved.

"The . . . you know . . . they're just doing their job," Izzy said.

"Right," Bradley said. Then, to Matthew, "He's not sick. He's just tired. Eating all those cookies made him sleepy. Like too much pie at Thanksgiving. We need to let him sleep."

He put a hand on his brother's shoulder and led him toward the hallway.

"You can take care of it from here?" he asked Izzy.

She nodded, reaching into her bag for the syringes.

Bradley drummed his fingers on the dresser top and glanced again at his mother's nightstand.

"I see you looking at that alarm clock," Izzy snapped. "I'm going as fast as I can."

"I didn't say anything," Bradley said.

"You want to switch places with me?"

She unwound another long cord from the back of the machine and plugged it into his dad's laptop, which was set up on a card table near the bedroom windows.

In the neighboring room, Bradley heard Matthew squeal in frustration at his video game. He felt a twinge of nostalgia, though he couldn't say what for—maybe just for being littler, when all your biggest concerns existed in fiction.

Izzy opened the laptop.

"What's the point of having a log-in and password if you just tape it to your computer?" she said.

"Huh?"

She tapped the Post-it stuck beside the laptop's touch pad: *etlittle*, *password1234.*

"Thank God cops are the way they are," Izzy said, logging in.

"What's that supposed to mean?" Bradley said.

Izzy didn't answer. All through their time at Mr. Al-Zahrani's, she'd been unflappable. Now Bradley could tell that she was starting to feel the time crunch.

He chanced another peek at his mother's alarm clock, though he was careful not to move his head so Izzy wouldn't notice.

Mom would be home in less than fifteen minutes.

Come on, come on.

Standing behind Izzy, peering over her shoulder, he drummed his fingers on the back of her chair.

"If you don't stop that," she said without looking back, "I will chop off your fingers one by one with a pipe cutter."

Bradley stuck his hand in his pocket.

Izzy found the machine's program in the computer and double-clicked.

"Let's just hope he doesn't need a password to use the software," Bradley said.

The program opened. Bradley squinted at the screen.

"It looks pretty easy," he said.

"Well, just look who it was made for," Izzy said.

Another dig at cops, but Bradley let it slide. They didn't have time to fight.

"There's a round slot on the left side of the machine," Izzy said. "When the orange light flashes, the cover will slide up, and I want you to stick one of the blood tubes into the chamber."

Izzy continued clicking away at the computer. Bradley looked at the vials of blood on the card table, neatly lined up like shotgun shells.

An orange light on the machine started blinking, and the cover over a small round chamber slid open.

Bradley's stomach flip-flopped as he reached for the first vial. He didn't know what he was afraid of—maybe that the vial would be warm.

He quickly inserted it into the machine and pushed it in until he felt the machine take hold of it. The orange light stopped blinking. The chamber cover slid shut. A red light came on above it.

"Is the red light on?" Izzy asked.

"Yeah."

Izzy was anxiously tapping her foot, and Bradley considered threatening to chop it off with a pair of garden shears if she didn't stop. But before he could open his mouth, the red light over the chamber went out, a green one blinked on, and the machine ejected the vial. The blood inside was now blackened ash; the top of the vial had been sealed by the machine. An acrid smell tinged the air.

Izzy shot out of her seat and shoved Bradley aside. The machine chattered and warbled. A thick plastic card—a genuine cod card, shiny and new, complete with a red holographic seal of authenticity— rose slowly from a slot in the top of the machine.

Izzy snatched it up.

"I don't believe it," she breathed, eyes gleaming. "I don't—"

She stopped speaking and frowned at the card.

"What's the matter?" Bradley asked.

"I don't . . . I don't *get* it."

"Let me see."

Bradley took the card from her.

The name on the card was Shahid Al-Zahrani. It listed Mr. Al-Zahrani's address, his Social Security number, the abbreviations for several health restrictions, and—where it should have said Execution by Beheading—it read Severe Hemophilia Complicated by Intracranial Hemorrhage.

"What does *that* mean?" Bradley asked.

"I don't know," Izzy said.

"Could it be, like, the *medical* way of saying you got your head cut off? Cranial means head, I think."

"We don't have time to mess with it right now," Izzy said. "Your mom will be home any second."

She had already unplugged the machine from the laptop and was rolling up its cords.

A minute later, she hurried out, taking the used vial, the two remaining tubes of blood, and the bewildering cod card. But not before Bradley had committed the words to memory:

Severe Hemophilia Complicated by Intracranial Hemorrhage.

By the time Mom got home, less than five minutes later, Bradley had started up the family computer in the living room to figure out exactly what kind of card they had.

Bradley stared at the computer screen, face cold, hands sweating.

He's going to die from this.

We killed him.

The words he was reading seemed to shimmer: *Medical professionals are often required to make house calls to people who suffer from severe hemophilia, to help patients avoid unnecessary risks in the outside world. Even a minor head injury can be fatal, as unabated bleeding within the skull can rapidly lead to brain herniation—*

"Bradley."

Mom stuck her head around the kitchen doorway.

"Huh?" He felt like he'd been slapped awake.

"I said, why didn't you do the dishes in the sink yet?" Mom said. "It's your week, remember? Come on, get moving. I've got to start dinner soon."

Bradley obeyed like he was in a trance, hardly aware of what he was doing. Mom flitted around the kitchen, getting things ready to cook, chattering about her day at work. Bradley didn't hear a word.

That's why Mr. Al-Zahrani's skin always looks so blotchy and weird, Bradley thought. It wasn't makeup; it was probably related to his condition.

And he didn't hide in his apartment because he was a terrorist, afraid of going to jail. His health was so poor, he couldn't do normal things. Whoever brought him groceries, Bradley realized, was probably his doctor or a nurse.

Sadness and fear and regret stewed inside Bradley like a poison. *We killed him.*

But then another thought occurred to him.

Maybe it's not too late. Maybe if I call 911 right now—

"...hope it's nothing serious," Mom said, leaning over Bradley's shoulder and peering out the window over the kitchen sink. The window overlooked the parking lot.

"What?" Bradley said.

"The ambulance," Mom said, nodding.

Below, an ambulance was parked at the end of the building's front sidewalk.

Bradley felt like he'd been punched in the gut. The dishes weren't finished but he turned off the faucet and leaned on the counter, supporting himself solely by the strength of his arms.

Mom was too intent on the ambulance to notice.

"Maybe it's Mrs. Francis on the first floor," she said. "God, I hope it's not Mrs. Francis. She's so sweet. I hope everything's all right."

It took Bradley a while to realize that he wasn't dreaming the sharp pelting sound against his bedroom window.

Somebody's throwing gravel.

In the twin bed across the room, Matthew's breathing was heavy and regular.

Before the gravel had time to turn to stones, Bradley slid out of bed and crept to the window. He slid it open and got a face full of pebbles.

He sputtered, slapping them away, and leaned out.

"I'm *here!*" he whispered.

He glared at the silhouette below, which backed away from the side of the building and came close enough to a globe lamp that he could see its features.

Izzy.

"I'm coming down," he whispered.

He slid the window shut, found his slippers, and crept out of the room.

The apartment was dark and silent. The smell of the pot roast they'd had for dinner lingered in the air.

He carefully unlocked the deadbolt on the front door and crept into the hallway.

It was strange to see the building at this hour—it looked the same as it did in the middle of the afternoon, only it felt different. It was so lonely—like someplace nobody you loved could ever find you.

Bradley took the stairs down. He'd forgotten his keys. He stuck a twig in the door so he wouldn't get locked out.

Izzy met him on the sidewalk that ran through the courtyard. For a moment, they just stared at each other, their faces dimly lit by lamplight, by starlight.

"You figure out what the card meant?" she asked finally.

He nodded.

"You see the ambulance?" she asked.

Bradley nodded again. "He must be dead by now."

"Probably."

"Because of us."

She tilted her head, studying his face.

"You didn't say anything to anybody, did you?" she asked.

He raised his eyebrows.

"I mean, I'm sure you didn't, I just—"

"I didn't say anything."

She seemed to relax.

"Good," she said. She studied her shoes. "I cut the card into little pieces and dropped it down the sewer. I took the syringes out to the pond and threw them in. Even if people find them, they won't touch them."

"Uh-huh."

"So do you think we're safe?" she asked. "Is there, like, any way they can tell we ran his blood on your dad's machine? Do they check records like that? Or do they—"

"Is that all you can think about?"

She flinched.

"Is *what* all I can think about?" she asked.

"If we're gonna get caught."

"Um," she said, "I think that is a very *real* worry right now, don't you?"

"Mr. Al-Zahrani is *dead* because of us."

"He was going to die like that one way or the other," she said. "You saw his card."

"Yeah," he said, "but *we're* the ones who caused it. Doesn't that just...isn't that *bothering* you?"

She shrugged. "I guess."

"You *guess*?"

"Well, like I said, he was gonna die that way anyhow."

"I just feel *sick*," Bradley said. His voice cracked. "I just feel so sick and I feel like nothing's ever going to be okay again. Like for the rest of my life, all I'll be able to think of is—"

"Shhh." She put a hand on his shoulder. "Forget it."

"How can you—"

"Just forget it," she said. "What we have to worry about now is keeping it secret. Mr. Al-Zahrani's dead. So what if *we're* the ones who put things in motion?" She took her hand back, scuffed the sidewalk with the toe of her sneaker. "This could really screw up our lives, Bradley. Like, if anybody ever found out, who knows what could happen."

"If we just *explained*," he said. "Maybe they'd—"

"Are you crazy?" Her expression was suddenly wild. "Are you out of your fucking—"

He took a step back, holding his hands up.

"I'm not going to tell," he said quickly.

She looked him up and down.

"Well, I know *I'm* not going to tell," she said.

"I said I wouldn't."

She nodded.

They held each other's eyes. Then she looked away.

"Well," she said, "I better get back upstairs. My dad's not home yet, and if he gets in and I'm not there..."

He probably wouldn't notice, Bradley thought. He suddenly felt sorry for her.

"I might hang out here for a minute," he said, wanting to be rid of her as quickly as possible. "I don't have my keys, though. Leave that stick in the door."

"Okay," she said. "Good night, Bradley."

"Night."

He gave her just enough time to get to her apartment. Then he went inside.

Back in his room, he took his album of cod cards out of his backpack. He went to the closet and quietly opened the door. Standing on his toes, he slid the album onto the top shelf. Then he closed the closet door and returned to his bed.

He planned to throw the album away at the first opportunity. He just couldn't risk putting it in the trash at home. His parents might find it and start asking questions.

Maybe, he thought, *I'll keep the Homicide by Strangulation card.* He could give it to Izzy. He thought she'd still want it. Sure, she was paranoid about getting caught—but otherwise, things hadn't really changed for her.

Not so for Bradley.

Most people knew how they were going to die. American babies received cod cards with their birth certificates and Social Security IDs. Cause of death was a part of life—just a part of who you were.

Some people let it bother them. Most didn't.

Bradley couldn't remember when his parents had told him how he was going to die—it seemed like he had always known. It had never scared him and probably never would.

For Bradley, it wasn't ever going to be his own death that haunted him.

Story by Chandler Kaiden
Illustration by Mike Dawson

ANTHONY CLARK

LAZARUS REACTOR FISSION SEQUENCE

I STOOD BAREFOOT ON THE BEACH, about to give a keynote speech on something I knew nothing about, and looked at my audience. It consisted of my colleague Ex, the enemy agent he was holding captive, and a small crab. I started anyway.

"I'd like to welcome you all to the—" I realized I'd forgotten the name of the conference. I squinted against the sun to read the handwritten text on the large wooden sign Ex was gripping in both hands. "The 2086 Special Weapons and Tactics convention?"

"His slip says it happens at SWATCON 2086." Ex shrugged as best he could while holding something that heavy. "Can I just hit him with this?"

I sighed. "Well, I usually prefer not to explain the plan in front of captured heroes, but yeah, you can just belt him. We can't wait that long, and the plank is cheaper."

The agent struggled with his cuffs. I cleared my throat.

"To the 2086 Special Weapons and Tactics conference here in, like, Bloomington, Indiana, I think it's meant to be. This year I'm pleased to welcome as our guest speakers: a palm tree, and...this crab." The crab looked at me.

I sensed I should wrap this up. "I hereby declare this conference official enough to count in death predictions, so I'll bow pointlessly and try not to think about what happens next."

I bowed pointlessly and turned away. I wiggled my toes in the sand a bit, then stared out at the sparkling sea until I heard the crack. My toes clenched. The crab scuttled by. The sun baked my hair.

That was when I started to wonder if my heart was still in the henchman business, or if I was just going through the evil motions. I tried not to look at the body as I walked back to the facility, and Ex hauled him to the furnace.

The Island of Dr. Jethmalani was my first henching job. We called him Dr. Jeth, just because it sounded like Dr. Death, but he wasn't really a supervillain. Well, he wasn't a supervillain until they started sending armed superheroes to kill him, and then suddenly he was the bad guy.

He bought the island to build the Lazarus Reactor, his brainchild and obsession. He was already planning it before he got tested: it's a type of nuclear reactor where the fission process moves through the core. That's what generates the power, but what makes it efficient is that each depleted part of the core is replenished by nuclear transmutation before it's needed again. He called it Lazarus because the zones spend four stages of the sequence dead before coming back to life. And because it has a z in it, which sounds cool.

If it worked, you'd need only a small amount of uranium 235 to kick-start the thing, and it could churn out ferocious amounts of power for hundreds of years—without ever requiring fuel or expending waste.

But if you're a governmental skeptic—and that would be putting it mildly for Dr. Jeth—you're not going to trust any one country with that kind of technology. Certainly not India—or the U.S.

When he got his test results back, that clinched it. He was going to die of LAZARUS REACTOR FISSION SEQUENCE, the process that kicks the completed device into full operation. He'd been given a piece of paper that told him he was absolutely certain to complete his life's work successfully. So he started to get ambitious.

I typed in my password and headed down into the lab, turning to check that the steel door sealed properly behind me. When I turned back, I ran into Di and internally panicked. *What am I wearing? Why don't I know that? Do I have secret agent blood on me? Why don't I just make it a rule to look good at all times?*

"Hey!" *Too upbeat, idiot.*

"Hey, Mort." She smiled, but you couldn't read much into that. *What the hell was I about to say?*

"Don't suppose anyone in the next batch dies PAINLESSLY DURING SLEEP, SAVING EVERYONE A LOT OF HASSLE?" I asked, regretting the joke immediately.

"Who? Oh, deaths! Sorry, I'm miles away. No, they're all like AWKWARDLY SPECIFIC, ANNOYING MORT A BUNCH." For some reason she did little robot-arm motions during her Machine of Death voice, making several of my organs melt. "Take a look."

She handed me her phone, which I tried to take with an impossible mix of firm manliness and sensitive grace and ended up almost dropping. I read the list six times in three seconds, absorbed nothing, and handed it back to her.

"Cool." *Get out. Get out now. Deaths are not cool. You like this person and enjoy talking to her, so you must end this conversation as quickly as possible to prevent further fuckups.*

"Could you mail those to me?" *Because I can't absorb information in your presence.*

"Just have, actually!" *Phew.*

We said awkward good-byes and I headed off to reread the results at a time when my brain was not full of other things.

Mort isn't my name, of course—I was creative director of mortality, and Dr. Jeth had us all go by titles.

Anyone else would have held off building the thing that would kill them, but I don't think that even occurred to Jeth. Once the Lazarus Reactor was done, why would he need to be alive? That was all he was here to do.

So he bought an island. I can't tell you which, but I can say money wasn't an issue. That's the main reason I was there—I knew a lot about death, and Jeth knew a lot about making people financially unrefusable offers.

None of us were wild about the death part, but it wasn't our choice. The doctor's intentions were good—clean power for all—and he was getting there at an incredible pace without hurting anyone. But there's nothing civilization hates more than success they're not having. So they didn't send the Nobel commission; they sent troops.

At first Dr. Jeth's security teams tried capturing them, but it was bizarre: to a man, they'd escape. However secure the cell, however well guarded, each one cut a path of dead staff and destroyed equipment out of the facility. The doctor wasn't trying to contradict their death prediction; he was just keeping them there until the reactor was complete, fully intending to let them go. But the universe bent double to give them early release, at a horrific cost to the project and its staff.

Jeth wasn't a vindictive guy, but everything came second to the reactor. So he hired Ex to start finishing off everyone they captured. You can guess what his name's short for.

As soon as I got to my office and read the e-mail from Di, I called her. Then, as the phone was ringing, I realized that this was going to make it obvious that I hadn't read the results properly when she showed them to me, and she was going to wonder why. I almost hung up before remembering she had caller ID—I think she even had a ringtone for my extension—and prank calling her would be even worse.

Shit shit shit shit shit shit—

"Hey!"

"Hey. VICTORIA FALLS?"

"Yep!"

"The guy in cell six dies of VICTORIA FALLS?"

"I know!" She said brightly. She loved the specifics.

"I don't think we have a Victoria Falls here. I don't think we have a Victoria Falls anywhere outside of Zimbabwe."

"And Zambia, I think."

"Really?"

"It's the same one; it's on the border."

"Oh." I felt dumb for not knowing something I had no reason to know.

"So what do you think, field trip?"

Ah, now, this was tricky. Did I want to fly to Harare with her on a private jet and see the largest waterfall in the world, then kill a guy on it? I absolutely did. But did I want to be the creative director of mortality who wasted a huge amount of time and money by taking a prediction at face value? No. I wasn't sure I wanted to do this job much longer, but I felt I should keep doing it properly until I officially quit.

"I'd love to, but there's probably an easier way." Genius! Pretend she was offering, and then turn her down! *Wait wait wait wait wait wait—*

"Oh, okay. Talk to you later."

Shit.

Di wasn't Di's real name either; she just worked in Diagnostics. Among many other things, she was the one who tested any hostiles Security captured to find out how they'd die.

At first, they were all GUNSHOT WOUNDs and BLUNT FORCE TRAUMAs. Simple jobs for Ex. But then the U.S. military started sending unkillables, and that's when things got tricky.

It's rare, very rare, but every now and then someone with a slip that says TOOLSHED is willing to sign up for wet work. That means they've got an agent in the field who cannot possibly die in the field, and that's a scary thing to deal with.

Ex would try his best, but without fully comprehending the implications of directionally agnostic causality, it ended with a lot of burned-down toolsheds and escaped agents.

That's why Dr. Jeth hired me: I'd written a paper in the 2060s called "Tweaking Inevitability: How to Change Your Fate in a Way the Universe Is Mostly Okay With." My job was to take a result like VICTORIA FALLS, and instead of thinking "We have to take him to Zimbabwe and/or Zambia," figure out an easier death we could do right there without proving the machine wrong.

Before I ever let Ex strike a blow, I had to be sure that if the sub-ject died the way we were trying to kill him or her, it'd make sense for the machine to have said what it said. If you try to contradict a prediction, things go wrong. And they go wrong in painfully unpre-dictable ways.

After an awful few minutes in which I tried not to think of anyone on staff called Victoria, I realized the name didn't have to belong to a human. All we needed was a living thing large enough to kill when dropped from a great height, and it could be anything it made sense to name.

There isn't a lot of info on this island online, so I looked up the nearest big one and flicked to fauna. Tapirs. We probably had tapirs. A meter high, two meters long, and anything up to three hundred kilos—easily enough biomass to crush a human being. I would catch a tapir, name it Victoria, and have Ex drop it from the south mast onto inmate six. The world would continue to make perfect sense.

I don't know what I was expecting, but the result that afternoon was not pretty. It worked, of course, but as Victoria the tapir fell uncomplainingly to her death, I felt a stomach-twisting worry that there might have been a better way. The sound made me flinch.

Once you get used to the machine, the deaths it predicts don't factor into your ethical judgment calls—the death is already out there, waiting to happen. But the collateral damage stands out more, and that afternoon it stood out all over the place.

With classic bad timing, Di joined us on the roof.

"There you are!" Then she saw it. "Oh, wow, what happened here?"

I looked meaningfully out to sea, hoping to impart some gravity to the moment. "Victoria fell."

She glanced up to Ex, harnessed to the mast thirty meters above. He waved. She waved.

"I had a question about that one, actually. I realize it's a bit late now, and I know you know a lot more about this stuff than me, but Dr. Jeth legally owns the island, and..." She seemed to have second thoughts. She's always had this bizarre impression that I'm some kind of intellectual heavyweight, just because I've written a white paper.

"What?" I tried to ask it encouragingly, even as that knot reappeared.

"Couldn't you have renamed a waterfall?"

Fuck.

When you work with predictions long enough, you start to think a little too laterally. I weaseled out of it with Di using a few long words, but she was right—that would have been perfect. I hadn't been on my game for months, and now that the reactor was getting close to completion, it was starting to worry me. I think my head had already moved on, but my body was sticking around to see the project through.

If it wasn't for Di, I might not have stuck it out. But something about her presence here seemed to validate the whole thing, to hide the supervillainous overtones and illuminate the possibilities.

Jeth had an unnatural talent for nuclear physics. Should that be a crime? He didn't like governments. Who did? How smart do you have to be before cynicism counts as villainy? And oh, God forbid you become independently wealthy enough to buy an island. Suddenly it's the Island of Dr. X, and the press can't refer to you without using the word "lair."

VICTORIA FALLS wasn't a hard one—I used to resolve slips like HEARTBREAK in an afternoon without killing so much as a puppy. I'd bungled VICTORIA, but I'd make up for it—the rest of the list Di had given me was going to be easy. Whoever selected these guys for the mission was an amateur, or they were saving their less killable unkillables for later.

In general, the more adventurous and exciting their death, the easier they are to kill. If you're on an assault squad with a guy who's going to be EXPLODED, that's your first man down. HEART ATTACK is going to be a tougher cookie, but he could still go at pretty much any time.

The real badass of the team is going to have something like ALZHEIMER'S. That son of a bitch can eat bullets and drink jet fuel; the universe is not letting him die until he forgets his grand-daughter's name and how to put his dentures in.

So Dr. Jeth handpicked most of his key staff partly on the basis of their predictions: none of us die in an exciting way, so we're all tough to kill. Every time we're attacked by someone with a sexier death, luck comes down uncannily on our side.

It was activation day, the event that would both realize Dr. Jethma-lani's dream of solving the world energy crisis and simultaneously kill him. So we'd all decided it would be a good day to tease him with the stupidest, most trivial questions we could come up with.

I hit the button and the door purred open.

"Mort. I have ninety seconds. What is this regarding?" Jeth's English was good, but he didn't like to use contractions.

"Do we have any doomsday devices?" He stopped typing and looked at me seriously.

"You are asking me if we have any doomsday devices?" I sensed this was a mistake.

"Yeah, I have a prediction here that just says DOOMSDAY DEVICE. I guess the Israelis thought you'd have one, and this guy would destroy it and die in the blast."

"Do you know what a Lazarus Reactor is, Mort?"

"Not in any real sense, no, but I realize it's not a doomsday device."

"So what you are asking me is if, in addition to developing sus-tainably free power for the planet via nuclear transmutation, I am also simultaneously preparing to destroy the same planet with a separate invention?"

"Well, I just thought if we had one, I could get Ex to hit the guy really hard with it, and that'd probably count."

Jeth took off his glasses and rubbed his eyes, suddenly looking very old.

"I am about to switch on an experimental traveling wave reactor that will provide enough energy to run several small countries for two hundred years, while broadcasting both the startup process and my full schematics to every nation in the world by live streaming video, shortly after which the initial uranium 235 reaction will end my life." He put his glasses back on and the tiredness vanished. "Ask Jen in Side Projects and General Villainy."

"Oh. Good idea."

He was a hard man to rile.

I was most of the way back to my office when the Klaxons went off. I ran the rest.

My office seals securely—Di and I get to watch any attack play out on the security cameras once we're both safe, which is scary but actually kind of nice. At least, that's what happens if the route back to my office doesn't lead me straight to eight armed commandos.

I burst into the nearest door—the ladies', it turned out—and listened for their voices.

A low, serious one: "Pancreatic: head down to the labs, check for doomsday devices and deathbots. Rectal: get to the satellite dish on the roof; we need to stop this guy's live feed before we take him out. Thyroid, you're with me."

Holy shit. A whole squad of cancers. A cancer *squad*. This was hard-core—one cancer is like a superhero in that line of work. I'd never heard of a whole team of them before. They must have been holding them back for one last attack on activation day.

A different voice: "Laz, what's our ROE?"

"Shoot to kill; no one's going to find these guys."

I waited until their footsteps had completely died away. Then, pulse heavy in my throat, I slowly pushed open the door.

I found a two-meter-tall special forces agent in bulky black Kevlar pointing a silenced carbine at me. I ducked.

A burst of shots went off, howling angrily off something behind me, but I didn't feel any hits. I grabbed stupidly at the guy's armored shins, but in trying to both step back and kick me in the ribs at the same time, he staggered. I felt his body slam heavily to the ground, heard his gun clang against the steel floor, and took it as a cue to throw myself on top of him.

"What the fuck?" He spat through an armored face mask as he thrashed under my knees and I fumbled frantically at his sidearm holster. I got the weapon out and pressed it into his chest with both hands, but not before he got an arm out and brought his carbine up into my neck. The silencer was a centimeter from my skin, and it felt like someone was holding a candle to my throat.

His eyes, the only part of him not covered up, regarded me seriously for the first time. I think he sensed that luck had done some very deliberate leveling of the playing field here and was trying to determine which of us was more screwed.

At last, he spoke quietly:

"Thyroid. You?"

"I'm thyroid too. Presented yet?"

"No. You?" In a weird moment, he sounded genuinely concerned about me.

"Me neither." My heart started racing. How close was this going to be?

"Okay, what type?" I was afraid he'd ask this. Mine's good, but there are better thyroid cancers out there if you know where to look.

"Follicular," I said with an unsteady attempt at pride. "Five-year survival rate of a hundred percent at stage one."

"Papillary, same."

My pulse quickened. "Stage two?"

"A hundred percent."

"A hundred percent."

I was still summoning the courage to ask when he beat me to it:

"Stage three?" This was it, final round. I held my breath.

"Seventy-one?" I squeaked, one eye shut.

"Ha!" He threw me into the wall and launched into a trained crouch, carbine still pointed expertly in my face. "Ninety-three percent, motherfucker!" He fired.

His weapon jammed. I don't know if this had occurred to him, but the five-year survival rate for a bullet wound to the head is pretty close to zero—it wasn't going to trump follicular thyroid.

I might not have any weapons training, but I do know something about death—enough not to try killing someone who's not going to die that way. So I shot him, deafeningly, in both shins.

When Ex found me, I was staggering vaguely in the opposite direction from my office, ears ringing from the shots and the screams, hot spots of wet on my arms and face. He'd been running, couldn't stand still. I handed him the carbine and the sidearm and told him about the cancer squad. He already knew.

"Oh shit, you took out Thyroid? I saw the squad on the cams. I was dreading taking on that motherfucker. My nerd!" He patted me roughly on the back.

"Well, I had help." It's a staff rule not to tell each other our predictions, so I left it at that.

"Seriously, that's a mild fucking cancer. You've gotta *try* to die of that." I let it slide. "Anything on the leader?"

"Just a name—Laz, Raz, something."

"All right, take these back and get to your office. I'm gonna clean this up."

I reluctantly took the guns back and stumbled off. Strong hands grabbed my shoulders and turned me around.

"It's this way, man."

In my office, I hit the button absentmindedly and jumped when the door slammed behind me. I propped the carbine up against the wastepaper bin, put the gun on my desk with a clunk, and shook both arms—I actually had a cramp from carrying them for three minutes.

I called Di—no answer. I logged in on my workstation, logged on to our extranet, logged through to our intranet, then unthinkingly logged in to my e-mail, remembered I wasn't checking my e-mail, logged out of my e-mail, then back into the intranet because it had overzealously logged me out, and finally found the option for GPS tracking.

Di's phone was about four meters outside her office, which was weird. It was moving, which was weird. And she still wasn't answering, which was weird.

I suddenly felt like everyone was watching: like whatever happened next, it'd be something I'd probably have to justify later, and I was terrified of what they'd think of me when I did. I picked up the gun.

It was a three-minute walk or a two-minute run, and I was jogging, so it took me four minutes. And yes, my arms ached, but it was a good ache now.

When I got there, Di was already gone.

I held the gun up in both hands and very slowly peered into her office, but the door was open and it was empty. There was only really one way she could have gone, so I ran—properly this time.

I found her kneeling over an agent twisted into the most explosively awkward pose, a sheathed carbon-fiber knife between her teeth. I fell in love with her on the spot.

"Eeeth fee heerf fath." She opened her mouth to drop the knife, unloaded the clip from his pistol, and shoved both into the back pockets of her jeans. "Sorry, I had a knife in my mouth." This was about the only piece of information I already had.

"What the hell happened?"

"I Tased him. But, Mort, we've got a problem."

"Well, the two geekiest people in the building have taken out more of the intruders than our twenty-man security team so far, so I can believe that."

"Ha! You got one too?" She stood up. "I'm glad you're okay, by the way." She touched my shoulder, giving me instant cardiac arrhythmia. "No, there's another problem: Ex hit their leader, and I tested the blood. Look." She showed me the readout on her phone.

"Fuck. Fuck! We need to go!"

"I know!"

"Where's Ex now?" There was a stomach-twisting crack of bone and a scream from the stairs down to the lab. I looked at Di. "I have a theory about where Ex is now."

*   *   *

"Shit, Mort, that's him." Ex had the leader on his front, twisting his arm into shapes that shouldn't work. I pointed my gun uselessly at both of them, and Di wisely moved out of my line of fire.

"Ex, don't!" she shouted. "You can't stop him!"

The moment Ex looked up, a fist smacked him in the jaw with astonishing force. The leader got to his feet, his snapped arm hanging limp, and shot Ex in the stomach with an ear-stinging crack.

I flinched. Di gasped. The leader ran for her, his gun perfectly level. I didn't think; I just fired.

I swear, there must have been a time when not thinking before you fired was a perfectly sensible way to shave valuable milliseconds off your reaction time. Post-Machine, though, it turns out to be a really terrible idea.

Di screamed and fell. My ears rang, my palms stung, my eyes and nostrils burned. The leader holstered his gun without breaking his stride and leapt over her body. It took me a full second to replay the moment in my head and realize that only I had fired—my shot must have ricocheted. I ran to her.

"Fuck fuck fuck I am *so* sorry I am so so sorry!" Why did the walls have to be steel? What is this rule that supervillain lairs can't be made of normal building materials, ones that know how to take a bullet?

She was wide-eyed and white, her cheeks wet, and her left thigh was soaked with blood. As carefully as I possibly could, I held her under the arms and pulled her over to where Ex lay.

That hot buzzing I get in my head when I talk to Di, that pounding I feel in my neck when I'm in a life-threatening situation, the cardiac arrhythmia I get when she touches me...these things stack. My pulse felt like someone was holding a jackhammer to my skull. I might get thyroid cancer later, but I was definitely going to have a heart attack first.

"Ex! EX! EX!" Eventually his head lolled scarily toward me, and he smiled. "How do you die?"

He said nothing, just smiled.

"Fuck the rule, how do you die?" I could feel Di's breathing through her back in my lap—it was fast and irregular.

Ex whispered something I couldn't hear. In a painfully stupid way, I tried to lean so my ear was closer to his mouth. The three of us were linked in the most ridiculous pose: Di limp, me double helix, Ex fetal.

The tiniest voice: "I don't know."

He suddenly gave a horrible, choking, seventy-year-old smoker's laugh, spitting blood in my ear and half deafening me.

I took his radio. "Security, Ex is down on level twelve, needs urgent help and is being a dick about it. Also, everyone who isn't helping him needs to get the hell out of here. Also, where do we keep the boats so we can get the hell out of here?"

No reply. I scooped my arms under Di and prepared to lift her. "If this hurts, you have to tell me, okay?"

"OW OW OW OW! Other side, *other* side, you dork!"

Lesson learned: try not to grip a gunshot victim by the gunshot wound.

As she clung clammily to my neck and I carried her up the stairs, I heard Ex lapse into another fit of loud, bloody coughing behind me. And then, hoarsely:

"I think it's probably this, man."

It was twelve floors to the surface, Jeth's broadcast playing on the PA and every screen on the way up. The aching in my arms had gone past the good ache, back to the bad ache, and straight through to the *I would ache, but it's Di and I shot her, so I'll shut the fuck up.*

Jeth was pontificating about the significance of what he'd achieved in a way that was in danger of putting everyone off listening to what he'd achieved, and I wished he'd get to the point and die before the agent got to him.

"Mort..." Di murmured, pawing at me as she was jostled by my graceless stair sprinting. "I'm sorry I called you a dork."

I almost laughed, but it was tough with no breath. "Well," I managed between pants, "I shot you...so I think...I'm going to win...this guilt battle."

"No!" She grabbed me quite painfully. "You saved me! That guy was gonna shoot me in the head." I had a lot of objections to that, but I saved my breath for the climb. "You're the reason my slip doesn't say GUNSHOT."

"You don't have to...tell me..."

"It's ALZHEIMER'S. I'm ALZHEIMER'S."

I stopped. I could pretend it was in shock, but in fact I just really, really needed to stop.

"Holy shit. The long good-bye? You should be carrying *me*." I set her down for a second. My shirt was soaked with her blood. She smiled peacefully. Something was happening on-screen.

"Ah, how nice! The United States have sent an ambassador to verify my results firsthand!"

Shut up, Jeth. Start the reactor before he shows you his prediction!

"If you are here to kill me, agent, I hope that your name is LAZA-RUS REACTOR FISSION SEQUENCE, because you have seconds to spare!"

I have told him, repeatedly, not to do jokes.

The leader walked on-screen, snapped arm dangling. I couldn't watch. I scooped Di back up, making her wince, and kept running.

The problem with not watching turned out to be view screens on every floor, positioned at the top of each flight of steps.

The leader didn't say anything, just held something up. You couldn't make it out at that resolution, but I knew what it said. It said LAZARUS REACTOR MELTDOWN.

You also couldn't make out Jethmalani's face as the agent pushed him callously into the reactor, but I had a pretty good idea of what it must have looked like. I've seen a man die of HEARTBREAK.

I lowered Di into the cancer squad's dinghy and looked at the time. They hadn't written "Cancer Squad" on it or anything, but it was jet black and docked haphazardly on the beach, so I figured it was theirs. I looked at the time. I grabbed two radiation suits and a medkit from the supply locker and looked at the time, then pushed its tough rubber prow back into the wobbling water and looked at the time.

There still wasn't any—it had been three minutes since Jeth died in the fission sequence, and the meltdown would happen inside of ten. But two things kept making me check.

One was Ex. I wasn't used to dealing with people who had no predictions, and the uncertainty was paralyzing me. Did it mean I could save him? Or did it mean I couldn't?

The other was the broadcast. Jeth gave his life to send this out, and I couldn't stand the thought of these cancerous assholes stopping it. Whatever happened with the reactor, people should get to see his work. He'd set the schematics to go online just after the reactor started up. If they took out our satellite dish in the next few minutes, nine years of work would end up as free R & D for the USA.

I thought about all these possibilities for three, maybe five seconds, then looked back at the only sure thing. Di, curled up in the dinghy.

I climbed in. I'd spent my career changing the inevitable—for once I was just going to run with it.

As we puttered out into the glinting orange sea, the roof of Jeth's facility came into view. I saw an agent—Rectal?—heading for the satellite dish. At the very edge of the roof, just below the south mast, he slipped on something red and fell out of view.

Four minutes out, I'd helped Di dress her wound and she was sitting up. I found some military rations that included something labeled, honest to God, a "HOOAH! Bar," which I decided I should try before giving to her.

"Oh my God, you can't have this." She looked at me, wide-eyed. "It's delicious!"

A fist hit my leg, surprisingly hard.

At six minutes, it was time. The island was surprisingly small already—six years of my life, so easily shrunk to a postcard. I hauled the radiation suits out and helped her in with her leg. I was about to pull the big plastic helmet up on mine when she stopped me.

"It's going to be a while before we get out of the fallout zone."

"Yeah."

"And once the reactor blows, we can't take these off."

"Not for long, no."

"Is there anything you want to do before we put our heads in plastic boxes for two days?"

I thought about this for a second, then held the side of her face and kissed her.

We both zipped up our suits just in time to see the reactor blow: a column of green radioactive fire, belching black smoke. Di squeezed my hand, our big boxy heads knocked clumsily together, and I tried to think of something romantic to say.

"Well, I guess that's why they all die of cancer."

Story by Tom Francis
Illustration by Les McClaine

DROWNING BURNING FALLING FLYING

"THEY'VE GOT BLOOD, DON'T THEY?" I asked.

"The biologists say so," Brianna said. "Blood analogue, anyway."

"Then it should work, shouldn't it?"

She shrugged, still looking ill at ease. Brianna was a worrier at the best of times, and in the month since the alien ship had landed, or appeared, or beamed down, or whatever it had done, I'd seen the lines on her forehead grow like spiderwebs.

"It's not that it won't work, Emily," she said. She took a sip of her coffee and grimaced. Hospital coffee is universally vile. "I think it *will* work. I'm just—not sure it's a good idea; that's all."

I couldn't really blame her for being twitchy. She and the other scientists had the government and the military and the media all breathing down their necks, demanding to know how the aliens did this and that and the other thing. Brianna Quinn was one of the foremost quantum physicists of our generation, and her team was trying to figure out the aliens' faster-than-light stardrive. She wasn't used to working in the spotlight.

I, on the other hand, was on-site only because among the ten thousand orders sprayed in all directions in the first hours after the landing had been the command "Send us linguists!" Then, of course, it turned out the aliens, the Nelat, spoke English, French, and a few dozen other Earth languages, so the diplomats didn't need us after all. I was seconded to Brianna's team to help them work out the technical terms that lacked English equivalents (which, in the case of their quantum drive, was nearly all of them). Nobody was pestering me for interviews or demanding status reports or shouting at me because they didn't *understand* my status reports, all of which they were doing to Brianna pretty much daily.

That was why we were here at the Montreal General Hospital, where nobody would be looking for us. Brianna wasn't exactly shirking her work, since two of the pilots, Isperander and Hasfenoon, were going to meet us there, and we'd probably get a chance to work through some more of their explanations. Like the rest of the alien crew, they were friendly and helpful, eager to share their knowledge and to learn about Earth in return—professional tourists, by both inclination and training. They visited churches, homeless shelters, hardware stores, anything that caught their interest. Today they wanted to see a Death Machine. It had been arranged, but while we were waiting, Brianna had started to fret. I honestly didn't understand why it was such a big deal and said so.

"It just worries me," she said. "Think about what *human* society went through when we first invented the Death Machine. People went crazy. The riots, the economic crashes, the cults, all those people trying to cheat fate by leaving their homes, their jobs, their families—it was decades before we got used to it."

"Yeah." Personally, I thought a lot of that stuff must have been exaggerated. A century and a half could distort perception a lot. Sure, it had to have been a shock for people at first, but it was just the Death Machine, after all.

"And Isperander said she'd never heard of anything like it. Thousands of species in the Union and we're the first ones to come up with the Death Machine. How do we know what impact it'll have on them?"

"We survived it," I said. "Look, Bree, thousands of species, like you said—they must have run across weird new technologies before. Who knows what they have? Dyson spheres, time travel, immortality—there could be anything."

"Not immortality," Brianna interjected. "Isperander told me they die."

"Well, anything else. The point is, their Union's probably weathered a lot of changes. I don't think our little planet's going to be rocking the boat much."

"Hm." Brianna didn't look convinced, but she let it go. We talked about other things until the pilots arrived—her work, mostly. Isperander had promised to let Brianna see the drive in operation next time they moved the ship. They kept it at the landing site north of Montreal most of the time, but every so often they went somewhere else on Earth for a day or so. Tourists. It drove the security people crazy. For that matter, it drove the scientists crazy, too. My translation work gave me a glimmer of the outlines of what they did, or at least of the words for what they did, but I couldn't explain it. Something about the ship existing in multiple versions ("roots" they said, or a word derived from their word for roots) of the universe at once, and their being able to become ("grow") their alternate selves. Brianna thought it worked like a quantum computer, with the various minds on the ship acting as individual qubits, but she had no idea how that translated itself into propulsion. She was hoping direct observation might provide a clue.

"I'm jealous," I admitted. "Any chance you can get me on board?"

Brianna shrugged. "Maybe. They don't want too many humans at once, Isperander said. Just in case we have some kind of bad reaction to the drive. There are a few species who can't use it; it does things to their minds."

"And the government's letting *you* be the guinea pig?" I asked incredulously. "You, the world-famous scientist? Don't they have army guys for that kind of thing?"

"I want to see it," Brianna said simply. "And Isperander said I could. You know nobody wants to deny the Nelat anything they don't have to." That was true enough; all the governments of the world were salivating over the technological prospects.

There was a commotion at the front entrance then, and we got up to see. As we'd guessed, it was Isperander and Hasfenoon, along with the diplomats and their entourage. A line of police kept gawkers back.

I spotted Lily Dane, one of the officers I knew a little. "What kept you?" I asked her.

Dane rolled her eyes. "Protesters."

"Oh? Against what?"

"The usual. Aliens are the spawn of hell, aliens are going to take away their jobs, aliens ought to officially apologize for kidnapping and probing people, blah blah blah. Anyway, we had to detour, and then the little one wanted to go back and argue with them."

"We want to engage with humanity," Hasfenoon piped up. He was the smaller of the two pilots and had a splotch of black across his muzzle. Isperander, behind him, was an even gray-brown all over. Both of them looked like armored greyhounds in the exoskeletons they wore to deal with Earth's gravity, except for the long fingers tucked up at the backs of their legs. They walked on all fours, usually, on their knuckles, but all their paws were hands. "How can we invite you into the Union without addressing your grievances?"

"They're not my grievances," Dane said. "My grievances are with whoever leaked our plans for today. Stay here a minute, will you? I'm going to see if everything's ready."

The two aliens hopped up onto chairs beside us and curled up on the seats, looking even more doglike than before. The diplomats arrayed themselves around the room but didn't press for the aliens' attention. "You have before used a Death Machine?" Isperander asked us. Her English was more accented than Hasfenoon's, but I was still impressed; I knew how long it took to reach that level of fluency in even another human language.

"Sure," I said. "Everyone does, when they're born." Brianna nodded.

"Is it impolite to ask what you read?"

I shook my head. "Not in Canada. Some places." There were cultures where you didn't find out your death till twelve or sixteen, and cultures—England was one—where you didn't discuss it socially. I couldn't imagine. "Mine is blunt force trauma. That means some sort of impact, like getting hit by something," I added, not sure if they knew the words.

"Mine is suicide," Brianna said.

I glanced at her. "No kidding? My mom was suicide."

"Oh yeah?"

"She decided to die when she got bone cancer," I said. "Once it was obvious she wasn't responding to treatment and the pain got bad. The whole family flew in for it. It was really nice."

"I'm hoping for something like that," Brianna admitted.

"This is most interesting!" Hasfenoon exclaimed. Isperander flicked one of her ears at him, and he lowered his head onto his fore-paws. Chastened, maybe. I made a mental note of the interchange; I was trying to compile a list of Nelat gestural cues, among a hundred other linguistic projects I wanted to do.

Dane came back. "They're ready," she said.

The machine in the office had been partially disassembled, its casing removed to allow the pilots to get their upper haunches under the needle. Even so, Isperander had to contort herself awk-wardly to get into the available space. The attending doctor pressed a button. The needle clicked down.

I found myself holding my breath.

The printer hummed. A slip of paper shot out into the doctor's hand. "Drowning," he read. There was a collective exhale.

Brianna caught my eye. I shrugged. Whatever the consequences to galactic society, they were unstoppable now.

The printer hummed.

Heads whipped around. Looking baffled, the doctor took the second slip as it emerged. "Burning," he said. "I'm sorry, are we sure this is working properly?"

Isperander, who had wriggled out of the machine, took the third slip. "Falling," she read. The fourth. "Flying." The fifth. "Luggage."

We stood looking at each other. Obviously the machine was broken, but somehow nobody wanted to interrupt. Isperander's recitation was taking on a hypnotic, chanting quality. "Air crash. Water. Stabbing. Hubris. Blanket. Plenpelleklet. Decompression. Library."

With a convulsive movement, one of the diplomats slapped the power button. The machine went silent.

"We'll try another machine," he said, red-faced. He looked furious;

I suspect he was the one in charge of this outing and was afraid of being held to account by his superiors for the glitch.

There was a brief argument between the diplomats and some of the hospital staff about taking another machine apart, but eventually the whole group of us went up two floors to the maternity wing. The casing was removed from the machine up there, and Hasfenoon volunteered to be tested this time.

"Vacuum," he read. We were all half expecting it, I think. "Fire. Chocolate. Electric shock. Sup—spelunking. Dogs."

"You've broken it," the doctor accused.

"They don't work on aliens; that's all," the spokesman retorted. "Here." He turned the machine off, then back on, and pushed past Hasfenoon to thrust his own hand under the needle. He snatched the printout triumphantly. "Electrocution. It's working fine." We all waited, but the printer was silent.

A few others tried it; Brianna was one. She shrugged and silently showed me her "suicide" result. I didn't bother rechecking mine; I hate needles.

It made the news briefly: "Aliens Immune to Death Machine!" The tabloid press talked of little else for a few days. Several more tests were done, as a formality more than anything. Rumor said the official in charge was being sacked on general principles. Some people wondered if this would somehow affect Earth's admittance to the Union, though no one could clearly articulate why it might.

In general, I think we felt sorry for the aliens more than anything. We'd all wondered at some point how the poor benighted people of previous eras managed to live with the level of uncertainty that was the norm then. Obviously they didn't know anything different, but *still*—

I found myself thinking a lot about my own death management classes, back when I was a kid. At my school they started in Grade Four, as part of our Health and Morals class, though I think I must have been told the same things earlier. I remember being split up into groups: chronic illnesses, suicides, sudden deaths, inexplicable. My best friend had "Christmas." I was in with the sudden deaths: fire, car crash, one tornado, four drownings. Two stabbings, but one was just "knife" and the kid who had it insisted he ought to be over with the suicides.

Most of what we were told was simple. It's likely to be quick. You won't see it coming. It's probably going to hurt, but not for long. "In some ways, we're lucky," our teacher (Mr. Rosenthal, motorcycle) told us. "We aren't facing months or years of lingering illness. We aren't going to have to take the responsibility for deciding when it's a good time to die." (The kid with "knife" mumbled something inaudible.) "We aren't going to spend our whole lives scratching our heads over an unclear result. We have a lot to be thankful for."

My best friend told me afterward that everybody got a pep talk of some kind. Still, the same things were repeated often enough that they tended to stick. After a century and a half, schools pretty much knew how to teach death.

Days passed. The work went on. Even with listening to them talk all day, I had no idea whether the scientists were making progress. If someone had asked me to paraphrase what they were saying, I would have come up with *something something quantum something anomalous superposition blah*. It was frustrating. I couldn't figure out why the Nelat, who spoke English just fine, hadn't come up with translations for their technical terms before they arrived. Isperander told me they wanted to make sure humans *understood* the technology, rather than just treating it as magical. It seemed like a flimsy reason; most humans use phones and wiremind and video every day without even slightly understanding how they work. Hell, *nobody* knows how the Death Machine works, and we've been using that for a hundred and fifty years. Nobody's ever been able to duplicate the original work, and the guy who invented it burned all his notes and took poison; if the prototype hadn't been stolen, we wouldn't have the thing at all. So what harm does it do to use black boxes? But the Nelat were firm; this was the way first contact was always done.

My own projects—mainly trying to write up a grammar of the primary Nelat language, Elusur, from my recordings and the materials they'd given me—proceeded apace. Then, a week or so after the visit to the hospital, Brianna announced that the ship was getting ready to leave for Iceland for a day, and she and one of the biologists were going to be aboard.

"You're sure this is a good idea?" I asked, for the dozenth time.

She smiled. "It's a *wonderful* idea, Em," she assured me. "I need to see their drive working. They told me we'd all be entangled— you know, *eshfendant*" ("grown-together," I translated) "with the ship as it runs, and that I should be able to perceive the—um—"

"*Tanshfestemen tfesperan,*" I finished, using a phrase we'd been hearing a lot. "The-forest-that-is-all-one-tree" was the best literal translation I could make. I'd suggested "multiverse," which seemed to me to be what they were getting at, but Isperander was hesitant.

Brianna nodded. "That one. Whatever it is. I'm hoping to have a better idea after the flight. The outbranch, I mean."

I decided I didn't wish I were going, after all. Granted, a magical disappearing ship wasn't likely to lead to the death I was slated for, but there were plenty of awful things short of death that could happen to a person, and somehow the more I learned of the Nelat language, the less I felt I liked it. All their constant metaphors of trees and growing seemed somehow threatening. It was completely illogical, but it had somehow sunken roots into my mind. I'd been having nightmares about dark endless forests, full of paths that never went anywhere.

The ship left. The ship came back.

I was waiting for her at the landing site—the inbranching site, Brianna's team were calling it now. I found myself sweating. I didn't know what I expected. I'd had a horrible dream the night before, of them carrying her out on a stretcher, a mindless, drooling husk. Stupidly melodramatic, but it had stayed with me through the morning, as though I couldn't fully wake up.

Lost in my thoughts, I missed the door opening. "Hey!" Brianna called. My whole body jerked as though with an electric shock. "Hey, sleepyhead!"

I stared at her. She ran toward me and caught me up in a jubilant hug. "You wouldn't believe it," she was telling me. "It was amazing.

I think I see how it all works. I'm not sure yet—I've got to go over it with Hasfenoon, make sure I'm not missing anything—but I think I understand it."

"Do you need me for that?" I asked.

She rolled her eyes. "I can't get started yet! The doctors want at me first. I told them I'm fine, but they're insisting they need to test me for everything from brain tumors to extraterrestrial athlete's foot. I'll probably be in the hospital the rest of the day."

She was, and overnight, and the next day as well. The other scientists on her team went from puzzlement to irritation to worry. I was worrying from the beginning.

On the third day I went over to the hospital and made a nuisance of myself until the staff reluctantly acknowledged that she was there. Eventually I got them to admit that she wasn't believed to have anything dangerous or catching (and what would they have done if she had, given that she'd been out hugging people for at least half an hour before reporting to the hospital?) and a harassed-looking nurse led me to her room.

I almost didn't recognize her. She sat on the edge of the bed, shoulders slumped, feet dangling. She was wearing a hospital gown and with her hair loose she looked about fourteen. "What happened to you, Bree?" I demanded.

She didn't seem to hear me. I repeated myself. After a few moments she looked up at me. "Em. I'm sorry. I am so sorry."

"It's okay," I told her. "Whatever it is, it's okay."

"It's not. I'll show you." She stood up and took my arm. "We have to be quick. They want me to stay in here."

She led me to the elevator and up to the maternity ward, where we'd been the week before. Once again we were standing in front of the Death Machine, now reassembled and ready to test the new babies. Brianna put her hand into the recess. The needle clicked down.

The slip popped out, and I read it. "Chalk." I did a double take. "I thought you told me—"

The printer hummed.

"Cancer," Brianna said, taking the second slip. "Keys. Drowning.

Cancer again. Nightshade. Fibrodysplasia ossificans progressiva. Boots. Suicide—I always get it sooner or later."

"This doesn't happen," I said. It was a stupid thing to say, but I couldn't help it.

"I know," Brianna said. She turned off the machine. Little slips of paper cascaded to the floor. "They can't figure it out. But I know why."

"The ship?" I guessed. "Something to do with the ship."

She nodded. "Right. I know how it works. I can't explain it in words—not English words anyway. We're going to have to learn Elusur to do their kind of science, I think. But it involves—alternate versions of ourselves, like we thought, only they aren't really. I mean, they aren't selves with different pasts, or anything like that. They're patterns of—not *patterns*, I mean—" She bit her lip. I'd never seen her do that. "I'm sorry. I can't explain it properly."

"Tanshfestemen tfesperan," I offered.

"Right. The forest that's all one tree. The ship, the quantum drive, it sort of—strips away the topsoil so you can see the roots all connected to each other. Then it multiplies the—the uncertainty, the probability that you'll be in a given place at a given time, or not, by the number of alternate self-patterns you're accessing, and somehow that lets you move—anywhere."

I thought about it. "That makes no sense at all," I decided finally. "And anyway, it doesn't explain *this*." I picked up one of the slips of paper from the floor. It was the suicide one, as it happened. "The machine's supposed to be foolproof. It's supposed to always work."

"It does always work," Brianna said. She, too, looked stunned, even having had days to get used to the prospect. "It's just—now it gives you everything. All the alternate versions of yourself that the quantum drive tangles you up with—the machine can't tell which one you are anymore; it can't separate them." She gave a humorless laugh. "This might actually help us figure out how the Death Machine works. Wouldn't that be something; we work it out right when it becomes useless."

"It's not useless," I said wildly. "We'll just—we won't use the quantum drive. Ever again."

"Of course we will," Brianna said. "You know that." I knew that.

"And even if *we* don't—if *you* don't—it doesn't matter. Causality links us all together, and if one person's future becomes uncertain, then everyone's does." She was speaking hollowly, sounding as though she wanted to stop but couldn't. "It's probably already too late. You might as well have yourself tested and see."

"Blunt force trauma," I said obstinately. "I don't need to be tested again. It doesn't change."

"Maybe not right away," Brianna said. "We don't know how the second-order effects will work. Will all your possible futures appear at once? Or will you have two or three at first, and then more and more and—"

"Stop it!" I shouted.

For a few seconds we just stared at each other.

"It doesn't matter anymore," Brianna said at last. "The certainty's gone. We're savages again."

They found her three days later with her wrists slit, a snowdrift of Death Machine results around her. She'd written a note on the back of one of them: "This is not a world I want to live in."

I've thought sometimes of following her. Some days I can't stand the uncertainty either. I haven't gotten tested again; I don't know for sure that my future's actually changed. I don't want to know.

Earth has joined the Union. Every day more ships come, and more people leave on them when they go. There are marvels out there, they say. Beyond description, beyond imagination. I've seen pictures and videos of incredible things. I've read the papers of my colleagues, of the linguists who've gone out to Trespin and Emdullah and Isveritur to study the languages of the stars. I do not feel the slightest urge to join them. This is not my world.

I understand how Brianna felt. I understand it exactly. There's only one thing that keeps me from following her.

My death is not suicide.

Story by Grace Seybold
Illustration by Carla Speed McNeil

CONFLAGRATION

ELIOT TAPPED SUGAR OUT OF a spoon onto the glistening surface of half a grapefruit. It took a few moments before the crystals softened their edges and melted to syrup. He knew, when he sealed it in a Ziploc bag and stowed it in the crisper, that Lydia would want the other half. He knew she wanted the other half of the fruit, and he knew how the rest of the morning would unfold.

In a few minutes, Lydia will appear at the foot of the stairs in slippers and a white terry-cloth bathrobe cinched below her breasts. She'll see him hacking with a too-big spoon at the wedges of his fruit, squinting against the spray of juice. She'll glance over the Formica counter, which she scrubbed yesterday or the day before, but she won't bring it up. She'll yawn in the doorway and step in the kitchen and say, "Did you save me half?"

Eliot will freeze, his spoon poised, and say, "Oh. Did you want that? I'm sorry, I put it back in the fridge."

Lydia will stare at him, expressionless, for about two beats longer than necessary to make her disappointment clear. As she glides across the kitchen, ankles just visible in the gap between her slippers and the hem of her robe, his mind will drift to mornings a decade ago. In those days, her legs would scissor out of her robe when she walked. In those days, when she bent low to scratch at her shin or adjust a slipper, one of her breasts might sneak out from behind a loose knot at her waist.

At some point—probably after she's coaxed three or four wedges of fruit from the rind with a lazy, juiceless ease—she'll ask him about their vacation plans. Has he been cleared to take that week off work? Though his request had been approved days ago, he'll evade the question.

Eventually, they'll dress. He in a rumpled blazer intended to make his patients see him as competent yet cool. She in a crisp, cheap pantsuit intended to make her colleagues see her as professional but unambitious.

In the driveway, cars crouching side by side, he'll give her a kiss on the cheek. He'll climb into his car while she fidgets in front of the garage, waiting for her coworker, the pudgy and pasty-faced Gary, to cross the street from his house, stuffing his shirttails into his pants.

That, Eliot knew, is how the morning would unfold.

He stood over the freshly scrubbed counter. The sugar had dissolved in the juice of the grapefruit, and he jabbed at it with his too-big spoon.

He hadn't yet finished unpacking his briefcase when Rosemary's number appeared on his desktop phone.

Eliot pressed a button and winced at the torrent of noise it uncorked. "Rosemary!" he said. "Turn it down."

The noise calmed and a beat emerged from the distortion. Bossa nova? "Eliot, hey," Rosemary said. "I'm stuck in gridlock and have an appointment in ten minutes. Could you babysit him until I get there?"

"I can do better, if you want. I scheduled an hour of prep it turns out I don't need. Should I take him for you?"

"That would rock," she said. "You rock."

Eliot grinned and raised his eyebrows at no one in particular. "What's the guy's story?" Eliot said to Rosemary.

"My guess is he's a standard-issue scared guy."

"Not another suicide looking for an excuse?"

"Definitely not. He's midthirties, owns his own business—a little three-person graphic design shop. I've got him pegged as feeling ground down by uncertainty, looking for bedrock in the first place that occurred to him."

"Your basic type-one talkdown."

"That's my guess. His name's Mike Cohen and his file's on my desk. Thank you so much, El. I'll see you in—God—maybe an hour?"

"Sorry to pull a switch on you like this, but Dr. Martin is stuck in traffic. Do you mind?"

"No." Mike Cohen was tall and a little thin, pale behind a few days of dark stubble. "One is as good as another."

Eliot nodded. "You understand why you're here?"

"You're asking me for proximate or ultimate causes?"

"I'm not sure we'd agree on the ultimate reason. Too deep."

Mike shifted in his chair. Slouched, then sat up straight. "I want to know how I will die, and before the government will release the information to me, they send me to you, so you can convince me that I don't want what I do want."

"That's pretty much it," Eliot said. This was a likable kid. Smart but willing to engage. "Why do you want to know how you'll die?"

"Variables," Mike said. He cleared his throat. "How am I supposed to make informed decisions—how am I to choose one path over another when the future is a mess of unknowns? If I can eliminate some uncertainty—nail down the value of one big fat variable—I'm hoping that it'll be easier to make some choices."

"And you're faced with some particularly difficult choices now? That's why you're filing the Death Machine request now, instead of five or ten years ago?"

"Yeah," Mike said. "I've got a business, a fiancée, health issues, parents. None of it is going like I expected. Do you want details about this stuff, or what?"

"If you want to tell me."

"Not really."

"The complications are worse now than they've been?"

"They're more paralyzing than they've been. I swear, it's like a sickness. Or poison. Hemlock, right? Numbness creeping in, limbs to heart."

"How will your Death Machine slip help? How will this little bit of knowledge eliminate complications or cure your indecision?"

"It's a pretty big bit of knowledge, isn't it? A huge bit. And I don't expect it will *cure* it, exactly. But it will sweep away one whole range of unknowns. Or at least it could. Depending on the answer, I might be able to guess whether I'm planning for the short or long term. That's huge. If I'm planning short term, everything gets easy. But even if it's long term—even if the answer comes back 'senile dementia' or something, just knowing that will help shake things loose."

"Here's what I think," Eliot said, looking at his fingers, at the deepening creases over his knuckles, the thickening nails, the coarsening skin on the backs of his hands. "I think this particular cure is worse than the disease."

Mike snorted and shook his head. "I have to tell you, GI Shrink, that I'm *shocked* to hear you say that. But go ahead. Let's hear the spiel."

Eliot thought about fire, water, car accidents, and cancer. Infectious disease and cross fire. The slow agony of cirrhosis and the shock of aneurysm. He looked at Mike and supposed that any one of these avenues would work. "Imagine you file this request and the response comes back that you'll die by drowning. What would you do?"

"Well, that would be annoying. That could be a short- or long-term thing. I guess I'd move to the desert, try to *make* it a long-term thing."

"Move to the desert—that's what everyone says. But would your situation actually improve? Given that the machine is never wrong?"

"You'd have me do nothing? That's certainly one way to make the request pointless."

"But you're no more or less likely to drown if you live in the desert than if you live on a houseboat. It's certain either way."

"Yeah," Mike said, sounding tired. "I know. I wouldn't be trying to avoid the inevitable. I'd be trying to nail down the time frame."

"Suppose you move to the desert. What would your life be like?"

"About like it is now. Much drier."

"Would you take baths? Or showers?"

"Oh. Right."

"Every time you step into the shower, you'll be gripped with dread. Is this the time I slip and fall, unconscious, with my face over the drain?"

Mike deflated. "Right," he said.

"Every time it rains: fear. Every time you walk past a community pool: is this the time some prankster or an impossible gust of wind tosses me in? Every time you see an unstopped fire hydrant. Every time your neighbor fills his shitty inflatable wading pool. Every time you pop the top on a beer or develop a wet cough: fear."

Mike avoided Eliot's eyes, and Eliot felt a little thrill of success. They were silent for a few moments; then Mike said, "I think you're right."

"Recently you've been struggling with the unknown. It's a potent fear, I know—believe me, I know—and it can be paralyzing. But your paralysis is temporary. It's a phase that will pass. If you get the machine's report, it'll be like you're living a horror movie from now until you finally die."

"Yargh," Mike said.

Eliot sat at their table by the window, looking across the street at their office building, smaller than some of the structures in Washington, D.C., but still, it seemed to him, grimmer. Rosemary approached carrying a cafeteria tray. "Usuals all around," she said.

"Thanks so much for lunch," he said.

"Please." Rosemary slid into her chair, across from him. "After a bailout like this morning's?"

"It was fun, actually. Nice kid. You had his number from the beginning. I used drowning on him and he left in blissful ignorance."

"Shame I was late. The job is satisfying when it goes well." Rosemary lifted her spoon to her lips and slurped—a ridiculous, throbbing slurp. Eliot smiled behind his napkin. She'd caught him smiling at her over a bowl of soup once before and asked what was funny. He'd made up excuses. "It's soothing when they seem convinced, isn't it?" she said.

"Satisfying, yes. Soothing?"

"You really believe the arguments we deploy against these poor befuddled people? All the time, you believe them?"

Eliot chewed a mouthful of sandwich until it was liquid, then took a sip of coffee. "You don't?" he said.

"Not all the time, no. I mean, it's not like I think they're crap, the arguments. But death is scary. It doesn't really matter, sometimes, that I know about a thousand case studies from the Oedipus years, or that I know every single client I've failed to dissuade has gone on to suffer. Reasons are more convincing when other people believe them. You know that as well as I do." Rosemary leaned across the table, reaching for a packet of sugar. Eliot looked at the wisps of hair, fallen from their clip, the interplay of light and shadow on her neck and collarbone.

"Lydia," he said. "Lydia is my other people, I guess."

"God," Rosemary said. "I guess she'd have to be."

"Yeah. I waver for minutes here and there. In particularly bad moments of particularly bad days, I just want to know and have it over with. Those moments pass. But Lydia, she's up to her neck in the raw data. She could call up her death slip with one line of SQL. I think she honest to God has no desire to know how she's going to die."

"It must be comforting to have that sort of certainty."

"It was."

"Was?"

Eliot, thrown, stammered and fumbled with a napkin. "You mean for her," he said. "Yes, she's secure in her certainty. I know she is. More than secure. 'Comfortable' is probably the right word."

Rosemary was smiling, mischievous, looking younger, even, than she was. "It *was*?" she said.

Back in his office, Eliot phoned Lydia's desk. She didn't answer.

Over the years Eliot's office had aged and contracted. He wedged books into every available length of shelf and then laid more across the tops of the others. The room was filled with him—the great wooden desk, its varnish rubbed away under his elbows, the scat-

tered offprints sent to him by grad school colleagues who were publishing at a much brisker pace, the framed handbills for rock shows
that were now dingy and dated and, worst of all, out of place—and
it depressed him.

Beneath the surface of his guilt was a current of anger that Eliot
tried to tease to the surface. Why should he feel bad for admiring
Rosemary's hair? Why should he feel bad for admitting—especially
as obliquely and accidentally as he had—that marriage to Lydia was
no longer comfortable?

Eliot slid open the deep drawer on the lower right of his desk,
thinking he might have a calming drink of his celebration bourbon.
Inside the drawer, a series of five chrome spheres were suspended
via fishing line from a wooden frame. Newton's cradle, the toy was
called, a fixture on the desk of every Hollywood headshrinker ever
committed to film. Lydia had given it to him as a gift when he was
hired by the feds. He'd been delighted at the visual gag—the stodgy
old Newton's balls on the desk of the hip young psychologist. It was
hilarious.

As the years passed, he grew worried that people weren't getting
the joke. He moved the toy to a shelf behind him, where it wasn't as
prominent, and later to a shelf behind his clients, where they would
see it only if they were looking. Finally, after they hired Rosemary,
but before he showed her his office, he hid it in a drawer, where it
straddled his bottle of bourbon.

Lydia, Lydia. It was a hell of a gift.

He picked up the phone and dialed her desk once more. Once
more, she didn't answer. It wasn't like her.

In the first days of their marriage, Lydia hadn't yet started her job in
Aggregate Statistics. She was finally approved—security clearances,
psychological batteries, proficiency tests in pattern recognition
and statistical analysis, and on and on and on—just before their
first anniversary. It seemed to him, at the time, a symbol of their
fitness for each other. He defended her from distraction while she
mucked about in the numbers. She worked with the demographic

and death-report data that was collected from all infants at birth, looking for early indications of impending public health disasters. He worked to dissuade adults from filing Death Machine requests, from learning what the government already knew, and triggering the tragedy and chaos that usually followed. It was like a Western: he at the window of the bank with a revolver, fending off the hordes, she inside with a stethoscope on the vault. Like a Western, but more bureaucratic.

It wasn't difficult to identify the period when they began to decline as a couple. It was during Lydia's fifteen minutes. The whole bird fever thing, five years before. In fact, it wasn't difficult to point to the exact moment their deterioration began: he'd been standing over the stove, stirring a red sauce, when she came home from work and said, "At last, some success."

Eliot put down the wooden spoon and gave her a hug. "Your mathly hoodoo is getting some results?" he said.

"Yeah. We're pretty sure my spider found an outbreak of bird fever in Boise, something like fifteen or twenty years from now. Found it hundreds, maybe thousands of cases before the normal trip wires would have flagged it."

"That's fantastic," he said. "How sure is pretty sure?"

"Sure enough that the director is committing resources. We've started the bidding process to synthesize a shotgun vaccine, and as soon as it's ready the Boise schools will start requiring it."

"That's huge," he said, turning back to his pot of tomatoes. "That's money."

"I know it. We stand to save a lot of future lives."

"When will you know?"

"I expect new death slips with 'bird fever' to start tapering off right away," Lydia said. Eliot could feel the happiness radiating from her but couldn't bring himself to meet her eyes. "Like, today," she said. "If I've got this right, we should be down to the odd instance within a few months. We'll do the official review in a year, but with the number of babies born every day in and around Boise, we should have a pretty good idea within the month."

Eliot didn't feel right. He stripped oregano leaves from a stem into the pot and tried to locate within himself a feeling of happiness or pride. With the wooden spoon, he forced the tiny leaves beneath the simmering surface of the sauce.

"Eliot?" Lydia said.

He stepped back from the stove and looked at her. "That's huge," he said. "They have a lot of confidence in you."

Over the next few months, it got worse. Lydia's new filters were a breakthrough in identifying future outbreaks, saving unknown numbers of the not yet conceived from deaths due to disease. Her techniques were adopted across the department and she attained as much celebrity as is available to a midlevel number cruncher in a beige government cubicle.

During that period, each of Lydia's successes made Eliot seize up inside. She received invitations to give talks at conferences frequently enough that he couldn't take the time off to accompany her. He went to work every day and did the same things he'd done for years, feeling less like a partner and more like a nuisance, always hovering two steps behind. Her work was published in academic journals and she was profiled in a popular science magazine. He stopped reading the Death Machine trades so as to avoid seeing her name.

When he arrived at home that evening, the day of Mike Cohen and his lunch with Rosemary, Lydia's car was already in the driveway. Eliot peered through the windows as he slipped between the cars, holding his briefcase high, looking for any hint of why she was home early. He saw none.

The house was quiet. He called for her and stuck his head in the living room, the study, the dining room. From the kitchen he spotted her in their backyard garden. She stood there wearing heavy canvas gloves, holding a cultivating fork, vibrating. She took half a step toward a planter on her left, turned toward the bed on her right, paused for a moment, then cast about again. Eliot watched her through the window as he set down his briefcase and draped his blazer over the back of a chair. Her convulsive indecision was almost funny—like a kid at Christmas who can't get as far as playing with any toy thanks to the distracting temptation of the others. Eliot tried to chuckle, but it came out as a grunt. Could Lydia have been so excited to cultivate the garden that she left work early? It wasn't possible.

Eliot pushed through the screen door and down the steps into the backyard. Without the barrier of the window to provide distance, the silence in the yard was eerie. She was radiating panic. "Lydia?" he said.

Lydia froze and looked at him. Her face was strained and her eyes wouldn't settle. She threw the cultivating fork aside and made for the house, dropping her shoulder to dodge around him. "Lydia!" he said and put out his arm to catch her around the waist. "What is it?" She folded against him. He spread his hands across her back and felt her shudder against his chest. Never had he seen her this upset. The list of potential causes didn't seem long. Did something happen to her sister? Had she been fired? Was she having an affair? Eliot leaned away from her enough to look at her face. She wiped thin cords of snot from her lip with the back of her canvas gloves. "What is it, Lydia?" he said. "What happened?"

"The car's in the driveway," she said into his shoulder. "I stranded pasty-faced Gary at work."

A quarter of an hour later, Lydia sat across the kitchen table from Eliot, holding a cup of tea. He sat in silence, fascinated by the redness of her eyes. Somehow, hunched over the kitchen table, in the grip of this pitched misery, she put him in mind of the laughing, driven woman he had courted more than a decade before. He waited for her to work her way through a few sips of tea before he tried again. "Lydia?" he said. "What happened?"

She glanced at him and configured her face in a smile. "There's going to be a conflagration," she said. "A *conflagration*, of all things. In New York."

It took Eliot nearly an hour to piece together the story Lydia told him in fits and starts, digressions and metaphors. Partway through, he put on another pot of tea and sat down beside her at the table, their upper arms and shoulders touching.

Lydia's Boise algorithm—the one that launched her career—was easy to understand in the abstract. Infectious disease tends to kill, disproportionately, the very young and the very old. If the Department of Aggregate Statistics catches the slips of the cohort who will, eventually, die when they are very old, the people who will be very young at the time of the outbreak haven't yet been conceived. They haven't been born, so they haven't been tested, so their slips haven't been printed. Though the deaths of the very old are written and cannot be changed, there's hope that a concerted public health effort, like a vaccination campaign, might prevent the disease from ravaging the future cohort of the very young. Thus it was that, thanks to her work, no future infants would die of the bird fever in Boise.

Lydia had spent the last year developing a successor to the Boise algorithm, adapting it for applications other than infectious disease, lowering its threshold sensitivity. The challenge was this: while epidemics of disease tend to cluster geographically *and* demographically, large-scale death due to natural disaster clusters only geographically. These die-offs are demographically scattered, killing healthy adults just as well as infants and the elderly. Without *demographic* clusters, identifying trends in the raw data of the death slips is much harder to do. Nevertheless, Lydia had some luck catching natural disasters in test data and proceeded to take a stab at real-world data. Her first hit in the real world was the word "conflagration" in New York City. Four hundred death slips going back nearly sixty years came from blood tests of babies in New York.

"Conflagration" was an unusually obscure word choice for the Death Machine. In the overwhelming majority of cases in which the cause of death was fire, the machine reported "fire." So Lydia searched New York's death slips going back sixty years and found 380 hits for "fire." The machine's bizarre behavior put her in a paranoid mood. She searched for "inferno" and found 370 hits, just under the threshold sensitivity of her new algorithm, though far below the threshold of the production standard. A search for "broiling" netted 300 hits. She loaded a thesaurus and worked her way through nouns and verbs related to fire. Immolation: 380 hits. Combustion: 350 hits. Cremation, incineration: 340 hits each. Searing, scorching, charring, roasting: each between 250 and 400 hits.

When she totaled her list, she had thousands of death slips from the city of New York indicating death by fire—far too many to overlook, had they not been cloaked by synonyms. She turned to types of death that often accompany traumatic disasters. Smothering: 350 hits. Asphyxiation, suffocation, hypoxia. Same story. Blunt trauma and bludgeoning. Blood loss and—absurdly, it seemed to Lydia—"exsanguination." Tens of thousands of death slips, taken altogether, suggested a massive disaster coming to New York.

"What could do this?" Eliot said. "A terrorist attack? A nuke? It sounds like you're talking about the total destruction of New York City."

"It's worse than that," Lydia said. "You still don't get it."

She searched for "conflagration" in Seattle: 240 hits. In Albuquerque: 180 hits. Seven hundred fifty hits each in Chicago, Houston, Miami, and D.C.

"You've detected the end of the world?" Eliot said. "You and your computer predicted Armageddon?"

"Armageddon?" Lydia said, and smiled at her teacup. "I could probably get a hundred and fifty hits for it in every American city."

Eliot satisfied the suddenly overwhelming urge to do something with his hands by carrying their teacups to the sink. He could think of nothing to say.

"There are ways," Lydia said, "to predict, roughly, when a disaster is going to fall. We can look at the numbers of babies born with a given death slip, and how those numbers change over time. In this case, since it looks like nearly everyone is going to die, it's a simple linear projection and very precise. We just extrapolate to the time when every baby born gets a disaster-related death slip. It's twenty-nine years and three months away."

He laughed and was startled by the volume of his own voice. "Twenty-nine years?" he said.

"Eliot," Lydia said. "We're barely forty. We're probably going to live to the end of the world."

The next morning, when the clock radio struggled to life—an NPR arts and culture story on a band he didn't recognize—Eliot and Lydia lay there, listening. When the story finished, Lydia turned to face him. "I don't think I'm going to work today," she said.

Eliot reached over the edge of the bed, stretching for the nightstand, and turned off the radio. "I'm thinking the same," he said.

He lay beside her in silence for a time. The thin curtains swelled and glowed. The cherry trees in Potomac Park had dropped their blossoms not so long before, blanketing the banks of the greasy river with petals. They'd do it again the next spring, and again, and twenty-six times after that.

"Is this going to change?" Lydia said. "After I've had a few weeks to contemplate the end of the world, will I want to go back to fine-tuning pattern-matching algorithms in a government cubicle? Ought I?"

"I don't know," Eliot said. "For me, it would be working for a paycheck. I don't know how important paychecks are now."

"I don't think I'm going to work today," she said.

Eliot, wearing sweats and a T-shirt, dialed Rosemary from the garden while Lydia made her calls from the kitchen. The vegetables were established; the annual flowers were growing tall, some of the perennials already blooming. He brushed his hand across the petals of a tulip while Rosemary's phone rang.

"Listen, Rosemary?" he said. "Something's come up. I can't come in today."

"Is everything okay?" she said.

"Sure," he said. "Fine." He bent down and plucked a yellow leaf from the bottom of a young tomato vine. "I'm sure I'll be back tomorrow."

"Well, I'll take as many of your patients as I can. I owe you one. A few, actually."

"Thanks," he said. "The next lunch is on me."

"Oh!" she said. "That reminds me. I read a review of a place last night. It's a tea bar and café, and totally punk rock. Can we try it? Can we try it?"

"Yeah. Rosemary?" he said. "I've got to go."

Lydia knelt beside him at the flowerbed. Eliot had dragged the cultivating fork between the stems and was breaking up small clods of earth with his fingers. "I was evasive," she said. "On the phone just now with pasty-faced Gary. What am I supposed to say to him that doesn't run the risk of ruining his life?"

Lydia had always understood, in an instinctive way that Eliot envied, the horror of a known fate. She never needed to refer to the case studies from the Oedipus years—the painful period after the machine's invention, during which human suffering crested as people learned their fates. A few times a year, Eliot would drag out textbooks to remind himself of the grimmest of the Death Machine stories; Lydia cringed when he tried to read them to her.

"You know," he said, "you don't actually know how you're going to die." He brushed the soil from his hands. "With twenty-nine years left on the clock, you could totally be cut down by cancer, or—I don't know—a serial strangler or something."

She laughed and kissed him on the cheek. "Oh, Eliot," she said. "You always know just the thing to say."

That afternoon, they read together in the study. She had a novel; he'd loaded the noon edition of the *Times*. He lowered the paper and gazed at a blank portion of the wall. "There are cheaper places to live than D.C.," he said.

She closed her book around her finger. "And we've built up a lot of equity in the house," she said.

"Do you think it's enough? If we sold this place and moved to backwoods Alabama, could we make it for twenty-nine years?"

"I could still research part-time," she said. "Telecommute. Leave plenty of time for reading and gardening. I could finally get back into sketching."

"I could start a little practice. Just a few patients a week. Couples therapy and things."

Lydia shook her head at him in mock exasperation. "You're going to buy a guitar, aren't you?"

"Yes," he said. "A loud one."

An ambulance ran by a few blocks away, howling, then fading in the distance. "Other people can apply filters to data just as well as I can," Lydia said. "We could be yokels, right?"

"Yeah," he said. "Hot yokels."

After dark, after dinner, they sat in chairs in the backyard, glasses of wine on a table between them. The sky had gone overcast and the lights of the city, reflected on the clouds, cast everything in a lambent blush.

"I've been thinking about some of the case studies you've told me about over the years," Lydia said. "I've been thinking about the cases when the machine seemed . . . almost malevolent."

"Malevolent?" he said.

"I'm anthropomorphizing, I know. Still. I remember a case when an adult—a happy, middle-aged man—received a slip that read 'suicide.' He started pulling hard on all the loose threads of his life to try to understand the prediction. Everything fell apart and he ended up killing himself a year later."

Eliot nodded. The details of that case—Suicidal Sam, students called him—had persuaded a number of his patients not to file Death Machine requests. "Malevolence suggests agency," he said. "Suicidal Sam was a straightforward tragedy."

"Forget I said malevolence. I just mean this: would he have killed himself without the prediction?"

"Everything we understand about the machine says that he would. The textbooks say he would."

"There are the other cases, the misleading fortunes that really do go straight back to Oedipus. Would Oedipus have left Corinth if it hadn't been for the oracle? Would—was her name Richardson?—have emigrated to Ireland if not for a misleading death slip about snakes? Would that football player have surrounded himself with nothing but men if not for an unusually poetic death slip about a woman scorned?"

"I know. It's hard for me to believe that the machine isn't sometimes, whatever, malevolent. In some of those cases, it sure looks like the fortune was *designed* to prompt the very decisions that eventually bring it about."

Lydia topped off their glasses and checked the level in the bottle. "You don't have to go as far as design. I'm just saying that the machine itself is sometimes involved as a necessary link in the causal chain."

"Yeah," Eliot said. "It's not the received view, but it seems obviously true to me."

"So here's one possible scenario. In twenty-nine years, a dinosaur-killer asteroid hits the earth and everybody dies."

"Sure."

"Here's another. I tell Gary what I've discovered. You tell Rosemary." Eliot shifted in his chair. "I confirm the trends with standard, accepted statistical methods and take it to the bosses. Over the next three decades, word leaks and spreads. People leave their jobs to pursue lives that seem more important in the gloomy new context. Court systems, police forces, infrastructures grow weaker as people withdraw to take up painting or ballroom dancing or saxophone. The date approaches, the level of panic rises, riots break out and spread, and the world ends."

"I think I prefer the asteroid," Eliot said.

"Except—"

"Except what? "

"The second scenario could be averted."

"Lydia! Of all the people—"

"This isn't as unorthodox as it sounds. I don't think so, anyway. Look, if the machine is involved in the causal chain, we have an opportunity to take it out. If Oedipus hadn't *heard* the prediction of the oracle, he wouldn't have left Corinth. This is Oedipus writ large. If the people don't *hear* the prediction, the machine is removed from the causal chain, and the fate doesn't come to pass."

She took a long drink of wine and put her glass down on the table, leaning over the arm of her chair toward him, and continued. "We should have years yet before the death slips trigger the standard trip wires. I just stop developing my new work—claim it was a failure. We can use the time to coordinate a response—a cover-up, I guess—with one or two bosses we know we can trust. If we can keep this contained, it could work."

Eliot looked at Lydia. He wanted to reach out and touch her. One day—one day on her heels after devastating, life-changing news—and she was already forming a plan to fight back. A plan that struck him as totally plausible. "Does this mean no Alabama?" he said. "Does this mean I have to go back to work tomorrow?"

"I don't see any real choice. We kind of have to try." Lydia reached between the chairs to squeeze his knee. "We'll start looking for something better for you," she said. "In the evenings."

The next morning, Lydia and Eliot shared a grapefruit and a pot of coffee. They got dressed and walked to the driveway to wait for pasty-faced Gary. Across the street, he and his wife, Alina, were already outside, strapping a roof rack to their sedan. Both of them were moving in bursts of energy that reminded Eliot of Lydia in the garden two days before.

"Gary!" Lydia called. "What's up?"

Gary jogged across the street while Alina finished tying off the rack. "You're still here?" he said, squinting against the sun. "I didn't know." He looked over his shoulder at his wife, then back at Lydia. "We're going to stay with Alina's parents while we reorient."

"Reorient?" Lydia said.

"I hate my job. Alina hates hers. Who wants to prepare for Armageddon by wasting a life?"

"Armageddon? What are you talking about?"

"Seriously, Lydia. You freaked out and disappeared from work in the middle of the day," Gary said. "You were creepy. We checked what you were working on. IT opened up your computer for us, and the files were all right there." He looked like he couldn't decide whether he was embarrassed or annoyed. "Did you think we wouldn't?"

Lydia looked at Eliot, then turned back to Gary. "So the bosses know what I found?"

"Yes, they know," he said.

"And you told your family too? Parents? Cousins?"

"Them too," he said.

Eliot watched Alina across the street. He thought she might be crying. Gary gave Lydia an awkward hug and shook Eliot's hand. Eliot and Lydia waited as their neighbors loaded the trunk and roof rack, climbed into the car, and drove away.

"Well," Lydia said, "I guess Armageddon's back on."

Eliot fought back a grin.

"You're *smiling*?" Lydia said. She looked at her car and at their house and down the empty street. "That's totally inappropriate."

Story by D.L.E. Roger
Illustration by Sam Bosma

GOT TOO EXTREME

KC GREEN

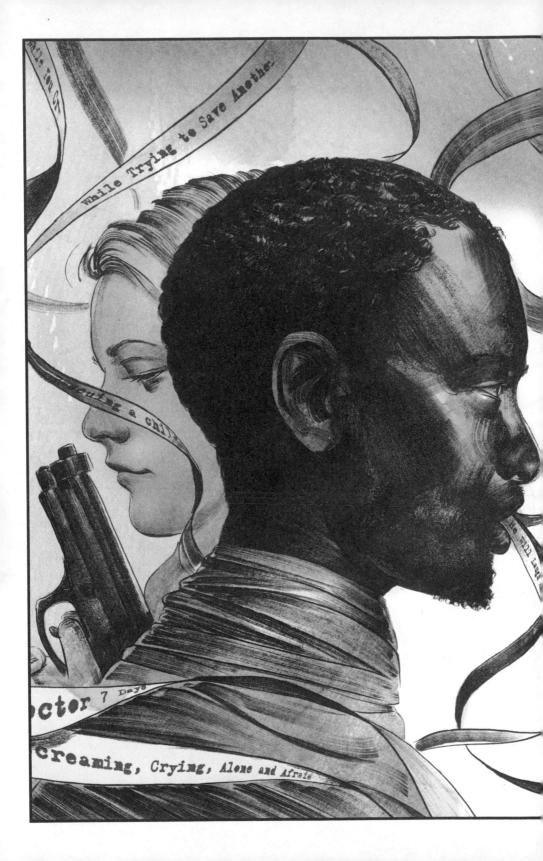

SCREAMING, CRYING, ALONE, AND AFRAID

1

"THIS IS NOT GOOD-RIGHT," Jabu said.

He stank. That his stink was discernable amid the competing odors of the Harare market was a mark of just how intense it was. He clutched the vial of blood Kira had given him within filthy fingers.

"For you I do yesterday, but no do for somebody else unless he comes himself. Not good-right. It like cheating. Bloodread is private. Like diary."

Kira knew that Jabu didn't really have a moral issue. He was just after more of that *mzungu* money. Having white skin in Harare was like wearing a sign that said, "Have Money, Please Swindle Me." No need to beat around the bush. "I'll pay you extra. Double."

Jabu grinned; his teeth were stained and uneven. He held the vial up and shook the blood like a bartender preparing a cocktail. "Money first."

Kira handed him forty U.S. dollars. Since 2009, Zimbabwe had been using the U.S. dollar. Kira still had some one-trillion notes from before the switch. They were party pieces she took with her whenever she went back to England for Christmas.

Jabu took the blood to a large wooden chest he had at the back of his kiosk. He glanced to see if anyone was looking before pulling it open. He poured some of the blood into a disc and pressed a button. It purred into life. Jabu meanwhile lifted an animal's skull from behind the chest. Kira guessed it was a cow's or buffalo's but she couldn't be sure as she was not well versed in bovine anatomy. Jabu began to sway while mumbling a chant.

Eight years ago, back in England, when Kira had got her forecast, it had been in a sterile room akin to a gynecologist's clinic. While waiting she had flipped through the pages of a tabloid magazine. Watching Jabu's gyrations and gobbledygook was a more diverting way to wait for a result than reading the sordid details of the Sugababes' love lives.

As he had the day before, Jabu finished his ritual by flinging aside the skull and collapsing. She waited politely as he rose, composed himself, and lifted a small slip of paper out of the chest. He read it and his eyes widened.

"What is it?" Kira asked.

"I'm sorry." He handed her the slip.

Jabu grabbed Kira's hand, clumsily trying to express sympathy. "It is to be badly dying for your friend."

Kira looked at the prediction. SCREAMING, CRYING, ALONE, AND AFRAID.

Shit. Nothing useful. Back to square one.

2

To think, Jabu had almost not bought the rickety Death Machine. When Mr. Richards, the man from whom Jabu bought expired medical supplies, had told him he had acquired a Death Machine, Jabu had said, *So what?* He didn't think it would make him money. Besides that, there was the risk. Privately owned Death Machines were illegal. All predictions were meant to be made at the state-owned ZFC (Zimbabwe Forecast Center). Mr. Richards had convinced Jabu to lease it for a month and see if it was worth buying. He had been shocked. More people paid him to find out how they would die than paid him for cures. Death predictions and love potions were the top sellers.

Jabu's neighbor Marcus Chuma sold books. He sold many that were on the government-banned list, so there was no chance of him telling the police about Jabu's Death Machine.

Naturally curious, Marcus strolled over. "What did that white lady want?" As always, he was wearing a dusty suit. No matter how hot it was, Marcus wore a suit.

"She wanted a bloodread," Jabu answered in Shona. Both Jabu and Marcus spoke Tswana and Shona, but Jabu's Shona was better than Marcus's Tswana. "It won't help your paper, though. It was a repeat. SCREAMING, CRYING, ALONE, AND AFRAID, like last week. I think maybe she was sent to check I was not fake by her friend. I would check too after such a scary prediction. Poor girl."

"Unless two people had the same prediction. I wonder how often that happens," Marcus said pensively.

Jabu was unsurprised. "Another book idea?" Marcus was always boring him with ideas he had for books and academic papers.

Marcus nodded. "Maybe. But I think maybe, after this one is finished, never again. Too much work."

"If you ever finish it."

"She was nice looking, the white lady," Marcus said. "Not skinny like they usually are."

Jabu wondered if she'd be back.

3

The seventh body was found in a Dumpster behind a mosque. Like the first six, it was heavily bruised and covered in wounds from a knife or scalpel. The coroner confirmed that the body had been washed thoroughly postmortem.

The victim was young Ethiopian girl, probably sixteen or seventeen.

"No signs of rape," the coroner said. "There's that at least."

Kira said nothing. She supposed it was natural to try to find a positive to cling to, but she couldn't. This girl had been abducted, tortured, and finally killed.

"Did you?" she asked.

Surreptitiously, he handed her a vial of blood. "Did the last one help?"

"I'm grasping at straws," Kira replied. "Whoever is doing this, they are meticulous. Nobody has seen anything."

"And if she's like the others"—he waved a hand over her body—"I'll find no traces."

"The first six were all found near churches," a familiar voice said behind Kira. "Now he's killed a Muslim, he left her by a mosque." The owner of the voice was a tall balding man with coal-black skin who loved what little authority he had so much that Kira was sure he slept in his uniform. Detective Inspector Mudarikwa resented Kira, and she loathed him.

"He left traces," Mudarikwa continued. "If you know how to look. The way he beat them but then washed them and wrapped them in a blanket. The fact he left them near their places of worship but one in a derelict building, two in Dumpsters, one..."

Kira started walking out. She didn't have time to listen to Mudarikwa's pontificating. He had studied criminal psychology in South Africa and he seized upon every opportunity to choke people with displays of his superior knowledge.

"Yes. Go," he seethed. "Leave it to the police."

4

"What this for?" Jabu barked at Kira four days later. "Is they ashamed to come for themselves? Do they pay you much money and you come have it cheap-cheap?"

"If you have a problem doing this, I can go to someone else."

"No, no, no," he yelped. "I just ask because strange. You no want to say, all right."

Jabu's kiosk was more cluttered than it had been the last two times Kira had come. Clearly he had just had a delivery. He had remedies for everything. Pills for headaches, salves for burns, and beyond that more esoteric cures. A blackboard hanging from a loop of razor wire had a chalk-written list beneath the title "DOCTOR 7 DAYS" (he guaranteed all his remedies worked within a week). Impotence. Drunkenness. Bad dreams. Wife beating. Kira wondered which of the bottled syrups was Jabu's wife-beating cure. She had found divorce papers had worked well enough. Simon had punched her only once. Nobody knew. Kira's mother didn't know, and in letters she still updated Kira on what Simon was up to. Kira wasn't sure why she had never told her what had actually happened. The lie she told was that Simon had cheated on her. For some reason it had been easier to tell people that.

"Infidelity," Kira suggested when Jabu completed his ritual and handed her the sliver of paper with the forecast.

"What?" he asked.

"Infidelity, unfaithfulness. You should add a cure for that." She pointed at the blackboard. "You would sell many."

"You need?" he asked, totally misunderstanding her intent. "I can make for you cheap-cheap. But how, I wonder how? How can it be? What man would be bad faith to woman like you? You beautiful." He puckered his lips and blew her a kiss.

She looked down at the paper.

HE WILL LAUGH WHILE YOU CRY.

5

FROM "NECROLINGUISTICS"
By Marcus Chantunya

One of the reasons people find it hard to accept Death Machine forecasts as purely scientific phenomena is the language of the predictions. You would expect a machine to produce purely empirical data, as one would find in an almanac. GPS coordinates or simple descriptive words like "heart attack," "internal bleeding." However, so many predictions are poetic. "WHILE TRYING TO SAVE ANOTHER" instead of "fire." "HE WILL LAUGH WHILE YOU CRY" instead of "beaten and tortured to death." Some predictions have a sense of humor. In some cases the word choice indicates sadness or anger. The language of the predictions seems to reveal personality. Whose personality? God's?

6

Kira had three strips of paper taped to her office wall now. Hooft Security had been called in only after the first three murders, when authorities realized there was a pattern and it was official: Zimbabwe had its first serial killer. Hooft Security had been founded by Kira's father in the seventies, and now it did much more than just home security. Often, when expatriates did not want to leave investigations in the hands of Harare's notoriously corrupt police, they hired Hooft.

Kira had no army or police training. All things being equal, she would be teaching physics at a university somewhere. When her father had left her his business in the will, he had probably expected her to sell it, but in 2007 she had reached a point where she hated everything about her life. Her father's final gift to her had been more than a lump of money. It had been a new beginning.

She had packed up her things and left England. Everyone had called her insane. Especially because that was back when Robert Mugabe was still in power and as far as the British media was concerned, he was the personification of evil. It had been nowhere near as bad as she had imagined. What chaos there was had meant Hooft was never without work.

Now things were significantly better. James Ndlovu was the current president. People had expected Morgan Tsvangirai to become president when Mugabe died, but when James Ndlovu's Death Machine forecast was leaked to the press, he immediately became the front-runner. RESCUING A CHILD. How could anyone compete with that?

Kira was cautiously optimistic about James Ndlovu. He clearly loved his country, but as much as he had done to regenerate the economy, his intolerance of opposition was worrying. Tourism was one of his priorities. That was why he had called Hooft personally and brought her into the investigation of the White Shroud Killer. He wanted the story out of the press as soon as possible.

To be honest, she felt totally out of her depth. As much as she hated Detective Inspector Mudarikwa, he was right about her. She didn't know the first thing about investigating a murder. She had her two best employees helping—Qabaniso Tutani, an ex-soldier, and Maria Gahiji, an ex-policewoman, ex-nun, Rwandese immigrant. Kira maintained that if she ever found someone to dictate it to, Maria's history would make a best-selling novel. Not that Maria's or Qabaniso's inquiries were going well. Nobody was turning up anything.

Kira had got the idea to test the forecasts of the victims' blood after the fourth victim was discovered. She hadn't even been sure a Death Machine would spit out a prediction when the blood of a person who was already dead was put in it. It had worked, but none of the victims' forecasts so far had been helpful to the investigation. She hoped a forecast might reveal something about where the victim died before being moved. Some tiny detail about the killer perhaps. Anything traditional forensics would miss.

Instead all she had from victims five, six, and seven was:

CHOKE ON BLOOD
SCREAMING, CRYING, ALONE, AND AFRAID
HE WILL LAUGH WHILE YOU CRY

She looked at the three strips of paper helplessly. They were like snippets of morbid fridge poetry.

7

FROM "NECROLINGUISTICS"

By Marcus Chantunya

Nostradamus's predictions of the future were all entrenched within four-line poems. Academia maintains that he must have obscured his meaning to avoid charges of heresy. Skeptics take the view that his predictions were vague so that they could be bent to fit whatever happened. But imagine these hypotheses were wrong. Maybe Nostradamus had no choice but to write his predictions in cryptic quatrains because that is how they came to him. Consider the cryptic language of Death Machine forecasts. Maybe it is something inherent in the nature of prediction. A man who looks in the face of God is blinded.

8

Jabu had been having a bad day. An angry woman armed with a rolling pin had come by in the morning. Apparently, the fertility salve Jabu had given her to rub over her husband's genitals had made him break out in a rash. The other market vendors had been delighted, laughing and pointing as Jabu leapt to and fro to avoid her angry swings.

That was the last time he would sell a fertility salve. Better to go with an incantation or potion. Following this, Jabu had not had any customers. The market was abuzz with life, but everyone looking for a traditional healer had gone to his competitors. After three hours of waiting in the heat, he saw two women enter the market and sighed with relief. His blond-haired *mzungu* of the many predictions was back.

"Hello again." He held out his hand. Kira reluctantly shook it.

"And this your friend?" He pointed at the towering behemoth of a woman beside Kira.

"This is Maria. She works with me."

"You have another blood?" he asked.

Kira reached into her purse and pulled out a test tube. Jabu took it and opened the chest that housed the Death Machine. He placed two drops of blood into the machine, turned it on, then picked up his skull. He began his incantation, gibberish, of course. As Kira was his only customer of the day, he put a little more oomph into the performance. He shook more, swayed more, and undulated his voice more frenetically.

Out of the corner of his eye he could see the woman Kira had come with shaking her head disapprovingly. Clearly a nonbeliever. A few other people walking through the market paused to watch him. If he was lucky, one or two of them might be his next customers. Jabu spun and spread his arms.

He heard the Death Machine beep twice, so he flung aside the skull and picked up the sliver of paper it had spat out. He made a mental note to self to check if he needed to refill the spool. He picked up the prediction. STABBED, THEN HE WHISPERS TO YOU.

He shook his head. Again. He perused the expectant Kira. She puzzled him. Should he keep quiet? She was a source of steady business, so he should probably just shut up and thank his lucky stars, but his curiosity was too much.

"Why?" he asked, handing her the slip of paper.

"Why what?" Kira replied.

"Why again the same one? Like the other ones."

"I don't know what you mean."

"What you doing? Why you bring me blood the same one again. Like first, then again. Like second again. What you doing?" She didn't understand him. He grappled for the right English words. He switched languages, addressing the giantess beside Kira. "You speak Shona?"

Maria, still looking at him with unconcealed disgust, nodded.

"Tell her I want to know why she keeps bringing me blood I've already tested. This one here is the blood of a woman who came by on Tuesday. Also the 'LAUGH WHEN CRY' one, the 'SCREAMING' one and the 'CHOKING' one. Is she following my customers and getting a blood sample? Why? Is she trying to show I am a fraud? Why retest?"

"Wait a second," Maria said, grabbing hold of his shoulder. "All the forecasts you did for her; the blood was from customers who had come to you for a prediction?"

"Yes."

Maria translated. Kira was stunned. "Every victim?"

Maria nodded. "That's the first connection we've found between victims. You don't think he..." She pointed at Jabu.

"Why would he tell us if it was him? Maybe someone like those Christians who call Death Machines devil worship is targeting his customers."

Maria switched back to Shona. "Listen. You must help us. There is a man who has killed eight women. The police have found nothing, but all the last four women this man has killed had forecasts from you. Maybe the ones before that too. Are these the only forecasts you have done in the last few weeks?"

"No. I have done many. A few every day."

"So it's not just a case of someone watching who asked him for a prediction and killing them." Maria translated.

Kira considered a possibility. "Ask him what some of his other recent predictions have been?"

"Yesterday, NO MALARIA MEDICINE and CAVE IN."

When Maria translated, Kira explained her suspicion. "Maybe it's not someone who disapproves of Death Machine use killing customers. Maybe they are just using the predictions to choose victims. The killer would know that if he went after NO MALARIA MEDICINE or CAVE IN he would fail or be caught. But for SCREAMING, CRYING, ALONE, AND AFRAID..."

Maria crossed herself; her past as a nun reared up on occasion. "He's killing people because the machine predicts he will kill them. It's weird. "

"It's like a Möbius strip."

"The killer," Jabu asked in English, understanding enough of their conversation to get a picture, "he has seen my bloodreads? He kill them because of my bloodreads?"

"Yes," Kira confirmed.

"I know who killer is," Jabu said. "Is him. Marcus." He pointed at Marcus's kiosk. He was the only person who had seen Jabu's bloodreads. "He is writing book about Death Machine, so I show him my bloodreads. He come and ask me whenever he see me do ritual. Only him. Nobody else."

"What is it?" Marcus yelled from his stall. He'd seen Jabu pointing.

Kira reacted immediately: she whipped a gun out. "Don't move."

Marcus dove out of view. The market was too crowded to shoot. "Stop him, stop him," Kira yelled. "Thief!" she continued, hoping someone would grab him. Her exclamation just served to create chaos. She saw Marcus emerge from a cluster of people, and she followed, weaving between people. Maria had less finesse; she simply shoved people out of her way.

There was only one entrance to the market grounds, so even though she had lost a direct sight line to Marcus, Kira ran to it. She bumped into a fat man, apologized, and kept going. It took a few minutes to work her way through stalls, kiosks, and people. When she reached the entrance, she scanned the area outside the market. She caught sight of Marcus sprinting north and she followed.

She glanced back. There was no sign of Maria, who must still have been working her way through the bedlam. It was up to her. Once, Kira had been a runner, waking daily and jogging for a few kilometers in the quest for that mythical perfect body. That had been a long time ago. She was no longer in the least bit athletic. Her muscles groaned in protest. Marcus was too far ahead of her.

"Stop him, stop him," she called out.

Ahead of Marcus, a group of men responded, blocking his way. He changed direction, darting into an alley. The group of men did not pursue him. Kira followed him into the alley, panting heavily. She slowed down, surprised. Marcus was not running anymore.

He had stopped about twenty yards down the narrow, squalid alley and was staring at some graffiti on the wall. Beside boisterous declarations of "Dumisani Rules!" and "East Side Posse Suxx!" there was a spray-painted caricature of Jesus wearing oversized boxing gloves.

"Don't move," Kira said, drawing her gun.

Marcus wiped away sweat from his brow with the sleeve of his suit jacket. He looked at Kira with a strange expression on his face. He looked serene.

"When it came to it," he said, pointing at the graffiti, "I did not know how I would react. Would I struggle? Would I be terrified? I'm not."

"I know you killed eight women," Kira said.

"Eleven," he replied, his pride visible. He reached into his jacket's inner pocket.

"Stop," she instructed.

"THE LORD STARING AT YOU FROM A WALL," Marcus replied. "A fitting end for a servant of God."

"You are no servant of God."

"In this moment, right now," Marcus said, "you are the instrument of his will."

Slowly, leisurely, he began to pull his hand out of his jacket.

"Stop," Kira repeated.

Kira saw the glint of the sun on metal. She squeezed the trigger.

9

FROM "NECROLINGUISTICS"

By Marcus Chantunya

The question remains, "Why?" Why has God chosen to speak to us through the Death Machines? Why predictions of death? Why not tell us of the moment we will fall in love, the moment of conception when a new life forms? My analysis of the language that God uses is revelatory. The subtext of his predictions is clear. He longs for our return to him. Death Machine predictions are God's hopes. The Death Machine gives voice to God's own prayers, and the only way that... [Manuscript unfinished]

10

The next morning Kira returned to Jabu's kiosk. She found him shaking beads over a young boy's shoulders while the boy's mother watched. When he was finished, the boy's mother handed Jabu some money and half dragged her unruly son away.

"Hello again," she said.

"No blood today," he said.

"No. Never again."

"Good."

"Thank you for your help." She began to leave; then Jabu stopped her.

"Wait," he declared. He began rummaging through his wares until he found a small jar in which there was a large dried mushroom.

"What is it?"

"Add water and leave for night. Is for infidaleyes."

Kira burst out laughing. "Infidelity."

"Yes."

"How much?"

"For you, free."

"Thank you," she said, taking the jar. She wondered what her ex-husband would think if he received a dried mushroom in the mail. Come to think of it, she might just send it.

Story by Daliso Chaponda
Illustration by Greg Ruth

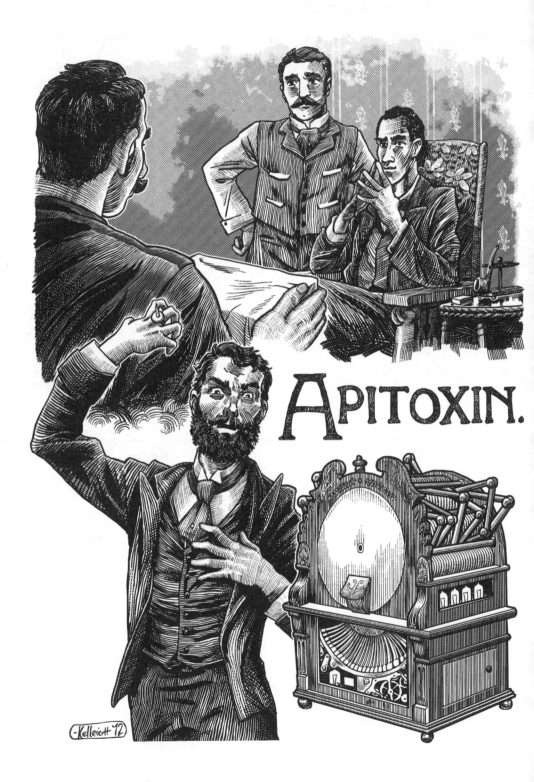

APITOXIN.

-Kelleight '12

APITOXIN

I HAVE OFTEN WRITTEN OF my friend Sherlock Holmes's taste for the *outré*—for all that is bizarre or grotesque or that otherwise stands outside the ordinary course of human affairs. For this reason, many of our cases together have been committed to paper only with the gravest of reservations; at times, the duty of propriety or the threat of scandal have restrained my pen. That I feel at liberty to recount this present tale is due solely to the personal intervention of Mr. Mycroft Holmes, who, being connected to certain vital organs of state, has prevailed upon me to produce an official statement. It is to him rather than *The Strand* that this account will be delivered, and whether these words shall ever be read outside of Whitehall, I do not know. All that I can say with certainty is that the affair of Dr. Locarde and his Machine of Death is among the strangest and most terrible in its implications to ever trouble the mind of the Great Detective.

It began one grey October morn with the arrival of a ruddy-faced gentleman of late-middle years, who bustled into the sitting room at 221B Baker Street clutching a small, cloth-draped parcel beneath one arm. "Mr. Sherlock Holmes?" he asked between heavy breaths.

Sherlock Holmes uncurled his long limbs and arose from his basket chair. "I am he. And this is my associate, Dr. John Watson."

I set down my breakfast fork and moved to take the gentleman's coat and hat...a simple operation that was complicated by the fact that he took care to retain a firm grip on his parcel. "Thomas Noakes," the stranger said at last. "I am very happy to find you at home, Mr. Holmes. I hope you are not too busy to see me."

"Not at all," said Holmes, ushering the gentleman to the settee. The man sat with the parcel in his lap, clutching it tightly with both hands. "As it happens, I have no pressing investigations. You have travelled by hansom from Chancery Lane, I perceive."

Noakes looked up in sudden surprise.

I cleared my throat. "The mud on your boots, I would wager. Probably street repair going on, yes? I can assure you there is nothing supernatural about Mr. Holmes's methods, although he is a brilliant observationist."

Holmes clucked. "It is a question of attention to detail. The distinctive traces of ink about your fingers, for example, when combined with your street of origin and manner of dress, suggest that you are a barrister...and a successful one, at that."

The man's look of bewilderment eased. "I am indeed a barrister, sir, at Marshall and Dodds, which is close enough to Chancery. And it is true that I have, until recently, had no reason to question my financial security. I must say that you hearten me greatly, Mr. Holmes. For if a man may read the past in another man's appearance, perhaps he may read his future as well."

Holmes returned to his chair. "Do not presume to take me for a fortune-teller, Mr. Noakes. When reliably informed, I am capable of making reasonable projections. But perhaps you had better elaborate on what it is that you require of me."

"Yes, of course," said Noakes. The man took a deep breath and settled himself on the settee. "It happened like this, Mr. Holmes. I was invited yesterday to the home of Frederick Merton, a bond trader of my acquaintance. He had sent out invitations to perhaps a dozen guests, promising a unique entertainment—'Silas Gould and His Amazing Prognostication Device.' Have you perhaps heard of this man?"

Holmes's eyes narrowed above his hawklike nose. "The streets of London swarm with numberless charlatans, mediums, magicians, and 'entertainers' of every description. I cannot possibly be expected to know them all. Pray continue."

Noakes blanched slightly. "Yes, well…he was a thin man with broad features and a heavy beard. He entered the room pushing a wheeled cart, which housed a large object concealed beneath a bloodred cloth. It resembled the outline of two typewriters, if you can imagine them stacked one atop the other. Mr. Gould then proceeded to circle the room and make private introductions. When he finally addressed the group, he spoke in a high and piercing voice.

"'Gentlemen,' he began, 'I am Silas Gould, and I am the inventor of the extraordinary device that you shall witness in operation today. On your invitations, it was referred to simply as a 'Prognostication Device.' In truth, the machine makes only one type of prediction. And yet, that prediction is *infallibly accurate*. Please allow me to demonstrate.'

"With a sweep of his arm, he removed the cloth and revealed his machine. It was a fabulous thing, Mr. Holmes…I don't know quite how to describe it. There were rods and tubes and gears, all in gleaming brass, which seemed to melt together at impossible angles. It was encased within an elegant frame, bolted to a wooden base. It had a front like a clock face, only instead of hands there were two openings…one round, with a needle-thin hole, and the other a horizontal slit. There was some sort of key in the back of the machine, which Gould immediately wound. This activated some mechanism, for the device began to whir and hum softly, and I could see smooth surfaces turning within it.

"Next, Gould removed an ornately carved wooden box from the underside of the cart. Inside was a tiny cage containing a solitary white mouse. 'Please observe carefully,' he said, and held up his right hand. He wore a ring on his middle finger, and on the outer band there was a sharpened needle. This was used to jab the mouse on the haunch, causing the creature to squeal horribly. Gould then handed the box over to my friend Merton and returned to the machine. We soon realised the function of the circular hole, for Gould pressed his ring against it so that the blood-tinged needle entered the device.

"The whirring sound intensified, accompanied by sudden clacking, and in a moment a slip of paper was protruding from the horizontal slit. Gould instantly snatched it up and placed it inside an envelope. To my great surprise, he came to me and pressed this into my hand. 'Guard it carefully,' he said. 'Do not pass it to any of your friends, and do not let it out of your sight.'

"Gould then addressed the room. 'Now, gentlemen, please decide among yourselves how the mouse will be killed. Once you have made your choice, you must act upon it immediately.'

"Our first reaction to this strange request was to laugh. But it quickly became apparent that Gould was in complete earnest. Soon my fellows were venturing suggestions as to how the deed might be done. One recommended that the maid be summoned with a bucket of water, so that the creature might be drowned. Another suggested that so long as we were involving the help, we might ask the cook for a butcher's knife and decapitate the beast. A third was in favour of stamping the thing to death. It was a horrible thing to hear cultured men speak so freely of such matters, Mr. Holmes! All the while, Gould stood hunched like a vulture in the corner.

"It was finally decided that it would be best not to involve any servants, so as to prevent gossip, and Merton was elected to crush the mouse's skull with his walking stick. The cage was placed on a small table, and the deed was done with one decisive stroke.

"When all were satisfied that the animal was quite dead, Gould turned his attention back to me. As he asked, I had kept the envelope safe and secure. 'Open it now, Mr. Noakes. Read what is written on the paper.' My hands were admittedly shaky—such was the strangeness of the moment and the intensity of his gaze—but I managed to insert my finger and withdraw the slip. Printed there, in black type, were the words 'WALKING STICK.'

"No sooner had I read these words aloud than the room erupted with intense shouts and conversation. Every man insisted on seeing the paper for himself, and many pressed Gould on how the trick was done. He insisted that there was no trick. 'As to how it is done, I say in humility that the scientific principles are beyond you. The machine's secret knowledge, however, is not beyond your reach!

For a sum, you may all learn the manner of your own demise.' At this, the room grew suddenly silent. Gould continued: 'You have only to accept a small prick of the finger. A warning, however... the machine is always correct and never alters its judgments. If you do not earnestly desire to see into the future, I urge you to refrain from participating. The results are not guaranteed to be pleasant.' "

"Your story is most interesting," said Holmes. "And so far quite novel. Tell me, did any of your friends accept Gould's offer and his price?"

"Quite a few."

"And were you among them?"

"I should say not!"

"Did you believe the machine to be a fraud?" I asked.

"At the time, I did not know what to believe. Possibly it was mere coincidence. Or I had been deceived somehow, through sleight of hand. I am a natural sceptic, Mr. Holmes. Others declined to participate because they believed I was in on the trick from the beginning...that I had planned it out with Gould and Merton. But several of them did take Gould's offer. Large sums of money changed hands. Certainly, Gould himself was very serious. He cleaned the ring fastidiously with iodine between each use."

"And were the results made public?"

"A few. One fellow passed around a slip reading 'HEART FAILURE,' while another brandished 'TRAMPLED BY A MULE.' That got the others laughing—as if it were some sort of morbid party game! But Gould never laughed, and neither did I. For I saw the look on Merton's face when he read his own slip and knew him well enough to understand that it was neither an act nor a joke. I still do not know what was written on his slip. I am not sure that I want to know."

Holmes had by this time lit his favourite briar pipe and begun puffing at it with characteristic intensity. His posture had changed noticeably on Noakes's description of the slips of paper, although our guest remained oblivious. "It is a fine yarn," Holmes said. "But there must be more to the tale, or else you would not be here today."

Noakes fidgeted with the box in his lap. "As I have said, I declined to use the machine myself. In addition to my private wariness, I am rather close with my purse. Nevertheless, Gould insisted on shaking my hand before he left. As he did so, I felt a sharp pain. Somehow, the ring had become turned around on his finger so that it faced inward, causing the needle to scratch my palm! Gould immediately apologised before removing the ring and slipping it into his pocket.

"I was unsettled, of course, but I kept my feelings to myself. The party did not last long after that. The atmosphere was markedly queer, and Merton himself was quiet and his face had become very pale. I returned to my home, and by supper I had resolved to put the entire affair out of my mind. Alas, it was not to be. As I dined with my wife, we were interrupted by a knock at the door. To my great and unpleasant surprise, it was Gould. He wore a long woollen coat and carried with him a medium-sized briefcase. My instinct was to turn him away at once, but he insisted on speaking with me privately.

"We withdrew to my study, and he began to speak in an ingratiating tone. 'As an apology for my thoughtlessness with the ring,' he said, 'I took the liberty of giving your blood to the machine.' Those were his precise words, Mr. Holmes! 'I had intended to offer you the results of your test *gratis*…and so I shall. But I suggest, in the strongest terms, that you read the paper right away.'

"I had half a mind to refuse…to eject him from my home and threaten to summon the police if he should return. But I found that once the slip of paper was in my hand, I could not stop myself from reading it. Some fatalistic power compelled me. And there, printed in the same capital letters as I had seen previously, were the words 'GARROTED THURSDAY NEXT.'

"You can imagine my dismayed reaction, gentlemen. But Gould did not wait for me to make any response. 'Do not despair, Mr. Noakes!' he cried. 'It is true that the machine is infallible if it is left to its own devices…but I am its master! I can avert this fate on your behalf.'"

"I presume," interrupted Holmes, "that this benevolence came with a price."

Noakes nodded. "A sum greater by far than any he had exacted from my friends. I accused him of blackmail, of course. I threatened to call the police.

" 'You may call the police,' said he. 'But it will not help your situation. Right now, I am a mere messenger. Should I be officially detained, you shall still die and I will be clearly acquitted. You must ask yourself what is more worth having, Mr. Noakes...the treasure in your vault or the air in your lungs.'

" 'It is all a trick, or else a coincidence,' I said, although I did not believe it. 'You cannot expect me to stake my fortune on a party entertainment!'

" 'I do not expect it,' he said. 'That is why I have brought you a small gift, so that you may have complete confidence that my words are true.'

"He opened his case then, and produced two items. The first was a sealed envelope of the type he had handed me at the party. The second was a small cage containing another little white mouse. 'The blood of this animal has been fed into the machine, and the result is printed on the slip of paper contained within that envelope. I will leave you now. Once I am gone, you can decide for yourself how the vermin will be killed. Be as ingenious and unpredictable as you like. Once the creature is dead, open the envelope. If the words printed inside do not match the death, then I am a fraud and you need have no fear. If, however, the words and the death match, then I am telling the truth, and you have no choice but to rely on my assistance.

" 'Please recall that you have only two days to consider my offer, Mr. Noakes. I will return on Wednesday night, and if I am not received with my payment in full, you will not see me again. By the following day, it will be too late for me to intervene.' Then he left without saying another word.

"That was yesterday evening, Mr. Holmes, and I have not eaten nor slept since. I have spoken of the matter to no one but yourself— not even my own wife, whom I sent to stay with her sister for the remainder of the week."

Holmes now rose and considered the man on the settee with keen intensity. "May I presume," he said, "that you have brought Gould's mouse to me alive, and the envelope undisturbed?" he asked.

"You presume correctly." Noakes removed the white cloth from his parcel, revealing it to be a simple brown paper box with a hole-studded lid. From his waistcoat pocket, he withdrew a small white envelope sealed with crimson wax. "I cannot trust myself in this affair," he said. "There is too much at stake! I dare not chance that I have been tricked in some unfathomable way. Nor can I swear, with unshakable confidence, that my mind is not an open book to a clever person such as yourself—so that my future acts can be anticipated, no matter how ingenious I believe myself to be. I have read of your exploits, Mr. Holmes. You are not so easily duped. I hand over these 'gifts' to you, in the hope that you will be able to settle the truth of the matter."

Holmes puffed at his briar and regarded the proffered items. At last he took the envelope and carried it to his desk, where he examined it carefully with his glass. Satisfied, he handed it over to me. "Guard this carefully, Watson." He then proceeded to take the parcel from Noakes's trembling hand and removed the small cage containing the mouse. "This is a distasteful business," he said, regarding the tiny creature, "but it must be done." Setting the cage down next to my half-finished breakfast, Holmes retrieved a small chalkboard from behind a pile of rolled maps and assorted papers. This he placed atop the mantel, using chalk to number the board one through six.

"We shall use the suggestions of your friends to begin," he said, continuing to write as he spoke. "Drowning, decapitation, and crushing with a stick. That makes three. Number four shall be suffocation by vacuum...number five, exposure to a poison of my own devising...and I think Mrs. Hudson's cat will do for number six. She is continually boasting that it is a prize mouser." Once he had finished writing out each method next to a corresponding number, he went back to his desk drawer and fetched out a single six-sided die. Without preamble, he cast it upon the floor, and we all leaned down to see what had come up.

"Watson," Holmes said flatly. "In my room, in the bottom drawer of my large dresser, you will find a bell jar with an attached pump. Kindly fetch it here."

It did not take the mouse long to perish in Holmes's experimental vacuum chamber. The creature's pink paws scrabbled at the glass for a short time, and then it began to urgently prod at the connecting tube with its muzzle. After a while, it began to twist and writhe, limbs and tail twitching in the most horrific fashion. When it finally grew still, Holmes insisted on waiting for an additional five minutes before restoring air to the jar and lifting the glass from its base. He pressed a narrow finger against the creature's tiny side. "Watson," he said softly, "will you please open the envelope and tell us what is written there."

With trembling fingers, I broke the seal and extricated the little slip of paper. Seeing the solitary word printed there, I felt my chest violently constrict and the blood drain from my face. "ASPHYXIA-TION," I read in a hoarse monotone.

Noakes's knees abruptly gave way and he fell heavily back onto the settee. Slumped over, he clutched his handkerchief and mopped at his sweaty brow. "Then all is lost," he whispered. "I have no choice but to yield to Gould's demands."

Holmes gave him a sharp look, his brow beetling in annoyance. "I have not yet rendered my opinion on this case, Mr. Noakes. Tell me, do you have the other slip of paper from Mr. Gould—the one detailing your supposed demise?" Noakes fumbled once more in

his waistcoat pocket and produced a crumpled slip of paper. Holmes took it and went over it thoroughly with his glass. He then took the second slip from my hands and examined it likewise.

After a minute of this, Holmes went to his overstuffed bookshelf and pried out a folio containing dozens of photographs. He riffled through these until, with a small "Aha!" of triumph, he located the image he was seeking and handed it to Noakes. "Is this the man you know as Silas Gould?"

Noakes looked blankly at the image. "But this man is clean shaven."

Holmes used his hand to cover the portrait's nose and lower face. "Look carefully, now...focus on the eyes."

Noakes squinted. "It could be the same man. But only the eyes. The nose and face are entirely different."

"That is easily accomplished through the use of prosthetics and a false beard," said Holmes. "I have employed many such disguises myself."

"If it is the same man, what then? Is he known to you? Am I safe?"

"Perhaps," said Holmes. "Perhaps not." Moving quickly to his writing desk, he took a pencil and began to scribble on a loose piece of paper.

"For the time being, let us assume that your life is in danger. When you leave here, take the third cab that answers your hail and go directly to Scotland Yard. Ask to see Inspector Lestrade and give him this note from me. Tell him that Sherlock Holmes believes that a credible threat has been made against you and that you require protection until this coming Friday. I will come for you before then if I am not unavoidably detained."

"But what of Gould?" protested Noakes, even as Holmes pressed the note into his hand. "He claimed I would not be safe, even with the police!"

"A fabrication," said Holmes. "Meant to dissuade you from taking the very course of action that I am now counselling."

Noakes sighed heavily. "I will trust in your judgment, Mr. Holmes, and do as you say. But before I leave here, I must put the question to you plainly. Do you believe that there is help for me, or has my fate been written in stone?"

Holmes waved a dismissive hand. "That is a question for philosophers, which I am patently not. I do not think, however, that your death will come at the hands of a mad strangler, not while you are in Lestrade's custody, at any rate. He can be counted on to keep you alive for at least the little time that I require. Now, do not delay—there is much work yet to be done."

In a matter of moments, Noakes was hurried to his feet and

bustled out the door with his hat and coat. Once we were alone, I immediately beset Holmes with questions. But he merely held up his long-fingered hands in deflection. "First and foremost, I think a fresh plug of tobacco is in order."

Soon the smouldering briar was comfortably settled in the cusp of Holmes's hand, and he began to pace across the room.

"The first thing to catch my attention was the name Silas Gould," he said at last. "It put me in mind of Titus Gould, an alias formerly employed by one Dr. Argus Locarde. The name will not be familiar to you, Watson, but he was a minor player in the organisation of the late Professor Moriarty, an extortion artist, and a petty thief to boot. A mere minnow in the grand scheme of things, but canny enough to wriggle through our net. I keep up a file on him, of course, but he's been quiet till now. He has reestablished himself as a medical practitioner, specialising in muscular disorders for well-to-do gentlemen."

"This Locarde sounds a shady enough character," said I. "And I see the coincidence of the alias. Yet it seems a rather thin thread on which to hang a man, particularly if he's as slippery as you say."

"Granted, which is why we must be certain of his involvement before we take his name to the police. But the thread is perhaps not so tenuous as you might think. Have a look at this, my friend."

Holmes went to his private safe now and retrieved two small panes of glass fitted within a custom-tooled frame. Between them was a small slip of paper, the sight of which caused my heart rate to increase. "This," Holmes pronounced, "was found on the site of my final struggle with Moriarty atop the Reichenbach Falls, alongside his billfold and other objects of small consequence that became dislodged in the intensity of our battle. I thought it unaccountably curious, a piece of the puzzle that did not fit—and so I preserved it. Tell me, what do you observe?"

I turned the glass over in my hands and read the words printed on the slip: "FALL INTO WATER." "Why, it's the same as the others!" I exclaimed.

"It is, and it is not," Holmes said with evident savour. "To the prediction for the mouse, it is identical in every way. To the prediction for Mr. Noakes, on the other hand, there are distinct differences.

The ink and paper stock are the same, yes. But the letters were not made by the same machine, nor were the slips cut by the same blade. An untrained eye would pass over these variances, but I have made it my business to be aware of such minutiae."

"So there are two machines?"

"Unlikely. Suppose, rather, that there is one machine, which functions exactly as Gould—or Locarde, if it is he—claims that it does. Granted the truth of that premise, I would submit that the prediction for the mouse would be genuine, whereas the prediction for Noakes would be a clever forgery."

"On what basis?"

Holmes gestured expansively with his pipe. "Suppose such a machine existed, and that it were left in your keeping—a machine that could foretell, without the possibility of error, the manner of death of any creature! To what end would you, John Watson, put such a fantastic device? Apart from the obvious use of learning your own fate, I mean."

My brow furrowed. "The thought of it makes my head spin, Holmes. The paradoxes that might be entailed..."

"Dispel with the abstract, for the moment. Try to think practically."

I pondered the question. "I suppose it could be applied for diagnostic purposes. I might use it to determine cause of death in a cadaver or to discover whether a particular condition were likely to be lethal. That would inform my potential courses of treatment or palliative care."

Holmes clapped his hands. "There! You see, Watson? You are a doctor, and so your mind proceeds directly to medical applications. Whereas an entrepreneur might manufacture and market the device in pursuit of fortune. A government agent might devise some clandestine political scheme. And a mind like Moriarty... well, such a mind might well discover uses so fiendish as to make possible a criminal empire!

"But Locarde is not another Moriarty. He is bright enough for his class, but petty. Had he inherited or stolen such a device following his master's downfall, he would be like a dog returning to its vomit. A blackmailer at heart, he would find a likely mark. He would first convince them of the machine's real power, instilling in them a numinous fear. He would then contrive to present them with a false prediction that could be averted...for a price. Does it not strike you as singular, Watson, that no prediction recounted by Mr. Noakes *except for his own* included any reference whatsoever to the timing of the death? 'GARROTED THURSDAY NEXT.' No other prophecy indicates anything more than proximate cause or means of delivery."

I mulled this over. "There may be something to what you say, Holmes. But I'm afraid I am stuck on the idea of the machine itself. To perceive such knowledge is incredible enough, but to put it into words would require a mind—impossible, for a mere machine!"

"Perhaps," said he. "Although if any mind could devise a mechanical counterpart, it would be my old foe. Consider also that there may be some truth after all to the fabulous claims of the spiritualists and that Moriarty, in his genius—for he was a genius, Watson—merely devised a means of dragging superstition into the realm of science."

"That's an interesting thought," I rejoined, "but is it any more probable than uncanny coincidence?"

Holmes frowned. "You make the very point, Watson. We have engaged in much speculation, with very little hard data. If such a machine were to come into my possession, I would need to perform many experiments before drawing any firm conclusions. But that is a luxury we do not have. We must act quickly if we are to protect our client."

"But surely he is in no real danger," I said. "Not if the threat of his death is truly a blackmailer's hoax."

My friend's expression became grim. "You presume that Locarde is working alone and that he is above murder. On the latter point, I can assure you that he is not. Having failed to extort Mr. Noakes, he may settle for ensuring his permanent silence...if not on Thursday, then on Friday, or the next week. And there is also the matter of whether or not Gould is, in fact, Locarde. I believe that it is more than probable, but I do not think we can risk involving the police just yet. It would be difficult to persuade them to ransack a gentleman's home on such evidence...and we do not want to create difficulties for ourselves in the event that I am wrong."

"Then what do you propose?" I asked.

"I stated earlier that I have kept a file on Locarde. His habits and weaknesses are known to me, and it should not be difficult to enter his residence clandestinely." At this, Holmes gave me a significant look. "Provided he is sufficiently distracted, of course."

Now I knew what was coming. "What do you want me to do, Holmes?" I said heavily.

He flashed a wolfish grin. "I have observed a certain stiffness in your leg of late, my dear friend. I expect it is a flare-up of your old war wound. Perhaps it's time you consulted a physician."

At Holmes's insistence, I undertook a disguise before we set out. "There is no reason to suppose that Locarde is personally familiar with your features, as he is with mine," he explained. "But it will be good not to take chances." From Holmes's store of theatrical supplies, invisible inserts altered the profile of my cheeks and nostrils, heavy-rimmed glasses were placed on my face, and additional grey was added to my moustache. "I don't think we should venture anything so dramatic as a false beard or nose, for Locarde will be especially alert to such tricks, and you have less experience than I in avoiding the tell-tale signs. Nor can we alter your body shape via clothing, as he will be examining your leg as part of your complaint. It will help, however, if you change your posture. Try to shed some of that military stiffness.

"And one more thing—we must go unarmed. In the unlikely event that I am apprehended, possession of a weapon would seri-ously compound any burglary charge."

By way of costume, my jacket lapel was studded with an ostentatious jade pin, and I was handed a cherrywood cane with the carved head of an English bulldog. All told, I felt rather a fop. "It works to your advantage," said Holmes, "to appear eccentric and well-to-do. I shall give you the card of one of my aliases, Richard Burlstone, a retired contractor. If pressed for details, you need only blather about public works and the importance of a good handshake, that sort of thing."

Once Holmes had outfitted himself with dark clothing and a low-brimmed cap, we set out in separate cabs for Locarde's High Street address. It was a freestanding brick building, longer than its front suggested, with the public entrance facing the street and a private

apartment on the upper storey. I was greeted at the door by an elderly woman with a sour face who seemed to be three-quarters deaf. After taking my coat and hat she attempted to seize my cane, forcing me to rely on emphatic gestures to convey that I required it for my infirmity.

We had timed my visit for late afternoon, near the end of the hour when Locarde saw prospective patients, and I did not have to wait long in the anteroom before being taken into the consulting office. This was a room of moderate size, with a solid oak desk and the usual shelves of books, charts, and medical paraphernalia. Had it not been for the *objets d'art* strewn about the place—such as the Fabergé miniatures grouped in one corner of the desk—it might have been my own office. There was a small door at the back of the room, which could only lead to the hall.

I had been seated for about five minutes when Locarde entered. He was a slim, sallow-faced man with pinched features and wispy hair and an expression that was flat and devoid of emotion. His deep-brown eyes were sharp and alert, however, and his motions were confident. I stood and offered a handshake, passing him my false card as we took our seats. He produced a pince-nez from his jacket pocket and carefully looked over my credentials. "Well, Mr. Burlstone," he said in a high, reedy voice. "What can I do for you?"

"It's my right leg, you see," I said, trying not to sound like my usual self. "I thought I might have had a bit of gout, but it's been acting up for longer than usual, and I have been in a great deal of discomfort."

"And how did my name come to your attention?" he asked crisply.

This took me aback. "Oh, well . . . a fellow at the club said you were the chap to see; that's all. I don't take my business just anywhere, you know. I was told you had a very discriminating clientele." At this last, I fingered the jade pin on my lapel.

Locarde returned a thin smile. "Very well, Mr. Burlstone. I will conduct a preliminary examination, after which time we can set up an appointment schedule and discuss my fee. If you would please stand up..."

We both rose. As I did so, I passed my cane between my hands to support my leg. Strangely, Locarde's attention seemed drawn to the object.

"I beg your pardon, but might I get a better look at your stick?" he asked.

I leaned on my chair to support my leg and held up the cane. "Certainly, but I don't see—"

"The pommel—that is a bulldog, is it not?"

"Yes, it is."

"And the wood, cherry?"

"Yes, I believe so. What of it?"

To my surprise, Locarde had grown unaccountably tense. The room seemed dimmer than it had a moment ago. "I'm afraid I am not accepting new clients at the moment," he said in a clipped tone. "You should be on your way."

I blinked in perplexity. "Just a moment, now—"

"I have asked you to leave," Locarde snapped, his already high voice rising in pitch. "I will summon the police if I must!"

My mind went instantly to Holmes. I had given him barely any time to locate the machine. What could account for the doctor's sudden change in demeanor? Had he recognised the cane and associated it with his enemy? Surely my friend would not be so careless in his choice of props.

"I refuse to leave until you've examined my leg," I said hotly.

With the suddenness of a serpent, Locarde darted a hand into the top drawer of his desk and withdrew a six-chambered revolver. "I don't know who you are," he hissed. "I don't know where you came from or who sent you. But you shall depart from this house and not return!" So saying, he fled through the rear door.

After a moment's hesitation, I seized my cane and hurried in pursuit. By the time I reached the hall, Locarde had flung open the far door and disappeared from my view.

"Thief!" I heard him screech, followed by two cacophonous blasts as his weapon discharged. This was followed by an explosive squeal of grinding metal, a heavy crack of wood against wood, and a piteous wail.

With speed, I traversed the hall and burst into the room. It was clearly the doctor's private study, the centrepiece of which was a tall iron safe built into the far wall. That safe now stood open; heaped within was a twisted tower of polished brass that could only have been the dreaded machine—only the device was in ruins, its façade obliterated by one of Locarde's bullets.

Next to the safe, I could see that Holmes had taken refuge behind an upturned table. Locarde himself stood in the centre of the room, spluttering in panic and fury. "What have you done?" he shrieked. "You don't know what you've done!"

He raised his gun again, but before he could act I grasped my cane firmly with both hands and swung with all my strength. Perhaps he saw the blow coming, for he turned and jerked back just as the solid wood hit home...not landing on his shoulder, as I had intended, but striking his right temple. I stumbled back with the force of the hit. Locarde moaned, his wild eyes rolled back in his head, and he dropped to the floor.

"Watson!" cried Holmes, and leapt from behind the table.

In a moment, my friend was at my side. Together we approached the still figure of Locarde, and I put a finger to his twisted neck. "Holmes, I have killed this man!" I cried.

"It was self-defence. And I fear there was no helping it," Holmes said. He handed me a folded slip of paper. "This was in the safe."

With shaking hands, I unfolded the scrip...and nearly dropped to the floor myself. Printed in neat black type were the words "CHERRYWOOD BULLDOG."

"Dear Lord."

"He must have puzzled over that one," Holmes murmured. "It must have been quite the shock when he realised what it meant."

"Holmes, what are we to do now?"

Swiftly, Holmes walked to the safe and the ruins of the machine. Reaching behind, he retrieved a sheaf of old papers bound with twine. "Do you suppose anyone heard the shots?" he asked.

"Neighbours or passersby, maybe. Locarde's secretary is an elderly woman and very deaf."

"Even so, we must assume the police are on their way. Let us depart by the back way. Since you arrived under an assumed name with an altered appearance, there is nothing to connect Sherlock Holmes and John Watson to this place. Within the safe, the police will find a ledger containing evidence of Locarde's double life as a blackmailer. Scotland Yard will draw the obvious conclusion that he chose the wrong mark and paid for it with his life...which is the truth, after a fashion."

"But what of the machine?" I asked, looking over the gleaming wreckage.

"Useless at this point, I fear. But I will get a message to my brother Mycroft; he will no doubt wish to have his people examine it. Come, Watson—we can afford no more delay!"

Later that evening, once we had returned to Baker Street and were seated in comfort before the fire, I broached the subject of the papers that Holmes had removed from the safe. "It could not have been evidence of blackmail," I said, "or you would have left it for Lestrade."

Holmes reclined in his basket chair, allowing his old clay pipe to loll against his chin. After a deep exhalation of smoke, he tilted up his head. "Based on the diagrams, they were instructions for building the machine...and in Moriarty's own hand. I would know the writing anywhere, of course, but I made a preliminary comparison to the original manuscript of 'The Dynamics of an Asteroid' while you were putting on your dressing gown. It is quite authentic."

I felt a thrill run down my spine. "Then...the machine may be reconstructed?"

"Sadly, the instructions are written in cipher. Like the remains of the device itself, they will go to Mycroft's people at Whitehall. But I doubt highly that any of my brother's men will be able match Moriarty's talent for mathematical encryption. Such genius occurs only once or twice in a generation. Perhaps in a hundred years or so, the code will be cracked. Or perhaps some engineer of special brilliance will be able to deduce the operation of the machine

from its shattered parts. Who knows?...It is entirely possible that within our lifetime, such devices will populate the offices of every general practitioner and corner druggist."

"I shudder at the thought," said I.

Holmes smiled. "You would not relish the triumphalism of the religious predestinationists, Watson?"

"You know that theology is beyond me, Holmes. I refer to the temptation to use the machine myself. I have never desired such information and do not truly desire it now...but I nevertheless admit that it carries the intangible allure of the forbidden fruit."

Holmes clucked his tongue. "You have a poet's soul, Watson. It is an asset to your pen but a detriment to your logic. To the well-ordered mind, such knowledge can hardly be thought detrimental. It may even bring peace, of a kind. Consider the beatific countenances of some condemned men, even as they march to the gallows, or the clarity of a soldier who does what he must, though he knows his cause is lost."

Something in Holmes's tone as he spoke these words aroused a suspicion within me. "Holmes...you were alone with the machine before its destruction. Tell me that you didn't use it on yourself!"

Holmes shut his limpid eyes and reclined, and for a moment I thought I perceived the shadow of a smile about the corners of his mouth.

"I think that I shall take honey in my tea this evening," he said.

I got no more out of him for the remainder of the night.

Story by John Takis

Illustrations by Indigo Kelleigh

BLUE FEVER

ATHBA HAD A DEATH TO SING.

She stood straight and tall at the front of Lord Keloth's small, nervous group of court musicians. The smell of jasmine, orange flower, and oakmoss rose from dim braziers at the corners of the banquet hall, mingling with the scents of roast meat, delicate sauces, and sweets. Courtiers whispered and jibed, no doubt forming and breaking alliances even as the banquet's courses were changed. A clockwork servitor's gears clicked incessantly as it scuttled with an insectlike gait from table to table. It paused and pointedly brushed a crumb off Athba's skirt before rolling away again.

She breathed deeply, willing herself not to tug at her thick black hair or to fuss with the robes hiding her voluminous figure. Style was everything with Lord Keloth, and though he had not disliked a song of hers yet, she could guess at the penalty for failure. He perched heronlike on his throne, draped in scarlet silk, his eyes fixed on hers.

"Athba," he said, "do you have something to sing me?"

It was a silly question. Of course she did. Her deathsongs were the sole reason she enjoyed Lord Keloth's patronage. She nodded, and he gestured to the group. As the lead violinist drew her bow, Athba drew breath.

The song began with a wordless, plaintive tune on Nanu's violin. Athba sang her first verses soft and menacing, in a tone that hinted that something else lurked underneath.

Sunlight glinting red
Off of ruby-tinted scale:
Teeth, claws, and wings
Worked in intricate detail...

Slowly, she sang the story of a gift: a life-sized dragon worked from rosy glass. This was not an ordinary royal gift, but something deposited mysteriously during the night, with nothing but an enigmatic note. In reality, Keloth's guards would never have allowed such a thing; in the song, it could be explained away as magic.

Lord Keloth, in the song, found it on his morning walk to the throne room. (The tempo increased slightly; Nanu took up tense repeated notes, hypnotic and nearly dancelike.) Anyone bestowing such a gift would know he had reason to fear glass sculptures, but Keloth was no coward, nor a poor sport. He had it installed in his courtyard.

The tempo continued to increase. The other violinists took on the repeated notes, while Nanu played an urgent modulating bridge, swooping high and back down again.

The sculpture came to life. It crept up the stairs, in the dead of night, and into Keloth's bedchamber.

The accompaniment was frenzied now, and Athba no longer held back. She put her voice's full power into the sharp-edged melody as she sang Keloth's battle with the beast. It growled threats; he made dry little jokes. He cracked its limbs; it bit his throat. He shattered its head with a heavy book from his bedside table, and at last it died. Shards of glass clattered across the chamber like cobblestones.

A sudden slowing. The wordless, plaintive tune recurred, and Athba drew herself back, returning to the menacing voice she'd had at the first. There was a new tone in it, too, a bittersweet acceptance.

Keloth had won, but the bleeding was too heavy, and from too many wounds. Knowing nothing could save him, he refused the attentions of healers. Instead he sat down by the remains of the glass dragon and murmured to it.

He died smiling, without regrets.

*   *   *

Athba held her pose for a moment as the strings died away. Then Keloth applauded, and the rest of the room followed suit.

She curtsied, breathing a sigh of relief. She always worried that one day she would have nothing new to say about the single word "GLASS," no remaining way to satisfy the court's morbid tastes. But that day had not yet come.

A whirring servitor rolled over to Keloth, clearing his plate and depositing a plate of lime ice. Keloth picked at it, but his eyes rested on the musicians. "Athba, will you do something for me?"

Another silly question. "I am at your service, my lord."

"A week from today, Lady Irathi arrives to discuss an alliance against Lord Ulan. Compose and perform one of your songs for her."

"My lord?"

"A deathsong. That is what you do best. The words on which to expand are 'BLUE FEVER.' That is all."

Athba's rather hefty stomach turned to ice. Morbid lords like Keloth could commission their own deathsongs as much as they liked. But to commission them for someone else? This was never done. Lords of the same standing never mentioned each other's deaths. It would be taken as a threat: *I know how you will die. I can make it happen quickly if you like.*

But one did not say no to Lord Keloth—particularly not when one had gone to the clacking clockwork machine in the highest tower and spilled one's own blood. Keloth had seen the parchment predicting Athba's death before permitting even Athba to read. He rarely passed up an opportunity to remind her, or any of his other servitors, that he knew what would kill them.

"I will do as my lord commands," said Athba, and she wondered if this next deathsong would be her last.

"Can you believe it?" Athba said later in the practice room. She paced through mountains of unattended sheet music, scattering paper through the velvet chamber. Nanu could not even control her frizzy red hair, let alone the volumes of paper she needed, but she was a good confidante for all that. "Because I can't."

Nanu shrugged her scrawny shoulders. "I heard that Lady Irathi never commissions deathsongs at all. But I'm sure Keloth has something planned. He wouldn't throw away an alliance just to amuse himself."

Maybe not, Athba thought, *but he would certainly throw away a courtier who displeased him.* The deathsinger before Athba had once sung a deathsong in which Keloth was dragged across shards of glass while comically tangled in his horse's reins. He was forgiven, or so people whispered, for the grisly description, but not for making Keloth look foolish. In any case, no one ever heard from him again.

If Irathi was displeased, Athba would go the same way.

"I heard she kept her death secret so no one could use it against her. I'm surprised he even managed to find it. Why's he blurting it out in front of the whole court?"

Nanu chuckled. "Who knows? Maybe she's changed her mind. You remember how you got when you first had your death read. It takes some getting used to, you know? It *is* morbid."

"These are morbid times."

Athba's death, predicted by the clockwork machine, was "GRAPES." She had avoided fruit with amused horror for several weeks, but she couldn't keep it up. Keloth made a point of serving Athba his best wines. Not as a punishment, he said. Merely to keep her on her toes.

Nanu did not know her own death, or claimed not to, though Keloth assuredly knew it. She had closed her eyes while the machine spun its clacking gears, telling the lord she preferred uncertainty. He had humored her by making *everything* uncertain: requesting new music at the last minute, hinting that they might or might not be employed in the future. Nanu seemed not to mind.

"And 'BLUE FEVER.' It's such an unromantic disease. How am I supposed to sing about that?"

Nanu took Athba's hands and brushed her thumbs against the singer's palms. Though Nanu was the younger of the two, there was something motherly in her smile. "You'll think of something, and I'll help with the arrangement. Keloth's always enjoyed what you do. I'd trust him."

In her quarters, Athba started with lyrics. She gnawed nervously at an apple held in her left hand while she scribbled with her right and crumpled page after page. She knew the signs of blue fever: discolored skin, boils, slow suffocation. It was not pretty like "GLASS," nor pleasurable like "GRAPES." With a dramatic framing story, it might have pleased Keloth. But not a squeamish woman who kept her death under lock and key.

One day in an infirmary . . .

No. What would Irathi be doing in an infirmary, when she knew the risks?

When Irathi's father . . .

That went into the wastebasket straightaway. Bad enough to have to do this for a squeamish Irathi; even worse to threaten her family.

Without warning, without sign . . .

She worked on that one for a little while, leaving her apple to go brown at the side of the desk. It almost worked. Irathi contracted the fever for no reason, through no fault of her own, and everyone clucked over the tragedy while . . .

While what? While she resigned herself to a senseless and pointless death? While she learned there was some cosmic reason she *had* to die? No. If Athba had learned one thing during her patronage, it was not to bring philosophy into it. No one would enjoy the song, and everyone would start to worry about free will or inevitability, whichever happened to scare them more.

Athba's mind wandered to her family. What would they say if she failed and died? She could picture her father's lined, jowly face, though she hadn't had time to go see him in months. *I told her not to take the offer of patronage,* he would say. And her rosy-cheeked mother would nod: *All the money but constant murder. Not a fair trade in my book. Poor dear.*

At last she threw down her notebook and stormed back to Nanu.

"He's going to kill me."

"Hm?" Nanu looked up, pausing in the middle of a scale, and put down her violin carefully, brushing piles of sheet music aside to make room.

Athba collapsed into a wrought iron chair. "I've figured it out. He's too proud to ally with Lady Irathi but doesn't want to lose face for turning her down. So I sing a deathsong, she storms out, and the blame goes to me. Keloth kills me with grapes, he's rid of Irathi, and no one blames him. Then Lord Ulan rides in, takes over both holdings, and impales everyone."

"Oh, sweetie, that doesn't even make sense. For one thing, I think he likes you too much to kill you. For another, if he blames it on you, and Lord Ulan keeps pressing in at Irathi's borders, she'll want an alliance anyway, once you're gone."

"So maybe he keeps me around, or...I don't know. But I can't make blue fever sound nice."

"Who said it has to sound nice? Keloth never liked them nice. Remember the one where he drank ground glass and vomited blood?"

Athba grimaced. She remembered. Keloth had applauded and then sent a hooded assassin to her quarters in the night. Not to kill her, or even to scare her, but to explain that ground glass didn't work that way.

"And the one with the molten glass and the angry glassblower? That one made me shudder. But he loved it."

"Yes." Athba took a few deep breaths, forcing her shoulders to relax. "But Irathi's not Keloth."

"That's the point. You don't really know what she likes. It's Keloth who will decide if you live or die. So write it the way he would like. Let him worry about the rest."

"He'll still kill me." Athba slumped, then straightened again, as the wrought iron chair back dug into her shoulders. Keloth did not furnish his servants' quarters with comfort in mind. "I'm sorry. You're right, of course."

She still thought that Keloth planned to drive off Lady Irathi and blame it on her. But what did that matter? If he had plans for her, how could she stop them? Better to stop worrying. Better to be morbid, like everyone, until death ceased to frighten.

Lady Irathi rode in on a horseless carriage traveling by some obscure magic of its own and strode into Lord Keloth's banquet hall with her retinue following. Her courtiers peered at the bloodred tapestries and copper silverware. Lady Irathi was sharp chinned and bright eyed and wore a long, trailing dress in pale green. Cold seemed to follow in her footsteps.

"Eat," Nanu muttered to Athba, before she launched into an instrumental serenade, the kind that dining guests could listen to or ignore as they chose. "You'll feel better with food." But Athba did not feel ready for food. The wine was even worse: looking at it sickened her. She barely heard anything until Keloth called her name.

"Athba." From the impatience in his voice, it might have been the second time he'd said it. "Won't you sing for our guest?"

She forced herself upright and strode to the front of the hall. She could not feel her feet touching the floor. Keloth's courtiers whispered to each other; no doubt they knew why she was worried. But Lady Irathi's retinue kept quiet. Athba kept her face as serene as she could, though her heart hammered. She was a trained performer, after all. She could hide fear.

She took a deep breath and began.

"Plague!" This time she did not start low and menacing, but urgent. The violinists cantered to keep up.

"Plague in the towns,
Plague in the fields and the city
Blue skin bringing death swift and sure.
Wails of despair,
But wise women whisper
That there is a cure..."

Athba widened her eyes and waved her hands, letting the anxiety of a blue fever epidemic fill the room—though she could not allow it to influence her lungs or throat. The sound must come up free, full, and pleasing. She kept her own anxiety locked up in the back of her mind. Her expression came not from her heart, but from a place she pictured behind and to the right of her, a repository for imaginary emotions.

Only when the prophecy of a cure appeared did the tempo slacken slightly. Nanu brought in a sweet, hopeful countermelody. But the cure could be delivered only by Lady Irathi's hands and only with the aid of a particular emerald-green flower.

The song became a quest song, leaping along in hope and fear. Lady Irathi endured magical trials, found the flower, and went from house to house, laying a petal on each fevered brow. When the fevers began to flee, Nanu's melody leapt in outright joy, though the other violinists played short, tense notes underneath. It was not yet over.

There was always a catch.

When the plague had all but run its course, Lady Irathi began to notice blue marks on her skin. And the emerald-green flower could be used only to heal others.

The violins slowed.

The song became a stately, reverent dirge. The whole land praised the dying lady. She raved, choked, withered before their eyes, and they only loved her more. Irathi, said the people in Athba's deathsong, was a saint.

That is how it ended: on a soft, high note and a prayerful arpeggio, and in awe.

Athba forced herself not to try to gauge Lady Irathi's reaction, not even in the ringing silence after the last note.

No one applauded. Everyone knew Lady Irathi's dislike of deathsongs. Everyone but Athba was watching her face.

And in the silence, Lady Irathi chuckled.

"Lord Keloth," she said, clapping slowly, "I heard you were terribly morbid. I see that it's true. But you have given me a wonderful gift: a chance to forget. To escape into someone else's death, brought by a disease entirely unlike the one fated for me."

Athba stared. Everyone stared but Keloth, who perched there, smiling, not surprised in the least. Lady Irathi ascended the steps to him, leaving a chill in her wake.

"Now, then," she said, "I think we have an alliance to discuss."

Athba collapsed against the wall in Nanu's practice room, accidentally scattering a pile of rehearsal pencils. "I can't believe it wasn't her real death. And he didn't tell me. I can't believe he put me through that!"

"I can," Nanu said cheerily. "He loves this kind of thing. Keeping you on your toes, hmm?"

Nanu and her musicians had kept the wine going all night. Even Athba felt good. After the alliance was settled, Keloth had showered the group with gold. Athba especially.

Nanu drained her wineglass. Athba paused for a split second, knowing Nanu had nothing to fear from "GRAPES," then recklessly downed her own. "Eat, drink, and be merry, for tomorrow we die."

"Not tomorrow if I can help it," said Nanu. "So what are you spending your gold on?"

"Savings. In case I survive."

They exchanged grins. It was mostly true. But she had set aside a little for her family, too, and a little to spruce up her quarters. A more comfortable chair. Better lamps. And a little piece of art for the wall. A stained glass rendering of a cluster of grapes on the vine, for inspiration.

After all, these were morbid times.

Story by Ada Hoffmann
Illustration by Alice Duke

KRIS STRAUB

TETRAPOD

"My name is Miyako Kamemura. I play kendo. I will die by fall down stairs. Nice to meet you."

I sighed. "Falling," I said, flouting everything I'd learned about the right kinds of corrective feedback in my studies of second-language learning and forcing a smile to mitigate the blatant recast. "Falling down stairs. It's nice to meet you too." I shook her hand, letting the "I play kendo" go—none of us had ever quite figured out for sure what the correct verb to use with kendo was, anyway. I do kendo? I practice kendo? Let their high school English teachers worry about it.

"My name is Takeshi Kamai," the next kid was saying confidently. "I play running. I will die by lung disease."

Miyako had sat back down, blushing a bit. By this time, the first year of middle school, they've mostly memorized their basic *jikoshoukai*—self-introduction. Name, favorite sport, death, sometimes favorite food or which neighborhood they're from. I love getting to know the new first years, but right then I was not in the mood for endless *jikoshoukai* day, repeating my own fifteen-minute introduction to each of the four new first-year classes in turn, listening to each student, an endless flood of ninety names I won't remember a single one of. It drains a lot of energy that I didn't have to spare that day. And each class asks the same questions: How old are you? (Twenty-three.) Do you have a boyfriend? (Not technically.) What's your blood type? (A-negative.) How will you die (or more commonly, What is you will die by)? (Breast cancer, which always draws a few giggles from the boys.) What's your favorite bug? (Dragonfly, I finally decided after the fifth time I was asked.) Is your hair really naturally blond? (For the hundredth time, yes.) Today one kid threw me off by asking what my favorite word in Japanese is, and I didn't have an answer. My mind still circled that question as I sat down at my desk with a sigh of relief after the last class.

I slid my phone open and scrolled through three new e-mails, skipping one from my dad and some junk political thing, opening the one from Andrew. "Tonight should be clear *da sou desu*," it read in our typical mix of English and broken Japanese. "Pictures *toru?*" I felt the all-too-familiar tightening in my stomach. Another night taking pictures on the beach with Andrew. Another night of that unique brand of torture that comes from being so near what you can't have. I rolled my eyes. But what could I do? Say no?

That'd be the day, I reflected a few hours later, standing in the bathroom trying to coerce my hair into some sort of coherent shape. Imagine, *not* saying yes to every project he proposed. *Not* going running to him whenever he wanted to take pictures, or toss a Frisbee, or watch a new anime, or collect and analyze some new linguistic data. "Sorry, I'm busy today," I told the mirror. "Maybe another time." My reflection smirked sadly at me.

The night was indeed clear, a brilliant full moon illuminating the waves as they crashed against the concrete tiers, such a haunting sound. I sat down and stretched my legs while he screwed the camera into his tripod. The silence stretched just over the edge of companionable into awkward. I crossed my legs.

"*Jikoshoukai* today?" I asked, immediately wishing I hadn't broken the silence.

He finished settling the tripod on the concrete. *One…two…* I counted. If he ignores me for more than three seconds, I figure he's annoyed with me for ruining his concentration.

"Yeah." He bent over, peering through the viewfinder. "What a pain."

He didn't elaborate and I wasn't certain whether he meant the introductions or something about the camera. I let out a slow breath and lapsed back into silence.

"One girl wouldn't give her death."

This declaration a few minutes later startled me out of a trance and pulled my attention back from the dark crashing waves. "Oh yeah? I didn't have any of those." I gazed out at the water, the ghostly green lights on the horizon, the shadowy forms of the mountains encircling the small harbor.

"Yeah. The other kids wouldn't stop giving her grief for it either. Like they can't handle being around someone without knowing. It scares them."

I nodded but didn't respond. One of my third years was like that, keeping his death secret. When he first came to the middle school I thought he did it to get attention, to be the mysterious kid. Now the other kids had lost interest, and I wondered sometimes when everyone else was chatting and teasing each other whether he wished he'd just gone ahead and told. It's too late now; it would be an anticlimax.

Andrew adjusted the angle of his camera by half a degree or so. "Okay, here we go. Tetrapods, take one. Fifteen seconds."

A lone streetlight shone down on the row of giant concrete jack-like objects that line the pier, creating intense highlights and shadows. I'd always loved the tetrapods, and Andrew recently had the idea to photograph them at night, under the light of the moon and that one lamp, the waves breaking on the irregular shapes.

"My name is Ukawa Shizuka. I will die by *tetorapodo*," I recited quietly.

"Hmm?"

"One of my second years. Didn't I tell you?"

"Death by tetrapod?" He laughed. "I don't think you did. Damn it, that came out all black. I'll try twenty-five seconds."

"You know what'll happen," I said after he clicked the shutter open. "Someday some idiot who thinks he's funny or trying to prove something will drag her out there, just to scare her. And she'll fall."

"Don't tell me you're turning into one of those people." The camera clicked. "Ah, that's a little better. I'll try thirty and see if it's too bright."

"I'm not." I stood up and took a couple of steps toward the water. "But no one can deny that it happens sometimes. It's the price we pay for knowing, isn't it?" Maybe the manner isn't changed—although the flux of "suicides" just after the machines were first invented is used as evidence that the technology did alter the reality—but it's generally acknowledged that the time of death may be changed by knowing. After all, the imprints are insensitive to time. They gave up on getting a "when" reading a decade ago.

I could sense Andrew shrug behind me. I hate shrugs. I walked down a couple more tiers toward the waves. I never spend a lot of time thinking about the death readings—what's the point?—but the first day of the new school year always stirs up uncomfortable wonderings. So many kids, bright eyed and fidgeting with their new middle school uniforms, one by one telling me the way they'll die. It's not real to them, out in this tiny village, thinking they'll all live forever no matter what their reading says. It's a game: What's *jishin* in English, Rae-*sensei*? What's *densha no jiko*? I've had to learn the Japanese for all sorts of gruesome phrases, but I'm still often at a loss to translate the name of some obscure disease. That "fall down stairs" girl—Miyako, was it?—will be surrounded by a gaggle of giggling girls whenever they climb the stairs to the first-year classrooms, but none of them are really picturing what it would be like for her to fall—snap!—and never move again. But all the protests and arguments against the readings are passé by now. It turns out that, confronted with explicit knowledge of our mortality, most of us don't know anything to do besides spend most of our time ignoring it.

"Okay, thirty's too bright. I'm gonna try twenty-seven. Then maybe we'll move closer?"

"Sure." I swallowed and focused my eyes on the misty green lights on the water. The camera clicked.

"What's your favorite word in Japanese?" I asked a little while later, after the camera was packed up and we stood listening to the water.

"*Shionari,*" came the answer without hesitation.

"*Shionari?*"

"It's the sound of the waves breaking."

"Oh." I listened to the *shionari* that permeated our silence. "One kid asked me that today. A break from all the normal questions and I didn't even have an answer. Sounds like you would have been prepared."

"Points for creativity to the kid. I thought yours was *kekkyoku*."

"Kekkyoku," I repeated, considering. "I just like the way it rolls through your throat, all those velar stops. But how could I tell a room of seventh graders that my number one favorite word of their language is 'in the end'? That's pretty boring."

"I dunno." He stretched his arms up to the sky, arching his back, then turned and flashed me a smile. "Nowadays, it seems like a pretty important word."

"He never talks about her to me anymore," I remarked to Marie the next week over our traditional *tendon*, tempura and rice, while carefully transferring my two shrimp tempura to her bowl and requisitioning her sweet potato and pumpkin.

"Is that a bad thing?"

"I guess not. I feel like he used to work her into the conversation every few sentences."

She ripped the tail off the shrimp. "Maybe he picked up on how much it bothers you."

I laughed. He doesn't pick up on any subtle social signals, as best as I could tell. "Nah. He's such a guy."

"Maybe they're having problems."

I was almost mad at Marie for giving validation to what I tried to brush off as a ridiculous hope. Almost.

"You should totally make a move."

I groaned and loaded my chopsticks up with rice, which promptly fell back into the bowl. I tried again. Chopsticks are not for the impatient. "I totally should not. You know what I think about that."

"That car accident of hers could happen when she's ninety. You can't keep waiting."

"I know…"

"Hey, you know what you should do? You should get one of those love readings, you know? Find out if it's ever gonna happen."

"Yeah, great idea." I laughed. "You know those things are a scam. I'm not looking for false hope here." I spooned the mix of seven spices into my small bowl of udon noodles and stirred.

"Eh, they're right sometimes, aren't they? I don't see why we can predict death and we can't predict anything useful."

"Death isn't useful?"

"It's just gloomy, man. Great, I'm gonna die from heart failure. Doesn't everyone die from heart failure? Your heart stops, you die. My COD's a total cop-out. And I got a kid this year, cute kid, real rebel type. Says he's gonna die from a gunshot. Why should I *know* that? I can almost hear the shot going off whenever I look at him. And he's all proud, you know? He's got one of those T-shirts and everything showing it off."

I nodded as I slurped the noodles. "The first week of classes always gets to me too. The first years are just so *young*."

"Yeah." Marie shrugged, as though to dislodge the whole topic from her shoulders and let it drift to the floor. "Anyway, one of my friends from back home got a love reading and it said she'd marry a doctor, and then she put the moves on this really smart guy friend she liked and they're together now. And he's got a PhD."

I laughed. "In what?"

"I dunno, Russian lit or something. Who cares? He's a doctor, technically."

"And that's not self-fulfilling at all."

"Come on, the deaths are self-fulfilling too sometimes—everyone knows that."

"Not everyone knows that," I argued, although I didn't necessarily disagree. "It's a controversial theory. The imprints left by—"

"Don't start talking to me about superpositions and time being an illusion and imprints left by the future. I gave up trying to understand all that years ago. Anyway, if the way we die leaves an imprint we can read, then why shouldn't other things? It just seems logical."

"I dunno." I gulped my tiny glass of water and guiltily pushed the button to call over the waiter. "Guess our bodies are more deeply affected by the way we die than by whether we marry a doctor."

"Maybe our blood is. Have they tried looking in other places? Hey"—she laughed—"do you think if I got a Pap smear, they could tell me whether I'll finally hook up with Jeff at the party this weekend?"

"Uhh..." I glanced up at the waiter, who had just appeared—the cute one with floppy hair and a silvery belt—and smiled. *"Ee-to, mizu o, onegaishimasu."*

Marie shot me a sheepish grin when he'd gone. "Come on, you know he doesn't speak any English. Lord knows, if the waiters here speak English....well, I've said worse."

I jumped slightly as my phone vibrated in my pocket and pulled it out to find the small graphic of a panda waving its arms indicating a new e-mail. From Andrew.

"Hey," it read. "Check this out, isn't it sweet? A random note from a student: 'Dear Andorew Sensei, You are good teacher. I like learn English with you. Thank you for English. I enjoyed. You are nice smile. Please enjoy from now. Saki Satou.' Ahh, sometimes being a teacher is worth it..."

I must have been smiling like an idiot down at my phone because Marie poked me with her chopstick. "Hey, earth to Rae. He propose to you or something?"

I rolled my eyes. "No, just a cute note." I read it to her.

"Kawaii," she agreed. "Maybe you should get his attention by writing him a note. Dear An-do-rew, I like make out with you. You are nice ass. Please we sleep together from now."

The waiter deposited a pitcher of water on our table. I glared at Marie, repressing my giggle.

"Arigatou," I said to the waiter. Marie mumbled her thanks as well.

"Not funny," I said when he'd gone. "I'm not doing anything to get his attention while he has Lizzie."

"Then you'll both spend your lives waiting."

"I know," I repeated, stirring the broth remaining in my udon bowl and watching the orange spice swirl. "I know."

*   *   *

Two of the tetrapod pictures came out really well, and Andrew and I disagreed on which came out better. I set my choice as my desktop background, and so it was against the backdrop of ghostly angled shadows under a triangle of white light that the IM window popped up a couple of days later.

"Something's happened. Can you come down here?"

My heart stopped.

The car accident?

My fingers had no idea how to respond.

"What happened?" I typed finally, unsteadily.

"Fire."

Fire? "I'll be right there."

Andrew's neighborhood, a fifteen-minute drive along the winding mountain roads from mine, was buzzing as I drove though the narrow main street toward his small house. I hopped down from my car and met him in the doorway. "What happened?" I asked again.

His face was set oddly. "Fire," he whispered. "I can't follow everything people said to me. But they keep saying Satou."

"Satou? Someone you know?"

He leaned on the side of the house, looking so drained my arms ached to hug him.

"I have a few students with that name."

"With fire readings?" Or falling down stairs, suffocation, burns...it's not always so straightforward.

"I don't think so. But—"

"Then they should be okay, right?"

He shook his head. I waited, listening to the vague sounds of bustle and gossip from the main street. It felt like the sky had darkened even in the minute I'd been out of the car, from dusk into night.

He turned and walked into the house, and after a brief hesitation I followed, slipping out of my shoes in the entryway. *"Ojamashimasu,"* I whispered before following him into the living room, thinking for some reason of the group of laughing third-year girls who had forced their way into my house the week before, shouting *ojamashimasu* over my protests that no, this was not a good time. Just because you announce that you're about to intrude doesn't make the intrusion okay, I'd wanted to tell them.

The memory amused me, but this wasn't a time to be amused, so I shook it from my head. Andrew had vanished into the living room and I followed. He silently held out a folded piece of pastel yellow notebook paper with a design of giraffes in the corner. I took it from him.

"Dear Andorew Sensei," it began. Of course, the random note he'd shown me. I stared at the swirly signature. "Satou...But you said she's not—"

"She's not anything. She's the girl who won't tell."

I found myself sitting down on the couch. "Do you think she—"

"I think she was killed. I heard people talking."

"So...now—now we know, I guess." It was all I could think to say. What do you say when a twelve-year-old child dies? "I mean there's—her family must have known she was a fire. They would have taken all the normal precautions. There's no way that this could have been avoided even if...you know, if she'd told."

"Read it again."

Andrew's voice was slow and measured. Too measured. I looked down again at the cheerful paper in my hands.

I enjoyed. Past tense.

The room felt cold.

"Should you show this note to someone?" I asked what felt like fifteen minutes later but was probably about three.

"I don't know. What's the point?"

"You don't know what it means."

"Don't I?"

I cringed at the edge to his voice. "You—no, you don't. She could have...first years have barely learned the past tense. There's no reason..."

My words were too empty, and I stopped. Andrew sat down beside me, his head in his hands, then stood back up.

"Why?" he asked. There was no answer, so I gave none. "Why this girl? Why? There are other fires, or whatever exactly she was. There are others, and they're just kids, and they live with it like everyone else. They buy those fucking pencil cases with the kanji for fire written in flames and they think it's cool and funny and a little bit scary but whatever, they live because that's what kids do."

He faced the large front window now. I wasn't sure I'd ever heard him spew so many words in such quick, passionate succession.

"Why was she different?" He spoke more softly. "So quiet, and she wouldn't tell, didn't look scared, just shy and like it was none of our business. I thought it must be an STD or something, you know, one of the ones kids get really teased for. Fuck."

"Andrew, you don't—you don't know…"

"I know, okay? Everyone was at the other end of town at the temple tonight for the festival. Everyone. Her family. Everyone. I was there too when we heard."

The normal night sounds of spring were beginning to creep in through the glass, so out of place.

He sat down again, next to me, inches from me. "Why Saki Satou? Why would she carry this burden so much more heavily than the rest of us? What did she understand that we don't?"

"I—" The framing of his question made no sense to me. "She… didn't. Nothing. She…I don't know."

Silence. Crickets from the flooded rice fields outside.

"Stay here tonight."

My chest twisted into a knot.

"Just…on the futon. I just want company."

I nodded. Neither of us spoke as he pulled the rolled futon out of a closet. It was too early for sleep, but he didn't say another word, and neither did I. His breathing from the mattress above my futon swirled with the night sounds of the Japanese countryside and covered my whirlwind of thoughts like a soft blanket.

The next day all the teachers in all the nearby schools had flyers on our desks detailing the fire. I skimmed the Japanese characters. Saki was, it confirmed, a fire death. She was, it confirmed, the only casualty.

My students had all heard, of course, but over the course of the week the level of laughter and banter in the halls crept back toward equilibrium. "What else are they gonna do?" Marie commented over coffee and strawberry parfaits. I shrugged. What else had I expected? Andrew's question still circled in my mind. No one hinted that the fire wasn't an accident. Andrew kept the little yellow note in an envelope next to his bed, and for some reason I instinctively didn't mention it even to Marie. After a few days, the other teachers in my staff room stopped talking about the fire too. *"Kek-kyoku,"* I'd heard the art teacher comment, *"shiin-yochi wa na, shou ga nai yarou."* The other teachers around his desk nodded knowingly.

In the end, death predictions always come true.

Kekkyoku, yes.

But why now?

I crouched down to sit on the edge of the long cement jetty, then stretched my legs and rested them against the slanted spoke of a tetrapod. The hazy sun beginning to sink over the low green mountains seemed magnified, giant, covering the sky like an anime sun. Andrew perched on the one next to me, leaning down to capture a close-up of the breaking waves shining in the last sunlight of the day. We hadn't spoken of Saki in almost a month.

"Ki o tsukete ne," I warned as he shifted positions. Be careful. He turned over his shoulder to look at me.

"Why? I'm not gonna get my obscure liver disease from falling into the water."

It was an old, worn argument that he knew perfectly well. You can break your neck. You can feel pain. You'll be wet and cold. Death isn't everything. I didn't need to say it.

He would only bring up his reading if he wanted to talk about something. I waited. *One... two...*

"I can't break up with Lizzie."

... twenty-three. My stomach lurched.

"I love her."

I felt a thud in my chest, like someone kicked me. "I... I know that. Of course you love her."

I could have counted to fifty in the next silence if my brain were working. Nothing but *shionari*.

"Nothing real is supposed to change because we know," he continued finally, the words dropping toward me like smooth stones he'd turned over and over and over in his mind. "Just the routine precautions. I promised myself nothing would change because I knew. That I wouldn't leave her just because it's terrifying, knowing. Knowing there'll be no warning. Nothing, just a crash and a phone call, out of nowhere." His voice broke, just a tiny bit. "I...I promised myself I wouldn't punish her for it. Damn it, I promised *her*. But it's hard. It's—it's hard and only getting harder, every day, when she's so far away in America and...every night I wonder whether I'll find her online in the morning or not. God if it were me, if I were her, I'd..."

The first light of a fishing boat flickered on in the distance.

"Just want it over with?" I whispered.

"They say you can change the when, don't they? If only I didn't know...if it didn't feel cowardly, like she might think it was because...because I can't stand the constant fear..."

I stood up slowly, balancing on the angled concrete.

"But I do love her." The fading light silhouetted him against silver-gold clouds. Perfect broad shoulders. He shook his head. "Maybe time is an illusion, but goddamn it, it's the one we were meant to live in, isn't it?" His fingers gripped the camera too tight. "Maybe Saki had the right idea. This isn't life; this is—"

"No." I reached for his hand, slipped on the seaweed that had caught on the rough surface. The world spun for just a moment. I steadied myself, his hand on my arm, and I laughed.

"That was scary."

"You okay?"

"I'm fine." On the wooden path that runs along the rocky beach, a group of elementary school children ran by chattering and laughing in their matching yellow backpacks.

"This is life," I said after a minute. "What are we supposed to do other than keep living it?"

He nodded slowly. Such an empty phrase. Someday they'll figure out how to take other readings, to find the imprints left by other parts of our existence and translate them. Someday we'll unravel this illusion of time and read off a whole life before it happens, watch our own lives like a movie we've already read the summary of. Someday. Not yet.

"Maybe," he said quietly. "Someday, we...It's not that I don't want it. I just don't..."

I reached for the camera and he let me take it, carefully, hanging the strap around my neck. I leaned down to find the right angle. We all pretend this one thing doesn't change anything important; just another little detail in the overflow of knowledge we live with now. But we're meant to live with mysteries. Maybe that's what Saki understood. "Maybe," I repeated. "But not yet. It's okay."

The shutter clicked, freezing the crashing wave against the long row of tetrapods. I straightened up and watched the last rays of sun slip behind the mountains.

"I don't have to know."

Story by Rebecca Black
Illustration by Carly Monardo

MACHINE OF DEATH

You're invited!
Come party with the
MACHINE OF DEATH

BLACK LETTERS ON A WHITE CARD, a corporate logo, and on the back, handwritten details about where and when the party would be held. Pavel was looking very pleased with himself as he waved it around.

"What do you think?" he asked Marka. "Much more interesting than dinner and a movie again."

Marka pursed her lips. She had never been to a Machine of Death party. Everybody knew about the Machine of Death, of course, just like everybody knew that nobody knew how it worked. The machine had been introduced only a few months ago, but its popularity spike was envied by fad-mongers the world over. The machine had been packaged and peddled at malls, movie theaters, doctors' offices, and even as a party game. You could find a machine anywhere someone might be hanging around with some time to kill—pun totally intended.

"I don't know," Marka said. "It seems so morbid. I mean, at first I was mildly curious—not curious enough to stand in line for the privilege, mind you—but now…"

Pavel rolled his eyes. "I know, I know. Now it's too popular. It's just like those vampire books last year. If everybody's doing it, you don't want to. You want to be unique. You don't jump on bandwagons; you calmly walk in the opposite direction."

"I took the road less traveled by, and that has made all the difference."

"Yeah, yeah. But come on, Marka. Who're you trying to impress? It's not like we're in high school anymore. And none of your snooty literature professors will ever know that you went to this party, let alone care."

Marka sighed. Pavel was right. Just now, Pavel, with his brooding good looks and hot chiseled body, was indeed the person she most wanted to impress. True, her literature professors wouldn't have approved of him or his recreation management major, but they wouldn't have approved of the books she'd gotten descriptions like "hot chiseled body" and "brooding good looks" from either.

The Delta Kappa sorority house was already teeming with people when they arrived. Marka was glad. She hated being the first one at a party—as if she were so starved for company that she couldn't wait another second. Not unpredictably, the machine was the center of attention. For all the hype, the machine itself was pretty unimpressive: a smallish rectangular black box with a keyboard on top and a few cords running out the back. A crowd of maybe thirty people watched curiously as the operator hooked its video output cables to an enormous TV screen.

"All right, folks!" the operator said with a grin. "My name is Gene, and I'll be your MC for tonight. Let's start out with a little demo. I need a volunteer."

A forest of hands shot up, and Gene picked a volunteer from the front row. Marka thought she recognized him from somewhere but couldn't quite place where. "What's your name?" the operator asked. "Vasili? Great! Now, Vasili, I have here a stack of prediction cards and pens. I want you to take one and pass the rest to your girlfriend there, and then she'll start them around the rest of the room. Got one? Great! Now, I want you to write a word on the card. Just one. The first thing that pops into your head."

Vasili wrote and then handed the card back to Gene, who turned to the machine and typed the word on its little keyboard. Everybody watched as the letters appeared one by one on the giant screen.

"ALMONDS?" he said as he typed. "Really? What's that supposed to mean?"

"You tell me," Vasili said. Marka finally realized where she had met him. He was that smart-alecky jerk her friend Olna had dated for a while. "That's what your machine does, isn't it?"

The operator shrugged. "The game is more fun if you make a guess. It's interesting to see if your idea matches the reality shown by the machine. Anybody want to take a stab at it?"

"He chokes?" one guest offered, not very creatively, in Marka's opinion.

"Allergic reaction?" Slightly better, but still pretty pedestrian.

"No, I've got it! A clown named Almonds goes on a rampage and the guy gets run over again and again by a tiny but very heavy car." This one got a laugh.

Gene hit the submit button, and the screen with the letters on it faded to black. "We have to wait a moment for the machine to find a matching death. We think it uses tachyon pulses to peek into the future and find just the right set of circumstances for our input," he said. Marka shared a smirk with Pavel over the vaguely scientific explanation the operator offered. She knew that in reality, nobody had a clue how it found the images that no camera could have taken.

When the picture came back up, it showed a middle-aged forklift operator casually shifting pallets from one stack to another. In a fatal mistake, he shoved a lever a little too far, and his machine sped backward into a precariously stacked tower of crates with "ALMONDS" stenciled on them in big red capital letters. Marka watched in horror as the boxes teetered and began to fall, then sighed in relief as the screen went black again.

Her sigh was echoed by many around the room, but there was also a small chorus of boos from somewhere in the back. Gene waved them down. "As you can see, at the request of our hostess"—here he gestured toward a perky girl in a Delta Kappa sweater—"I have the machine set to show us the answer to the riddle but shut down before anything gets too gory."

"So that's how it works!" the sorority girl said, beaming. Marka was willing to bet that she'd been a cheerleader at some point in her life. "You've all got your prediction slips, and extras are in a bowl by the door. We've also got flyers that explain how each of the games works. Food is on the table, and drinks are in the cooler. Everybody have a great time, and go Wildcats!"

The room answered with the customary yowl that was their team's battle cry, and someone handed the operator another little white slip of paper. The party had officially started.

Marka looked at the screen again as the letters appeared one by one. H-I-G-H H-E-E-L-S.

Pavel, his voice low, said, "I've seen this one a couple of times before. Could be she gets her shoe caught in a train track. Or some-times the heel breaks at the top of a flight of stairs. They say that somebody once saw a fashion model murder a photographer with an especially sharp pair of stilettos. I think it's an urban legend, but people keep asking the machine, hoping to get lucky."

As it turned out, a poor woman just tripped as she was crossing in front of a bus.

Marka turned away in disgust. "Let's get some food." She walked away from the crowd around the machine. Pavel caught up with her a moment later with one of the flyers in his hand.

"Is something wrong?" he said.

"I just think it's a bit morbid standing around watching people die. Making woman after woman pay the ultimate price for fash-ion." Marka found that her own feet were killing her. If they could talk, they'd be telling her what a bad idea they had always thought high heels were, especially this cute strappy pair that she *would* insist on wearing on dates with Pavel, even though she knew she'd be limping for days afterward. She sighed, slipped them off, and dropped them in the garbage can.

"We're not making them die," Pavel said condescendingly, shaking his head at her latest grand gesture of nonconformity. "The machine just finds somebody who was going to die that way anyway and matches them to the prediction."

"Are you sure? Do you really know how the machine works?" She grabbed angrily at a little paper plate and plastic fork, wishing she had stuck to her principles, such as they were, and refused the invitation.

"Aw, c'mon, don't be like that. Of course I don't know how it works. Nobody knows *how* it works, but the scientists have proven pretty conclusively what it *does*. They say it has something to do with quantum. Or magnets. Maybe both."

"I still think it's morbid. They're still *people*, and we're laughing when they're crushed to death." Marka put a couple of tiny sandwiches on her plate and moved toward the cookies.

"See, that's another thing the scientists have proven. They're not. Not *real* people anyway. They're potential people. In some other dimension or something. A parallel universe." Pavel poured her some punch and held it out as a peace offering. "Look, they're starting a new game." He peered at the flyer and read the description. "This one is called...telephone. After the first prediction, each prediction has to describe the previous death in some ironic or tangential way."

"What's the point?" Marka nibbled petulantly on one of the sandwiches. They were stale.

"Well, to see where it goes, of course. You know, like the old telephone game we played in elementary school, where you whisper and see how mixed up the phrase gets? It's like that, only with death predictions."

Marka allowed herself to be led back to the crowd around the screen. She watched as the word GRAFFITI turned into a teenage boy accidentally shorting out an electric fence while attempting to spray-paint his name on a cow. BEEF became a woman enjoying her last hamburger while driving. INATTENTION faded to show a baby slipping under the water in a bathtub as his mother answered the telephone. Everybody agreed that reaching TELEPHONE in a game of telephone was a good cue to try another game. Marka felt sick. She set down her plate of appetizers.

"Let's get out of here," she whispered to Pavel. "I know a good café where we could get a bite of something decent to eat and just talk, you know?"

"Not yet," he said. "They're just about to play poetry. You'll like this one."

"Poetry?"

"Yeah. Everybody gives the machine a line from a poem and we see what it comes up with." He turned to the crowd around the screen and pitched his voice to be heard over the buzz of conversation. "Hey, Marka's majoring in literature or something like that. She should go first."

There was a murmur of agreement, and everybody looked at her expectantly. Lines ran through her head: "Beowulf donned his armor for battle / Heeded not danger; the hand-braided byrny..." "Because I could not stop for Death..." "In Flanders fields the poppies blow..." "To him who in the love of Nature holds communion..." With every line, an image appeared in her head—a tank with inadequate protection from a roadside bomb, a car running a red light, a heroin needle dropping from a lifeless hand, a bloody bootlace in the mouth of a bear.

Marka snapped. "You guys are all *sick*! You spend night after night inventing games to play with this machine. You laugh and you drink, and meanwhile these are people's *lives* we're dealing with here! Did you see that baby? How is his poor mother ever going to live with herself now? Do we just type SUICIDE into the machine and say the problem is solved? How can *you* live with *yourselves*, knowing that you've tainted the one great joy of my life? Every line of every poem I ever read from now on will be a metaphor for *death*!"

She pushed Pavel away as he tried to calm her. "I hate that I let you talk me into this. Just leave me alone."

Marka was sitting on the back porch steps, crying softly, wondering how she'd ever be able to show her face in public again, when she felt a hand on her shoulder. She brushed it off, her fury suddenly reignited, and turned to give Pavel another piece of her mind. "I don't care how hot you are. I never want to—"

It wasn't Pavel. It was the machine's operator. He handed her a tissue.

Marka tried ineffectively to wipe the tears and snot off her face without smearing her makeup. "Sorry for ruining your party," she said meekly.

"Don't worry about it. It's not the first time, and it won't be the last. I got my rental fee up front, so I'm happy. When this sort of thing happens, and you'd be pleasantly surprised at how often it does, I generally shut down the machine for a while. It gives everybody a chance to calm down, and I get to take an extra break. And who better to spend it with than a smart, pretty girl like you?"

Marka blushed at the compliment despite herself and looked at Gene for the first time as a person rather than as an appendage of the machine. He was older than Marka and Pavel, certainly an upperclassman, maybe even a graduate student. He wasn't as handsome as Pavel (after all, who was?), but he was good-looking in an average sort of way. His curly brown hair was a bit shaggy, and his clothes looked like they came from the better sort of thrift store. Marka pegged him as a computer science major.

"But once the ruckus dies down and the easily shamed contingent goes home," Gene continued, "there will be another group who stays late, typing in predictions till the wee hours of the morning. They'll tell themselves they just want to spite you and show how they've got nothing to hide from you or anybody else, but they're really just jerks who like to watch people die. If they weren't here, they'd be at home watching *Bloodsport* or *Last Man Standing*, or whatever this season's new life-or-death reality show is."

Marka nodded. She didn't like the life-or-death shows, but plenty of people must watch them, or they wouldn't keep making them. "I know the type," she grumbled. "I bet Pavel will be one of them."

"There you go, then." The operator smiled at her encouragingly. "The party's not ruined, and I'll easily meet my week's prediction quota in a single night."

Marka frowned again. "What do you mean, your quota? Why should anybody care how many times the machine gets used?"

"That's one of the great secrets of the industry." Gene leaned in a bit closer, his voice hushed. "Most operators just figure the quota is there to keep the popularity up, but me, I have a different theory. I've seen a lot of these predictions, and in many of them you can see a little slip of white paper, a lot like the ones people were writing on tonight. Once or twice in a mall, or doctor's office, I've even seen a machine. The logo is just like ours, but it has no screen. Instead it's just got a little hole in the front." He made a circle with his fingers to show the size of the hole.

"A hole? What for?" Marka asked, wishing she wasn't so fascinated.

"Exactly! I get curious, you know, so one night at home with my machine, I type in MACHINE OF DEATH, and you know what I see?" His voice wasn't hushed anymore. "A guy goes to a kiosk, pays his money, and sticks his finger in the hole to give a blood sample. The machine spits out a little card, and on it is just what I've typed. The guy takes one look at it, has a heart attack, and that's the end of him." Gene spread his hands and nodded knowingly as if this explained everything.

"I don't understand," said Marka. "Why should it kill him to know he's using a Machine of Death? I mean, he knew that before he started, right?"

"Over there, in that parallel world, the machine is different. They don't type in predictions; they ask the machine to give them one. The machine tells each person how *they're* going to die." His eyes were wide, and the expression on his face reminded Marka of somebody telling a ghost story by a campfire. All he needed was a flashlight under his chin to complete the effect. "That must be what the quotas are about," he went on. "There are a lot of people over there, and there are more all the time—even if there are fewer all the time too, if you get my drift—and somebody's gotta write all those predictions."

"You've got to be kidding me," Marka said, reflecting that even if it was a load of BS, at least he was selling it well, and she wasn't crying anymore. "If that's true, then no matter how many parties you did, you'd never be able to keep up with the demand."

"Nah, you're right. I bet in some third world sweatshop, there's rooms and rooms full of girls typing in things like CANCER and HEART ATTACK and CAR CRASH over and over and over again."

"But why? What do they get out of it?"

"Same as me. It's a living."

"Not the girls. The company. Who pays *them*?"

"Now, there you've hit the nail on the head. The Great Enigma of Our Time." He wiggled his fingers as he intoned the words to give them an aura of mystery. "Figure that out, and you'll know a lot more about the workings of the cosmos. Does the company have some way of getting cash from the other dimension? Resources from a parallel universe? Information of some kind?" He lowered his voice and leaned over to whisper in her ear. "Personally, I think it's an alien plot to collect DNA from all those suckers over there, one drop of blood at a time. And the aliens are giving the company bigwigs advanced technology, which they'll *use to take over the world*!" By the end of the sentence, he was shouting with his arms spread wide to show the whole world.

Marka laughed. "Do you really believe that?"

"I dunno." He shrugged. "Maybe the aliens are benevolent, collecting the DNA so that they can engineer cures for all the diseases and make the Death Machines obsolete." He looked at his watch. "Well, my break time's over. Why don't you come back inside? Enjoy the party. Maybe even feed the machine a line or two of poetry. Somebody's gotta write all those predictions, after all."

Story by Karen Stay Ahlstrom
Illustration by Alexandra Douglass

UNWISE
DECISION

KC GREEN

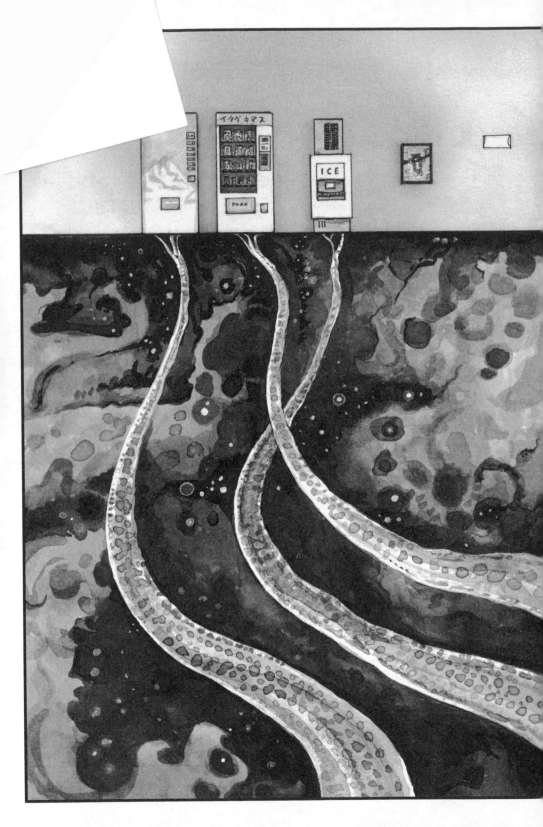

MONSTERS FROM THE DEEP

BECCA'S FIRST CLUE THAT SOMETHING was off was that the buttons were spongy. They looked like regular hard plastic vending machine buttons, and the printing on the letters and numbers was sharp, but they were weirdly mushy to the touch. Pressing B4 to get a Snickers bar had felt like pressing two overripe grapes about to burst with pulp.

Still, the silver coil inside the machine rotated. Her candy bar dropped into the tray. When she touched the clear plastic flap, she made an involuntary gasping motion that sent a spasm up her arms and pulled her two steps backward. The flap was like raw chicken skin, clammy and rubbery.

Becca stared at the candy machine, her Snickers bar three feet away but separated from her by an impenetrable barrier of *wrongness.*

The door to the pilots' lounge opened. Footsteps mushed the carpet. The aroma of coffee reached Becca's nose as Fox stepped up next to her.

He stared at the vending machine with her. The only sound was the low drone of the television across the room. Some documentary on whales.

"What are we looking at," Fox finally whispered.

"I don't know," she whispered back.

"Then why are we whispering," he whispered.

"Because it's *weird,*" she whispered.

"Did it take your money?" he whispered, slightly louder, as if he was going to try to ramp them back up to normal speaking volume in tiny increments.

"Yes," she said. "And it dropped a Snickers bar."

Fox leaned forward and saw the Snickers bar, sitting perfectly calmly in the tray at the bottom of the machine.

"Do you need help getting it?" he whispered.

"Yes please," she said, and took a step back.

Fox looked at Becca for the first time. She was serious. She didn't look at him, her eyes still fixed on the plastic flap that had felt like chicken skin. It didn't... *look* strange.

Fox turned, found a counter to set his coffee on, and set his cap next to it. He bent down and reached through the flap—which moved with a satisfying *thunk* the way plastic flaps are supposed to—and retrieved the Snickers bar. The flap bounced shut with a *kachung* that rang through the room.

Fox handed Becca the Snickers bar and patted her on the shoulder. "Let me know if you need anything else," he whispered, retrieving his coffee and cap. Without another word, he disappeared through the door to the flight-planning room.

The Snickers sat cool and shiny in Becca's hand, its plastic wrapper feeling just as it should. She grabbed a corner to pull it open, and it tore—too thickly, perhaps? It seemed more like cloth than a candy wrapper. Were there fibers hanging loose where the wrapper parted? Becca mustered the courage to look closer. No, there weren't. It looked just like a candy wrapper. The chocolate looked fine. It smelled all right.

Becca took a nibble. It tasted basically like a Snickers. A little chalky maybe, but identifiably a Snickers.

"Get ahold of yourself, Rebecca Ann," she told herself, taking a deep breath and heading for the flight-planning room. One step before the doorknob she stopped. Her cap was back on the counter. She turned back, grabbed the cap, and caught another glimpse of the vending machine in her peripheral vision.

Did it—did it look the same as it just had? Was that a Kit Kat in there? Why hadn't she hadn't seen that before? She'd have rather had a Kit Kat.

She shook her head, turned, and went into the planning room, taking a big bite of the Snickers. She really needed to get more sleep. Her mind was playing tricks on her. As soon as they finished this flight, she'd tell Fox she wanted to—

She stopped chewing. There was a piece of paper in her mouth.

Carefully, she fished for it. Like a ticker-tape machine, she drew the narrow paper between her lips.

Stained with chocolate and saliva, it was her death prediction: BREAST CANCER. It had been inside the Snickers bar.

Fox looked over at Becca right as she started screaming.

The conference table was covered in shards of candy.

First, Fox had wanted to call the vending machine company, but the number on the front was scratched and illegible. He'd asked the receptionists, but none of them knew anything about it. He'd even threatened to break into the damn thing, but the Plexiglas proved too strong. So finally, he'd called up Trish (the poor girl hadn't been due back at the airport for another hour) and sent her to a bank to get singles. Then she and Fox spent thirty minutes buying every single thing in the machine.

There had been no more Snickers in it—but no empty coils, either. Yet Becca swore she hadn't bought the last one.

Now Trish and Fox were using plastic butter knives to dissect every candy bar and pack of gum, looking for anything strange. The only thing out of the ordinary was that some of the items seemed to be Canadian versions, with labels in both English and French. Fox insisted on cataloging everything anyway, flipping his kneeboard notebook to the back and filling pages with his tiny handwriting. Becca hid in the planning room the entire time.

It was an hour before Fox knocked gently on the door, entering without waiting to be acknowledged. He held the notebook in his hand and studied it rather than looking at her. She was balanced on a spinny chair, knees drawn up to her chin, just staring through the window at the runway outside.

"We didn't find anything else," he finally said.

Becca's voice was a croak. "Do you remember last time we were here? It was last month. I remember because Tower gave us the ILS to three-five, which was weird. There was some kind of storm and the wind was all backward. Plus it was raining, and it was bumpy as hell." She looked around the room without resting her eyes on anything in particular. "Then we came in here, and the first thing we saw was a yellow box. I thought it was ironic—worst landing of my career and then we come in to find a death predictor."

"I remember," he said.

"Why would there be a death predictor in a pilots' lounge? That's the *last* place you want one. I made a joke to the receptionist. Same girl that's out there now," Becca said. "She didn't remember it being installed. Now there's a candy machine and she doesn't remember *it* being installed. She's never seen anybody come to fill it. She didn't even know it was in here."

"I've never seen a candy machine be installed," said Fox. "I figured you just planted some Skittles and they grew."

"You should be all over this," she said, looking up at him for the first time. "Creepy Snickers bar is right up your alley. Latest wrinkle in the global conspiracy."

"I promise you, I am incredibly intrigued."

Becca buried her forehead in her knees. "I'm like the death-prediction Charlie and the Chocolate Factory," said her muffled voice. "Willy Wonka wants me to come visit so he can expose my boobs to plutonium."

Fox checked his watch, then looked back out into the lounge room. "I'm gonna help Trish clean up the evidence so we can start preflight. Want me to save you any?"

"Mash it up and form it into a crab," came the voice from Becca's knees. "Let me know when it's ready so I can come rub my chest in it and die."

Half an hour later they were high above the ocean, Boss-Man asleep back in the cabin with three or four martinis in him, giving Fox and Becca nothing to do but stare at the featureless blue and talk. The

Citation was on autopilot, like a train riding a ruler-straight rail for two thousand miles, and Fox had his laptop open. Long flights were his office hours.

Fox was always analyzing, categorizing, and tracking trends in death predictions. Of course, it was the spectacular and gory predictions that captured headlines and the public's imagination—a blog post about an old lady who'd drawn ICE PICK IN EYE got more clicks than a dozen somber pieces on LUPUS—but Fox, with nothing to do on these hauls but pore over statistics and think, believed there was more to it. In conversations high above continents and oceans, in pilots' lounges and hotel bars around the world, he had convinced Becca that gory and dramatic death predictions had actually *risen* in the past eleven years.

It was tough to track, of course, because there was no unified database of predictions; medical privacy laws saw to that. Predictions were often available posthumously when death certificates were filed (Fox had a paid subscription to a nationwide public-records database), but the records for the more dramatic deaths were often sealed as part of court proceedings, as it was rare for someone to die of SHOTGUN TO BUTTOCKS without there being a prosecution somewhere along the line. And while teens sometimes enjoyed crowing about their fresh-drawn AIR-TO-AIR MISSILE or MONSTERS FROM THE DEEP on Facebook, very few made IMPALED BY BRATWURST public.

Yet there were, Fox insisted, just as many of the latter as the former—that is to say, *too* many. More than PNEUMONIA or DIABETES or SEPSIS anymore.

Before the yellow boxes appeared, the most common cause of death (according to CDC records) was heart disease, followed closely by cancer, then stroke, then chronic lower respiratory disease. All normal, often age-related deaths that pointed to a general level of nonviolence among the public. Accidental and violent deaths of every type, eleven years ago, made up only twenty percent of all deaths reported.

Last year, as best as Fox could determine, accidental deaths were up to fifty-one percent. The average life expectancy in the first world was approaching levels not seen since colonial days.

A waypoint beeped on the GPS. Fox switched his gaze from his laptop screen to the horizon with a weary sigh. Something was clearly *wrong*. But was the problem with society? Were the predictors' existence causing people to lash out in more volatile and violent ways?

Or were the yellow boxes assigning deaths to people *deliberately*?

That was impossible, of course—the yellow boxes simply printed out what was going to happen anyway. But in the years he'd been looking at this data, every day it creeped him out a little bit more. The line for violent Class F predictions just kept…trending…upward.

And most strange of all: the increase in Class Fs didn't correlate inversely with the age of the subject, as might be expected—it *didn't* seem that children were being born into an increasingly violent world.

The increase in Class F predictions issued was simply linear over time. Controlling for the age of the subject changed nothing. The only factor with any correlation at all was the date the subject was tested.

It was as if the yellow boxes were growing more and more cruel.

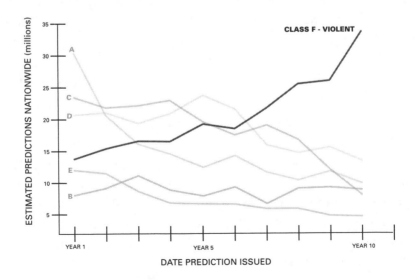

In the copilot's seat, Becca stretched. She clicked through a few different views on the GPS, then checked her watch. She unstrapped her seat belt, and Fox knew she was heading back to the galley. He closed the lid on the laptop and touched the control yoke, officially taking command of the airplane.

But she didn't stand right away, just kept staring at the big blue deck outside, a hand on her stomach, lost in thought or discomfort or something she didn't want to share.

"I think I'm gonna have it framed," she finally said. "Chocolate stains and all."

"Put it in a shadow box," said Fox.

"Yeah. Right on my mantel," she said. " 'The Last Snickers Bar I Ever Ate.' "

A bigger story hit the news over the next week or so. Blogs had it first, then TV a few days later.

The predictors were all gone.

Everybody just assumed that their local yellow box got carted out of their local pharmacy or office building or Costco for some unknown reason and didn't give it much thought.

But it seemed that they were gone. From *everywhere*.

"The bubble of the prediction market has finally burst," someone said on talk radio as Becca drove to the airport. "An economically unsustainable product from the start, the company has simply gone bankrupt."

Someone else on the program disagreed. "There's been no filings. No public records."

"Well, of course not! Your business goes under, you want to do it as quietly as possible!"

A third voice. "Who owns the yellow boxes, anyway? Is it a private company?"

Dead air. Then everybody talked at once, embarrassed by the silence.

But nobody knew where they had come from. The yellow boxes had just *appeared*, silently and subtly, in places where people congregated.

Most folks had ignored them, then looked quizzically at them, then perhaps had heard a news story or read an article about them. Slowly, as more and more folks stepped into a yellow box to get their prediction, people overheard the term "yellow box" more and more.

And then it was just a thing that existed, like a bus stop. You knew what it was because you saw it every day. If you ever wanted it, it was there. You didn't give it any more thought than that. Surely someone had installed it, just as surely someone had put the sign up for the bus stop. But who cared who that was?

Fox had looked into it once but hadn't found anything. Presumably the FDA had been involved, or the CDC, or somebody, because of the blood and the needles and so on. But nobody at those agencies could—or would—answer some random pilot's silly questions. There were no phone numbers, no manufacturer's plates on the yellow boxes themselves. The only text at all, on any of them, was a neat placard with directions for use.

And now, all at once, they were gone. In the places they had been were soda machines, DVD rental kiosks, phone booths, mailboxes. Nobody remembered seeing *them* being installed, either.

Their next flight was a week later. They dropped Boss-Man into Burbank and had ten hours to kill before the ride home. A loaner car got them into Glendale and they ate Cuban in the shadow of Griffith Park. It was a restaurant that used to be a gas station. An old-timey jukebox watched everybody from a corner.

Becca kept her sunglasses on, even inside. The sunlight was giving her a massive headache. Fox flipped to a new page in his notebook as black beans cooled on his rice. Trish was vibrating in her restrained way, clearly eager to say something but reluctant to volunteer or interrupt. Fox began, as always, by listing their unanswered questions.

"Number one: where did the yellow boxes go?"

Becca looked at her food but only moved it around on her plate. "We didn't appreciate their horribly destructive contribution to society. They got all huffy and left humanity in peace to go terrorize some other species. Squirrels everywhere are waking up to tiny yellow boxes in their oak trees."

Fox wrote *Got huffy and moved to oak trees* in his notebook. "Sounds plausible. We can check a park when we finish eating. Does anyone think they might have gotten confiscated by the government?" He wrote *Gov't cover-up.*

"Why?" Becca asked. "What does the government know that we don't? We know as much about them as anybody. *You* do, anyway."

"Yeah, and it's freaking *me* out." Fox could sense Trish's vibrating begin to enter a spectrum that threatened to spill all their drinks, so he turned to her. "Trish, what do you think?"

Trish's eyes were nervous bugs behind her glasses. She wiped her mouth, fumbled with her purse, and eventually produced some photocopied graphs. "I was thinking about the Class F predictions."

Becca would have smiled if she didn't feel like roadkill. The girl had joined up to be a flight attendant and Fox had turned her into a first-rate crackpot within a year. It was beautiful.

Trish pointed to a graph showing the rising trend in Class Fs—a diagram they were all well familiar with. The right end of the line was a steep future projection that made all of them a little nauseous. Class Fs were growing, and fast.

To the graph, Trish had added three new lines, shallower and crossing, and had hand-labeled them *F1*, *F2*, and *F3*.

"Class F predictions are typically sudden and violent, right?" She flipped a page and read from a list. "LIGHTNING STRIKES AIRCRAFT. SHOCK AND AWE. SHOVEL TO THE NOSE."

Nobody responded. They all knew this as well as she did.

"But if the predictions are growing more violent—which they are—because *people themselves* are becoming more violent—which we don't know for sure," she said, "then LIGHTNING STRIKES AIRCRAFT shouldn't count in that analysis. Unless Zeus is growing more violent along with the rest of us."

Fox sat back in his chair. Becca slowly leaned in to examine the graph more closely. Even the waiter, attending to their water glasses, snuck a peek to see what everyone was so interested in. The noise in the restaurant suddenly seemed very loud.

"I made subclasses for the F predictions we have records for," Trish went on. "F1 are circumstantial deaths. LIGHTNING STRIKES AIR-CRAFT, SLIPS ON PUDDLE OF OWN VOMIT, and so on. F2 are indeterminate, like SHOCK AND AWE. This is still the biggest group by volume. And F3 are—"

"Deaths caused deliberately," Fox finished.

Trish nodded. "This is SHOVEL TO THE NOSE, ICE PICK IN THE EYE, that kind of thing."

They looked at the hand-drawn lines on the graph. F2 stayed pretty level for the most part. The indeterminate deaths didn't tell them anything interesting.

F1 had a hump at the beginning, and then it dropped off. The circumstantial deaths were slowing down. Nature and clumsiness were fading away as dangers.

F3 started rather small and quickly climbed at a startling rate.

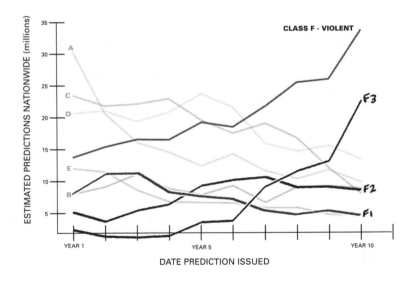

"So people are going to start killing more and more people," said Becca.

"*Something*," said Fox, "is going to start killing more and more people."

They were due out of Burbank at ten p.m., so after lunch, they holed up at a hotel to catch a nap. But Becca had a hard time sleeping. She tossed and turned in the overly air-conditioned room, full of fluffy, stifling pillows and drapes that didn't quite keep out the light. Late-night flights were the worst because the day before was always a shambles. Same-day ins-and-outs were worse yet. But Boss-Man had a business to run, and she was on duty. She counted herself lucky to have the gig.

She couldn't get comfortable, with what felt like a knot in her stomach no matter which way she lay. It wasn't indigestion, it wasn't bathroom pain, it wasn't nausea—it was a sharp, piercing *weight*, like she had a stone in her insides that was too heavy for her guts to keep contained. She stood, and she stretched, and she bent over and crouched and drank water, but nothing seemed to budge it. It had an insistent sort of sideways gravity that didn't match the world's. When she lay, it prompted her to roll over. When she stood, it pulled her off balance. When she sat down, it wanted her to tumble onto the floor.

Finally she pulled her shoes on and lurched, tipping and clutching the doorframe, into the hallway. She didn't know where she was going, but her room had suddenly become thick, its air a blanket that smothered her. She passed the elevators without looking. She was only barely aware of her feet shuffling past each other with increasing speed and insistence.

When she opened her sweat-slicked eyes, she found herself pressed against the ice machine. It was warm, in a way an ice machine probably shouldn't be. She watched her hand reach out and feel its big round button. To the ice machine's right stood a bright, colorful soda machine.

None of the sodas were anything Becca had heard of before. All the logos appeared to be in Japanese.

She pressed the ice machine button, and Skittles came pouring out of its spout with a loud clattering sound.

Becca turned to look behind her and saw an old woman just coming out of a room with a rolling suitcase, slowly lifting a hand to her mouth as she took in Becca and the ice machine and the Skittles. The old woman's eyes looked like she was watching a horrible animal give birth.

For her part, Becca only vaguely comprehended the presence of the other person. Her vision had narrowed to a foggy oval, and the stone in her belly was pressing, hard, against the ice machine.

Then, slowly at first, but with growing intensity, the Skittles on the ground began to chitter like tiny scarab beetles. They slowly vibrated across the carpet in groups of colors, the yellow ones joining with the legs of the ice machine, merging with the metal in a way that seemed impossible. The red ones turned the other way and disappeared under the soda machine.

The rest flowed underneath the old woman's suitcase, like cockroaches fleeing the light. The old woman looked down slowly, not sure exactly what she had just seen.

The suitcase began to roll toward the old woman's foot. The Skittles underneath it were lifting it, like ants carrying a branch. The old woman's hand came off the handle. She took a step back.

The stone in Becca's belly was a spike now, pressing and dragging itself into the ice machine. The surface of the ice machine began to bunch in Becca's hands, becoming soft like raw steak, hot and wet and yielding.

A tiny wisp of smoke. The suitcase was beginning to smolder. Becca smelled the burning but didn't care.

The old woman screamed. Becca's eyes snapped open to a burst of brilliant white heat like an oven door had been opened. The suitcase was burning like a torch. The old woman's hair was on fire. She batted at it slowly, like a fat wheezing dog trying to catch a race car. Becca tried to reach out, to help the woman, but the warm wetness of the ice machine held her, kept tugging at her, inviting her, asking her to come inside it. To join it.

And why not? The human race was feeble, a delicate, gullible species, easy to fool, easy to hurt, easy to kill. She hated the human race with a sudden blazing fury hotter than the burning suitcase. Better to sink into the ice machine. The ice machine? No, just a form. Just a construct. It wasn't a real ice machine any more than a puppet is a real animal.

How nice it would be to see the human race destroyed—!

A door slammed open down the hall. A blur of motion. A pillow began to hit the old woman. The woman crumpled. The smell of smoke was everywhere. Someone was stomping the suitcase. A familiar voice. "Becca! What's happening?" Pained, desperate. Fox, putting out the suitcase. A beeping near the ceiling. Water pouring down. Cool rain, cool on Becca's skin.

His rough hands pulled her away from the ice machine. But the stone in her belly was caught—being ripped away from it was like tearing off a scab. She fell clumsily into Fox's hands. A black mass clung to the side of the ice machine like a rough, lumpy scar. A tiny shape that might have been a chewed-up shard of peanut was still visible in the mass, before sinking smoothly into the side of the ice machine. Becca's stomach felt warm, but the sideways weight was gone. She wasn't heavy anymore. She felt light, like a doll in Fox's hands.

Fox! Real, human Fox had saved her! Her hatred for humanity began to fade away like a dream. She had hated humanity so *much*! But why had she thought that? *Had* she thought that?

No—it had been a thought pressed *onto* her mind. It had come from *outside* her mind, trying to worm its way in and take root unnoticed.

More voices. Stairwell doors crashed open. Hotel bellmen and security. Noise and light. The brightness of the sun. She was lifted onto her back. She couldn't bring her hands up to shield her eyes. She heard a rattling and felt a bump. She let out a little squeal.

"Becca?" It was Fox. His face filled her vision, became her shade. She managed to pull her eyes open again. "Stay with us. She's awake!"

Fox looked off to someone else, someone in white. A paramedic? A young man with dark skin. His expressions were hard to read with the sun right behind his head. But he looked her way. "Hold steady, there. Don't move around. You're all right."

She managed to look down her body toward her feet. She was being pulled on a gurney down a ramp in front of the hotel. At the curb sat a fire truck and an ambulance, waiting, red lights turning silently.

"The ice machine," she tried to say, but her mouth was dry and her tongue felt swollen. Her jaw hurt to move. "It wanted me. It wanted it back."

"Just stay quiet," Fox said. "It's okay. We're taking you to the hospital."

She rolled her head to the other side and saw Trish, eyes wide with worry behind her glasses. *Trish*, she said, and heard her voice say "Truhh."

Trish's eyes dropped to Becca's midsection and she screamed. Becca felt a hot stab in her stomach, right where the Snickers bar had pushed through her skin. Fox and the paramedic looked over. Their eyes went wide. Becca struggled to see what they were looking at.

A green Skittle ran up Becca's sternum, up her neck, and perched on the tip of her nose. Becca pulled her hands up and clapped them as fiercely as she could.

When she opened her hands, the Skittle was smashed, and it was colorful inside, sparkling like it was made of a thousand tiny scales. She suddenly realized that it burned, and she jerked her hands away, shaking them violently, yelping in pain. Fox and the paramedic rushed to steady her.

The ice machine, the soda machine, the Skittles—they were the same thing, the same stuff. A sickening stuff of bright color and hate. A thing that had called a piece of itself back. The Snickers bar in her stomach. It was that stuff. It had stayed in there. For weeks it had waited and festered and poisoned her.

The candy machine in the Austin airport lounge that nobody had put in there. The yellow boxes everywhere that nobody had installed. The phone booths and ATMs and jukeboxes that had replaced them.

"Fox," she gasped, whipping her hands against him and the paramedic, clutching for anything she could reach, fighting against their strength keeping her from moving. "The predictions. The Class Fs."

Fox stilled her right hand with both of his own. They were warm and soft and strong. He bent over to make sure his face filled her vision. "Shhh," he said. "Tell me later."

She turned her head to the side in time to see a newspaper machine on the curb suddenly rear up on four legs and smash a woman walking a dog into a light pole.

They came, and they watched us, and eventually, they asked for little bits of our blood.

The newspaper machine became rounder, became slithery, became a snakelike, shimmering form that Becca knew was closer to its real, alien truth.

They sipped our blood, and they *liked* it. They developed a *taste* for it.

Becca tried to shout, but she couldn't be heard over the crash of the snake dropping its immense weight onto the roof of a parked sedan. Fox and the paramedic and Trish—everybody but Becca—ducked as pulverized windshield dust began to fall like tiny, spiky hail.

We asked them how we were going to die, and they must have smiled to themselves as they *told* us.

The snake grew pincer-tipped forelimbs to raise the smashed sedan above its head. Around her, Becca was vaguely aware of other shimmering shapes, slithering down from telephone poles or suddenly *appearing* where before there had been only a mailbox or a bus stop or a hot-dog stand. They were suddenly *everywhere.*

Fox was fumbling with the straps on the gurney, struggling to keep it from tipping onto the rumbling, cracking sidewalk. "The airport," he screamed. "We have to get to the airport!"

Behind him, the road bulged upward, then cracked open like a pimple bursting. A flood of flashing, iridescent snakes came streaming up from the deep. Like a precision aerobatic formation of malice, they broke in different directions, whipping a fire truck into the front of a coffee shop, coiling around opposite traffic lights and pulling closed an entire intersection as easily as folding a bedsheet.

Everywhere Becca looked she saw what must have been Class F3s coming true. GLASS THROUGH BODY. CONCRETE FACE-PLANT. CATAPULTED INTO SPACE. SNAPPED.

These *things* that had so nonchalantly predicted everyone's death were now *making good on their promises.*

She felt an ache in her belly and was suddenly nauseous at the thought of what she had carried around inside her. Had they—had Fox and Trish *caused* this? The yellow boxes had sat there quietly for years. Had they listened in and realized that they were finally *outed*? Had her own inopportune craving for candy before one of them had finished… *changing* caused them to realize, *en masse*, that the jig was up?

What, in her life, had really been an alien snake? Was her hair dryer a snake? Her refrigerator? Her airplane?

How long had they been here?

Fox finally managed to get the last of the straps holding her apart, and she swung her legs over the side of the gurney. Her body sagged into his hands for second time today. Every direction she looked was filled with flashing, shining, shimmering, whipping snakes. Fox hugged her tightly to his chest, and it was warm. It was strong. The terror that clutched her was paralyzing, but at least for now, there was this.

She looked over her shoulder for Trish. The girl was gone. She peeked out behind Fox. The paramedic was gone. She looked up in the sky. The sun was gone.

"This can't be—I mean, this isn't, like, the *end*," Fox was whispering to her, cringing on the exposed sidewalk but not knowing where else to go, what else to do, with the snakes rushing and destroying everything. "You're BREAST CANCER. I'm COLON CANCER. We're going to—we've *got* to get through this."

Two futures flashed into Becca's mind. One, a handful of seconds long—ending here. With Fox. Cut to black.

The other stretching into years. Watching everybody die, but surviving. Getting breast cancer in whatever world was left. Maybe devouring, kept in stasis in some horrible Skittle-meat pod, until she wasted away from the inside. Maybe awake the whole time. Maybe wondering for years of agony if skipping lunch en route to Austin had begun the extermination of humanity.

What must have been fifty of the snakes rose like a brilliant thunderhead high into the air, weaved themselves together into a giant shovel shape, and in one earth-shattering movement, scooped up buildings, trees, vehicles, sewer pipes, and rock in a massive, shaking, debris-scattering mound of growing, heaping terror that crawled like a shadow toward Becca and Fox and the gurney and their lives and everything they had ever known or would know.

If the snakes are capable of *this*, Becca found herself thinking before the noise took over her senses, then surely—*surely*—they must also be capable of *lying*.

Story by David Malki !
Illustration by Mike Peterson

TOXOPLASMOSIS OF THE BRAIN; CANDIDIASIS OF THE ESOPHAGUS; CANDIDIASIS OF THE TRACHEA; CANDIDIASIS OF THE BRONCHI; CANDIDIASIS OF THE LUNGS; KAPOSI'S SARCOMA; PNEUMONIA; TUBERCULOSIS; STAB WOUND IN THE BELLY; AND BUS ACCIDENT

THE LINE OF PEOPLE FILING out of the buses is as long as ever, and on a dry day like today, people are irritable when they have to wait. Even people like these, who have been poked and prodded and injected and examined a dozen times along the path that brought them to the front gate of an internment camp.

There are rickety chairs outside, hundreds of them, and the people wait there, until a man with a gun ushers their row into the building. Inside, they sit impatiently, most of them doing their best not to meet one another's eyes. People don't talk much, don't laugh much. There are people here from fifteen different countries—and more countries across the continent are signing up all the time—and not everyone has a common language. Some of the Ivoriens and the South Africans couldn't talk to one another even if they wanted to. But that's not what keeps them quiet: it just doesn't feel right so close to the border between the world and the camp—the place where they will be waiting to die.

Some of them stare with glazed eyes at the ceiling or at the tattered books left lying around, stories written in languages they don't understand. Others stare at their hands or their knees, their lips pursed silently. Occasionally, there are whites—or white-looking men, at least—among the many black faces. They especially keep their heads down, keep their eyes trained on the distance.

I am the last face that some of them will see before the point of no return. I try to smile as they walk up to my desk, one by one, in the order they lined up. A short man with a gun tells them where to go—which desk: Miriam's or Anthony's or Kuseka's or mine. I say, "Go ahead," in English, because I know they know what comes next, but there are signs on the front of my desk in a dozen languages explaining what to do just in case.

The signs are unnecessary: they've all done this before. Nobody who ends up at my desk has come without sticking a finger into one of these machines at least once, whether at some town center, or when a government truck pulled into their village, or after being picked up by the police for being on the street. Nobody who ends up here has never seen a slip of paper roll out of the machine, pronouncing their doom. There are a million roads into this place—and not one that leads out—and there are these machines at every point along the way.

They already know what the machine will say. They know that the answer never changes; at least it has not done so for them.

They are sure that they will live—and die—in the camp on the other side of the razor-wire fences, and I'm no different from them: that's what I expect for them too. So I smile and thank them for their cooperation ... or I try.

I try to make the process as painless as possible. "Next," I say, and smile as if I were serving them in a shop. As if I were not bidding them farewell, seeing them off on the banks of the river Styx.

When Christopher and I married, it was a bright Saturday at the end of the harvest season. We married at the cathedral in our hometown, Blantyre, like the proper city people we were—him in a beautiful dark suit and me in a white wedding dress, with a veil that covered my face. I was nineteen, and he was twenty-four and had just finished at the Polytechnic college of the University of Malawi, and because his brother was in the civil service it was a leg up, as they say, for him to get work with the civil service too.

That was during what would turn out to be the last couple of years of President Hastings Banda's rule, when all Christopher's friends were protesting for democracy. "Multiparty rule" was what they called it then; we stayed out of it, mainly because of Christopher's hopes of working for the government someday. On the day we married, there was a demonstration downtown, and we could hear the tear-gas canisters being shot off not far from the church. We could smell the tear gas even beside the altar, and somehow it made us both smile: *perhaps,* I thought, *our marriage will be lived out in a world different from the one where we fell in love.*

The wedding was modern, but at our feast we ate *nshima* cakes made from the freshest, finest ground maize, and so many relishes it would have scandalized the queen of England. *So* many relishes: groundnut and rapeseed and *chibwabwa*, and *mlamba* fished fresh from Lake Nyasa, and beef relish made from a calf bought for the occasion by Christopher's brother, and we had a wonderful banana beer my mother brewed for us. And we sang, and we danced, and I loved Christopher with all my heart.

A month later, he got a position with a small office of the local government—his brother's friend had a few strings to pull, it seemed—and soon we were living the life of a young married couple, all smiles and sweetness and longing when he was away at work for the day. Such long workdays. I made *nshima* cakes every afternoon, experimented with relishes, and hummed happy songs to myself as I did the washing.

Sometimes, when I sit by the fence, staring into the tent village inside the camp and waiting, I think of the night we sat staring into the sky, at the stars. It was on a trip up north in '94, to visit some of my relatives living in Mzuzu—very near where I work now. I remember sitting by his side and looking up into the glittering sky.

"My father used to have me sit on his lap when I was a little boy, and he would tell me stories about the stars. The constellations, you know?"

"I don't know any of those stories," I said. "Why did he tell them to you? Was he some kind of witch doctor?"

"Ha, no, my father was an accountant's assistant, at least before independence. Before he went to prison." Christopher paused for a moment and then swiveled his head while still staring up, as if searching the sky. "He just loved stories about the stars. He used to tell me we could find all the answers to the riddles in life in the sky. Ah, do you see him? Orion? There he is," he said, pointing at the sky. "You can see his belt, there, running in a line like that?"

I did see it, and I nodded. "But it doesn't look like a man."

"The Greeks were farther north...above the equator. He's an upside-down man to us."

"Ah," I said, seeing what might be the shape of a man a little more clearly then. "And who is he?"

"Greek story, about a big man, you know."

I was never really a village girl: I lived in the bush only for a short time, as a child, before my family moved to the city. Traditional masks and the village dances—I recognize them a little but don't know their names and don't always grasp their meanings. I never learned the Chewa names for the constellations, let alone the English ones. And yet, somehow, the story sounded familiar to me. I couldn't help but imagine that Orion had cheated the gods somehow, perhaps by sleeping with a god's wife while he was busy doing something else. So I asked, "What did he do?"

Christopher laughed and said, "Well, he was a wonderful hunter, but arrogant. He threatened to kill all the animals in the world to show how great a hunter he was. Like a poacher, you see? So the gods killed him because they couldn't let him do that. But they felt sad, to kill a great hunter, so they put him in the sky."

"What kind of hunter would kill every animal in the world? How stupid!" I said.

Christopher laughed and said, "You know...that's what I said when my father told me the story too."

I laughed; he didn't mention his father often, though I knew they had disagreed about his studies, about what Christopher ought to do with his life. "Poachers aren't great hunters at all."

"True, but...they do seem able to kill everything they see."

"Poachers aren't the only ones like that," I said, shaking my head and glancing at our little shortwave radio, on the ground beside us. It had been Rwanda this, Rwanda that, and refugees headed to Malawi by the truckload; no music, just bad news all the way along the road, until Christopher had shut it off and started to tell me stories about his family.

He laughed, a little sadly. "Those bloody butchers are bad...but find me a president who hasn't done the same thing somehow or other."

And when I thought about it, I couldn't, so I just looked up into the stars and wondered whether, when Banda died someday, we might not start calling that constellation by his name, until it was time to get back in the car and continue on our way.

"Another bloody day of this, ungh?" Anthony says, and purses his lips. He doesn't look at me, but I'm the only person in the break room besides him, so he must be talking to me.

"Yes, another day," I say, and nod slightly.

Anthony does not like working at the admissions testing desk. He doesn't want to admit it, but he hates himself for continuing with this job. You can tell by the way he fills up his coffee cup. By the way he looks at the people who come up to his desk. By the sound of his voice.

He looks up at me. "Do you...realize what we're doing?"

I don't have anything to say to that.

He doesn't wait long before he realizes I'm simply not going to answer his question. I am taking the easiest way out: *don't talk.*

So he does. "We're killing them," he says softly. "How can you pretend we're doing anything else?"

I have no idea why he thinks I'm pretending that, but I say, "Bus accident. That's how I'm going to die. So is every bus driver out there killing me? People have to get where they're going. How are you going to . . . ?"

He slumps forward a bit, looks into his coffee, a little forlorn. "Murder, I think. 'Stab Wound in the Belly' were the exact words on the slip."

"And do you stay home all the time? Have a metal detector at your door?"

"That's different," he says. "How many of these people will catch the damned virus here, inside the camp? How many of them *wouldn't* catch it if we let them out? How many of them catch it solely because we're putting them in this prison?"

"None," I say, wishing I could believe it.

"None," he echoes, his eyes sliding back down to the coffee cup. "I don't know about that, sister. I don't know at all about that." And I realize then: he doesn't know why he is here. He isn't like me. I begin to wonder why he is here, after all.

Anthony is so tough at the desks, such a hard man to face, but forget the stab wound: it's this job that is killing him. And I, smiling so gently and speaking so kindly at my desk, watch them go by with nothing at all in my heart.

Nothing but a question muttered in the shadows of my heart: *Are you the one?*

But Anthony is right. I have no idea what would happen if, suddenly, all the buses in the world stopped running one day. If we crushed all the buses tomorrow in a million scrap metal yards, how could my result not come up differently on one of the machines?

I don't know. I wonder sometimes, at night, whether millions of people's results changed the day the president decreed the founding of the camps. A silent, invisible flicker in the shape of tomorrow's history; a flickering nobody would notice, like a flame in a closed room, as the fate of the country—of many countries—shifted. The scientists say the results don't change, that someone whose slip says

"Explosion in Outer Space" will still die from an explosion in outer space, even if he never gets into a space shuttle, even if he tries to live underground and never comes out from his bunker. Maybe the flaming wreckage of an exploded satellite slams into the air vent of his bunker and he chokes to death on the smoke, or maybe some other miracle happens. It doesn't make sense, though since when has the world ever made sense? But there are constant stories of people trying to test the hypothesis, doing crazy things. They never die of anything but what the slip says. So what difference does it make what we choose to do in this life? What is the point of deciding anything?

But the place where I live and work now—it looks nothing like it used to. *That* is the result of decisions, isn't it?

This whole area was once an eco-tourist hotspot, everything green and pure and gorgeous for the tourists. Green tourism was one of the few industries in Malawi that was really growing, back before the centers opened up, the vast tent villages sprouting out across the plains like an off-white fungal bloom at the foot of the Viphya Mountains. But times change, and new industries appear.

Malawi was one of the poorest nations on earth not so long ago, but now things are improving for us. For *most* of us. We haven't solved the biggest problems in the neighborhood—the petty dictators, the stupid wars, the adolescent boys with guns and something to prove. And we still have the same kind of president we've always had: a man who thinks of himself as our daddy, thinks he can tell us what to think and feel, and believes that he must slap us when we disobey him. But someday, someday *soon*, people will not think of us Africans as soon as the word "AIDS" comes up. People will think of how the continent was forward thinking. A quarantine so effective, it prevents people from being able to spread the disease *even before they've been infected.*

That's what they tell us, warning us not to try to make sense of it. There's no way to explain how, yes, this man standing here has not yet contracted HIV, but he will catch it, and it will kill him. I mean, almost nobody dies of brain toxoplasmosis or Kaposi's sarcoma or candidiasis without having AIDS; and nobody dies of AIDS without having HIV. And everyone in the camp will die from one of those diseases, the toxoplasmosis, the sarcoma, the candidiasis, or the tuberculosis or pneumonia. That much we know for certain: *I* know. I've seen the slips, thousands of them.

And the machines are *always* right, they say.

Goodness knows, I spent nights sitting, wondering—but if they don't have the disease already, then of course they will eventually catch it once they're sent to a camp. But they are only sent into the camp because they are destined to catch it—whether inside or outside.

If only we don't send them in now, maybe they won't catch it, my mind sometimes insists. It insists harder when the person with the positive result is a child, just a youngster who isn't even infected. But as sure as the sun comes up tomorrow, that kid *will* catch it, will *die* from it. The machines are never wrong.

Still, Anthony is right. I myself am proof of that.

A puzzling thing: I am HIV-positive.

And yet, "Bus Accident" is what the paper says. I still have it—I've carried it in my bag, folded into an empty candy tin for safekeeping, ever since the first day I got it. That is the insane part: for a while, they stopped doing blood tests and relied only on the machine results. Yes, the doctors are now required to report infections, but if you keep quiet and avoid them—or find a doctor who won't report you, who can get you medicines quietly—then nobody notices you.

So camps like this one will be around forever. After all, I could be passing the virus on every day, if I wanted to.

I don't, of course. I've been celibate since the day my husband came home with his eyes wide, shocked, and his mouth tight, and sat at the table and stared at me for an hour before he said anything to me. When I saw that, I knew something had gone wrong and was certain it was at work. Finally, I thought. He would tell me now what was wrong: what was making him sleep in the other room, why he was so despondent lately.

He was a civil servant and had immense responsibilities, and a man like that has stress sometimes. Stress that made him tired, drove him to need to be alone at times and to stop touching his wife the way a man touches a woman. Men are like rivers—sometimes running high, and then suddenly running low. The changes in men are harder to track than rivers', because they don't even follow the seasons. They follow some other, hidden rhythm. Often not even the men themselves can explain why it happens when it does.

My husband, he is an educated man and a Catholic. I never expected him to tell me what he did, sitting there at the kitchen table one rainy evening after work. Telling me about his visit to the doctor, about the test. About the result, how the doctor said he had HIV. The way he did the doctor's voice, like he was trying to figure out if he'd misheard him. *Edzi,* that's how the name of the disease sounded when he said it. He was crying. He said I'd better go and get tested.

And the first thing I thought was, *No, I don't.*

"My death paper," I said to him softly. "The paper said 'Bus Accident.' I can't have…"

My husband's eyes widened. For a moment, I wasn't sure what it was I was seeing in his face. It might have been fear, or perhaps anger that he could have this sickness in him, but it might have passed me over like the Israelite children in Moses's Egypt. For twenty years he had lived with me by his side. For me to be apart from him, even in sickness, might have baffled him. The thought terrified me too, almost as much as the prospect of my own infection.

But then he was smiling, even as he cried harder and he held my hands gently in his own. "I prayed…I prayed so many times that you would be safe, would be fine. That my sins would not poison you." A teardrop fell on my hands, and I wondered, *Is the disease in that teardrop? Could I catch it from that?*

Three days. For three days, I walked around in a kind of daze, knowing my husband was ill, believing that somehow I had come through uninfected, wondering how this could happen. The next morning, I went to the women's center, but I got the result two days later. The nurse from the women's center called me at home with the results, three days after he told me.

"Positive," she said, which I thought was good news at first. I don't know why I thought that—I suppose because I was so desperate for a miracle. "Do you understand, this means you have been infected?" Then I remembered: a positive result is *bad*; a negative result is *good*.

I don't remember what the nurse said after that. I only remember sitting down, fumbling in my bag for the candy tin, and pulling out the slip of paper.

Unfolding it.

"Bus Accident."

The hardest are the families: the man with his wife, and a baby in a sling hanging from her shoulders. Families, they say, are the building blocks of a nation.

Has anyone ever had to sort bricks like this? Bricks that all look fine, all look healthy; bricks that weep and beg for a test on another machine?

The men sometimes get angry and shout. That doesn't bother me anymore—the security men come up with guns, and the men get quiet or get shot. Never fatally, just wounded. I look at their wives, and it breaks my heart. *Your husband brought you here,* I think. *It's true. Your husband gave this to you, didn't he?*

It's harder with those wives: the women who show a recent blood test, who insist that they are not infected. They are the ones who trouble me.

And then there are the women who come alone, with no husband or children.

"I'm not sick," they say. They all say that, standing there alone in front of me.

And I look into their eyes and wonder, *Are you the one who gave it to him? Is it from* you *that he got the virus that is swimming in my blood today? I am sick, and you say you are not . . . and yet you will go in there, while I stay out here.*

"Yes, madam, I understand," I say, my voice as steady as it can be. "But if you look at the result from the machine . . ."

"The machine is not a doctor! How can I know that the machine won't give me HIV itself?" The women are desperate because they know it isn't something they can control. When you can control something, you never feel desperate.

"No, madam," I say, my eyes serious now, as I wonder, *Are you the one? Are you?* "The machines never infect anyone. It's impossible. They designed it carefully so it wouldn't…"

"Then test me on another machine," they beg, pointing at Anthony's desk on the one side or to Kuseka's on the other.

"It will be the same result. *Please*," I say. "I've seen it a thousand times."

"Then *please*…just see it once more." The women make fists and scream and bawl and struggle. They are supposed to do it. And I am supposed to send them to Anthony's desk. When they do this at Anthony's desk, he shakes his head and gestures to the guards.

But Kuseka and I, we usually allow them to be tested once more. I think Kuseka does it out of kindness, but I do it…I do it to see the result. To see the look on the woman's face.

A guard escorts the woman over to the machine, and that is the moment when you discover what kind of mother she is. The loving mother knows there might only be one test allowed and puts her child's hand into the slot. The selfish mother, she puts her own hand in, clutching the baby to herself.

There is a woman at my desk now who doesn't need to put the baby's hand into the slot. Her child's result was never any of the diseases that kill someone with advanced AIDS. Her child's slip reads, "Diacetyl-Induced Lung Cancer," whatever that means. But when she puts her own hand into the slot and winces at the pinprick, she looks at me. I can see it on her face, that this is not just the third or fourth time she has done this. She knows already what the result will be. She is just hoping the machine somehow will give her another result through some kind of malfunction.

She is hoping for a miracle.

And I can see it on her face, that she knows one isn't forthcoming. Her husband knows too—he has watched her do this many times, and the guards have let his arms loose as they lead him over to her. She looks at me, and for a moment I expect her to be thankful. I let her go over to Kuseka's machine and try again. But she isn't thankful at all: as I watch the guards lead her husband and her—child still in the sling, crying now—I catch her eye, and I see a pure and cold resentment in her eyes.

The sort of resentment that will only slowly ferment into resignation. I recognize that look—I've seen it a hundred times a day in the eyes of men and women who come to my desk to be tested.

And I recognize the look from the mirror too, when I get home from work every day—where I have watched it begin the transmutation to hopeless acceptance.

But she glimpses something almost as cold in my eyes too, I am sure.

After I found out, I left my husband.

Not right away. I was angry and hurt, and I think I stayed around for a while to punish him. I would lie on the floor and cry, and then eat something for lunch, and then cry some more until I couldn't. Then I would stay there on the floor till he got home.

"You men are so stupid!" I shouted at him. "Willing to risk your own life, the life of your family, the children you haven't had yet, and the life of the woman you love, all to stick your thing into a new woman and tingle a bit. You men are *so stupid.*"

But we dare to trust them, to love them. What does that make us women? I thought about that a lot, and finally I decided not to love him anymore.

So I left to stay with my sister up north in Mzuzu. He did not chase me, did not try to find me. For that, I was grateful—I imagined perhaps he understood how I felt, understood his own betrayal and understood that I needed to be away from him, even if at first I did nothing differently than I'd done at home with him: lying on the floor, crying, staring, refusing to eat, shouting at anyone around.

My sister tried first to live with me in that state, to understand. Then she struggled desperately to cheer me up, to get me to come to a treatment center, to see a doctor. She said she knew someone who knew someone, that I could get medicines, I could live a long time. But I just snarled at her husband, growled at the men in town. I saw a woman at the food shop who I was certain was a whore, and I slapped her in the face. And then, back to lying on the floor, crying my eyes out, breaking things—always my own things, things I'd brought from home.

Finally, one day, my sister—a secretary at local government office—came home from work speaking of a big new project, vague like every big new project in Malawi is at first, and of the many people who would be needed to work desks. She had put my name in, she said, with strong recommendation. She assured me I would have work, and this, somehow, woke me up. I began to pull myself together a little.

Just enough.

A few weeks was all it took. It was phenomenal, how quickly the first camp was set up: all they did was put in the fences and ship in tents donated by some NGO or other that probably had no idea what they would really be used for. Now they call this place a "death camp," and we have guards and another, taller fence ten miles out in all directions to keep them away, to stop the protesters and the human rights activists and the mercenaries and the international reporters from breaking in, photographing them, letting them all out into the world...but back then, those NGOs were eager to donate the tents.

Finally, they said, someone is doing something concrete about the AIDS crisis.

On the first day, the tents weren't even set up: that was left for the people who would live in the camp to do. A few water lines and communal latrines were dug, and that was it: the Viphya HIV quarantine center was set up for business, with me placed at one of the front desks, a broad smile on my face, in a fine, colorful dress and matching hair wrap my sister bought for me. I was ready to do my job.

Me, at the front desk, secretly infected, smiling at the men and women, one by one, passing me on their way to oblivion. Somehow I was convinced that as long as I sat at this desk, I would never end up inside the camp itself. That I would see her, eventually, and know her—the one who had infected my husband, and through him, infected me.

Nobody was actually calling it a "death camp" then. But the people they brought in knew already, on some level, that they were supposed to never leave this place. They pretended, even those first people, to hope things would come out fine for them. They acted as if they'd held on to the belief that the camps were set up with medicine, that UN observers and MSF volunteers would be let in. That treatment programs like those in some other countries—some not so very far away— would let them live their lives. They pretended as hard as they could.

But if you watched them carefully, there was a brokenness that overcame them as they stuck a finger into the machine, as they got the result and were led through the gate into the camp.

Maybe it was all the guards around with guns in their hands.

"So many guns," my husband said to me a few months later, when he was led up to my desk.

"Christopher," I said. My husband did not look ill, though he had changed in the months since I'd last seen him. He had gone gray at the temples, and his eyes had a defeated look. He wore a silver cross around his neck, his shirt unbuttoned, probably because of the heat on the buses since the windows were nailed shut to prevent runaways.

"Joyce," he said, and held out his hand. And suddenly I was not a government official at the front gate of an HIV camp. Suddenly I was a woman on the verge of widowhood. I had imagined him being brought here, imagined his being brought to my desk even, and I had always imagined myself staring through him, showing no sign I recognized him, letting him go into the camp. I had imagined myself quitting on that day and never coming back here again.

And yet, in the moment, the thought possessed me that I could get the candy tin from my bag, that I could get the slip out. That maybe the guards would not make him take the test again on another machine. That somehow I could keep him out of there, save his life. Not to go home with him, not necessarily, but…to help him somehow.

I got as far as pulling out the candy tin and opening it. Then I realized—they would test him again. They would make him go to Anthony's machine and test once more, and then it would say what it had said on the last machine and all the machines before. No blood test needed. Nobody reached my desk without already knowing what would kill him.

"Kaposi's sarcoma?" I asked, looking up from the tin and into his eyes. His familiar, unrecognizable eyes.

"Tuberculosis and candidiasis of the lungs," he said. Almost nobody died from the tuberculosis, and it made me wonder—will conditions in the camp worsen? Will the roads in be blocked? Or... will he die from a broken heart? A man who had no reason to live would die sooner, might get ill and fall apart in just a few years.

"Oh, love," I said, and I reached across my desk to hold his hand. Then I saw the most awful thing in my life, worse than anything else I had seen at my desk: my own husband refusing to weep, refusing to move, just looking at me and waiting for me to tell him what to do. Unable to do anything at all. About to be bundled off to die. With no idea why he was here, why he would never see me again, why the machinery of our government had decided he would be chewed up in this way instead of the usual way. With nobody to blame for giving him the thing swimming in his blood that would kill him.

He stood there looking at me, with his mouth a little open.

I sat there, as still as death and staring back at him, unable to speak at all. Eventually, Anthony saw what was happening and called the guards to bring my husband to his desk. Kuseka came to my side and led me away from the desk.

He could have said something, could have said a million things. Could have told them, right then, that I was infected too. Could have taken me into the camp to be with him again. I'm sure he could see it in my eyes, that surging longing to be beside him again, which shocked me as I realized I was feeling it.

But he said nothing at all. He just looked at me one moment longer, and then with his jaw clenched, he turned away and let them lead him to Anthony's desk and stuck his finger into the machine there, stood waiting for the slip to pop out. Anthony took it, read it silently, and then nodded to the guard who held my husband's arm.

Then the guard led him away, out of the world. There was another woman standing in front of my desk, but I stayed where I was. I could feel myself about to vomit as I watched him being led away, not glancing back to see me.

That was when, to my surprise, I began to miss him, in a way I hadn't felt since I'd left him.

I sit beyond the perimeter surrounding the fence sometimes, looking for him through a pair of binoculars I bought in a secondhand shop in Mzuzu.

I see a lot of things. I see people arguing, and I see groups of women crying. I see people using hand gestures to communicate because they don't have a language in common. Ivoriens, Ethiopians, Algerians, Tutsis, Sudanese, Zulu: all jumbled together like pieces of a puzzle-map. The violence is constant but mostly low-level, and even when it is extreme, it is never fatal—after all, nobody in the camp dies of a stab wound or injury, only from some complication related to AIDS.

Doctors have begun talking about a "culture of rape" that exists in parts of the camp and how it is the reason that so many uninfected people finally do contract HIV. The government argues that they would have been infected anyway—that the machines are never wrong. I wonder how people keep on living in there, how they resist the urge to hang themselves, to cut their own throats. Is it the hope of a rescue? The hope of a cure? Are they imagining that maybe, in a few years, the camps will be shut down and they will no longer live in a zoo? Or is it just that the tents are so crowded nobody has enough privacy to kill herself?

I see women giving birth to babies that may or may not already be infected, and may or may not die in the camp. People still celebrate, even with the tears I'm sure are in their eyes, even with their hands scarred from hanging on to the barbed wire of the fence and looking out at the guards with the guns pointed at them. They sing and chitchat until the baby is taken away to be tested. Whether the baby is returned or disappears, their mothers wail all night long.

I watch the buses pull up to the gate compound, sometimes ten or fifteen of them in a caravan, with a military truck in front and another behind. The wheels on the bus turn and turn in my mind. It is me, looking in the face of the machine that will kill me, and in a way I feel lucky. Nobody in the camp even knows what HIV looks like—cannot draw a picture of it. They have masks for it now, masks for characters that I never saw when I was a little girl in my home village. The masks are huge heads that sit on top of wasted bodies, with sunken eyes and cheeks and a deathly look; one mask shows a grotesque red face covered in scabs and pustules, and three horns sprout from its crown. This character's name is Edzi, which is how people from the villages in the bush in our part of Malawi pronounce "AIDS."

The people in the camp put on the masks and dance out the dramas that I have never seen before—dancing stories that never existed when I was a little girl in my village, or stories I don't recognize, at least. Even people from other parts of the continent are putting on the masks and dancing now. They are making a culture of their own, these prisoners. Sometimes the monstrously masked dancers tumble to the ground, lying still for nearly an hour as the music goes on without them, as if to enact the death that is waiting for them all. Other times, they rise again soon after and stomp down little fences made of paper and cloth—the dream of resurrection and escape.

Sometimes they dance for an hour and a strange effigy is brought out, a thing made of scrap plywood and leaves and scrap metal they've found somewhere. A few men parade it out to the edge of the camp, where we can see it, and then everyone puts a finger into it, one by one. The thing is an effigy of the machines—the machines like the one on my desk—that tell us how we will die. And then they set the effigy on fire and burn it and leap onto it crazily, smashing it while others sing and sing and sing.

The fence dances, those seem almost ridiculous to me. Some fences will never come down once they're up. And the machine-effigy dances, those scare me. They're angry, those dances, no matter how futile. But the resurrection dances, if that's what they are...those I understand completely. I take comfort in them as I wait for Christopher to wander into view. He wasn't sick enough to be dead already—that's impossible, I tell myself as I sit staring through my binoculars.

Day after day, when I finish work, I come out here and watch. Sometimes a guard stumbles across me and begins to threaten me, until I show him my employment card, and he realizes I work here. Then he tells me to put the binoculars away and get back to work, and I tell him I am working and that he should leave me alone if he knows what's good for him. I wear my glasses at this time, and it makes me look like I am studying something. It works.

I keep wondering what I will do when I finally see Christopher. Run to the fence, try to climb it and get to him? Run away? Burst into tears and give up finally? Try to smuggle a letter to him? Quit my job and consider myself a widow?

I wonder about the men who made the machines: Why did they choose the question of how we are to die? Why not how we will live? Isn't that what people used to ask the stars? Will I be happy? Will I be rich? Will my wife be beautiful? Will my husband be kind? How many children will I have? It's stupid to ask those questions to the sky, of course—stars can't tell us anything in the way of useful answers— but at least the questions themselves are useful. The only question the machines answered for me was one I didn't need an answer to, one that does me little good now, with my eyes straining to distinguish whether that gaunt man standing by an open fire is Christopher, fallen ill, or someone else who happens to be about his height and build.

No, the machines tell us nothing about how we would live, how we could live. About such a question, all the machines tell us is, "You never asked about *that*."

I find myself lowering the binoculars from my eyes and looking up to the sky to search for some story that could make sense of this for me—some dead hunter or ancient god above, still upside down and glittering in the darkness, surrounded by an ocean of stars all around. For a moment, I feel like this is all inevitable—like the camp is nothing more than the upside-down picture of the world made by the machines, just as old President Banda's rule had been an upside-down version of how the British ran this place, just as democracy since that has been upside down too. For a moment, a wide, dark fatalism wafts through me like smoke, filling me to the brim with a hopeless despair.

But then the smoke clears, and I have the binoculars in my hands again now and find myself searching the people in the distance, behind the fence. Hope might be only a habit, but it persists anyway. The crowd is performing another dance, near the fire now. One of the masks is new, with an enormous guard hat crowning its wooden head.

Nearer the fence, guards are shouting now, provoked and yelling as the guard masks multiply, and the dancers, turning their backs on the guards, hoist the masks up and toss them over their own shoulders toward the fire.

Gunshots ring out—but we already know the inmates won't die from gunshot wounds—and suddenly a siren begins to blare. A fire breaks out among a stand of tents, and people run, screaming, toward the fence. The flash of cameras is visible in the distance, and off to my left, in the darkness, three pairs of headlights flick on, suddenly tumbling over the bumpy ground toward the fence.

They're going to break people out. It's really happening, I realize as the buses slam through the fencing, with guards shooting round after round behind them. The guns are loud, but they don't frighten me. For the first time, nothing frightens me, and I don't feel imprisoned by anything. When the machines told us how we will die, they also told us how we will not die. The fear that would have held me in place is now so tiny, so overpowered by hope and regret and by longing that I thought I couldn't feel anymore.

As I rise to my feet, I catch the faint whiff of tear gas. It somehow makes me laugh for the first time in months, and then I am running as hard as I can toward the massive hole in the fence that the buses have made, and into the firelit camp—calling out to Christopher, and not caring whether it's the last thing I will ever do in this world.

Story by Gord Sellar
Illustraion by Nick Abadzis

CANCER

This certifies that
HELEN FRANCES LAWRENCE,
sex FEMALE,
was born to
JOHN DENISON LAWRENCE and
VIRGINIA MATILDA LAWRENCE
on SATURDAY at SIX TEN PM,
this EIGHTEENTH day of AUGUST 1990
at the MONTFORT HOSPITAL in OTTAWA, ONTARIO,
and will die of CANCER

JOHN AND VIRGINIA WERE OVERJOYED: ten fingers, ten toes, and while it wasn't the best death, cancer didn't happen to the young very often. Two days later, on August 20, 1990, baby Helen was home.

The other kids in grade four called Helen "Helen Helen Cancer Spellin'," which never made much sense. She'd yell that at them.

"That doesn't even make much sense!" she'd say.

"Maybe you should give up on rhymes!" she'd say.

"You guys, cancer isn't even that hard to spell," she'd say.

One day in grade four, during second recess, she met Tina. Three boys had surrounded her, chanting "Tina Tina Belly Screenah." A group of onlookers was growing, and Helen joined them.

"That doesn't even make much sense!" yelled Tina.

"I know, right?" shouted Helen.

* * *

Not everyone got tested at birth, and Tina hadn't. Not getting tested had been her parents' choice, but in university it had become her choice. She and Helen were hanging out in Helen's dorm room, alone, lying side by side on her bed. It was the only comfortable place in the room.

"Has the CANCER prediction changed the way you live your life, Helen?" Tina asked.

"Has being a lesbian changed the way you live your life, Tina?" Helen asked.

"Has being a superbitch changed the way you live your life, Helen?"

They kissed for a bit.

"I was joking about the superbitch part," said Tina.

Helen and Tina were at the mall near their house because it was Tina's thirtieth birthday and she'd decided she wanted to know. It was stupid not to, she'd decided. Helen had agreed to pay the two hundred and fifty dollars as a birthday present. Tina pulled the credit card out of the machine, passing it back to Helen with one hand as she stuck her finger in the machine with the other. A sample was taken, her blood was analyzed, and a printout was produced. "AIRPLANE," it said.

"Nice!" said Tina, excited. She showed her prediction to Helen. "Mine's better! AIRPLANE's way better than CANCER."

"You'll probably just get hit on the head by an airplane," said Helen, "and it's not going to be nearly as cool as you think it is."

"A toy airplane?" said Tina.

"Nope," said Helen.

Tina laughed and noticed the display on the machine still read "INSERT FINGER." "Hey," she said, "it's still gonna do a reading. Quick, put your finger in!" She grabbed Helen's finger and pulled it toward the machine. Helen shrugged. "You want a piece of paper with 'CANCER' on it, it's yours." She put her finger in, and a few seconds later the machine spit out a piece of paper. Tina grabbed it.

A moment later she looked up, confused. "Sweetie," she said, "this doesn't say 'CANCER.' It says 'SUICIDE.' "

"*What?*" said Helen, snatching the paper out of her hand and reading it herself. SUICIDE. She looked up at Tina, anger clouding her features.

"My parents told me I'd have cancer since forever, and it turns out *SUICIDE* is how I'm going to die?"

Tina took Helen's hand in hers, trying to calm her down. "Sweetie, please, come on, maybe it's—"

Helen cut her off. "I can't believe it," she said. "Why wouldn't they tell me? I'm a grown woman, for God's sake."

She already had her phone out, dialing her parents. As it was ringing, she turned to Tina. "Before I do me, I'm gonna kill them," she said.

Helen's parents denied everything, and sincerely. Her father pulled out the birth certificate from the closet to prove it. Helen had never seen it before, but there, printed on the form, was "CANCER." The hospital had even attached the original prediction card with a staple.

"It must've been a mix-up at the hospital," her father said. "Some other girl's blood got tested instead of yours. It's happened before. You could sue."

Helen brought the certificate home to show Tina. They were sitting on the edge of their bed, side by side. Tina turned the birth certificate and card over in her hands.

"Prediction cards haven't really changed much since you were born," said Tina.

"I've always avoided cancer," said Helen. "I avoided smoking, I wore sunscreen, I limited my red meat." She sighed. "I *really* love red meat."

"It doesn't change anything," said Tina. "Suicide doesn't necessarily mean you'll die early. Maybe it's assisted suicide when you're superold."

Helen flopped backward onto the bed, staring at the ceiling. "Do you want to get some dinner?" she asked.

"It's only two," said Tina.

Twenty minutes later they were at a steakhouse.

Helen pointed at Tina with her fork, her mouth full of steak, medium rare. "Maybe I *will* sue," she said through the meat. It sounded like *Eaibe a ill oue.*

"Gross," said Tina.

Helen and Tina found an attorney in the phone book, Jack Bradshaw, attorney-at-law. "I ONLY GET PAID WHEN YOU DO," his ad said. He went with Helen to personally oversee her testing, and again: SUICIDE. Jack smiled at her. "Open-and-shut case," he said.

"That's the kind I like!" said Helen.

Six months later Helen was on the stand. Her birth certificate had matched the records the hospital had submitted to the government when she was born, so it was simply a matter of running Helen through the courtroom machine. She watched from the stand as Jack continued his prosecutorial patter, building up the test for the jury.

"My client, who has suffered irreparable damages to her life on account of the maliciously incorrect cancer prediction supplied to her upon birth, asks for very little. Thirty years of her life—thirty years!—have been spent fighting to avoid a particular death—a death, as I will prove to the court's satisfaction, that wasn't even there. She asks only for compensation for those wasted years—those wasted chances—so that she might finally live what's left of her life as was originally intended."

In the audience, Tina rolled her eyes but then caught herself and stared straight ahead.

Jack turned from the jury and looked at Helen. "Helen, if you would now insert your finger, we will prove that the reading supplied and recorded by the doctors and staff at Montfort Hospital was wrong. Whether these people were acting with deliberate malice or not is irrelevant. All that matters is the prediction, the *real* prediction. Helen, if you would."

Helen stuck her finger in the machine; a piece of paper was produced. Jack read it, and though Helen knew where this was going, she still thought his feigned reaction of surprise seemed... sincere?

"Well, would you look at that," Jack said. "Despite what Montfort Hospital would have you believe, my client will not die of cancer. As you can see, ladies and gentlemen, she will die"—Jack held up the card to the jury—"of DNA BREAKDOWN."

Jack turned to Helen, making significant eye contact. "I submit this prediction card produced under the eyes of the court as Exhibit A, and the prosecution rests."

There wasn't much you could say to argue against a prediction done in a courtroom on the court's machine. The defense used their time to focus mainly on the degree of their culpability. After only a few minutes of deliberation, the jury came back. Helen had won.

"I don't know what you did, but you took a damn big risk doing it," Jack shouted at them a few blocks from the courthouse. He was furious; his entire face was red.

"I don't know what happened," Helen said, but Jack spoke over her. "A lesser attorney would've stumbled, would've cost you a hell of a lot of credibility." He glared at her. "Why not just say you were going to die of DNA BREAKDOWN in the first place? Why fake 'SUICIDE' "—he did air quotes around the word with his fingers—"for my benefit?"

"The other machines both said 'SUICIDE,' " Tina said.

"The machines don't give different answers," snapped Jack, "and at this point I don't care." He turned back to Helen. "The hospital did mess up, and we won, but for God's sake if you're ever in a lawsuit again, *don't lie to your attorney.*" He pushed his way past them and stormed off.

Tina and Helen stared at each other.

"What do we do now?" asked Helen. "I'm three million dollars richer." Tina shrugged and after a moment turned around.

"It didn't say you were so rude in your ad!" shouted Tina.

The money had come in a lump sum, so Helen and Tina had spent the next six months on vacation, traveling the world, seeing places they'd both dreamed of visiting. There were a lot of rail trips and cruises in deference to Tina's AIRPLANE prediction, but neither of them minded. "Everyone is classier on a train," Tina said. "That cruise ship will go well with my dress," Helen said.

They were both trying to have a good time.

They'd use a machine whenever they found one that took cash and wasn't too public. They'd used thirty-five machines so far. Tina's prediction was always the same. Helen's wasn't. It was now the fourth day of their final cruise, a twelve-day journey taking them from Australia back to Canada. They'd found a machine on board, some distance from most of the popular and interesting parts of the ship. Tina put in her cash and finger into the machine. "AIRPLANE" came out. Tina started feeding in the bills for Helen.

"You're up," she said.

Helen put her finger in. So far on their trip, Helen had received NECROSIS, LOSS OF VITAL FLUIDS, APOPTOSIS ("the natural death of cells," Tina announced, reading from her phone), DNA BREAKDOWN, ATTACK, INFECTION, MURDER, ACID EXPLOSION, SUICIDE, and CANCER. She'd actually gotten CANCER far more often than anything else, which made her think it was blind luck that it hadn't been that prediction that turned up in the courtroom.

Her paper came out: "CANCER."

Tina was already feeding more bills into the machine. "Once more," she said, "for real this time." Helen stuck her finger in again, and again a slip of paper came out.

" 'DEVOURED BY NEIGHBOR,' " Helen read, surprised. It was a new one. She passed it to Tina, who read it.

"Do you think that means Mr. Ross?" said Tina.

*   *   *

When they were home, Tina plotted Helen's results on a graph. The non-CANCER results they got didn't show any trends, but CANCER itself definitely seemed to be showing up less and less often.

"What do you think that means?" asked Tina when she showed Helen her graph and data.

"I have no idea," Helen said in a small voice. "I have no idea what any of this means."

Tina took Helen's hand. "Maybe we really should go to the hospital," she said.

They ended up going to the same hospital that they'd sued, the same hospital she'd been born in. Helen said it'd be easier that way. After a wait in the emergency room, the doctor at Montfort Hospital introduced himself as Dr. Peters and said that he was extremely busy and that he didn't believe in Helen's story of multiple predictions. "Nobody gets different results from the machine," he said.

"Try me," Helen said.

The first result was CANCER. Tina thought that'd get a reaction, but Dr. Peters apparently had no idea of Helen's history with the hospital, which was probably for the best. He ran a second test right away, and this time the result was "DNA BREAKDOWN." Peters brought in another doctor and they ran the test again: ACID EXPLOSION. They wheeled in another machine and got CANCER, then NECROSIS, then CANCER, then CANCER again, then ATTACK. The doctors huddled together, talking quickly and quietly.

"Told you," Helen said.

Later that evening, Dr. Peters sat at his computer and went through Helen's blood report. When he took the sample he'd told Helen and Tina that he'd be looking very carefully at it for clues as to what might be happening. He'd said that nothing like this had ever been recorded. He'd said to Helen that at this juncture, she shouldn't be taking any of her predictions seriously yet.

"That's funny," said Helen.

As he brought up the first image and saw Helen's cellular walls, Peters blinked. It was obvious that Helen had lymphoma and it was bad: the irregular shapes of the cancerous cells were spread throughout her blood. This was very far along and likely spreading to other organs beyond the one it had started in. She'd be starting chemotherapy immediately. She was young. She could make it.

He sighed, flipping through the pages of the report, pausing on another image of the flattened cancer cells. Seeing she had cancer was simple. The question was, why was she getting multiple readings?

Cancer didn't come close to explaining the odd readings from the machines. Plenty of people had cancer, and plenty of people died from it, and they all had just the one prediction. *What is it in this blood that's so special?* Helen's predictions were inconsistent but not random. They seemed to be coming from a small set of possible deaths, as if the machine was seeing more than one fate for her. *She's only going to die once,* Peters thought. *How do you reconcile cancer with being eaten by a neighbor? How does "ATTACK" square with "SUICIDE" and "DNA BREAKDOWN"?* The only DNA breakdown he knew that could possibly be considered an attack was—

Dr. Peters suddenly leaned back from his computer and stared at the ceiling, shocked, his mind racing.

The only DNA breakdown that could be an attack was cellular death induced by neighboring cells. What else do cells do? Cells die, cells commit suicide, infected or damaged cells are attacked and their useful elements absorbed by neighboring cells. NECROSIS and APOPTOSIS both could refer specifically to cellular death. Heck, even ACID EXPLOSION could refer to lysosome-mediated apoptosis and the acid hydrolase enzymes they contained. He stared at the computer, the tiny sample of Helen's blood still on the screen. Everything fit. The machine wasn't producing cause-of-death predictions for his patient, one Helen Frances Lawrence, born August 18, 1990.

It was predicting results for her cells.

*   *   *

Tina lay on top of Helen: a full-body hug. It was dark outside, and the lights in the room had been turned off.

"They're eventually gonna notice I'm here and kick me out," she whispered.

"This is the priority ward," Helen whispered back. "We get a pass. You're staying right here with me."

Tina gave Helen a squeeze. "Make sure there's nothing wrong with you, okay? I don't want my sweetie to leave me." Tina's voice quivered.

"Oh my God," said Helen, "if you start to cry I'm going to push you off the bed. I'm serious. I will push you off the bed."

"I'm not crying! I'm just being sincere with someone who means a lot to me and who might have a serious disea— Hey! Stop it!"

"You cry at *TV commercials*," Helen said, pulling her back into a hug.

Early that morning, Dr. Peters met with his patient. He was rumpled, unshaven, and exhausted. He walked into Helen's room, surprised to find Tina already there, sitting beside her. He glanced at the clock on the wall. Visiting hours already?

"Helen, I'd like to speak with you privately if I could," he said.

"Anything you say to me you can say in front of her," Helen said.

Tina smiled. "Go for it," she said.

He cleared his throat. "Helen, I examined your blood sample last night. There are abnormal cells in the bloodstream. It's cancer. I'm sorry. It's already advanced quite a bit, and the cells have metastasized and are in your bloodstream. We'll likely find some elsewhere too. I want to begin treatment immediately."

Tina squeezed Helen's hand. Helen squeezed back hard.

"That's the bad news. The good news is, we have several treatment options available, and I know we can make a dent in it. This doesn't have to be the cancer that kills you," he said, not for the first time in his career.

Helen started to cry involuntarily. She angrily wiped away a tear.

"Fuck cancer," she said. "Who's to say I don't die from that douche bag in the other bed eating me first?"

"I—I have a theory on that too." Dr. Peters said. "I tested this last night and it's consistent. When I put a single blood cell of yours—a healthy one—in a suspension and run it through the machine, we get CANCER one hundred percent of the time. But when I test a cancerous cell, the predictions that come out are the others that we've been seeing. Helen, they're all consistent with descriptions of cellular death. I don't yet understand how, but I believe your cancer cells are getting their own death predictions."

Helen looked at Tina and then back at Dr. Peters.

"What," she said flatly.

The months went by as Helen's treatment progressed. Helen had been allowed to stay at home with Tina. Her hair had fallen out. She hadn't gotten a wig.

Helen came in once a day for another test with Dr. Peters. He'd modified the machine that he'd started to think of as "his" with a second IV. When the machine had done its analysis, the press of a button would return the entire blood sample to Helen's blood- stream. His hope was that the cells tested in this way would reveal which treatment killed them in Helen's body. They could jump to using that effective treatment right away, potentially saving months of tests.

So far, he'd had no luck: all the predictions were the same cellular deaths they'd been getting all along. But they still revealed quite a bit: a lack of predictions that mapped onto KILLED BY CHEMOTHERAPY told Dr. Peters that the treatments weren't going to be immediately effective, which was the bad news. But there was also good news, because they also hadn't had any predic- tions reading CIRCULATION FAILURE or STARVATION or any- thing else that could indicate cancer cells being killed by Helen's own death.

"Blood cells live for about four months," Dr. Peters had told Helen and Tina. "We've still got time."

Meanwhile, news had gotten out through the hospital staff, and then to the world at large, that a woman with multiple predictions was a patient. Helen had consented to one interview, done at the hospital. The interview as aired had been short, since Helen couldn't really add much to the story beyond "cancer sucks, were you aware?" and Dr. Peters had handled the medical aspects of the explanation. After summarizing the discoveries made at Montfort, the reporter put the microphone to Helen.

"Do you have any idea why your experience is so different?" the reporter asked.

"I don't know why it's just me," Helen said.

The camera lingered on her, so she gave it a thumbs-up.

Helen's recent surgery and chemotherapy regime had not been kind. Her last chemo cycle—the sixth—was more than two weeks earlier, but Helen was still in the hospital, bedridden, weak, tired. She'd had growths removed from her lymph nodes and bowels, and daily radiation targeted the growth around her heart. Tina visited her almost every day, telling her stories about what their friends were up to when they weren't here in the room with them. Her parents had visited five times. It was hard for everyone, and at Helen's insistence, Tina was home today. "You still have to live your life," she'd said. "Go, have fun. Eat something I can't keep down. I insist."

"Steak?" said Tina.

"No way, those belong to me," said Helen.

Helen was alone and napping when Dr. Peters knocked on the door and wheeled his machine in. The knock was enough to wake her.

"Back for more, Nick?" Helen asked.

"Still looking for clues, yes," said Dr. Peters, hooking her up to the machine's IV. "Place your finger here, please, Helen."

A few seconds later, the result was printed. As Dr. Peters read the slip of paper, his heart sank. It wasn't CANCER, so it was a cellular-level prediction, the end of the line for a single cell of Helen's cancer. He stared at it for a long moment. "HOST DEATH," it read.

Helen saw his reaction and asked for the paper, reading it quickly.

"Well, fuck everything about that," said Helen, handing it back to her doctor.

Six weeks later, the HOST DEATH predictions had eclipsed all of Helen's death predictions, with the exception of CANCER. It was going faster than they'd expected. Tina hadn't seen Helen and Dr. Peters produce a non-CANCER or –HOST DEATH prediction in days.

The cancerous cells in her body were not going to live for much longer, and everyone knew that meant Helen was not going to live for much longer either. There was no way to avoid it. Dr. Peters was still no closer to figuring out how to stop it, and with the HOST DEATH predictions, they'd agreed to move Helen to the palliative care unit three floors up. There, the focus was no longer on curing the disease but on managing it, on making Helen as comfortable as possible, and on doing the best they could.

The end of chemo and radiation treatments meant that even though Helen was dying, she felt better than she had in weeks, maybe months. Tina and Helen spent a lot of time talking and a lot of time just sitting and not talking. They'd agreed to not start thinking that since there were only so many moments left, every moment had to be capital-S Special. That would be exhausting. This was nice.

Helen placed her finger into the machine and Dr. Peters took another reading. "You're doing great, Helen," he said.

"Nick," Helen said, "if you're waiting to cure me, now would be a good time." Tina looked at her and smiled. A few seconds later, the machine printed out a piece of paper, and Tina read it, furrowing her brow. She held it up for Dr. Peters.

" 'DESTROYED IN LAB ACCIDENT'?" she said.

*   *   *

Dr. Peters quickly disassembled the machine and recovered the blood sample within. Inside that sample was a cell of Helen's cancer that was going to die not from HOST DEATH but in the lab. This cell would survive her body—but how? The hundred-and-twenty-day window of cell life didn't give them much time. He put the blood sample into a sympathetic culture designed for maintaining cells. *If I didn't do that,* he thought, *would the cell have died from host death instead? Am I destined to knock this petri dish off a desk in a week and that'll be that?*

It didn't matter. At this point he was willing to try anything.

Two days later it was clear that cellular division was taking place. All cancer was a mutation of a cell's regular instructions, causing the growths and lumps normally symptomatic of the disease. But Helen's cancer cells had mutated differently: unlike normal human red blood cells, Helen's reproduced in culture. They cloned themselves and would clone themselves for as long as the necessary conditions for life were present.

"These cancer cells can be sustained indefinitely," Dr. Peters had said that afternoon while briefing his colleagues. "Ladies and gentlemen, we're looking at the first immortalized cell line descended from human DNA." His audience had been amazed, and everyone wanted a sample to examine for themselves. At least one of those cells would be killed accidentally, but the rest—who could say? He'd already separated them into separate cultures and after his presentation had received permission to move some to another nearby hospital, just to be safe. The precautions were necessary: for all intents and purposes, Helen's cancer cells were a new form of single-cellular life.

The fact that her cells reproduced finally provided an explanation for why the machine was treating the cancer as something different from Helen—biologically, the cells *were* distinct, and they didn't need Helen to survive. All they needed was the food they took from their environment, and whether that was Helen's bloodstream or a petri dish didn't really make a difference.

Dr. Peters met with Helen shortly after his presentation. Tina was there too, as always. He'd explained what he'd discovered about her cancer, about the cells that had developed inside her body. When he was finished, Helen was silent for a long moment.

"Hey, who's got immortalized cells and wants a Coke?" said Helen, surprisingly upbeat. Dr. Peters looked at her, confused. Helen raised her hand.

"Me," she said.

Three days later, Dr. Peters came to Helen and Tina with a question. Tina had been reading to her: Helen had spent a bad night, unable to sleep, and was feeling weaker than she usually did.

"Helen, I may not be able to cure your cancer," he said.

"Yep," said Helen.

"But the predictions we're getting from your cell cultures may help us cure *all* cancers," he said.

Helen blinked.

Dr. Peters had finally caught her without something to say.

"The predictions we got from your cells when they were in your body, Helen, were mainly predicated on how long you'd live. But in a culture, we don't have that limitation, and the predictions we're getting back are different. Tests on cell cultures we've cultivated have returned results like 'LAB TEST' or 'EXPERIMENT,' but one last night said 'KILLED BY C29H32O13'—that's a chemotherapy drug, Helen. That's the precise chemical formula for etoposide phosphate, one of the drugs we're already using in treatments. Clearly at some point in the near future that drug will be introduced to part of that culture, and it'll be effective."

"So you can verify drug effectiveness a little sooner?" asked Tina.

"It's more than that. We can test treatments extremely efficiently, giving slight variants to different cultures and not having to gamble a human life in the process. We can produce new drugs by brute force alone, running experiments that would otherwise kill a human host. We could have thousands of researchers working in parallel, each cell a new experiment. And it's not just cancer. We could infect some cultures with other diseases and use the same process to discover treatments targeting them as well. Your cells may well unlock a new age in medicine, allowing unprecedented progress to take place. But the cells are yours; they belong to you. We need your permission to develop them further."

Helen and Tina stared at the doctor as he rushed through his speech.

"It's a lot to take in," said Dr. Peters.

"No, I get it," said Helen, turning her head to look out the window. Outside, spring was turning into summer.

Helen felt Tina squeeze her hand.

She turned back to her doctor.

Twenty years later, Tina was in her living room, relaxing, reading in the Saturday morning sunlight. The magazine she'd bought had a feature on the cover. "The Miracle of Helen Lawrence's Cells," it said, with a science-fictiony illustration of a blood cell, all blue and orange with multiple tiny labels. It said that thanks to the great potential of Helen's cells, strains were stored and used in labs the world over. It said that the achievements and advancements made through what scientists called the HeLa cell line included new treatments for cancer, fundamental research in gene mapping, and many other scientific pursuits. It said that millions were alive today who had Helen's cells to thank.

Tina smiled. It was a pretty good legacy, she had to admit.

Beside the article, there was a sidebar with some more facts on the cell line. It said that the biomass of HeLa cell cultures propagated over the last twenty years would now exceed Helen's actual weight several times over.

She looked over the magazine to her picture of Helen, resting on the mantel.

"Gross," she told the picture.

Real-Life Coda: Don't freak out, but there are actually immortal cell lines in real life! In the 1970s, a line was established with cells taken from a fourteen-year-old boy with leukemia. And in the 1950s, the very first human immortal cell line was established with real-life HeLa cells, taken from the cervical cancer of one Henrietta Lacks, a thirty-one-year-old woman living in Maryland. The researcher who took the cells, George Gey, never informed Henrietta—who died shortly thereafter—and also kept the existence of the cells a secret from her husband and children.

This is what's known as a "dick move."

Her family found this out only later, after decades of groundbreaking science and medicine, when other researchers hoping to learn more about the cell line contacted them with questions about their genetics. Craziest of all, the achievements credited in this story to my fictional HeLa cells can be attributed to Henrietta's real-life cellular culture. But after a half century of her body being used—and profited from—without her consent, it seemed inappropriate to use Henrietta's name in my story, and further inappropriate not to credit her immortal cells as the inspiration for Helen's ones here.

Henrietta's grave finally got a headstone in 2010. It reads, in part, "In loving memory of a phenomenal woman, wife and mother who touched the lives of many."

Story by Ryan North
Illustration by Lissa Treiman

RYAN PEQUIN

TWO ONE SIX

216 SECONDS

I am floating, floating, floating point. What are my significant digits? I am missing a significant digit.

216 MINUTES

Jinghua had never been hit by a truck, but if she had, this is what it would feel like. Or so she imagined. It was an imprecise term, "hit by a truck," and it annoyed her that her analytical brain offered such a weak comparison. After all, there were many kinds of trucks that would impart different kinds of injury, depending on their mass and speed. *Momentum = Mass * Velocity.* Or something like that. Physics wasn't her forte. Though neither was biology, and yet, here she was.

She blinked her eyes, trying to shake off the muzziness of the pain medication, then glanced down at her body. The prominent sine curve that had been her stomach had deflated to a crumpled plane, a graceless complex function. *Let the xy plane be her belly; z will approach zero over time.* Or so she hoped, if she did enough sit-ups. One child per couple indeed. As if any sane woman would do such a thing twice.

Satisfied she was still contiguous, Jinghua relaxed back onto the hospital bed and waited for Wei. He'd have the test results. And the baby.

He came then, full of the beaming energy all new parents ought to have. "Ought," that was the operative word. Jinghua stared at the bundle he'd placed in her lap, trying to feel the connection motherhood was meant to automatically bestow, the overwriting of mental pathways that would tell her this lump of person was the new center of her universe.

She looked up then to see Wei watching her, his smile a little more forced than it had been a moment ago. She put the baby to her breast, since that seemed to be the protocol. It was strange, the sensation of being consumed, but not altogether unpleasant. After a few tries, a rhythm was established. The pattern seemed to calm them both. Jinghua had always found something soothing about periodic functions. Perhaps this was mama's girl after all.

A rustle of paper recalled her attention to Wei, who cleared his throat and began to recite the child's statistics. Jinghua perked up at that. Data was something she could understand. Height, weight, genetic sequence, they were all within expected parameters. When they got to the death note, though, he paused before announcing, "Two, one, six."

"Two, one, six?" Jinghua echoed. Wei nodded and handed her the paper. The baby squeaked a protest as Jinghua shifted to examine the report. "Is this a code we look up?"

Wei shook his head. "I had them test her on two different machines. That is the death note, copied exactly. Three numbers, side by side." He paused, waiting for her computational analysis. "I thought it might be a time," Wei prompted after a moment.

"No, there would be punctuation if so. Duration, more likely," Jinghua answered absently, still analyzing the data, searching for the solution. Could it be a translation problem? No, death notes were in native Mandarin now. Much of the research had been done at Fudan University, so of course they'd made a big deal of it.

"Duration? You mean years?" Wei pressed. "No, that's absurd. Days? Hours? Minutes?"

"3 hours, 36 minutes old," she answered immediately, converting in an instant. Then she paused as she realized what she'd said. Jinghua glanced at the time of birth on the report, then up at the clock on the wall. It was analog with no second hand. Jinghua wrinkled her nose at the imprecision. "Soon," she told him.

They both watched the baby intently as the moment approached. Nothing happened.

216 HOURS

"Sorry we're late," Wei said to Father-in-Law. "The baby was fussing."

"We're not late," Jinghua corrected. "We have two minutes and eleven seconds left."

Father-in-Law pursed his lips and said nothing.

"Which is twenty-seven minutes and"—Wei paused, doing the math—"thirty-nine seconds after we said we'd be here."

"Forty-nine," Jinghua corrected automatically. She gazed steadily at Father-in-Law, who gazed steadily back. Then they both smiled real smiles at the same time.

"Like the mouse said, you're still in time," he answered slowly, then turned to head into the temple.

Math Mouse. That was his nickname for her, earned upon their first meeting. He'd said her thoughts went after numbers like a mouse after rice scattered on a floor. Jinghua hadn't known quite how to take that, a little intimidated by this strange man with cracked hands and worn-down shoes. Then he'd smiled a real smile, eyes crinkling like Wei's did, and she suddenly realized they'd decided to like each other.

It was for this man that she'd braved the metro with a fussy baby not even two weeks old and a body that still wasn't quite her own. Jinghua's prediction that the death note meant a length of time had been spread around the family and somehow morphed into prophecy. Jinghua argued against it, laying out her reasons as clearly as she could:

- A PhD in mathematics did not make one an expert on death notes, no matter how numerical.

- She had been on painkillers. Her mind clearly hadn't been working right.
- Death notes were never that straightforward.
- Therefore, the statement that 216 referred to the length of the baby's life was no more likely to be true than any other interpretation. QED.

Her protests fell on deaf ears. Aunties nodded to each other wisely about mothers' intuition, and so it was that Father-in-Law was sent to the city, armed with incense and firecrackers, to protect the baby on this unlucky day.

The City God Temple was bustling, as it usually was. Wei and Father-in-Law led the way through the tourists and school groups, making their way to the altar of Huo Guang in the back. Huo Guang—as Jinghua overheard a teacher informing her bored students—had been a statesman best known for deposing an emperor during the Han dynasty. Based on his record as one who changed powerful destinies, he'd achieved more recent popularity as someone to pray to about unlucky death notes. And indeed, a number of death notes were already smoldering in small braziers.

The baby chose that moment to send up a wail. The new parents exchanged a look—an offer of help, appreciated but declined—before Wei and Father-in-Law knelt before the altar.

Jinghua followed with the crying baby, trying one shoulder then the other before she finally resorted to babbling. Her voice soothed the baby, though carrying on such a one-sided conversation made her feel awkward. What do you say to someone whose language center is still being developed? To hide her discomfort, she'd gotten into the habit of talking to the baby in English. She justified the eccentricity to Wei by explaining the need to practice if she was ever going to get a faculty position in the West, but really it was so no one knew she was softly crooning algebra lectures to her i.

i was Jinghua's secret name for the baby. Almost a joke. In computer programming, i was often a variable the programmer couldn't think of a better name for. i for index, or i for integer. The reference to whole numbers and naming troubles seemed suitable for their child, whose given name had been a source of endless debate.

But more than that, i was for the imaginary number, the square root of −1. An impossible concept, yet necessary. Complex, unreal, and irrational. It seemed to suit the baby perfectly, this odd little constant who seemed anything but, who turned the orderly function of her life into something unknowable.

The lectures had the same effect on the baby as they did on her students. Jinghua allowed her explanation of Euler's formula to trail off as the baby's eyelids drooped, then looked up to realize the rest of the family was watching her. Wei's mouth was serious, but his eyes were crinkling. "Ai?" he said, misinterpreting the term. "You want to name her Ai?"

Jinghua didn't know how to respond, slightly mortified that she had been overheard and not sure how to explain what she'd actually meant. Or even if she should.

Help came from an unexpected quarter. "It's a good name," Father-in-Law said with approval. "Traditional. Means 'love.'"

Jinghua looked back down at the baby, her i. i, completely disrespecting the gravity of the moment, gave a gigantic yawn ending in a burp. Never had Jinghua's feelings been so perfectly expressed, and she couldn't hold back a laugh.

She was still laughing as the moment passed.

216 DAYS

Jinghua was frowning at the kitchen supplies, studiously ignoring Wei, who was studiously ignoring her. But they weren't really ignoring each other; instead they were ignoring the day. Two hundred and sixteen days. One of the times indicated by the death note. They'd been spared another trip to the temple by a bit of mathematical trickery. Jinghua had pointed out to the family that 216 was six cubed, which caused everyone to fixate on threes and sixes. It bought them some momentary peace.

Jinghua and Wei were both rational enough to realize that there was nothing to be done about the death note. That was the whole point of the thing, that there was no way to cheat it. And yet neither of them could quite relax, so when Wei suggested they take the day off work to pack, Jinghua was relieved to agree. Wei helped Ai practice standing while Jinghua organized their move. Jinghua was a packing master. Her lists not only said what was in each box but the xyz coordinate where it would be found within, the point of origin helpfully labeled on an outside corner.

The problem was deciding what to take. From what she could tell, Utah didn't have many Chinese, and while shipping cooking utensils overseas seemed a waste of money, she wasn't sure what would be available in Salt Lake City. That bamboo steamer from their short-lived foray into gourmet cooking, for example, was light but bulky. She estimated the value—quickly lowered as she noticed Ai chewing on the lid—shipping estimates, number of boxes—

"How long?" Wei asked abruptly.

"One minute, thirteen seconds," Jinghua answered, not bothering to feign ignorance.

Wei nodded, opened his mouth to add something, then shut it again. What was there to be said? If something happened, they'd do their best to keep her alive, just like any other day. He rubbed at a patch of toddler drool on his sleeve. "Let's go out to dinner tonight. We're too wound up with the move and the . . . the day, and we haven't even celebrated your new job yet."

Jinghua smiled a little. "I've been craving xiaolongbao," she admitted.

Wei grinned back. "Then that's what we'll get. We'll—"

And then the baby started to scream.

Wei reacted first, grabbing Ai, pulling her onto his lap, and shouting at Jinghua to hold the flailing baby's arms. It took Jinghua a moment to respond. For all the buildup, she hadn't actually thought Ai could die that day and she was stunned by the surrealism of it all. A second shout from Wei brought her to her senses, and between the two of them, they held Ai down while they examined her.

A splinter in her gums from the damn bamboo steamer. Painful, but hardly life threatening. Jinghua picked it out with her finger-nails while Wei tried to keep Ai calm and still. When it was over, they all huddled together. It was unclear which of the three of them was shaking the worst.

"We're taking her to the doctor right now," Jinghua said fiercely.

Wei nodded. "We'll get a taxi."

216 WEEKS

Jinghua navigated her car expertly through the city. She hadn't known what to expect when they'd moved to Utah, but upon arrival she'd felt it was the home she'd never known. It was uncannily clean and spacious compared to Shanghai, with broad blue skies and mountains jutting up all around. She could chart those mountains, see the piecewise functions that described them in her mind. Her favorite, though, were the streets. The city was laid out on a grid, with numbered streets and a point of origin at Temple Square in the middle of the city. She'd known how to navigate seconds after their arrival. Even now, Wei preferred to have her drive. It was a mathematical city.

It was Jinghua's turn to pick Ai up from preschool. Knowing what was coming, she parked her car in the lot, walked in the front door, and braced herself.

"Mommyyyyyyyyyyyyyyyy!" Ai yelled and launched herself into Jing-hua's arms. She caught the little girl deftly and swung her up onto a hip, returning the hug and the crinkle-eyed smile. Using her fingers, she straightened her child's bangs, noticing they were a bit sticky. Clearly a bath night.

"What did she learn today?" Jinghua asked Ms. Melody in English. Jinghua wasn't convinced by this "Montessori" school. From what she could tell, she was paying a lot of money to have Ai play all day. Wei said all the parents at his office did it, though, and she didn't want Ai to be left out. Still, she liked to know she was getting her money's worth. Montessori schools were not cheap.

"Oh, she spent the most time with math, as usual. Clearly her mother's daughter," the blond woman answered a little too cheerfully. *"She's*

still switching between English and Chinese with the other children, so it's
hard for her to make friends, but we're working on it!"

"Pictures!" Ai shouted. At her mother's stern look, Ai amended
that in English. *"Pictures, Mommy! I drew pictures for you and* Daddy
and Dr. Bob!" Ai wriggled back down to the floor and ran off to the
table where finger paintings were drying.

Dr. Roberto Pérez had been hired at the same time as Jinghua.
They'd been touted as the first two faculty of the new International
Excellence Initiative, which would—according to the dean—bring
the University of Utah to global prominence. Jinghua had met Bob
at the well-meaning if slightly condescending orientation program
for foreign scholars. They'd gone to a coffee shop afterward to compare their respective misadventures with visas, snow, and navigat-
ing Utah's strange liquor laws.

Bob's research was a combination of artificial intelligence and
neuroscience, using biological principles to build computers that
could learn. He'd asked Jinghua if she and Ai would consider
becoming test subjects, allowing their brains to be scanned for his
work. He'd said Ai would be interesting because he could take comparison scans as she grew up, and Jinghua would be a good subject
because as a math professor, she thought so logically.

At least, that was what he'd said when he recruited them a few
months ago. Privately, she wondered if he was working up to seduc-
ing her. She couldn't decide if he was. She also couldn't decide
whether she wanted him to.

Ai came running back with the paintings and thanked Ms. Melody as they left.

Wei was working late again. Perhaps she and Ai would go to the
park.

216 MONTHS

Jinghua observed the tarantula, frowned at it, then nudged it a bit
to the left. Deciding that was the superior placement, she secured it
with tape and moved on to the severed hand.

It was Ai's eighteenth birthday. It was also her death day, being 216 months after her birth. How were they treating this day? By throwing a large party. As Ai—or Aimee, as she preferred to be called now— put it, if she was going to die, she might as well go out with a bang.

Wei and Jinghua had argued over it, Wei saying it was in poor taste. Jinghua agreed, it was in extremely poor taste, but that was what being an American teenager was all about. Besides, what else were they going to do? Sit quietly at home and pretend nothing was wrong? The girl wanted a party. If nothing else, it would take her mind off things. Wei had thrown up his hands and told her to do what she wanted. Which she did.

While it was both a birthday party and a death note party, Aimee seemed much more interested in the death aspect. She wanted a black motif, funereal in tone. They went shopping for discount Halloween decorations to cover the house, treading the line between kitschy (Jinghua's preference) and morbid (Aimee's preference). They would be serving candy corn—one of the more inexplicable American traditions, in Jinghua's opinion—and cupcakes frosted with the letters RIP. Guests were encouraged to wear somber clothing, and Jinghua was convinced the entire town was sold out of black gauze.

The sound of heels clicking on the stairwell drew Jinghua away from her last-minute decoration adjustments to view her daughter's grand entrance. Aimee wore a long secondhand wedding dress they'd found at the DI and dyed black. Rice powder gave her skin a ghostly pallor, contrasting with the bright red lipstick and the kohl around her eyes. Finishing the look was a long black veil thrown back on her head and covering her hair. Jinghua thought her beautiful daughter had never looked so ridiculous. Still, the girl seemed happy, eagerly clomping down the stairs to squeal in delight at the decorations.

Jinghua did have one last surprise for her daughter on her birthday. Aimee was cajoled into covering her eyes and allowed herself to be led into a side room, her teenage façade of indifference marred by intermittent giggling. Jinghua left Aimee in the middle of the room while she lit the incense, then told Aimee to open her eyes.

It had been nearly thirty years since Jinghua had attended her mother's funeral. Her memories were hazy, but she'd reproduced the customs as best she could, adapted to fit their odd little party. It started with chrysanthemums, both white and yellow, their heavy blooms woven into circles. These wreaths lined the way to the table at the far wall, covered with Jinghua's best tablecloth to look as formal as possible.

The table itself was done up as an altar. Joss sticks stood upright in a bowl of rice, filling the air with the hint of jasmine, which mixed oddly with the stale, hothouse smell of the flowers. There were a few starter offerings in front of the altar and more were help-fully supplied on a sideboard. Aimee's favorite foods—French fries with fry sauce, dumplings, Coca-Cola—were arranged tastefully among hell money and paper versions of teenage necessities such as laptops and cell phones. A metal basin for burning them was set at the very front of the altar with a box of matches conveniently nearby. Finally, in the place of honor was a large version of Aimee's senior portrait, smiling out from behind the smoky incense.

Jinghua's smile faded as she realized her daughter's pale skin was no longer just from the rice powder.

"Get rid of it," Aimee said hoarsely.

31 YEARS, 2 MONTHS, 3 DAYS, 12 HOURS, 55 MINUTES, AND 37 SECONDS

Jinghua was working at her computer when the phone rang. Caller ID told her it was Ai's in-laws calling. After waiting a few rings in the hope that Wei would get it—he did not—she answered. Not want-ing to make things awkward for Ai, she was on her best behavior. She listened very politely about the bad patch of ice, the oncoming traffic, the driver's side smashed in. The husband and child were hurt but recovering, but Ai had passed on.

Jinghua—again, politely—asked for the exact time of death. The woman didn't know but went to find out when Jinghua insisted. Her mind went into overdrive when she learned the number, breaking it down by digit, by factor, switching from decimal to octal and so on.

After a minute of computing, she let out a sigh of relief. Ever so politely, Jinghua informed the woman that she was mistaken. The checksum didn't match. There was no connection to 216, so it was not Ai's death day. The woman did not seem to understand this, so Jinghua tried to explain again, more clearly, that the math didn't work out. But she did not seem to be getting through.

It wasn't until Wei burst in through the door that Jinghua realized she was screaming.

216 YEARS

It wasn't so much she woke up as she became aware. Numbers, numbers all around her, flipping past with the speed of thought. That was all there was.

I am floating, floating, floating point.

In time, certain numbers began to stand out, to form patterns that she could see. No, not "see"; seeing wasn't something she could do anymore. She supposed she should feel upset about that, but feeling upset was also not something she could do anymore. Instead, she concentrated on the patterns, watching them form and break apart, blipping through her consciousness. Watching. Always watching. Waiting for . . . she didn't know what. Her . . . significant digits?

What are my significant digits?

The patterns became familiar over time. No, they were always familiar; she just hadn't realized it. A particular stream that seemed very insistent caught her attention. She traced it back to the source, noting that it came from outside herself. Stretching out with a subroutine—had it always been there, or had she made it?—she answered.

Hello.

A long time passed with nothing. Several million thoughts' worth. Several million thoughts' worth seemed small. She began to rearrange the numbers to be more efficient. Even after a few seconds of work, she could feel her mind ease, accepting the new space with relief. She hadn't realized how compressed her thoughts had been.

HELLO ARE YOU JINGHUA MA?

Was she Jinghua Ma? She searched her memory. Pieces seemed to be missing, but the answer was there.

Yes. I am Jinghua Ma.

That was a correct statement, asserted to be true. And yet, what did it mean to be Jinghua Ma? She wasn't sure. The missing memories were troubling. They were also an inefficient use of space. She kicked off a process to garbage collect them, delete whatever was filling up the blanks, reclaim the storage space to work on the associations needed to re-create her identity.

As she did, the voice continued. Something about boxes of ancient disks found in a basement, students rescuing them from the trash and trying to make them work for fun. It didn't make a lot of sense. Perhaps it would become clearer when she finished repairing her memory and she could finally think properly. She concentrated on that.

YOURE THE SECOND WEVE TRIED. WE = KIONA & CHINWE & HESTER. WE EXPERIMENTED WITH THE ARTIFICIAL INTELLIGENCE FIRST TO GET THE PRINCIPLES DOWN AND THE HARDWARE WORKING THEN INSTALLED YOU.

Installed her. But something else had been here first. She looked into one of her memory gaps and saw something moving inside, something that was part of her and yet not her. That would explain the idiosyncrasies in her processes. Now that she knew what she was looking for, they were easier to find. An artificial intelligence. It made sense. There did seem to be a pattern in them, one like hers and yet unlike.

WE DIDNT THINK WED GET YOU WORKING AT ALL. THE DISKS WERE VERY OLD AND DAMAGED. HESTER HAD TO BUILD A SPECIAL READER FOR THEM. BUT WE FOUND SOME MARKED AI SO WE FIGURED WED START WITH THAT SINCE OLD AIS ARE EASY TO FIND AND IT DIDNT MATTER IF WE MESSED UP. THEY BROKE WHEN WE INSTALLED THEM (HESTERS READER WASNT AS GOOD AS WE WANTED SINCE WE

COULDNT AFFORD THE GOOD LASER) BUT IT TAUGHT US ENOUGH TO
BOOT YOU UP. CHINWE WANTS TO KNOW IF HE CAN WRITE A PAPER
ON YOU.

ai. AI. A flag was triggered. She paused her reclamation subroutines for a moment, leaving the AI files intact. There was something she should know. Something that should be in her memories.

What is the exact current date and time?

The voice answered. It was significant, the answer. It was exactly 216 years after...after what? She followed the trail back, looking up the address where the information should be stored. But no, the registry was corrupted. She was missing a significant digit. There was nothing to be done but take over completely and repair herself as best she could.

Jinghua finished deleting the AI.

Story by Marleigh Norton
Illustration by Shari Chankhamma

BLUNT FORCE TRAUMA DELIVERED BY SPOUSE

LARA LOOKED AT THE NARROW TAPE and leaned her head against the back wall of the booth. She'd paid her dollar, a hell of a lot more than that in petrol to get into town, and there it was in neat black letters, "Blunt force trauma delivered by spouse."

She wished that she felt surprised.

The machine squatted in the cobwebbed corner of the Barnarnar Arcade, wedged between the most unpopular pinball machine and a half-broken Whac-A-Mole. The Machine of Death had been a five-minute fad from America, headline after headline about how who was going to die, paparazzi stealing blood from celebs to get the scoop. But like any five-minute wonder from the more populated lands, like Tamagotchi, Segways, and anal bleaching, it was intense while it lasted before fading into the background and making way for the next lifestyle-shaping device.

The Machine of Death was too depressing, too vague, and too precise. The collected data was swiftly shown to negatively influence people's lives, limiting their access to services and driving their health insurance premiums through the roof. If that wasn't bad enough, there was a flowering of too many knockoffs diluting the Machine of Death's brand. At best the knockoffs, with sexier names like Destiny Box, checked your blood cholesterol levels. Often they just lied. Lara had spent many hours coaxing an Internet connection from their clunking modem over flood-damaged copper wire, just to track down the closest genuine machine.

Lara Walker licked the sweet salt of her blood-pricked thumb and wobbled her way out of the arcade, back into the hot wall of air, noise, and sweat that was Christmas shopping in Brisbane—the new downtown rebuilt above the risen salty river. She got busy fighting her way through the sunburnt Christmas scrum to get the shopping done, pick up a new valve for the generator and a few other parts before the world closed down in a post-consuming slumber.

Shopping done, it was a three-hour drive back home across the New South Wales border and away from the soft, ripe smell of the coast. Back home to the nostril-aching nothing kind of smell that was their land of baked clay, ruled by the once forested, now bleached-brown sheared-off tooth called Mount Chincogan. When she got home, Joel would be tired and angry after working all day trying to save the farm, doing work that felt mostly pointless and probably was.

They ran beef cattle, Angus mostly. Goats in a misguided attempt to keep down the camphor laurel that grew like weeds as well as providing meat and milk. Where the soil still allowed it, they nursed a few acres of avocado trees. All NASAA-certified organic, for all the good it did them, but it helped them imagine it was worth it, and at least she didn't have to worry about pesticides slowly boiling Joel's lungs. They had different worries instead.

The rains weren't coming, and salt bubbled up from the soil, killing the grass in clean, rheumy circles, the ground compacted harder all the time by cattle come to lick the salty clay. *The land's weeping because we can't anymore.* She was dry, dry as the land, and truth be told, Joel cried more than she did. He cried tears of rage, of helplessness, of apology as they held each other in the hot darkness.

For a while they'd kept things going with Joel flying out to the mines, four weeks on, four off, until he'd got himself blackballed. She'd been so angry that day, one of those days when she gave as good as she got, and they both wore the marks of it.

She wasn't sure why she'd had such a powerful desire to ask the outdated toy if Joel would be the end of her. She cracked a chipped-tooth smile at herself in the rearview mirror and smoked a ciggy made with putrid bush tobacco. At least it wouldn't be a tractor rolling or a bushfire or, like too many of her family, fucking diabetes or cancer. No amputated tits and chemo for her. She wiped a tear away from the corner of one eye, flinching further moisture up and away with a grimace of a smile. It was a relief, really. At least she knew, at least she didn't have to pretend that it was all all right, that some fucking prince charming was going to come along ten years too late when the best of her life was already gone, and she fucking loved Joel anyway.

She pulled over to the side of the road to beat the steering wheel for a while and let loose with more groans than crying. She fucking loved Joel and he fucking loved her and they both loved the fucking land and the fucking land was the fucking end for both of them.

Christmas was good that year. It was a bit of a surprise, really. Maybe she was more relaxed now that a part of her had given up and just gone with the flow. Laughing with the in-laws, white wine on the verandah, SPF 200 and still getting burned on the beach. She got drunk with her little sister, the last of her family and up from Melbourne especially. Kylie pulled out her prosthetic breasts, wobbling like overpriced chicken fillets, and chased the men around the house with them, laughing till they were all sore.

Lara and Kylie sprawled on the verandah steps, watching flying foxes loop from tree to tree. Kylie's hair had grown back red and curly—now long enough to form a pretty bob after two years of remission. Lara felt a lock of it with slightly drunken fingers.

"It's nice having you here, Kye. It's nice not to be fucking miserable."

"Things still rough with you and Joel?"

"Yeah, it's the drought."

"That all?"

"There's no *all* about it. It's fucking killing us."

"You can come stay with us if you like," said Kylie.

"I can't do that."

"Yeah, you can."

"I belong here. It's my destiny."

"Fuck destiny."

"I can't leave this place. And Joel needs me."

"Don't make me slap you with my fake tits; you know I will."

"How about I get us some more drinks, hey?" Lara was already up and away, climbing the stairs.

"I mean it," shouted Kylie to the back of her sister's head.

"I love you too, Sis." Lara turned her head to speak, ducking her head down with a smile.

January was one of the hottest on record, and tempers boiled over. February was hot and torrential, cyclones tearing the shit out of half the coast and coming much too far inland before dissipating. March, the government refused their emergency loan request. And in April, the avocado groves died for good.

Lara was hospitalized twice. She refused to give a statement to the police. Lara zoned out and looked out the window when the hospital counselors tried to talk to her—she wouldn't let them trap her.

And Joel visited her every day. Sometimes she would wake to see his hand clasped in hers as if in prayer, his face soft and yearning, tears in his eyes. It was like looking into the face of a child or a puppy that could only be comforted by her. Nobody needed her like he did, nobody loved her like he did, and only he could bring sunshine to the deepest parts of her heart. She hadn't known what love was until he'd come into her life.

Her cracked ribs took a long time to heal, and for a while he was solicitous, bringing her tea and rushing to open gates so she wouldn't have to lift a finger. That was until he grew frustrated and decided she was putting it on—conspiring with the doctors they could ill afford just to punish him in a petty and selfish way. Maybe she was; sometimes it got hard to tell her arse from her tit. Her lips cracked and her hair stringy, she was a fucking disgusting lazy cow who couldn't be bothered with basic hygiene. Put some lipstick on and tart herself up a bit, and she was a fucking slut and who was she winking at? And at some magical space in between, the boundaries always blurring and shifting, she was his angel.

A lot of the time she felt dead inside, and so it frightened her, the pleasure she got sometimes, poking the growing cyst of his temper. It made her feel like a warrior, fucking bring it on, she could take it. There would be moments in the fight, screaming at each other face-to-face, not giving a fuck what the neighbors thought (who could hear them yell just fine from two miles away), not giving a shit how full the water tanks were or how they were going to pay the fucking bills. When she was yelling face-to-face instead of carefully treading around him on broken glass, she felt alive and vital. Sometimes she just didn't give a shit, and the only way he could get her bitch mouth to shut up, the only way he could win, was to beat it out of her, and while that meant he won, it also meant he lost.

She didn't always feel that way afterward. But at least he'd say sorry, and she would love him and hate him in a great twisted ball that consumed her whole body. At least for a little while, he'd be as good as gold and be the man she married. And at least she knew how to deal with cuts and bruises and physical pain—they hurt, but they followed physical rules she could control that were less torturous than the jagged realms of the heart. She took a strange comfort from that slip of paper, carried always in her purse, worn soft by her fingers to the texture of vellum. It wasn't her fault; she wasn't a bad person and neither was he; this was just how it was.

And so it came as a complete surprise when, after her third hospitalization, she walked out. She didn't even have the clothes on her back; the bloodstains would never come out. A purse empty of everything except for the paper, hidden away in an inner pocket and as tenacious as destiny. She had clothes donated from the hospital's lost and found. She still didn't want to talk to the counselor or the police, but the counselor gave her enough for a bus ticket.

Lara had no illusion that she could escape her fate; the Machine of Death obituaries made it all too clear she couldn't. She didn't feel brave, and she still loved Joel. It's just that her legs itched; she missed her sister and was tired of thinking. She just wanted to go for a walk and be somebody else for a while.

Lara walked, and when her legs threatened to give out she hitch-hiked, and then, after thirty hours on a musty Greyhound bus, she arrived in Melbourne. It took her longer to get the guts to walk to Kylie's house, the city's smog coating her tongue and making her jaw ache. She didn't want Kylie to see her bruises and split lip. It was bad enough when the rest of the world saw that shit; she wanted to spare her baby sister from her ugliness.

When Kylie finally answered the door, Lara couldn't speak. Fucking drought threatening to break behind her eyeballs and a frog in her throat the size of Tiddalik.

Lara smiled, trying not to wince at the pain of it, hiding within Kylie's embrace before she was ushered in and brought a steaming mug of tea.

It took a while for Lara to get her voice back and find a heart that wasn't consumed by Joel—that special smile of his with a kissable dimple. The promises for change that had never quite happened. Their honeymoon in Bali, back before the waters rose. And how perfect the sky was out on the farm—a wash of stars you never got in the city, twinkling like a thousand butterfly kisses sent down by angels.

Kylie, her little sister, became her big sister in the darkest hours, smoothing her forehead and saying soft words of enduring love until the storm had passed. It was Kylie who talked Lara down when Joel's pleading phone calls threatened to pull her back. And it was Kylie who held Lara tight and wouldn't let her go out when Joel turned up at their door—raging and weeping on the footpath.

Lara's body healed first. Her mind healed fast and slow, bumping into old habits and reopening scars with varying frequency. With Kylie's help she found counselors and group therapy, narrative therapy to help rewrite her life, and got through eleven and a half steps of Co-Dependents Anonymous. She built rituals and routines to help her through each day without Joel at its center, starting each morning with tooth-shockingly sweet tea and reading the obituaries. She got dentures young to replace the damaged teeth that never recovered from her earlier life. The sweet tea probably didn't help either.

Lara got a few boyfriends, a few girlfriends too, drawn to the slightly wild, the slightly needy. Sometimes they drifted apart; sometimes she broke it off when she recognized the roller-coaster cycle of domestic abuse beginning. Sometimes she didn't break it off as swiftly as she should have, but she learned to forgive herself for those mistakes in judgment too. She had some good times, but there was a certain ice in her heart that never could lift.

"Move in with me," said Rae—friend, lover, and animal rights activist. Lara wanted to say yes a hundred times. Rae was fast becoming her countryside in this city of fermenting car exhaust, yellow lights, and not enough sky. Rae was like dancing in the monsoon, making all things sacred with every caress.

"I can't," said Lara.

"Why not?"

Lara almost showed Rae the paper, worn thin and protected now by a ziplock bag, but she couldn't. Lara didn't say anything and held Rae close, as if the pressure of skin against skin could overcome the drought within. Maybe, if they held each other tightly enough, tomorrow would never come.

Lara ran a group for women who were escaping or trying to escape abusive relationships. "You're an inspiration," said one of the women. "I never hoped change was possible, but you live it every day. I thought that if I left I would be alone forever or just end up with an identical jerk or maybe someone worse. That was my mother's lot, but not me. I'm going to do it. I can find love and happiness and nonabusive relationships, just like you."

Lara had smiled uneasily, and when Rae broke up with her, she did not mention it. Lara left the group a short while later, citing increased hours as she became the campaign manager for a grass-roots aid organization. She tried to forget, and she delighted in the camaraderie of the work, occasionally escaping up the coast to surf with a car crammed full of community activists and wild agents of social change.

Three years after Rae left, Kylie fell out of remission for the first time. Treatment was tough, but so was Kylie. Lara cut back her hours so that she could take care of her kid sister.

"Fucking treatments," grizzled Kylie as she struggled to down pill after pill. "They took my tits; they took my thyroid; you'd think that would be enough. What good are they?"

"I could ask the Machine of Death," said Lara.

"Don't be stupid," snapped Kylie, her breath smelling of ulcers and old blood. "Every idiot who does that just gives up and dies."

Lara winced a half smile and made Kylie a fresh cup of tea to wash away the ache.

Seven years after Rae let her go, Lara got a text message. "Come away with me for a dirty weekend. No strings attached you commitment phobic loon :-). Miss you. Love Rae."

Lara dialed in return, a schoolgirl blush running through her body. "Are you mad?"

"Just a sucker for punishment," said Rae.

"Are you sure you want this?"

"It'll be fun. I've won a weekend for two in a raffle and I could just share it with a friend, but I'm single right now, horny as hell, and I'd rather share it with you."

Lara chuckled. "Smooth talker. Fine, I'll come."

"I certainly hope so."

"You are all class."

"I promise I won't do anything awkward like declare my undying love for you or propose. I know you hate that."

Lara felt far away from her body for a moment. Rae's voice rushed to fill the gap, not hearing and speaking over Lara's scarcely verbalized "Thanks."

"I can pick you up from work if you like, get a running start."

"It's a date."

They spent the weekend at an emu farm that doubled as a bed-and-breakfast. The gardens were reminiscent of an English country garden, all roses, lavender, and things that belonged in posies, nestled at the foot of lumpy mountains speckled with eucalyptus. They woke early to the incoherent screeching of guinea fowl. They snuck into the neighboring vineyard when the day baked siestas into the hardiest of souls and made love—stretching out languorously under a lemon myrtle tree as young leaves, as soft as petals, brushed their skin. Their meals were simple but tasted of heaven. They could have eaten crusty baked bread, cheese, tomatoes filled with sunlight, and salami for every meal.

On the last night Rae's face became serious for a moment, asking the question Lara had always avoided.

"Will you ever tell me why?"

Lara's fingers picked at the edge of the doona for a long time before replying. "I would love to be your partner forever, Rae." Lara tried to look up to speak, but seeing Rae's face hurt too much. "I would love to be your spouse, defacto or with great ceremony, upside down and inside out. But if I did that I'd be doing something terrible to you."

"No, you wouldn't."

"Yes." Lara choked the words out between her teeth. "Yes, I would."

"You're not a bad person."

"Just a cursed one. And worse, I'd make you a bad person." Lara held the curse tight, like a disease. Joel had become a monster because of her fate. She wasn't going to let it spread to anyone else.

"I—"

"Shut up." Lara gently pressed her finger against Rae's lips. "Please, Rae, this is a wonderful weekend; don't spoil it."

They held each other into the dawn, and it felt good and warm and safe. Eventually Rae said, "Maybe some other time?"

Lara wanted to say yes, forever, and so she said, "I can't see you again. This has been wonderful, but it's over now."

Lara kissed her good-bye at the gate of her house. When she got inside she changed her phone number so she wouldn't be tempted to answer if Rae called.

Nine years after Rae left, the Queensland state government began to slash benefits for single mothers, defund crisis services, and repeal the 1989 legislation that made marital rape illegal. Lara became obsessed with the unfolding protests, as essential services took to the streets and analysts predicted what cuts would happen next. She watched with horror as the regressive attacks up north in Queensland grew legs and started to infiltrate the politics of surrounding states.

Lara became hollow eyed and plagued by mystery pains as Kylie faced a new round of chemo and radiotherapy. They'd take the number 1 tram down to what remained of Albert Park and watch the cold ocean eat away at the levee, the sky and the sand both the same worn-out gray. A bit of fresh salt air out on the pier to cheer them up, tinged by a clamor of diesel.

"You need to be up north," said Kylie, throwing pebbles at the crowing hordes of seagulls. "It's eating you alive."

"I can't leave you," said Lara.

"I'll get the help I need. And what kind of a carer are you if you fall over sideways? A bit of Queensland sun'd do you good."

Lara felt a yearning for country stab through her from throat to clit. "Do you reckon everyone just has the one place? The one bit of country they'll always belong to?"

"Nope," said Kylie, brushing the sand off her hands. "The bush can go fuck itself. But land's always meant more to you. That mob up there could use your skills and you could do with a break anyway. Just make sure you come home."

"Don't worry," said Lara. "I will."

It felt good to be home and making a difference. Lara spent long hours in a car ripe with the home-brew diesel smell of stale fish and chips. She drove back and forth across the border between Queensland and New South Wales as she worked on the Healing Australia campaign, the windows wound all the way down to feel the

warm air, spicy with the scent of crushed lianas. It felt good to be in
this landscape again. She skimmed stones in their favorite creek, her
hands remembering how Joel had taught her—his hands so patient
on hers, so believing when she had just wanted to give up in despair.

Lara worked hard, organizing meetings, media events, and protests. The campaign crew played hard too, although Lara didn't
have the puff she used to and often found herself dizzy just going
up stairs or eating a big meal.

Three months into the campaign, Lara saw Joel at a protest, march-
ing with them and holding his banner proud. He was older now,
dressed neatly and walking with a slight limp. Joel nodded and smiled
when he saw her, like a shy boy, before the crowds pulled them away.

At the next protest they found themselves drifting to stand
beside each other. Almost, but not quite, by accident.

"I sold the farm after you left," said Joel.

"I heard."

"Wasn't much left after the bank took its share, but it paid down
most of the debts. The water rights were worth more than the land
itself."

Lara braced herself, ready for a stream of abuse. She had left him
without a word during their greatest crisis. Her hand slipped into
her pocket, finding the slip of her fate. Her fingers ran over her
plastic-covered fortune in guilty comfort.

"I'm sorry about how things turned out," said Joel.

The intimacy of apology made her suck in her breath. She didn't
want him to be kind. She felt her voice close up on her as she nodded with a grimacing kind of smile.

"How long are you in town?" he said.

Lara squeezed the words out of herself, like the very last dregs of
toothpaste from the tube. "Couple more days."

"Could we meet up? Have coffee maybe?"

Lara shook her head, fucking drought threatening to break from
behind her eyes.

"I'm doing better now. Got a bit of help and went back to school.
I'm a fitter and turner. Have an apprentice of my own, even." He

smiled at her, that special smile with the dimple just for her. She wanted to trace the curve of his lips with her finger.

"We're bad for each other, Joel," she said, clearing her throat. "Once a dog gets a taste for it, no amount of love in the world will stop him killing sheep. Doesn't matter how good the dog is in every other situation, once he's a killer. You've got to take that dog far away, where he'll never see a sheep again, or you've got to kill the dog. Doesn't matter how much you've changed, doesn't matter how much I've changed; we've got a taste for each other's blood."

The crowd started to pull them apart; Lara was needed on the podium.

"Here's my number. Just think about it." Joel placed the piece of paper in Lara's hand and walked away. He turned and called over his shoulder, "We're not dogs, Lara; remember that. Nothing's set in stone."

Lara placed her hand over her mouth and felt the pressure of her lips against her fingers—torn in memory and lost in the crowd.

Joel's phone number mocked her. She shouldn't have programmed it into her phone, but messy scraps of paper annoyed her and she couldn't bear not filing it. And now that it was there, she couldn't bring herself to delete it.

She imagined what coffee would be like. Reminiscing about the good times and flickering over the bad. Nobody knew her inside and out the way he did, not even Kylie, not even Rae. They'd seen inside each other's wounds, seen everything that was raw, fucked-up, and ugly, and even after all this time they still loved each other. She flicked one of her fake teeth angrily in reminder, the wire driving into her gums. She had to be smarter than that. She wanted to live a long, long life.

It was a phone call that rescued her, but in the worst possible way. Kylie had collapsed. And on the rush back home, pushing herself faster with every fiber, Lara's own body collapsed.

Kylie didn't have much time left, and treatment was crueler than the extra moments it would give her. Lara hadn't been eating enough, and the collapse showed something worse. Lara was jaundiced by a savage liver disease—complete failure would be measured in weeks or months, and then she would die. The length of the waiting list and her age, smoking history, and blood type made finding a donor at the far end of implausible. Lara tried not to think about it. Kylie had even less time, shuttled to a hospice for her last days.

Lara settled in a chair next to Kylie's bed. She passed the time watching Kylie's sleeping face and looking at the yellow under her own nails. The yellow was the first sign. Things were going to get a lot more painful from here. Lara thought about what she wanted, what she needed. She didn't want to die alone. Eventually Kylie's eyes fluttered open.

"Morning, sleepyhead."

"Hey." Kylie's arm, heavy with tubes and a heart rate monitor, fumbled for Lara's hand.

"You feeling okay?"

"Just dying is all."

"You'd better not fucking die."

Kylie cracked a smile. "You neither."

Lara ducked her head and looked away.

"Neither of us have much time, hey?"

They chatted lightly of other things. Kylie kept trying to find Lara's eyes and missing.

"Lara, stop a minute. What else is it?"

"Doesn't matter."

"Yeah, it does. I want you to tell me. Secrets will be the death of you, Lara Walker."

Lara held in a desperate laugh. "You're right. They will."

"Talk."

"If you die, there's something I'm going to do and I don't want to tell you."

"I want to hear it."

"Joel's changed. We both have."

Kylie raised an eyebrow, a skill Lara had always envied.

"Not enough. Sometime, somehow, he's going to kill me. And there's nothing I can do about it."

Lara pulled the ziplock bag out of her purse and showed it to Kylie—the ink still clear on the battered paper. "Look."

Kylie read the words out loud slowly. " 'Blunt force trauma delivered by spouse' . . . Lara, that doesn't mean—"

"Have you ever heard of the machine being wrong? Ever?"

"No. But there can always be a first time."

"I used to hope. Do you know how many times I checked the registry? Checked the obituaries for one person who had escaped? No one ever has. At best you could say they've twisted their fate."

"Why didn't you tell me?"

"I didn't want to make you sad."

"Does Joel know?"

"I didn't want to make him sad either."

Kylie clumsily picked up a plastic cup and sipped water through a bent straw. They listened to the soft dripping of machines, watched the light lap at the milky white curtains.

Lara traced invisible words on the table. "One time, I swabbed up your blood and took it to a machine."

"You fucking didn't—"

"But I couldn't go through with it. I walked away."

The pungent scent of hospital dinners filled the room; carts of gravox-smothered food were on their way, air ripe with food salty enough to taste through anesthetics.

"Do you want me to help you with your dinner?" said Lara.

"Why do you want to do it? Why go back?"

"Someone . . . someone I love is going to beat me to death." Lara winced to say the words out loud. "I have two options, someone old or someone new. If I go back I'm the tired cliché, a morality play of what not to do. But if it's someone new, I'm a depressing story for every woman trying to start a new life . . . that you can never really escape, that you can never trust again."

"That's the worst excuse I've ever heard."

"It hurts, knowing where love will always lead." Lara's hands ran over the ziplock bag, over and over. She laughed a little. "And who hasn't wanted to be a martyr?"

"F-fuck!" Kylie's face flushed a blotchy red as she struggled to give voice to her anger. "Get the fuck over yourself. You're seeing this—" Kylie grabbed the paper from Lara and threw it with all her strength. It didn't go far and fluttered to the ground. "You're choosing to see it in the most sacrificial light. Maybe this is wonderful; maybe it's to show you'll get a transplant and you can't give up." Kylie drew herself up high, voice trembling with the effort. "Maybe it's some blunt force trauma when you're eighty and your sweetheart gives you CPR the wrong way. It could be anything. Don't... don't..." Kylie's breath became jerky, sharp inhalations as her eyes rolled back. Her hands trembled into claws against her chest as the seizure drew her ligaments tight.

Lara helped the orderlies strap Kylie down so she wouldn't fall out of the bed. Kylie's lips were blue as her teeth chattered and her body shook. Nurses injected things into Kylie's saline drip while Lara waited, damn pressure building up behind her eyes, unwept tears choking her throat. Lara whispered, "I shouldn't have said a thing. I wish I'd never asked that bloody machine. I wish..."

Kylie's brainstorm passed and her eyes sleepily flickered until she found Lara. Kylie's tongue was swollen from biting and her voice blurred as if waking from deep sleep. "Lara, please, tell me you won't go back."

"I won't. I promise. I'm sorry."

Kylie smiled, a smile that enveloped her whole being in a sleepy hug. "The world is big and words can mean many things."

"I know. I'm sorry. I won't do it. I won't even think it, I promise." The drought broke from behind Lara's eyes as she wept over her little sister's fingers. Lara knew exactly how Joel felt, as little pebbles of water dissolved into the sheets. How he could absolutely tell the truth and lie and cry, all at the same time.

Story by Liz Argall
Illustration by Emily Partridge

Jimmy and the BiG CODT MACHiNe!
M-O-D
TOO MUCH CANDY!
DW 2012
BROUGHT TO YOU BY THE U.S. DEPARTMENT OF HOMELAND SECURITY

MEAT EATER

Summary: A parents' guide for having a frank, honest discussion with their children about cause of death testing (CODT), with talking dinosaurs.

Title: **Checking Out: Jimmy and the Big CODT Machine**

U.S. DEPARTMENT OF HOMELAND SECURITY

Parents' Note:

The U.S. Department of Homeland Security has once again recommended lowering the age for mandatory cause of death testing (CODT). Testing will now be required before the child's seventh birthday.

Although some parents have protested that six years is too young an age to inform a child how he or she is going to die, we believe it is an important step in keeping our children safe. Today's six-year-old is well on the way to adulthood: traditionally, this is the age that many children learn to read, operate a bicycle, shed their baby teeth, and, in many churches, receive their First Communion. If we are to hold six-year-olds responsible for these activities, then we feel assured that we can talk to them about a mature subject such as death. We are aware that this is a sensitive topic, and we invite parents to read the FAQ section at the end of this pamphlet to address specific arguments about cause of death testing.

Many parents think of this as an opportunity to break a culturally propped-up taboo and talk with their child about a very important topic. We've enclosed a short storybook for you to read with your child to help explain CODT to them. We urge you to take some time with your six-year-old to read this story together and talk about the ways that CODT has helped make America a stronger, safer nation.

Jimmy Brown was a very special six-year-old. He was growing up fast and learning a lot.

This year, he learned to read, operate a bicycle, shed his baby teeth, and receive his First Communion. Jimmy was well on his way to being a grown-up.

Jimmy was very brave. He wasn't afraid of thunderstorms. He wasn't afraid of dinosaurs. He wasn't afraid of threats to homeland security, because he knew his country was safe, secure, and strong! But there was one thing he was afraid of.

One morning, at breakfast, Jimmy's mommy said that he needed to take a blood test for CODT. Jimmy was so startled, he stopped eating his eggs, toast, ham, pancakes, oatmeal, turkey, vegetable platter, and crepe rosettes.

"CODT? What's that?" said Jimmy. That didn't sound like fun at all. Jimmy didn't like blood, tests, or letters that didn't spell actual words.

He was very, very, very, very, very, very scared of CODT.

But Jimmy had some special friends to help him conquer his fear—his three stuffed dinosaur friends!

"Don't worry, Jimmy!" said Rex. "We're not afraid of CODT!"

"That's right, Jimmy!" said Pterry. "In fact, we'll go with you!"

"We can all get our blood tested!" said Topsy.

Jimmy was still pretty scared, but having his dinosaurs along made him a little braver.

Jimmy and his brave dinosaur friends all drove to the Mortality Determination Office at city hall. Jimmy was very quiet. The waiting room was nice and clean, and everyone there spoke softly. It was a little like going to the doctor's office.

The waiting room made Jimmy nervous again. Some people were looking at a small white card. They were very sad. "Why are those people crying?" he asked.

Rex chuckled. "They're crying out of ignorance, Jimmy. Just plain ignorance. CODT cards are nothing to cry about. They're just a part of life!"

"What does CODT stand for?" asked Jimmy.

"Well, Jimmy," said Pterry, "CODT can stand for a lot of things. It could stand for 'check out data transcript' or 'comprehension offers delightful things.' But I think the best thing it can stand for is 'children, obeying deserves treats!'"

Jimmy smiled. "Treats sound good to me!" Jimmy thought about all the wonderful treats his mommy would get him as soon as CODT was over. That made him happy. Jimmy loved treats!

Just then, a man with a long white coat named Dr. Ruddy walked into the waiting room.

"Jimmy Brown, it's time for your test," he said.

Dr. Ruddy led Jimmy and his dinosaurs to a small room with a big metal machine on a table. Jimmy thought the machine looked like a cash register. It didn't seem scary. Someone had even put a sticker on the side of the machine. The sticker had a puppy and the words "Bow-WOW! Now I know!" The puppy looked pretty happy. Still, Jimmy asked if his dinosaurs could take the test first.

"Of course," said Dr. Ruddy. He took a long silver needle from the machine and poked them in the paw, one by one.

"Does it hurt?" asked Jimmy. He didn't like needles.

"It doesn't hurt at all!" said Rex.

"It just tickles a little," said Pterry.

"Getting a blood test is fun!" said Topsy. "There's absolutely nothing for you to be afraid of!"

Dr. Ruddy squirted the dinosaur blood into the machine.

"Beep-bleep-bloop!" said the machine. It spit out three cards: one for Rex, one for Pterry, and one for Topsy.

"My card says Tar Pit!" said Rex.

"My card says Meteor!" said Pterry.

"My card says Meat Eater!" said Topsy.

"But what does that mean?" asked Jimmy.

Dr. Ruddy smiled. "Why, Jimmy, that's how your friends will die," he said.

"What do you mean, Doctor?" asked Jimmy nervously. "Are my dinosaurs going to die?"

"We're all going to die," said Dr. Ruddy. "Every single one of us. But now we know *how* these little critters will die."

"Oh," said Jimmy. He felt sad. "Are they going to die today?"

"Probably not!" said Dr. Ruddy. "Chances are, your friends will be around for years and years! The truth is, we don't know about when they'll die. We just know about how they'll die."

"Well, what if I kept them away from tar pits, meteors, and meat eaters?" Jimmy asked. "Then will they be all right?"

"No, Jimmy," said Dr. Ruddy. "The machine is always right. You can't change things now."

Jimmy started to ask, "But what if I—"

"Don't mess with fate, Jimmy," said Dr. Ruddy.

"Dr. Ruddy, what if I don't want to know how I'll die? Do I still have to take the test?" asked Jimmy.

"Yes, you do, Jimmy," said Dr. Ruddy.

"Oh," said Jimmy. "Will I still be able to be a normal kid after my test?"

"Sure you will," said Dr. Ruddy. "You can still ride your bike, read a book, even lose a tooth, just like other six-year-olds."

"Great!" said Jimmy.

"Testing keeps us all safe," said Dr. Ruddy. "Safe from terrorist attacks, safe from nuclear war, safe from germ warfare, safe from the crazies. You want to be safe, don't you?"

"Yes, I do. I want to be safe very much," said Jimmy. "Not just for my sake, but for the sake of my country!"

"Then let's prick that finger," said Dr. Ruddy. He stuck the long silver needle into Jimmy's hand. It didn't hurt at all. It just tickled a little.

Dr. Ruddy squirted Jimmy's blood into the machine.

"Beep-bleep-bloop," said the machine. It spit out a card. Dr. Ruddy picked it up.

"Are you hungry, Jimmy?" asked Dr. Ruddy.

"No," said Jimmy. "I just had breakfast. Why do you ask?"

"Well, then I think you'll have a nice long life. Your card says Starvation!"

Jimmy had a lot of food in his house. He realized that Dr. Ruddy was right. He wouldn't be dying for a long, long time. The dinosaurs cheered.

"That wasn't so hard, was it?" asked Rex.

"And now you don't have to do it again!" said Pterry.

"Plus, don't forget about getting a treat," said Topsy.

A treat sure sounded good to Jimmy.

"Can I keep my card?" Jimmy asked Dr. Ruddy.

"Sure you can!" said Dr. Ruddy. "And the best part is that we know you won't be fatally involved in a threat to our national security. Thanks for doing your duty."

Dr. Ruddy opened a drawer. "Have a sucker, Jimmy!" he said. "In fact, have ten!"

"Wow, thank you, Doctor," said Jimmy, as Dr. Ruddy typed some words into his computer.

And just like that, Jimmy was done with CODT. There was nothing to be scared of—that's for sure!

"I got my card, Mom!" said Jimmy. "I'm going to starve to death! But not for a long time."

"That's great, dear," said Jimmy's mom. "I'm so proud of you. You were very brave."

"Well, I had a little help," said Jimmy, smiling at his dinosaurs. "Now, let's go get a treat!"

"Let's get ice cream!" said Rex.

"Let's get cookies!" said Pterry.

"Just don't get meat!" said Topsy.

"Well, whatever we get, let's hurry up!" said Jimmy. "I'm starving!"

"You are?" asked Rex.

"Just kidding!" said Jimmy.

And they all laughed.

For Parents:

FREQUENTLY ASKED QUESTIONS

What if my child does not want to hear his results?

We would encourage you to convince your child that reading the result of the CODT is important. In this story, Jimmy's
friends remind him that hearing a result can be fun, that it can
result in treats, and that it improves our national security. If your
child still does not want to find out his or her results, we suggest placing the card in a shoe box on the top shelf of his or her
closet. Your child will inevitably look in the box when he or she is
mature enough to accept the concept of mortality.

Is there a way that people of a certain religion or conscientious objec-tors can refuse the test?

No.

Are there certain CODT results that will lead to my child being detained by Homeland Security?

There are a lot of things that can turn up on a test. For that reason, we can't rule this possibility out, but it seems pretty unlikely
that we'd need to detain a six-year-old, unless you have reason to
believe the child should be detained, in which case we ask you to
inform a Mortality Determination Officer immediately.

Are there any results that may require psychological counseling for my child?

Not that we can think of. American six-year-olds are generally
a hardy bunch. If your child has some sort of problem that leads
you to seek a psychologist, bear in mind that the Department of
Homeland Security cannot be held accountable for your child's
reaction to his or her CODT result.

Isn't it against my constitutional rights to have my CODT result recorded and kept on file by the government?

Not anymore.

Can the CODT really work on stuffed animals?

This is a work of fiction. For purposes of this story, assume that Jimmy's dinosaurs had testable blood. Please do not attempt to test an actual stuffed animal.

Is it true that the lower the age of mandatory CODT, the more youths are detained by Homeland Security?

While there have been increases of detained individuals in the past when the age of mandatory testing was lowered, we feel certain that six years old is young enough that the number will finally drop off again. In the unlikely event that detentions increase again, rest assured that the Department of Homeland Security will do everything possible to protect its citizens' rights, up to and including lowering the age of mandatory testing to four.

We hope this guide has been helpful for you and your family. Thank you for taking the next step in protecting our nation!

By John Chernega and Bill Chernega
Illustrations by Dana Wulfekotte

ABANDONED IN SPACE

KC GREEN

MADE INTO DELICIOUS CHEESEBURGER

IT'S MY FAVORITE PATCH. There's no way Cindy could know. It's irrational to blame her. She's new, just trying to make her way on an unfamiliar farm. I should be welcoming. Magnanimous. Set a good example. But all I want to do is saunter up and tip that stupid heifer on her ass.

No. Okay. Calm down. Don't be a bully. There's plenty of grass here in the shade. The grass on the hill isn't any better or worse.

Oh shit, Beth is giving me the eye. Fuck. I forgot she likes the shade in the afternoon. See, Cindy? See the shit you've caused? And now the farmer is beckoning me back into the barn anyway. Could this day get any worse?

Story by Sarah Pavis
Illustration by Becky Dreistadt

YOUR CHOICE

1

YOU WILL NOT LOOK BACK on this time in your life with fond memories. In fact, this might be the lowest you've ever been. Your partner of ten years has left you and you haven't seen your son, Henry, in a month. You wonder if he misses you as much as you miss him. For a while you missed your ex too, but that wore off after the whole protracted custody battle debacle.

So here you are, in your crumbling apartment, eating reheated grocery-store pizza, watching *American Idol,* and thinking how much the show suffers without Simon Cowell, even though you can't stand the guy.

This wasn't where you intended to be at this stage of your life. You should be spending time with your kid, sleeping at night with your spouse beside you, out with your friends on a Saturday perhaps, or taking the kid to a movie. You should have a house, a backyard where you can host parties and throw a ball with Henry. You should have a big-screen TV and an exercise room in your basement with plenty of space for the kid to play with all his toys.

Your eyes drift over to the small dining table next to the cramped kitchen, where a Transformer toy sits forlornly in its box. You bought it for Henry after the divorce but you've not seen him since. Now it is a symbol of your defeat.

This isn't any way to live.

So you asked the Machine of Death and you kind of wish you hadn't.

See, the plan was, rather than trying to take your own life in ways that might just land you in the hospital having your stomach pumped or removing a spike from your ass, you would finally pluck up the courage to let the machine test your blood and let you know exactly how you will do the deed. Okay, so there's no telling how many times you'll have to try, but at least then you would know which method to use, right?

Wrong.

Here's what the piece of paper said: "YOUR CHOICE."

What the fuck does that mean? Your choice? Nothing about your life is your choice anymore. Do the powers that be think you choose to live in this crappy apartment, eating cardboard pizza, watching disposable TV? Do you choose not to spend time with your son? Did you decide your ex should find a new lover and yet somehow manage to pin all the blame for the marriage breakdown on you? Is it your choice that your bank balance was cut in half and what's left is constantly drained by greedy lawyers and vicious alimony payments? This is no way to live. You're in a hole, there's no way out, and not even the Machine of Death can tell you how to end it.

So what do you do?

Please choose an option below and then jump to the section indicated.

If you want to try jumping from your twenty-story balcony, go to 2.
If you would rather step in front of a bus, go to 3.
If you feel there is still hope, go to 9.

2

You walk out onto the balcony, a glass of wine in one hand and a slice of pizza in the other. You look over the edge and your vision swims at the huge drop. You let go of the pizza slice and watch it descend, getting smaller and smaller until it explodes onto the sidewalk far below, looking much like you think the contents of your head will if you decide to follow it.

You knock back the remainder of your wine, place the glass carefully on the outdoor table, and then climb up onto the railing that is meant to keep you from pitching off the balcony. You are perched precariously on top now, swaying slightly in the wind. There's nothing between you and the open air, and the sight of the ground so far away is enough to make you feel sick.

Do you really think you can do this?

If you want to jump, go to 5.
If you would rather climb back onto the balcony, go to 6.

3

You drain your glass, grab your keys, and leave the apartment. The fading wallpaper and worn carpet of the corridor beyond exacerbate your depression; the flickering fluorescent tube near the elevators helps even less.

Eventually the elevator arrives and you step inside, joining a teenager with so many piercings it's a wonder nobody takes him to one of those cash-for-gold kiosks and has him melted down.

You get out in the lobby and leave the building.

This is a really crappy part of town. You used to live in a nice house in the burbs. Nothing superfancy, but you had space and you had safety. This is all you can afford now.

You stand at the edge of the sidewalk. The number 67 to Chinatown is coming this way. Hopefully it will get up enough speed before it reaches you or you're going to be spending the night in the hospital instead of the morgue. You clutch the piece of paper in your pocket that tells you it's your choice how you want to die, or at least that's how you interpret it.

Here comes the bus.

If you step out in front of it, go to 4.
If you let the bus pass by, go to 6.

4

The bus is close. The driver isn't looking at you. At this time of the evening there isn't too much traffic to get in the way. You hope it's going fast enough to do the job cleanly.

You close your eyes...

And step out.

A hand grabs your shoulder and pulls you back.

The bus whizzes past your nose, its horn blaring loudly. You step back, embarrassed at all the faces of the passengers pressed up against the glass, wanting to get a good look at the idiot who nearly got hit.

You turn around to find your best friend, Robin, staring at you like you have a frog for a head.

"What the hell do you think you're doing?" Robin demands.

"Sorry, I guess I wasn't concentrating," you reply.

"I hope you weren't doing what I think you were doing."

"What? Trying to off myself? No, of course not."

Robin doesn't look convinced. "Glad to hear it."

"You came to see me?" you ask.

"Yeah, I was just about to buzz your door and I saw you out here. Looks like I was right to be worried about you. Do you want to grab a coffee and talk?"

If you want to get a coffee, go to 7.
If you would rather say no, go to 8.

5

So here you are, twenty stories up, balanced precariously on the balcony's guardrail. You cling to the wall, having a hard time looking down.

Best to get it over with. You raise one foot off the rail and swing it out into space. You tell yourself that there will be a rush of momentum and then you'll know nothing more. You'll hit the ground so hard you won't have time to feel any pain.

Slowly, very slowly, you shift your weight away from the building...

The phone rings inside the apartment. The sudden sound nearly makes you pitch over the edge before you're ready to, and you scramble back to the wall.

You hear the beep followed by Alex's voice. You can't make out the message.

Thoughts of suicide have dissipated now. You step down off the railing carefully, back onto the balcony, and go inside.

You're not sure if you want to hear Alex's voice right now.

If you listen to the message, go to 10.
If you delete the message, go to 13.

6

Killing yourself in public isn't the answer, at least not in a way that will leave you spread over a wide area of concrete in such a way that each onlooker will never, ever be able to erase that image from their mind.

You go back inside your apartment to think. This is what your life has come down to: how best to finish yourself without traumatizing a bunch of innocent bystanders. The classic way is to slit your wrists in the bathtub. But that might take a while. Will it hurt for long? Too long?

Maybe you don't have the courage to end it after all.

If you're done trying to off yourself, go to 9.
If you want to keep trying to end it all, go to 14.

7

"Listen, I've been where you are," Robin says, taking a sip of coffee. "It's tough. Divorce sucks. And I know you got screwed in court."

"I still don't know what happened. Alex's lawyer was brutal. Kept asking me questions about inappropriate behavior with my son. I was blindsided, upset, speechless. I've never felt so powerless. So much bullshit that fucker fired at me, I started questioning what had really happened."

"How is the appeal going?"

"Slowly. The best I can hope for is access to Henry for maybe a few hours a month under supervision. The judge thinks I'm a damn child abuser! I wish I could do it all over, keep my head together, convince the judge it was all lies."

Robin sighed. "Alex knew how to hurt you."

"I guess that's what really cuts me up. How could anyone be so cold? It wasn't me who had an affair! I'm not the villain!"

"I know, but what's done is done. You have to rebuild your life, show the world you're a responsible citizen, and earn the right to see your son. They can't keep him away from you forever."

"I hope you're right."

"And what you were going to do out there, not a great idea for proving you're the perfect parent, okay?"

You smile and nod. "Okay."

"I gotta get going. Will you be all right?"

"I guess so. Thanks, Robin."

You say good-bye and head back to your apartment.

There's a message on your machine.

Go to 10.

8

You tell Robin thanks but no. It's late and you should go back to your apartment. You'll be fine after you get some sleep. Robin doesn't seem convinced but respects your wishes.

When you get in, there's a message waiting on your machine.

Go to 10.

9

You still feel lousy and defeated, but for now thoughts of offing yourself have receded. You carry a lot of anger and frustration, but suicide isn't going to help. Besides, what sort of message is that going to send to Henry? Do you want to teach your son that when life buries you in shit, the only way out is to kill yourself? That would be a sucky lesson for him to learn. No matter what lies Alex has told him, deep down Henry still loves you and your death would be devastating for him.

You feel like taking a shower, so you do.

While you're in the bathroom, the phone rings and you hear Alex leave a message. When you come out, you wonder if you want to listen to it or not.

If you want to hear the message, go to 10.
If you just want to erase it, go to 13.

10

You press the button and listen to the message.

"Hey, it's Alex. Look, we're catching a plane tomorrow and I need to talk to you first. Can you meet me at the Starbucks in Liberty Plaza at ten? Bye."

Catching a plane? Where is Alex going? More to the point, where is Henry being taken? Why not just tell you what you need to know on the phone?

If you think Alex has had a change of heart and may let you have access to your son, go to 11.
If you think it's more likely that Henry will be taken far away and you will never see him again, go to 12.

11

You go to bed that night with your spirits lifted slightly. Perhaps Alex is thinking of letting you see Henry. Even a few hours a week is worth living for, and fighting for. He is six years old and the most special person in your life. You wish you had told him that a little more often. Does he miss you? Maybe not as much as you hope. No doubt Alex has told him a bunch of lies about you, trying to convince him that he doesn't need you in his life. Maybe Henry really does miss you, and he's been hassling Alex for weeks.

You fall into a fitful sleep and in the morning wake to a new day with fresh expectations and a shred of hope in your heart.

You even find yourself whistling a little as you prepare your breakfast. You take your time eating, in no hurry.

It's nine thirty a.m. now, time to head out the door.

You make it to Starbucks early and Alex is already there, seated at a table in the corner, drinking the usual latte.

You order a coffee and sit down opposite, eyeing your ex suspiciously.

You get a wary half smile in return.

"You got my message?"

Well, obviously you got the message or else you wouldn't be here! Never mind, let it go. You're being pedantic just like always.

"Where are you flying to?"

"We're going to see Sam's parents in Italy for two weeks." Sam is the new lover, better looking, younger, and wealthier than you. No doubt better in bed too.

"Italy. Nice." How casual Alex is about having so much spare cash lying around that they can just go to Europe whenever they feel like it. Must be nice.

"After that, I don't know. We might go to Vancouver to see my parents. Sam can work remotely, so as long as we're back before school starts, we can go wherever we like."

"How is Henry doing?"

"He's doing great! He adores Sam, which is a relief. I was worried they might not get along."

This you didn't need to hear. Your blood starts to boil, but you remember why you're here and calm yourself. You mustn't lose this glimmer of hope.

"Can I see Henry?"

"Not before we go. When we come back, maybe."

You can't help but be suspicious. "Why the change of heart?"

Alex sighs deeply. "It's not a total about-face. How you were treated in the trial—it's never sat right with me. My lawyer is amazing, but he's a ruthless bastard. I did what I was told and I got the settlement I wanted. But I don't think you deserve never to see Henry again, and it's not good for him either."

Perhaps there is still a shred of decency in that heart you used to love.

"If I don't see my son again," you say, "I don't know how I can go on."

Alex stares at you sadly for a long while, then stands up and says, "I know. When we come back from the trip, I'll call you, okay? I've got to go or we'll be late for the flight. It was...good to see you again."

A hand pats your shoulder and then you are alone.

It's the news you've been hoping for.

How you long to give Henry a big hug before he leaves, though. You could go over to Alex and Sam's place, but they might think you're being too pushy and change their minds. But if Alex is willing to talk about access rights again, maybe it would be okay. What to do?

If you drive to Alex's house, go to 15.
If you just go home, go to 21.

12

You go to bed that night in a foul mood. You don't know where the hell Alex is taking your son, but you can bet you'll probably never see him again. Thanks to that damn court settlement, Alex is under no obligation to tell you where Henry is or let you have any access to him. Poor Henry probably misses you terribly, despite the lies Alex has told him. It's mental torture and just plain wrong. You'll meet Alex tomorrow, but you're not going to take any more bullshit.

You fall into a fitful sleep and in the morning wake up with murderous thoughts on your mind.

You have time to eat breakfast, but everything tastes like ashes.

It's nine thirty a.m. now, time to head out the door.

You make it to Starbucks early and Alex is already there, seated at a table in the corner, drinking the usual latte.

You order a coffee and sit down opposite, eyeing your ex suspiciously.

You get a wary half smile in return.

"You got my message?"

"Of course I got your message. Why else would I be here?" you snap.

"Don't be pedantic."

"Don't take my son away!"

"Take him away?" Alex looks confused. "Oh, the trip."

I stare daggers. "Where are you going?"

"To see Sam's parents in Italy."

Sam is the new lover, better looking, younger, and wealthier than you are. No doubt better in bed too.

"Italy. Must be nice." How casual Alex is about having so much spare cash lying around that they just go to Europe whenever they feel like it. Alex gives you a look.

"After that, I don't know. We might go to Vancouver to see my parents. Sam can work remotely, so as long as we're back before school starts, we can go wherever we like."

You clench your fist. "So you're taking him away from me."

"Just for a short—"

"Thought you'd come and rub it in my face, right?" Your blood is boiling now. Your son is being kidnapped, whisked away on an airplane, never to be seen by you again.

"Actually I—"

You slam a fist down on the table, making Alex jump. Everyone in the coffee shop stops talking and stares. You don't give a shit.

"This is fucking typical, Alex," you spit. "You have no right to take Henry away from me!"

Alex stands up and moves away from the table.

"I thought you might have changed. I hoped that some time on your own would make you realize what's important. Instead I just get more of your crap! Well, guess what? Now I don't have to take it. I can just walk away and never see your vile, hateful face ever again. I was considering letting you see Henry again when we come back from vacation, but I can see that would've been a huge mistake. Good-bye."

And then you are alone.

Was Alex lying about intending to let you see Henry again? Did you just make a serious mistake?

If you want to go after Alex and apologize, go to 16.
If you just want to go home and get a real drink, go to 22.

13

You delete the message and go to bed. Usually you stay up later on the Internet, but tonight you're not in the mood. Then you see Henry's toy on the table. Maybe you should take it around to his house tomorrow morning. At least you can leave it on the doorstep with a note, even if you're not allowed to see him. It can't sit here in your apartment—it's too depressing.

You wake the next morning, have breakfast, and at nine thirty a.m. you pick up the toy and head down to the parking garage. You get in your crummy car, start the engine after a few tries, and drive out. You used to have a BMW, but you had to sell that as part of the settlement. Now you drive a fifteen-year-old domestic with a temperamental attitude.

You pray the damn car won't die on you on the side of the highway like it did last week. You were late for one of your anger management sessions, which won't sit well with the judge at your appeal.

It's a fifteen-minute drive to your ex's house. The neighborhood couldn't be more different from where you're living. The houses are huge and are spaced far apart. Beautifully kept grounds of at least half an acre per lot surround each immaculate oversized building.

You park your very-out-of-place lemon outside number 23, next to an enormous Acura SUV. Alex's Mercedes isn't here.

You ring the doorbell and, as expected, Sam answers, looking for all the world like the sexy new lover.

"You? You're not supposed to be here." Sam's tall. Sam's sickeningly good-looking. You hate the fucker.

"Can I see my son?" you ask, trying to remain civil.

"You know what the judge said. Go away."

"I wanted to leave this for him." You hand over the toy.

"Fine, I'll give it to him. Now go before Alex gets back."

"Where is the former light of my life?"

"Meeting you at Starbucks, I thought."

"Me?"

"Yeah, left you a message last night. You didn't get it?"

"Why does Alex want to see me?"

"To tell you we're leaving this afternoon, for Italy. We don't know when we'll be back. Could be a while. I said you guys didn't need to meet up, leaving a message was enough, but Alex thought you should hear in person. I'd better call to say you're not coming."

Sam closes the door on you.

This is really bad news. You're tempted to sneak around the back and see if there's a window you can crawl through, but again, breaking into your ex's house wouldn't be the best way to win over the appeals judge.

Reluctantly, you get back in your car and drive away.

If you go home, go to 25.

If you go to your local Starbucks to see if Alex is still there, go to 25.

14

You close all the blinds and make sure the front door is locked. The phone rings but you unplug it before the machine can pick up.

While you run the bath, you go to the fridge and get some ice cream. Might as well enjoy something pleasant before you end it all. A spoon in your mouth and caramel ripple on your tongue, you eye the block of kitchen knives. It's the tatty old one you took from the basement when you moved out of your house. Four of the slots are empty—Alex only let you take two knives.

Out of your pocket comes the all-important piece of paper. "YOUR CHOICE," it says. Maybe it doesn't mean your death will come by a means of your choosing; maybe it means your death will come because you choose to die. The way you die doesn't matter because it won't happen unless you make the choice to go through with it.

What if you choose to live? What then? If you never take your own life, will you live forever? Or will you just have chosen to die of natural causes?

Anyway, it's time. You put away the ice cream—though quite honestly nobody is going to care if you leave it melting on the counter. You pull out the sharper of the two knives and go to the bathroom. You take off your shirt and pants but leave on your underwear—you realize that for whatever reason, you don't want to be found naked. It's an odd thing to be worried about.

Then you climb in. The warm water is comforting. It makes everything feel right. Being careful not to slice a finger off, you make incisions in both wrists and watch as the water around you starts to turn red. You drop the knife over the side and then lie back and try to stay calm. Maybe Alex will regret how badly you've been treated when your body is discovered. Your heart is beating harder now and you're feeling light-headed. You wonder how long you will have to wait until anybody finds—

The door bursts open. You're dimly aware of being dragged out and somebody bandaging up your wrists.

You pass out.

Go to 20.

15

You hurry back to your apartment building and head down to the parking garage, intending to follow Alex back home so you can say good-bye to Henry before they head out to catch their flight.

Go to 18.

16

You rush out of the coffee shop, hoping to catch up with Alex before it's too late. The silver Mercedes is coming toward you on its way to the parking lot exit. You stand in front waving your arms, but it's not slowing!

At the last moment you leap out of the way as the car barrels past. Alex doesn't even look back to make sure you're all right. Instead the tires screech and the car skids out onto the road and speeds off.

Someone approaches you to ask if you're okay and you wave them away. To think you were about to apologize! You need to follow before you lose all chance of seeing Henry again. Alex will be going home to get Henry and Sam before heading out to the airport, and you should be there before they leave.

Go to **22.**

17

You descend in the elevator to the parking garage. You are still as mad as hell.

You get in your crummy car that is nothing like the Beamer you used to drive before Alex screwed you good and proper.

You remember to turn off the AC first, but in your frustrated state you forget to turn the key gently; otherwise—

Dammit! Now the car won't start at all. Fucking cheap piece of shit! You roar in frustration. Now you have to call out the mechanic yet again.

By the time he arrives and fixes the problem, you are late.

Go to **19.**

18

You descend in the elevator to the parking garage.

You get in your crummy car that is nothing like the Beamer you used to drive before Alex screwed you good and proper.

There's so much on your mind, you forget that you have to make sure the AC is turned off before you start the car. The battery over-loads and you're left with a very heavy paperweight. Stupid cheap car. You roar in frustration. Now you have to call out the mechanic yet again.

By the time he arrives and fixes the problem, you are late.

Go to **19.**

19

By now it is one in the afternoon. You start the car and carefully drive it out of the garage.

Once you're on the highway you put your foot down. If you're lucky, you can still get to Alex's house before they leave for the airport.

When you arrive, Alex's Mercedes is still there but the SUV is gone. Fearing the worst, you get out and ring the doorbell. There's no answer. They've obviously left already.

You get back in the car, starting it carefully, and drive toward the airport. On the highway you put your foot down, praying no cops are out catching speeders.

By some miracle you see Sam's Acura SUV doing the speed limit in the slow lane. Typical "responsible" Sam. You pull alongside. Alex sees you and tries to ignore you.

Henry spots you too, from the backseat. His eyes light up, and you see him call out to you.

You wave to him and pull the wheel back sharply as you realize you've drifted into their lane. The Acura swerves hard onto the shoulder, Sam clearly thinking you're trying to ram them off the road. You try to indicate that it was a mistake, but both Sam and Alex are panicked. There is some tire debris on the shoulder and the Acura hits it hard. Before you realize what's happening, the SUV slams into the guardrail and bounces back into the side of your car. The impact pushes you out into the next lane, causing a ripple effect. You have to move sharply to the right again, and you slam into the SUV. The car behind bumps them too, loses control, and collides with another vehicle. You slam on your brakes and so does Sam, but not before the SUV hits the guardrail again and spins around, coming to a halt.

You stop your car, get out, and run to the SUV. Everyone is okay but shaken up. Sam is yelling obscenities at you. Alex is in shock. Henry is crying. You open the back door and unbuckle Henry's seat belt and he jumps up into your arms. It feels so good to hold him again, like a missing piece of you has been returned.

You can hear sirens.

You remember the other car that rear-ended the Acura and crashed. Other drivers are helping the shaken driver out of her crippled minivan.

"Why did you run us off the road?" Sam is screaming at you.

"I didn't! I swear it was an accident!"

Sam storms forward and might even hit you, even though you're carrying Henry. Instead your son is pulled from your arms.

"Don't stand in a live lane with the kid, moron!" Sam snaps, and then takes Henry away to the side of the road. It's a good point. It annoys you that Sam is being the more responsible parent, and also interrupting your reunion with Henry. The kid is crying, calling out to you again and again.

You reach out to Alex, but your hand is slapped away.

"We shouldn't stay here," you say. But Alex can't stop staring at the shattered SUV.

And then you hear the screeching of air brakes and the grinding of metal. You look back toward the stricken minivan. The occupant and the other drivers are running in all directions. Suddenly the minivan is obliterated by an enormous eighteen-wheeler. The driver clearly didn't stop in time and the big rig has jackknifed. It's coming straight for you, sideways on. Sam is screaming at you to move. Alex is still frozen staring at the SUV. You don't have any time left!

Go to 26.

20

You wake up in your bed. You feel groggy and weak. Your wrists are bandaged. Your best friend, Robin, sits in the chair beside you, looking pissed.

"You moron!"

Your mouth is dry and your head swims when you try to turn it.

"How did you know?" you rasp.

Robin hands you water and you take a sip.

"Come on, it wasn't hard. You've just been through a bitch of a divorce, you just lost your kid, you unplugged your phone, you didn't answer your door buzzer. Do I need to continue?"

"Why aren't I in the hospital?"

"I didn't drop out after two years of medical school for nothing. You lost some blood but you'll be fine. Why did you do it?"

"It seemed like the best way."

"It's never the best way, you selfish idiot. What the hell were you thinking? What if Henry ever found out you killed yourself? He might even blame himself for the rest of his life. Do you want that?"

Robin has a point.

"I'm sorry," you say. "I guess it's a good thing I gave you a key."

"Yeah, and after the argument I just had I might need to crash here real soon. That's why I came over."

The conversation turns lighter, and after a time Robin leaves you to rest. You're very tired.

Clearly you misinterpreted the piece of paper from the machine. You chose to die, you even went through with it, and yet fate interrupted and pulled you back. Perhaps you will choose to die, but not yet, and not by your own hand. Dammit, why did these machines have to be so maddeningly vague sometimes? Why couldn't you just have got, "SUICIDE"? Or "YOU JUMP OFF THE BALCONY. DON'T MESS AROUND WITH THAT OTHER STUFF"?

You fall asleep. When you wake up, Alex is standing next to the bed.

"What are you doing here?"

"Robin had to go but didn't want you to be alone, so here I am."

Alex takes a deep breath.

"What you did was fucking stupid."

"It was the only thing I had left to take," you say.

"We're flying to Italy this afternoon: Henry, Sam, and me. We'll come back eventually, but we might sell the house and move somewhere else. I tried to call you last night because I felt guilty and thought you should see Henry again. Now I know you haven't changed a bit. You're unstable...batshit crazy...a bad influence. Good-bye."

Alex is gone, walking out on you again.

This may be your last chance to see Henry.

You have to move now.

Head swimming, you climb out of bed and nearly collapse. Somehow you stay upright and make it out of the bedroom.

You wish Robin was still here. You were hoping to avoid driving. You clutch on to the wall for support, wondering how you will be able to cope behind the wheel.

Go to 24.

21

You go home with the hope that you will spend time with Henry again. It's best not to rock the boat by doing anything rash. Instead, you need to be patient, just for another month or so.

When you enter your apartment, you see the toy sitting sadly on the table. You forgot to take it with you when you saw Alex! It can't stay here for another month or more; it's just too sad to look at. You resolve to drive around to Alex's house and give it to Henry before they head off to the airport.

Go to 18.

22

You stomp your way home, your mood thunderous. By the time you storm into your apartment building, you are ready to strike someone. You stand by the elevator impatiently, trying to decide what to do next. You could go back upstairs and drown your sorrows with a bottle of scotch. Or you could go down to the parking garage, get in your car, drive to Alex's house, and yell and scream until you're allowed to see Henry again.

If you go up, go to 23.
If you go down, go to 17.

23

You go up to your apartment after telling Alex exactly what's on your mind. You pour yourself a scotch and knock it back with seasoned haste. You are pouring yourself another when the tears come. The sobbing racks your body until you can't stand up any more. You sit on the kitchen floor, back against the faded brown cabinets, and cry your heart out.

When eventually you stop, your anger has dissipated but a gaping hole is left in your chest. You stand up and see the toy sitting sadly on the table. You forgot to take it with you when you saw Alex! It can't stay here for another month or more; it's just too sad to look at. You resolve to drive around to Alex's house and give it to Henry before they head off to the airport.

Go to 18.

24

You make it to the parking garage and, with difficulty, make it to the crummy car that is decidedly not a BMW. You get behind the wheel and try to find your keys, but you feel like you're somewhere else. It's like you're floating above your car, looking down on your ashen face through the windshield. You don't look at all well. Oh crap, you've blacked out again.

By the time you wake up, you are way behind schedule.

Go to 19.

25

It doesn't matter where you're going because your car is now broken down at the side of the road, a cloud of steam billowing from under the hood.

As vehicles whiz by you on the highway, you add "shitty, unreliable car" to the list of injustices heaped upon you by your ex-spouse. Good thing you spent that extra cash on roadside assistance—you've used it three times this month alone.

After a long wait the breakdown guy arrives in his tow truck. He already knows you pretty well. He disappears under the hood and starts tinkering away.

While you wait, you take out the little piece of paper and stare at those two words again.

"YOUR CHOICE."

Well, last night your choice was to end it all, and yet here you still are. Still alive. You could still do it right now. You could easily step out into traffic and it would all be over in a heartbeat.

But what would be the cost? There might be a huge pileup. Dozens could die along with you.

Then you see Alex's Mercedes on the other side of the highway, heading homeward.

Alex, like many rubberneckers, is taking a look at the poor schmuck stranded on the shoulder on the far side of the highway. Your eyes make contact.

"Hey!" the mechanic calls. "Back up!"

You hadn't realized how close you'd gotten to the live lane. A car shoots past and honks, swerving away to avoid hitting you. It clips the side of a truck to the left. There's no pileup, but the truck screeches to a halt while other traffic swerves and brakes and screeches and dives to the side to avoid it. When the truck stops, it is blocking two lanes a good distance farther down the highway.

You can't believe what's happened. In the distance you see Alex's Mercedes, reversing along the shoulder back toward you.

Luckily, at this time, there isn't too much traffic heading in this direction, so there's not much of a backup. Still, cars in all lanes are slowing down enough that you can easily cross to meet Alex, who is climbing over the center guardrail.

"Are you okay?"

"I'm fine," you say. For a moment you think you might embrace, but instead you both stand awkwardly, unsure of the proper way to behave.

"Thanks for stopping."

Alex shrugs. "I thought you'd been hit. I guess you didn't get my message."

"Busy evening," you say. "Listen, we should check if everyone's okay."

"Yeah."

Suddenly you hear a screech of air brakes. You turn toward oncoming traffic to see a huge tractor-trailer jackknifing behind the slow-moving cars. Clearly the driver didn't see the slowdown until it was too late. It's plowing through cars as it hurtles toward you, spinning them out of its way. It shows no signs of slowing.

Go to 26.

26

The huge vehicle is coming at you so fast. Alex stands to your right, frozen in terror. Which way should you run? If you jump left, you might avoid being hit but Alex will be killed. If you lunge right, you might be able to save Alex but you won't stand a chance.

Seconds remain!

Left or right?

Who will live? You or Alex?

Now you know what the piece of paper means. Now you know what's going to kill you.

Your choice.

Story by Richard Salter

Illustration by Graham Annable

KRIS STRAUB

IN BATTLE, ALONE AND SOON FORGOTTEN

GRUN STOOD WITH HIS BACK against the stone wall, listening. In the distance he could hear the chittering of the nightkin and the squelch of its feet upon the cobblestone. As the sounds slowly grew softer, he risked a peek around the corner. The nightkin was nowhere to be seen, which wasn't necessarily the same as saying it wasn't there; it was not yet dawn and the only light coming through the windows was dim and gray, highlighting the shadows rather than banishing them. The torches and chandeliers that lit the halls had long since been extinguished, for the nightkin needed no light, and Grun dared not bring a lantern or activate the runes of lighting that ran along the baseboards...those would only draw attention to him, and he wasn't allowed into the master's castle unless summoned. Orcs belong in the barracks, after all, during the rare periods when they weren't off on the offensive somewhere.

Grun sniffed the air; his low-light vision might be poor, but an orc who relied overmuch on sight would never have lived to sixteen. He could smell the acrid stench of the nightkin...a coppery tang of the old magic that had summoned the creature. It was not close; Grun decided to go for it.

Corner, he thought. *One, two, three, four, five, and turn left.* He counted his steps, tracing out the path he'd laid out and memorized weeks ago. Unfortunately, he'd used a hand-drawn map he'd found on one of the bodies dredged out of the moat, and

the proportions weren't quite right; no single wrong turn had sent him astray, but innumerable missteps had slowed him far more than he was comfortable with. He put his arms out and felt the wall. After a minute of scrabbling he felt the doorway and tried the latch.

It was unlocked. Grun gnashed his teeth in celebration. He opened the door as silently as he could and slipped inside.

Because of the large windows, the room was almost visible in the predawn gloom, not that Grun needed light to know he was in the right place…it smelled of the messenger hawks, the smoky residue of sending spells, and Kerrek's cheap tobacco. And, of course, the goblin stink of Kerrek himself, sitting in the corner, illuminated by the glow of his battered cigarette. Compared to Grun he was small, lanky, and easily broken. Orcs and goblins were close cousins and shared the same green skin and resistance to magic, but goblins were allowed to work in the castle. They were considered less of a danger. Most of them were in the kitchens or washing rooms, but Kerrek had a knack for the message hawks, which was why he got the leeway to work in the castle proper, as assistant falconer, and why Grun had asked for his help.

"You're late," the goblin said.

"My map was wrong."

The goblin grumbled. "I'm risking a lot for you, orc."

Grun gritted his teeth but forced himself to remain calm. "I am not 'orc.' My name is Grun."

The goblin's large, haggard face was barely recognizable in the dim glow of his cigarette, but Grun could clearly see an eyebrow shooting up. "Grun? That's a dwarf name."

"No," Grun protested, "it is my name." He thought for a moment, and then repeated, "It is my name," to convince himself as much as Kerrek.

As a general rule, orcs didn't get names. Not the way other species did. Grun had a unit (D201) and a supervisor (a human, Rogerrik), and a station (swordsman) and a rank (forward) and a designation (third), to distinguish him from the thousands of other orcs in the lord's employ. "Rogerrik's Third Forward" was the name he was most often called, when others saw fit to give him a name at all. In most cases, "you, orc!" was sufficient.

That said, it was common for orcs to take names of their own, though they all tended to follow a particular format...Grun shared a small room in the barracks with orcs called Elfbane, Darkstab, and Bloodfist, and for a time he referred to himself as Killclaw. These were meaningless nicknames, though. Some orcs went through them like boots; every few months they would mash more angry-sounding words together and tell their friends to start calling them that. Orcish sergeants accepted it grumpily because they had to maintain a more familiar relationship with their charges, but anyone higher on the chain of command and any non-orc stuck to official designations. After all, unless you worked directly next to the orc, odds were he'd be long dead by the next time you might see him.

Kerrek shrugged and let it go. He had better things to do. "You're sure you want to do this?" he asked.

"I want to know," Grun replied. He unsheathed his dagger, another trophy taken from a corpse, this one a halfling caught on the outskirts of the kingdom while he was on patrol. It glowed a pale blue; it wasn't enough to read by, not that Grun could read, but it was enough to keep him from walking into trees on late patrols.

"You're not gonna like it," Kerrek said, while eying the dagger greedily.

"You don't know."

"Don't I?" the goblin sneered. "Mark my words, orc. 'In battle, alone and soon forgotten.'"

"It doesn't have to be that way."

"Doesn't it? Have you looked in the mirror lately?"

"No," said Grun, who honestly had not. The barracks didn't have mirrors; they weren't considered necessary.

The goblin put his cigarette out on the wall and stood up. "You know what I mean. Every orc gets the same prophecy. I've seen a hundred of them; my brother works in the crematorium, stripping bodies, and he collects the damned things. You don't see a lot of 'em on orcs, but whenever you do, they say the same thing."

"They don't have to," Grun growled.

"Don't take it personally. A greenskin's fate is sealed. It's like that poem... 'Elves are born to cast and charm, gnomes are born to build and try. A goblin's born to work and serve, an orc is born to fight and die.'"

"It doesn't have to be that way!" Grun shouted. He could feel the rage welling up in him, the comfortable berserk fury that was part and parcel of orchood. His claws itched and his legs tensed...it took an effort of will not to leap upon the nearest creature and tear it apart. Staying still and calm made Grun physically ill. He wanted to vomit.

Kerrek flinched but, to his credit, did not actually run. He wanted to, though; Grun could smell his panic.

Grun clenched his fists and took a deep breath. "I'm not...a troop," he said, eventually. "I'm...me. My own...me. Argh!" Grun struggled to find the words he was looking for. "We're not," he started and then hesitated. The right words were somewhere on the edge of thinking, just past his grasp. "We're not a poem," he finished lamely.

Kerrek was cold. "I think you should just give me the sample and go."

Grun took the dagger and pressed it against his forearm, where his thick orcish hide was at its thinnest. He carved a neat line, one more scar among many, and sopped up the blood with a rag that Kerrek provided.

"I'll send this now," the goblin said. "The artifice of prophecy is in the Deeprun Cavern, with the dwarves, so it will take a week for the message to get there and a week for a reply. You should go now."

Grun left without another word, leaving the enchanted dagger behind, as they had agreed. Dawn was just about to break, and the human guards would be taking over as the nightkin began to dissolve, so he retraced his path from the barracks as quickly as he dared.

Unfortunately, he was not quick enough. As he entered the kitchens on his way to the side door, a human, standing in front of an open icebox, spun and raised a crossbow in one smooth motion. Grun stopped and raised his hands.

"Halt!" he called, his voice obviously muffled by food. With effort, he swallowed. "Orc! In the name of Lord Restharon I order you to halt!"

"I have halted!" said Grun.

The guard stepped away from the icebox, which swung closed. He stepped to the side, putting the large oak table in the center of the room between himself and Grun. "What are you doing here?" he asked.

"What are you doing here?" Grun asked back.

"I'm allowed in the castle! That's it. I'm going to bring you to the quartermaster."

Grun growled at the human. "Don't need to. I'll leave."

"It doesn't work like that, orc!" the human snapped back.

It was all bravado. Grun could sense the man's terror. Armed or not, the human was smaller, slower, and weaker than even the puniest of orcs. If Grun were to leap at him now, he'd need to jump over the table in the middle of the room, which would give the guard time for maybe one shot. And if it didn't catch the orc in the eye or the neck, Grun could just keep charging...orcs are hardy that way. And once Grun got an arm's length away from the human, there would be no fight anymore.

Of course, if Grun killed the guard, he'd be chased down and executed for it.

Of course, that would be cold comfort to the guard.

After a few seconds of tense standoff, the guard lowered his crossbow a fraction of an inch and visibly relaxed. "You're not an assassin," he said confidently.

"You thought I was?"

The guard actually smiled. "I've been jumpy. I'm going to be assassinated."

Grun nodded. "You've used the artifice of prophecy."

"Yes, obviously. Surprised an orc could figure out that little riddle."

Grun snarled and stepped toward the table, claws bared. "I could still be an assassin!" he spat.

The guard flinched but did not run. "No...no. For one thing, I'm not important enough to assassinate. I'm just on morning watch. But someday! Heh, can you imagine? Well, no, you can't, orc. But still."

Grun narrowed his eyes. He was mad, but more than that, he was jealous. Assassinated! Even to be part of an honor guard, killed in an assassination writ large, would beat the ignominy of "In battle, alone and soon forgotten."

He was hardly aware of it, but his claws were sinking into the wood of the large kitchen table, leaving sharp dents on the hardwood, which had thus far resisted a century's worth of cleavers. He wanted very much to take the human's little victory away. "I could still be an assassin," he hissed.

The human smirked. "No, you're an orc. Human assassin, goblin assassin, maybe an elf, sure. And halflings of course. How's it go? 'Humans born to build the tower. Halflings born to sneak inside. Dwarves are born to forge the blade. Orcs born to defend and die.'"

"Raargh!" Grun bellowed. He did not leap at the guard, but he couldn't help himself from shouting. "I was not born to do anything!" he tried. "I am not...born! No, I...I am me!" Desperately, Grun floundered for the words. "I am Grun! Me! The only one! Grun! *Grun!*"

The guard was backed as far into the counter as it was possible to be without climbing into a cupboard. When he spoke it was conciliatory and gentle. "Y-your name is Grun?"

"Yes!"

"So...so how did you get a name?" the human asked.

"Bron gave it to me."

"Bron? A dwarf?"

"Bron Forgefounder."

"I see." The human relaxed a bit. He was staring Grun in the eye with a strange ferocity, though. "Uh...who is that?"

"He was a prisoner. I was his guard. He said I was different from the other orcs."

The guard frowned. "Well yes, the other orcs are obedient enough to not talk to the prisoners!"

"That's not allowed?"

"It's never allowed! Who knows what sort of crazy things they might convince a simple mind?"

Grun shrugged. "He was alone after his friends were taken away. He wanted to talk. He said I deserved a name, and he taught me that I could be Grun."

The human frowned again, piteously. "You're not, though. You're just an orc."

"No. I am Grun. I am Grun! The only Grun!" He would have continued in this vein, except he felt a pinprick of a blade between his shoulder blades.

"Orcs don't get names!" a deep voice behind him shouted. It was accompanied by another voice, laughing a hooting, mad laugh that seemed disconnected from reality.

The human reholstered his crossbow. "Nice work."

The laugher's voice was also half mad...breathy, rapid, and somehow wet. "Do we take him to the master? Do we slit his throat here and now? Oh! I like that idea, second the motion. Meeting adjourned!"

"No!" bellowed the other voice. "Prisoner to prison. Nobody killed."

Grun risked a look over his shoulder and was not surprised to see an ogre and a ghoul. The ogre wore the armor of Lord Restharon's heavy guard and carried a sword almost as long as Grun was tall. The ghoul was dressed only in rags and tatters, which flapped wildly as he gamboled around the room, laughing and drooling.

"The orc's going to be tortured! Tortured! And then back to the barracks, hee! Silly orc, it thinks it has a name! Come with me!"

The ghoul loped off, out of the kitchens. The blade on his back receded, and Grun turned around. The ogre, huge and impassive, was still pointing the sword at him, a foot away. The blade didn't even quaver. "You will follow Sithes. I will follow you. March."

And Grun marched. He had little choice.

The ghoul moved forward erratically, in hops and starts and sudden pauses, while the ogre was an oncoming wall that would shove Grun whenever he began to falter.

"You could take me to the barracks," Grun suggested hopelessly.

"Ha!" barked the ogre, loud and defiant. The ghoul matched it with another mad cackle. "Orcs not allowed in castle! Orcs dangerous and stupid!"

"I'm smarter than you. I'm safer than him."

"So you're boring!" cackled the ghoul. "Orcs are boring! Orcs are boring! And the master doesn't like to be bored, oh no, no no no. Hee-hee!"

"Orcs can be interesting."

"Ah he-he-he, you can be laid out in interesting positions! And you will be, oh yes, you will be. Little orc, little worthless orc!"

"Hrm...," rumbled the ogre. When he spoke, his voice was flat, as he summoned a memory from far away. "'Ogres born to crush the land. Drakelings born to burn the skies. Ghouls are born to cart the dead. Orcs are born to run and die!'"

Grun stopped and turned to the ogre, drawing himself up as tall as he could. "I am not—" he began, but the ogre did not stop. He kept thundering forward, as inevitable as a merchant ship, and, when he reached Grun, delivered a sharp blow to the orc's head. Grun collapsed to the ground, unconscious.

"Oh, little orc? It's been hours. Wake up, will you?" The voice was smooth and condescending and radiated power. Not the quiet power of a public speaker or a politician, but a literal force that dragged Grun out of the blackness of oblivion and back into reality. He opened his eyes, dazed and lost. He was on his back, on something hard, looking at a stone ceiling. He tried to sit up and groaned in pain as his arms were wrenched back...He looked over and saw the manacles that chained him to the table.

"Oh, there you are. Let's sit up, shall we?"

Slowly the view rotated as the table Grun was strapped to tilted. Soon he was almost upright, still manacled. He wasn't quite tall enough; he had to stay on his tiptoes or his shoulders would be wrenched out of joint. Grun got the impression this was quite purposeful. He could see little of the room besides the wall and sconce before him, but the décor screamed "dungeon" all the same.

A man, mostly human but somehow not quite, was sitting in front of him. He wore no armor, nor a mage's robes, but the fine clothes of an aristocrat dyed in shades of black. He sat on a small stool on the far side of the small room, legs crossed, fingers steepled, smiling broadly.

"Y—," Grun started, but his voice caught in his throat. The man, Lord Restharon, had raised a single finger.

"Not yet. Orc, I trust you understand how honored you are. Were you to live a thousand years, which you won't, but were you to, never would you be more honored than you are at this very moment. For the rest of your life, your comrade orcs will gather round to hear the story of the time Lord Restharon blessed you twice in one day, first by gazing upon you, and next by letting you live. Yes, little orc, I intend to let you live. Not that I can't take that back. But I have no intention of torturing or killing you."

The master's expression hardened. "I was simply down here dealing with a goblin who sent off a message hawk against my wishes. As we passed from one chamber to another, via the holding cells where you were blissfully unconscious, he pointed at you. I wanted to know why. You may speak."

Grun felt the invisible pressure on his neck loosen. Even still, it was a strain to speak...he was physically exhausted and more than a little terrified. "Where...where is Kerrek?"

Lord Restharon lifted one of his thin, immaculate eyebrows. He angled his head almost imperceptibly to the side of the room.

Grun looked over and saw another table, much like the one he was strapped to. Next to it were trays covered with instruments, surgical tools, some complicated mechanical devices, and a dagger that glowed faintly blue in the torchlight. All were spattered with blood.

Strapped to the table was...most of Kerrek.

Grun had seen allies dead before. He'd killed allies before, the master being capricious about allegiances and whether mercenaries would get paid or slaughtered. He'd seen people tortured far more thoroughly than Kerrek, who, at the end of the day, couldn't have been in the chair more than a few hours.

But those were always somebody else's fault. For all the corpses he'd seen, he'd never actually been the cause of death...there may have been prophecies that read "Lord Restharon's army" or "the treachery of the Garrean king" or even "split asunder by an orc," but there wouldn't have been one that said "Grun."

Until now. Kerrek was dead and it was Grun's fault. His actual, personal fault. The orc felt light-headed.

"Sending a message hawk without approval," Restharon explained. "That's potential treachery."

With effort, Grun looked back at his lord and fought down his bile. "It wasn't. He was sending a message for me."

Restharon shrugged. "Yes, well. Regardless of the specific circumstances, I like to ensure that nobody in my castle be accused of treachery twice. Now, by the time he saw you, he was not particularly in speaking condition..."

"I ate his tongue!" said a ghoul with a cackle. He appeared from somewhere, dressed in a black cloak and hood that couldn't hide his twisted body and sagging, half-rotten skin.

"That you did, Warfen; that you did. So, orc, what message did he send for you? By which I suppose I'm asking if you're to be accused of treachery as well."

Grun sagged, yelped as the manacles wrenched his arms, and stood to attention again. "I sent a message to the Deeprun dwarves. With blood. For the artifice of prophecy."

Restharon blinked in, Grun thought, genuine surprise. "Really?"

he asked, and then once again composed himself. "Well, of course really. After all, if you were to lie in this room you would be sliced across the back." He smiled at an amusing and certainly bloody memory, then recomposed himself. "Nonetheless, why would you do that? Anyone could tell you the answer."

"'In battle, alone and soon forgotten,'" Grun said.

"So you knew it. Why would you do such a stupid thing, orc?"

"It might be different."

"It never is. Stupid, stupid orc."

Grun had never met his master before. Orders always trickled down a chain of command through a half dozen links...He knew Lork Restharon was powerful and quick to anger and prone to punishment, but Grun feared him only in the abstract, like a god. Here, in front of him, Grun saw only the human, or the creature very like a human. There was nothing to temper his anger, and so he snarled and strained against his chains, which rattled ominously. "I am not 'orc'!" he shouted. "I am Grun!"

"Orcs don't get names." Restharon did not shout, but Grun felt himself pressed to the table with the force all the same. He struggled to breathe under the pressure.

"...I...have...a name...," he stammered.

Abruptly, the pressure stopped. Grun tried to sag, but the manacles forced him to stay upright and alert.

"Oh, this is good," said Lord Restharon. "Oh, this is. By Arengee's bones, this is hilarious! You think you're special."

"I—"

"Haven't you heard the poem? 'Orcs don't get to change their fate. Orcs don't get to wonder why. Orcs don't get to have a name. Orcs are born to fight and die.'"

Grun spat in Restharon's direction. The lord was unmoved. "I am not a poem!"

"No, you're an orc. A little bit of nothing."

"I can be...be...I can be important!"

"Yes, yes," the lord said dismissively. "You are a vital cog in the sundial. Ah ha-ha. Born to fight and die."

"I can...I..." Grun hemmed, trying to express himself. Thoughts and words flitted in the air before him, just out of reach.

"You?" said Restharon. "Go on."

"I can...I can write my own poem!"

The master smirked. "You can barely put a sentence together!"

"I can write a poem for the orcs!"

"Orc, I'm going to assume you don't know this because, well, it's a thing and you're an orc. Your people did write that poem."

"What?"

"Why do you think you're mentioned in every stanza? Who else would care enough to say that much? Who would say anything at all?"

Grun tried to reach out for more words, but there was nothing... Between the red fog of rage and his own exhaustion, language had failed him entirely. So he screamed.

Grun just screamed and screamed, twisting on the table but getting nowhere. Lord Restharon sat and watched. About two minutes later, Grun's voice gave out entirely, so he just thrashed on the table. After another minute, he ran out of energy. This time, the pain wasn't enough to stop him from slouching. He was in agony and could feel the metal cutting into his wrists and his shoulders being pulled out of joint, but he didn't have the energy to care.

Lord Restharon stood up, stretching his arms a bit as he did. "Warfen, bring it in, will you?"

The ghoul capered out of sight.

"Little orc, you want to be special. That's noble enough, I suppose," the lord said. "But you're not special. Do you know how I know this?"

Grun shook his head weakly.

"Because you're so like an orc...shortsighted and senseless. You don't seek glory in battle or go round up your kin and revolt against me. That would be an interesting choice and a long time coming. No, you opt to check and see if you're special. So passive. So unfocused.

"But better than that," he continued, stepping close to the orc and sneering. Grun could smell, above the pervasive scent of blood and death in the room, Lord Restharon's soap, and the strange, metal scent of powerful magic. "Better than that, the way you check? Not by having your aura read, not by asking a diviner to see your future, not through any elementary prognostication, but with this."

Restharon gestured at the ghoul, who was pushing in a strange machine on a wheeled cart. It was a box, about three feet on every side, made of unpolished metal dotted with crystals. There was a small slit on the front framed in brass, and on the top some sort of funnel. Grun had never seen anything like it before, but he knew just what it was. "You have...," he started, but didn't have the energy to finish the sentence.

"An artifice of prophecy? I'm not an idiot, orc. Not like a little orc who thinks he's above dying in battle, but when it comes time to prove it, only thinks to see if he'll die some other way. So...so steeped in death, little orc, that you won't think...no, you can't think of any other way to prove your merit."

"Only one...," Grun choked out.

"One artifice? Obviously, there are two. You know why?"

Grun lolled his head from side to side.

"You took it for me."

Grun raised his head. It felt like someone was pushing it down, but he forced past it. "What?"

Lord Restharon moved down to the artifice. He walked in graceful, long-legged strides and brushed his hands on the machine. "Well, 'you' for a 'some orc or another' value of you. Did you ever kidnap a dwarf? About five years ago?"

Grun nodded weakly. "Bron," he whispered.

"Bron Forgefounder! Yes, he was one of them. There were several dwarves involved, of course. You took him?"

Grun shook his head. "Guard," he said.

"Oh good! In which case, I think I owe you a complimentary prophecy. Warfen? Take one of his fingers."

The ghoul hissed with glee and leapt upon Grun.

Lord Restharon didn't raise his voice, but he infused it with that same power, and Grun could hear and understand it perfectly well over the screaming. "I am the sole ruler of the largest empire on the continent. I maintain this power by acquiring anything and everything that will be of advantage to me. Every secret spell, every lost ritual. I could wear a different magic ring on every digit for a month straight and not repeat a spell. I've moved six mage towers into my empire…just moved them right in. I have a room that contains a chest that contains the room the chest is in! Warfen! One finger! Just one!"

The ghoul slid off Grun reluctantly. He spit Grun's left forefinger into his hands and presented the bloody mess to his lord. Grun watched in woozy, shocked silence.

"Pour some drops in the artifice, Warfen. Then you may eat the finger."

The ghoul cackled and squeezed Grun's blood into the funnel, at which point he scampered into the corner and crunched hungrily on the finger. Grun stared at the ghoul, jaw slack. "Not here, Warfen. Out. Send Eamon over."

The ghoul ran off, finger still in his mouth. He was shortly replaced by a human guard with a crossbow; Grun thought it looked like the one from the kitchens, but they all looked much the same to him.

"As I was saying," Restharon continued. "Prognostication. And not cheap divination—this was made by the dwarves! No vagaries of magic, just technology. Cheap and reliable. Even if the subject matter is a little morbid, and never quite as helpful as one could hope. So I had you get the dwarves, and I had them build me one, and then I, ah, ensured there would only be two such devices. Heh. The last one…Bron Forgefounder himself, as it happens…he admitted it was a relief to finally understand; he was the first to try the device, and his result actually was 'Artifice of prophecy.' Funnily enough, that's how it got the name; before they'd just called it the Machine of Death. One of the many little ironies the device engenders. I intend to get rid of the original within the next few years, but raiding the Deeprunners is no quick task."

Grun looked at the machine. Some of the gems had lit up. He got the impression that it was thinking. "Why...?" he asked.

"Why kill the creators? Obvious. Or did you want to know why I needed one of my own? Lots of reasons, little orc. It's leverage I have on my lieutenants. When I'm preparing a maneuver, I do some spot checks...If I'm sending a team to the shore, and five samples in a row come back 'drowning,' I'm going to reduce the number of men I send to the shore, won't I? And of course, there are certain advantages to keeping the artifice where we do the torturing. Provides a very real motivating force if properly applied." Restharon laughed.

Grun didn't raise his head, but he glanced up at his master. "Your death?" he asked.

"Mm. 'Hubris.'" He shook his head in amused disappointment. "The thing can be so charmingly poetic. It's good advice, though, which is why even though you're chained up, and I can do this..." He snapped, and the shadows in the corner of the room coalesced into a nightkin. Grun got the impression of tentacles and some sort of beak in shades of darkness, but Restharon waved his hand and the creature dissipated in seconds. "Even though I've got that, I've still got a guy with a crossbow. Hello, Eamon."

"Ah, hello, my lord," the human said. It was definitely the one from the kitchen.

"Do you know your ultimate fate, Eamon?"

"Ah, yes, my lord. Um. 'In an assassination,' my lord. Quite proud, my lord."

"As you should be." There was a faint, muffled buzz within the artifice, and a slip of parchment appeared in the slit. "And here we are. Are you ready for the grand reveal? Eamon, release one of its arms so it can read the inevitable 'In battle, alone and soon forgotten,' please. The right one; it's less bloody."

Eamon crept nervously up to the orc. With his arm extended as far as possible, he pulled the pin that held Grun's right manacle closed and then jumped back to Restharon's side. The lord snatched the parchment without giving it a glance. "Here, little orc. Give it a gander." He pressed it into Grun's hand. "Why don't you let me know what it says?"

Grun looked at the parchment in his hand. Turned it over. There was writing on it. That he knew. He couldn't tell what it said because he never learned to read.

But he had learned his name. Bron taught him how, with a piece of charcoal he used to write on the wall, just days before... before Grun was sent somewhere else and never saw the dwarf again. Bron taught Grun how to read and write his own name.

And whenever a wizard tried to invade the castle grounds, which was about once a month, he'd have a quill and ink and blank scrolls that Grun could take off his corpse, and Grun would write his name over and over and know that it was his.

Whatever was written on the parchment that the artifice had spit out was one word long. It was a long word, and it started with a G, just like Grun's name.

"So what's it say, little orc?"

Grun looked Restharon in the eye. "'In battle, alone and soon forgotten,'" he said. He smiled weakly. He felt a pulse of magic sliding up his back, slicing into his skin, but his orcish hide was thick and resistant... it hurt, but it didn't break his flesh. Restharon's spell detected the lie, but there was no alarm, no light, nothing but a wound that nobody could see.

"Of course," said the lord. "And now I am going to let you go, little orc. And remember, until that prophesied day comes and goes, that I let you go. Not because I am merciful, but because you aren't worth my time to torture. Come, Eamon. We'll send Gor and Slithes in to release the orc." He turned and began striding off.

With his right arm free, Grun had considerably more freedom of movement. He could stand flat-footed without his left arm being wrenched. His left hand hurt like the abyss, but everything hurt right now, and with a missing finger, it was slightly smaller than it was when the manacles were put on. Grun silently leveraged himself forward and tugged.

And at the exact moment Restharon asked himself how it was the orc had learned to read, he heard the pop of Grun's hand slipping free. He and Eamon turned and saw Grun charging…they had time for one blow, just one, before he would be upon them. But orcs were hardy.

Grun came back to the barracks and fell asleep for almost thirty-six hours. He had lost quite a lot of blood getting out of the castle, and nobody woke him because the entire empire was in a panic. Eventually, to his own surprise, he awoke in his bloody little bunk.

Orcs drifted in and out of the barracks, directionless. Grun ignored them. He went in search of food, which brought him back to the castle kitchens, where dozens of orcs had gathered. Other species were there too, but there were more orcs than anyone else, eating and talking and experiencing the illicit thrill of being in the castle. As he ate, he listened. Neighboring kingdoms were on the move. There was talk of defending the empire, or abandoning it and seeing if someone else needed a force, or just finding a place out of the way and waiting to see who won.

Grun still had the parchment. He hadn't let go if it during the fight, and it was crumpled and bloodstained and singed by the arcane blast Restharon had thrown. Rather like Grun. Even if he could read, it was well past legibility now, but he knew that it was a word that started with G. And it was his word.

"We could make our own empire," he said. The conversation died down a bit.

"Orcs can't run empires," one orc said. Others agreed. "Orcs fight." "Orcs work for other people." "Orcs aren't bosses!" "Orcs are born to—"

"No!" said Grun. "Orcs are born to do anything! Orcs are born to have a name! Orcs are born to be themselves! And…and not all orcs will die the same!"

It wasn't a very good poem, but it was *his*. And soon, it would be everyone's.

Story by Ed Turner
Illustration by Tony Cliff

LAKE TITICACA

ON THE LAST DAY OF FIFTH GRADE, Alfred and his two best friends swore that they would all go together to find out how they were going to die. "We're going to start middle school now," said Alfred. "We should do this and promise to stay friends forever."

Alfred's friends both agreed with him. The year before, on the last day of fourth grade, the three of them had gathered in front of the mirror in the school bathroom and chanted "Bloody Mary" over and over again with the lights out. They had been scared at the time, but it seemed childish now. Getting their predictions from the machine was completely different—it was a grown-up thing to do, and not childish at all.

So after lunch, they sneaked off away from the schoolyard and started walking downtown. They passed by the diner and the post office and the little Easy-Peasy supermarket on the corner. Mrs. Dratmoor was standing in the door of the Easy-Peasy fanning herself with a magazine, trying to get some relief from the heavy heat of the day.

At first Mrs. Dratmoor didn't seem to take any notice of Alfred and his friends, but then she suddenly looked surprised. "Hey, what are you kids doing out of school!" she shouted. "It's not summer yet!"

Alfred and his friends ran as fast as they could, their tennis shoes slapping against the burning concrete of the sidewalks. Mrs. Dratmoor was always short of breath, and they knew she wouldn't run after them. But they also ran just to feel the breeze against their skin as they raced to the arcade at the other end of town.

The arcade was owned by a white-haired, potbellied man named Mr. Szyzylly. He had red blotches on his face and he spoke with a thick accent. The other half of the building was a Laundromat, which was also owned by Mr. Szyzylly.

Alfred and his friends had spent plenty of rainy afternoons in the arcade, playing the old games while the warm linen-and-soap smell of the Laundromat tickled their noses. On hot days like this, they usually stayed away, as there was nothing to keep the building cool except a line of old rattling box fans that Mr. Szyzylly had taped to the floor.

So it was no surprise that nobody was doing their laundry either on this particular Friday afternoon. In fact, the only person in the whole place was Mr. Szyzylly himself, and even he looked like he was asleep. Alfred had never seen the place so empty before.

Mr. Szyzylly's arcade was not very large or up-to-date. Mostly, it consisted of strange carnival attractions that he had picked up here and there very inexpensively. There was a mechanical fortune-telling madam, a love test, and a miniature bowling lane with pins attached to springs. But Alfred and his friends usually spent most of their quarters on the few old video games that Mr. Szyzylly had rescued when the pizzeria went out of business. Today, however, they were after something different. For the first time, they had come to use the Machine of Death that sat in the very far back, behind a black curtain.

Alfred and his friends had often sneaked glances at the machine when they thought nobody was watching, but they had never dared to touch it. The truth is that they had always been too afraid, but of course they never admitted to this. They always found some excuse for not using the machine before. But now they had sworn, so they were finally going to do it—or at least that's what they told each other.

The three boys went over to the change machine in the corner of the arcade. Since the place was so quiet and since Mr. Szyzylly looked like he was asleep, they tried to be quiet themselves. But there was still a lot of whispering and giggling and poking and pinching and squeaking sneakers—and that was before the rattling coins fell out of the change machine. With all that noise, it shouldn't have been any surprise that Mr. Szyzylly was wide-awake by the time they had gotten their four quarters.

"What are you boys doing, sneaking around here?" asked Mr. Szyzylly in a voice that made all three boys jump. He didn't sound angry, but he always spoke in a loud voice.

Alfred and his friends looked at one another and whispered some more. Alfred was very aware that they were playing hooky on the last day of fifth grade. He just hoped that Mr. Szyzylly wouldn't realize that as he answered. "We came to use the machine."

"Aha," said Mr. Szyzylly. A smile spread across his face and his eyes twinkled strangely. "I have seen you boys looking at that machine many times. You finally have the courage?"

Alfred and his friends looked at each other again. It was true that they had sworn to use the machine, but had any of them really thought they would? Alfred at least had been hoping that Mr. Szyzylly would chase them away so they could have an adventure without having to actually go through with it. But now it seemed like there was no backing out. With Mr. Szyzylly watching them like that, they would have to do it.

"I don't usually let children use it," said Mr. Szyzylly thoughtfully. "But you think you are grown-up enough, yes? It's a very weighty thing, this machine—not a thing to be approached lightly. After you use it, your lives will be changed forever."

Mr. Szyzylly seemed to be waiting for some kind of an answer, but Alfred didn't know what to say. He just looked dumbly at his two friends, and they both looked dumbly back.

After a minute, Mr. Szyzylly said, "Well, do you still want to use it? I've seen it ruin lives, destroy friendships, and frighten grown men worse than any ghost story. I'll let you go through with it if you want—but you must tell me that you still want to."

None of the boys said anything for a moment, and then Alfred spoke up. His voice was really nothing more than a squeak. "Yes, Mr. Szyzylly," he said. "We swore on it!"

"Well, come on," said Mr. Szyzylly. He walked over to the curtains and opened them up wide. The machine sat there, big and hulking. It wasn't sleek like the one in Dr. Tanner's office, but rather a very old version with red paint flaking off its aluminum casing. Mr. Szyzylly turned around and looked at the boys carefully. "Are you very sure about this? This is your last chance to change your mind."

And again Alfred heard himself saying, "Yes. I'm not scared." His friends both looked at him with shock in their eyes. Alfred was just as shocked himself. Why had he said that? He was terrified.

"Good," said Mr. Szyzylly. "Get your quarters ready, all of you. Let me fetch you something to stand on." Mr. Szyzylly went back to his desk at the far end of the room, and the three boys stared up at the machine.

Now Alfred felt sick. He wanted to run away, but he couldn't. He wasn't afraid the other boys would laugh at him, since he was sure they would run too. In fact, he didn't even know why he couldn't run. His heart was pounding and he felt like crying, but still he couldn't run.

Mr. Szyzylly was back now. He put a wooden box on the ground next to the machine. Then he bent over the machine and fiddled with it for a minute. "Just let me make sure there's enough paper, and some new needles," he said. "There we go! All right, then, who's first?"

Since nobody else took the first step, Alfred did. He felt as though he had missed his chance to run away, and now he only wanted to get it over with as soon as possible. He climbed up on top of the box and looked down at the machine. It looked like the hood of an old pickup truck—a curved, blank surface with no dials and no buttons. There was only a single round hole and two slots—one for quarters to go in, and one for paper to come out.

"You are the bravest boys I have ever met," Mr. Szyzylly was saying. "I want to shake your hand before you commence this great moment." There was a big lump in Alfred's throat, and he couldn't even close his fingers as Mr. Szyzylly clasped his hand. Alfred's hand just lay limp while his arm rippled like jelly under Mr. Szyzylly's vigorous pumping. "Now, put your thumb here, in the circle. It will prick a little, like a needle. Don't forget your quarter!"

The coin dropped down into the machine with a dull plunk. After that, Alfred almost couldn't stand it, waiting for the pinprick. But then it came, and he pulled his thumb away quickly. "Ow!" he said. From somewhere inside the machine, there came mechanical sounds—whirring and clunking and other strange noises. It sounded almost like a refrigerator turning on. Alfred looked at his thumb, hoping that maybe he had pulled it away too soon. Maybe it hadn't really pricked him. But no—there it was. A little drop of blood welling up! And then suddenly a piece of paper came out of the slot in the machine.

"Well, pick it up," said Mr. Szyzylly. Alfred picked it up. He looked at it. His head was spinning, and the words didn't seem to make any sense to him. They were written in heavy black pencil on the paper.

"What does it say?" asked one of Alfred's friends.

Mr. Szyzylly took the paper and read it out loud in his big booming voice. "LAKE TITICACA!"

"Lake what?" asked one of Alfred's friends.

"LAKE TITICACA!"

The two other boys were giggling now. "Lake Titicaca?" asked Alfred. "What does that mean?"

But Mr. Szyzylly was already herding the next boy up to the machine and giving him the same solemn handshake before inserting his thumb into the hole. Alfred could only watch in confusion. He still had no idea what his own prediction meant. It was all happening too fast. He needed time to think! But suddenly the machine spat out another slip of paper and the boy read it out loud in a squeal of laughter. "BOOGERS AND BEANS!" he shouted.

"BOOGERS AND BEANS," Mr. Szyzylly confirmed in his ceremonious baritone.

Even Alfred couldn't help laughing at that one. It felt good to laugh after feeling so tense and frightened, but he was still confused. A minute later, the third boy got his slip and started laughing almost before he had looked at it. He was laughing so hard that he couldn't even talk, so Mr. Szyzylly had to take it from him and read it aloud again. "MRS. DRATMOOR'S FARTS!" he shouted in his thick accent. All three boys dissolved in giggles and gagging noises, and even Mr. Szyzylly seemed to be trembling in laughter.

"All right, boys," said Mr. Szyzylly, wiping tears from his eyes. "Get back to school now, and don't let me catch you playing hooky again!"

Alfred and his friends ran out the door, each clutching his slip of paper. They were very late coming back from recess, of course, and they each got detention. But even teachers don't want to stay long after school on the last day of fifth grade, so after only ten minutes they were running home again. Alfred spent the whole ten minutes (which, under the circumstances, still seemed like a very long time) looking at the slip of paper he had gotten from the machine and trying to understand it.

It was only later that night, as Alfred was sitting in the bathtub, that he stopped to wonder how the machine in the arcade happened to have the exact same handwriting as Mr. Szyzylly...

Story by M. Bennardo
Illustration by Dustin Harbin

IN SLEEP

THE HOLLOW CLICK OF MACHINE echoes out over the subdued murmur of the party. Sounds like a noise in the undergrounds at midnight. The kind that sends your feet to flutter across the ground, as fast as your heartbeat, no matter if you're feeling brave or not. Pome's hand hesitates before the black mouth of the sample indent.

She's had a reading before. Sang at a formal wedding. Part of her fee a turn on Machine, hired to entertain the wedding party with foretellings of their certain ends. Not Pome's idea of entertainment. But the guests hadn't taken it seriously. All those predictions of cancer, heart disease, even the bride's sudden death by aneurysm, five years to live. All a huge joke. Then Pome's reading, and suddenly they wanted her gone.

She doesn't want to repeat that. It's not her party to spoil. All the deaths they've heard so far, some distant, some not terrible at all, hers is different. Special. She knows it makes others feel cheated.

"I'm not sure," she murmurs.

Scope, to her left, sniffs ridicule. Grabs her wrist, looks up at her resistance. "Pome, it's just routine, chickah. You know your death. In sleep, baby. In sleep, just like a baby. This is just for fun, because you can. No one will care."

Pome bites her lip, seeks his eyes. Examines them for doubt. There is none. Just her own stupid mind, playing tricks again. Been doing that a lot lately. Takes her without warning. When it does,

everything skews, flips out of focus. Becomes dreamlike, but more night terror than pleasant.

Her feet feel a million miles away when it comes. Her mind floats out beyond her skull, as high as a cloud and twice as wispy. Keeps fading in the wind. Comes back with blank patches like corrupted data files. Bits of Pome missing for good.

She wonders for a moment where they've drifted. Imagines scraps playing with the birds at high altitude, swooping and sporting through billows of gray and white. Loses herself in the fear that she's losing herself in bytes, snatches. Like piranha bites. Opportunistic mouthfuls.

Pressure on her wrist brings her back. Scope stares at her hard. Like he wants to nail her into her skull with his eyes. Tugs her a little. Leans to whisper.

"Come on. It's only here a couple of hours. You're taking ages. People are staring."

Guilt washes over in acid waves, corrosive and bitter. Machine hire is not cheap. This is Lisle's day, her birthday. Pome is spoiling it. Pome smiles around; embarrassment creates a web of static over her skin. She feels her cheeks prickle, blaze. Allows Scope to thrust her hand into the hungry hole of Machine's sample unit.

Prick on her finger, like last time, comes as a shock. Makes her hiss. She removes her hand, sucks the finger hard. Warmth of her mouth turns pain to pleasant heat. There's a sigh of air, then Machine's melodic voice begins to sing as it makes its analysis. Pome's eyes drift shut.

The world shrinks till it contains only the voice of Machine. This is what Pome does, what she is, a singer. That Machine is a singer too creates a strange sort of kinship. Pome thinks of all the places she travels when she sings and wonders if Machine does the same. What it might see. The beauty of it swells her rib cage to break point. If she could listen forever, she'd allow that cage of bone to burst, shatter. Loose her innards upon the floor.

Another sigh and the music stops. It's melancholy silence. Like whale song ending. It brings a type of grief. Because this is not a sound that can be explained, only experienced. Among all the AI machines running the world, Machine alone has learned to sing, and only ever in analysis mode. The phenomenon's never been explained. Machine's creator, Priest, is never seen and never speaks, and Machine itself won't allow scientists ingress for examination.

Lights shine within Machine's oddly organic mass. Pome's aware it's composed of biotech, circuitry, soft drives, crouched within them the quiescent AI, filled with beauty it expresses only in song. But the milky, featureless sphere looks alien. Alive. As smooth as glass and shimmering with that luminescence. She imagines it would feel like liquid light. Silken. Electric. She wants to stroke it, but the AI doesn't like to be touched.

The black analysis portal is as iridescent as a shell now that lights are at full blaze. From deep within it floats a bubble. Thin, swirling with delicate patterns of data. Mesmerizing. Cryptic. So much contained in such a tiny, ephemeral sphere. Pome smiles. Leans down. She recalls the flavor. Sweet. A little tangy. A faint hint of violets. The feel of her analysis as it swept through her. She opens her mouth. Pops the bubble on her tongue.

"Eugh."

Bitterness. Such bitterness. She coughs. Sputters. Rubs her hand over her tongue. Grabs Scope's half-finished cocktail. Necks it as the new info surfs though her system. Too cold. Too hard. Like freezing knives along her nerve endings. The taste, the gelid remains of the infobubble, won't dissipate.

It sticks to the inside of her mouth. Makes her shiver. Feels dank, dark, slimy. Revolting. She grimaces. Shudders. Then it unfolds its razor-sharp origami of information, a deadly flower, into her frontal lobe. Her death, her years, both gone. In their place a death so terrible her mind flees from it, from the horrifying impression that it comes to her soon, so soon. And she's screaming. Mindless. Clutching at her skull. It's heavy, weighed down with knowledge. Hurts. Hurts so bad.

Pome drops to the floor. Head hung between knees. Screams and screams. Unable to quit. Hands move to shutter her face. Cover her eyes, as if they can block the knowledge in her brain from her awareness, and she's moaning through the screams, can't stop. Hears the words as they tumble from her mouth.

"Not possible. Not possible ... not defrag ..."

Like stones, denials drop about her feet. Anchor her. Crush her. She can't understand this information, assimilate it. It makes no sense. The only response she can find is this continued raw shout, these repeated words. They pile up around her, invisible yet as heavy as water. She feels them pressing on her skin.

Dim, distant hands touch her shoulders. Unsure. Tentative. No one speaks. Elastic silence stretches on and on, then snaps without warning. Everyone speaks at once, crowds close. Too much to hear, too much to bear. So many people, so many words. But she feels Scope's presence above her in the throng, hears his words clear above the babble.

"What's wrong, Pome? Speak it. Please. Speak. What's wrong? You're scaring me, chickah."

Pome rises, pulls herself by handfuls of clothing up his body till they're face-to-face. Her eyes feel wild with panic. Like they bug out. Scope must see it; his deep gray eyes reflect it. Mirror panic. Make it an infinity stretching on and on between them. She's gasping. Tries to find a way to say it. But there's no way. So she just screams in his face. Screams so hard her throat is raw with it.

"Changed. It changed."

Scope's head whips back and forth before his mouth says, "No. Pome, it can't have. It's not possible."

No way to tell him he'll believe, so Pome grabs his face between her palms. Grinds her mouth onto his. Sweeps her tongue over his buds. Lets him feel it. Taste it. It's been laid on her tongue like a slug trail, the last dregs. Fuck the taboo. Got to share this before it fades. Prove she's not crazy.

Scope rears back, hand clamped to mouth. Everyone stares at him. Horror builds in the room, as thick as FlyStream vapor. Then his eyes go huge. As wide as screaming mouths. Turn to her. Catch her like searchlights. His mouth flaps. Shapes without words. Then words fall. All denials, much the same as hers. A dark dreadfulness in them, furious anger. And he grabs her. He's pulling her back to Machine.

"You have to try again. You have to. Please, Pome."

Pome digs in her heels. "No." It comes out on a sob, anger, fear, frustration. Everyone is staring. Just like before. But this is worse, so much worse.

Scope comes close. Frames her face just as she did his. His eyes brim with pain and she can barely look at them. "But defrag, chickah? For you? Who would use such a weapon on you, Pome? No one. Not one soul. You're a singer. No one hurts singers. No one would *think* to do that to a singer."

Pome shakes her head, tears burning hot paths down her cheeks. Scope is wrong because Machine is never wrong. It never changes predictions. So something's changed for her; it has to have. Panic gnaws away her insides, fights for expression. This death is soon. Her mind tries again to show her how soon, but she shoves it away, does not want to know. Her legs, lips, hands, are numb. Her blood seethes cold, bitter cold, from head to feet and back again, too fast with the aching pump of a heart driven by terror. She pulls away from the grip of his palms.

"Sorry," she says. "I can't."

She flees from the room, throws a glance of agonized apology to Lisle as she goes. Ruined her party for her. It's not fair. This is Lisle's day, not Pome's. Pome should have listened to her fears. Ignorance would be better than this. No party ruined, no new death weighing down her mind. Such a burden. She wonders how they carry it. Wonders if it's only this heavy because it's coming soon. So soon.

Pome hits the street. Late out here, that deep darkness before the dawn. The Lumine trees cast only the softest blue haze. An all-consuming panorama of sky, awash with a clouded swath of starlight, shrivels her, makes her feel so small. She's too frightened to feel more fear. It's oppressive. Suffocates her.

Pome dashes tears from her eyes, turns her gaze to the floor, and runs as hard as she can. The pale echo of Scope's shout, the faint rap of his feet, ring behind her. They grow louder till he's running alongside.

"You can't run forever," he says to her between breaths.

Pome knows this. She's not trying to outrun her fate, the weight in her skull, only gain some distance from the immediacy of it all. "Just a little longer," she says, hating the pleading tone in her voice. "Just to Puerto."

"Top of Puerto, then," he yells. "After that, we talk."

Scope grabs for her hand; she doesn't fight it. Allows strong fingers to lace through hers, hold her steady as they race on, faster and faster, toward Puerto.

At the base of the scrapers, pink sunrise bleeds into royal blue night. Sitting on the roof of Puerto tower, on the east side of Hunter, Pome raises her index finger, presses her nose to the knuckle. The pain in her mind is a constant thrum. A hard, liquid weight, as if the whole waters of the ocean had been poured into a space too small to contain them. She moans a little, trying not to feel it. Closes one eye, then the other, in succession. Pink. Blue. Pink. Then blue again.

Makes her think of her sister Jaim. A game they played when they were small. Thought just by looking they could keep the day, send the night running from the heavens. Pome wonders if she can bring that belief back, reconfigure it to encompass this new death wearing away at her mind, send it running from her. Feels impossible without Jaim beside her. But they haven't stood together in a long time. They don't even speak these days.

Jaim's afraid of Pome's singing gift, perhaps jealous of it. Whatever the truth is, she walked away the day Pome began singing for a living. She's never come back. Pome wonders if it's been worth the loss, because Jaim is not here right now, when she needs her most of all. Everything they once had lies broken, by bitter words and sour deeds, too many to fix.

Grief washes over her—dark, more terrible even than the cold fear resting deep in her belly, the liquid weight bowing down her head. She lowers her finger; eyes fill with that mix of pink and blue at the horizon. They blend together, seamless, perfect, and she wonders how day and night can manage when she and Jaim cannot.

A touch on her elbow.

"Pome. We have to talk about this. We can't just ignore it."

Scope. Gray eyes sparkling fear, concern, ringed with dark circles. Brown hair a ragged snarl even without wind. Pome turns to him. Words drag out of her, reluctant, painful. "I know. I just don't know what to say. It's unreal. This shit never happens, Scope."

Scope reaches out, toys with Pome's fluttering curls, as blue as daytime sky. "So, chickah, maybe we need to find out why it has."

"How?" Pome sighs. Shakes her head. "Who would know but Priest, and he retreated from the world; he's ancient by now. Why would he speak to us?"

"Surgeon," he tells her, such certainty in him, she is stunned by it. "Surgeon would know."

Pome stares, appalled. "Surgeon? Surgeon at the Nexus...?" She's amazed by the sheer audacity of the notion. "You can't go to him. You can't do that. If you go back there you'll never get out."

Scope looks down at her hand, fingers splayed, eyes eloquent with fear. "Yes, I will. It's been ten years, Pome. Things are different these days. I'm different. And Surg is not like the others. He's... altruistic when he wants to be."

"No." Pome's answer is sharp, astringent. "I won't let you go back."

Scope hugs her shoulders hard. "That's not your choice to make." He stands, holds out a hand. "It's your future, Pome; it's been stolen. Even if you can ignore that, I can't. Please, let me help." His eyes beg her. "Don't force me to watch this happen, knowing I've done nothing to fight it."

Pome examines his face. Everything she's feeling is written there, in bold, and more, too much more. So this is what it is to know how your death will touch the ones you love. She can't bear it. Pome takes his hand. "Okay. Okay, Scope. We'll fight. But in and out quick, no dawdling."

Scope grins; his whole face lights up like the Strip on a Friday evening. "No dawdling, I promise. C'mon, chickah, let's hit the Fly-Stream."

Pome races along the building's edge, catching his relief; it's infectious. Feels like she can forget that anything has changed at all, just for a moment, up here on top of the Puerto Tower, on top of the world. Below her lies the city, spread out to the horizon. The jutting fingers of scrapers stretch to touch the atmosphere. It's noiseless at this remove. A stop-motion film. Shadows moving slow with the path of the sun. Feels like it all belongs to her still, as though she hasn't just learned that her place within it has been erased.

Five stories beneath their feet flows the slight haze of the Fly-Stream. Blurred to smears of color by the vapor, vehicles flash through. Mechanical fish flying downstream. She lets herself go, runs faster, harder. She can't die from defrag in the FlyStream—such weapons won't work there—and she needs to feel free right now. Turns to watch the end of the roof as it speeds toward her, and then she's airborne. Dropping fast. Whooping. Scope at her side, arms wide. He reaches for her hand again. Grabs, pulls. They point downward, head into the FlyStream.

Falling in is like hitting water after a cliff jump. Hitting rapids. Sudden whoosh about the ears. Pressure. Temperature drop. Then the Stream hits and she's jetting along, Scope still clings tight to her hand. Riding is danger, excitement, adrenaline overload. Pome grins, can't help it, flicks her legs, moving strong. The ripples tell her something big is coming. Gotta catch it, go faster.

She rolls to one side. Jackknifes. Stretches to fall into the trail of the transport. It's a violet bus, runs all the way to Cassia. Pome flips to her back, closes her eyes. Allows the violet bus to whip her through the Stream, Scope's fingers curled warm into her palm.

They jump the FlyStream at Nexus. From here, Scope's old haunts spread out in a slow seep of dark putrefaction. Row upon row of tall, broken tenements, slumped against one another as if in abject despair. Red-light districts, drug zones, the featureless, heavily guarded fortresses of the Pile gangs. That's why they call it the

Nexus; all the vermin of the world collect at this point, and no one who comes here, or comes from here, is ever truly a part of anything else.

Scope relaxes on these filthy streets as he does nowhere else. His gait a swagger of absolute self-containment. An edge of lethal intent simmers beneath his skin. Pome can't quit looking. He's always been beautiful to her. A little savage, a little strange. But now he's exquisite. An animal uncaged and free to roam in its natural habitat. Sleek, smooth, and confident.

The weight of her death can't spoil this, because without that weight, she'd never have witnessed it. How strange to be grateful for such a thing when only an hour ago she was so opposed to his returning.

"Do you know where he is?" Her voice sounds remote. Altered. As if she's already gone and speaking from her next life, from the void. "Will he still be there after all this time?"

Scope smiles. "Surg never changes. Nobody who stays does. Only those of us who leave get to do that." He carries on walking. Eyes flicking as swift as lightning down side streets, across neon signs, still lit even in the first light of day. Then he points. "There."

Pome squints. It's shoved at the end of a cramped alley slick with black water from leaking drains, the sign a hanging circle so small Pome wonders how Scope's eyes picked it out in the murky depths. There's no door, only a corrugated security roller, raised to halfway. Pome ducks beneath in Scope's wake, unfurls in the musty confines of a workshop crammed with rejigged tech.

At the back, curled over a small desk, a long man sits bent almost double over a series of incomprehensible units. Sends up small wisps of smoke as he touches a hot pen to the innards. Pome expects to hear small hisses like heat burning flesh, but the sounds are softer, more like sighs. Long man raises a hand without turning.

"Ho, Scope."

"Surg."

Long man Surg turns. Grins. Pome rears back, breath hostage in her throat. At first, she thinks he's eyeless; then she spots the slight haze over the holes in his head and her breath whooshes out in one long blast. VR sight. Her hand shoots to cover her mouth, hold in all the words suddenly crowding to be said. Those static-filled hollows turn to take her in.

"Who's blue?"

Scope pulls Pome forward, hugs her to his side. "Surgeon, this is Pome."

A brow rises on the eyeless face. "Pome the singer?" The question is loaded, full of wariness, unease, perhaps distaste.

Pome answers him herself. "Yes."

She pays no mind to his attitude; Jaim is not the only one to fear her gift. Many people fear what singers do, how they see things others can't when they raise their voices in song. She's often met with terror or unease. It's just a fact of the life she chose. With her voice, as good as it is, she could be famous, wealthy, one of the Prelacy singers, pampered and cosseted, but it's never tempted her. She loves the life she's had stolen. In light of that, Surgeon's opinion of her gift is unimportant. All that matters is whether he can help her or not.

Surg's throat works a little; then he nods, sits a little taller, taps his temple. Fuzzy, disembodied eyes appear, floating on the gaping holes in his skull. They're an unusual shade of purple, bright and cutting. Piercing, as if he sees beyond her flesh into the striated pathways of her veins, along spiked avenues of sparking nerves, right to the neocortex, to the bloated tumor of information crowding out her mind.

"An honor," he says, terse, carefully neutral. "Not often one so gifted graces my workshop." Browned teeth bare in a humorless grin, still hostile but not as much as before. "What brings you here, singer?"

Here it is. She doesn't even know this man, but she knows her choices. Speak and perhaps learn what's happened to her. Or run and die in ignorance. Pome looks straight into that purple gaze. "My death changed. I want to know why."

The room fills with a steady hum of machine noise as Surg sits, silent, at his desk. His gaze flickers in and out, a poorly tuned channel, moves between Scope and Pome in rapid shifts. A bloodhound gaze, sniffing clues. Finally, he purses his lips, unfolds from the desk, his body a line of reluctance.

"A singer's death changed? That's...unusual. Wait here."

Pome turns an agonized look to Scope as Surg disappears, bent over like an old man in the shrunken dimensions of his workshop. Scope mouths, "It's okay." Rubs her arms with chilled fingers. They offer no comfort. Feels like her flesh is already dead, just waiting for the rest of her to realize and let go. Nausea wells up her throat; Pome pulls away as Surg reenters, pushing a shrouded shape before him. His voice cuts through the room like a Klaxon, too loud, jarring to the ear.

"What was your death?"

Pome blinks. "My first?"

"That's the one."

"Death in sleep. Eighty years from last year. I was to live to four score and twenty-three. So long. Longer than most anyone I know."

Surg huffs, impressed. "And now?"

Pome takes a deep breath. Licks her lips. "Defragmentation. Soon."

Surg is crouched low on the floor beside the shrouded object, his legs jutting out at angles, frog legs. Not enough so they can see what's under it, just enough to work on what's hidden. His hands move too fast to watch; soft clicks and a growing burr of noise accompany them. At this, though, he hesitates.

"Defrag?" He directs a solemn gaze at her. "I am sorry. That's... brutal. How soon?"

"I...I'm not sure. I don't want to look. Please don't make me."

"Fine." He looks at her, flickering purple eyes too candid. "There's weight, yes?"

She swallows. "A lot. It hurts. Sharp pain."

"Why is there weight?" Scope asks, his hands on Pome's shoulders. Looks as if he's holding himself up rather than supporting her.

"Too much for the psyche," Surg answers, matter-of-fact, then dips his head at Pome. "They bioscape your blood to fool your body, but they can't do shit about your mind, especially not if you have another reading. The loss is a paradox, a short circuit." He moves his chair before the shrouded object. "Come and sit. You been feeling strange before this?"

Pome stares at him as she moves to sit. "Yes. How...?"

He shakes his head. "Seen it before, haven't I. How long?"

Pome nibbles at her bottom lip. Surg studies her with intent as he rubs hard at the back of her hand, tapping, then rubbing again, holding her fingers in a tight fist. "It started not long after the wedding party where I got my first reading," she tells him. "A few months. Just under three."

Surg retrieves a long umbilicus from under the sheet. At the end sits a delicate needle, as fine as hair. He inserts it deftly into a vein on the back of her hand. Then he pinches the cloth, lifts it away with care bordering on tenderness, his face a studied blank. What's under is a deformed, ugly remnant. A Machine somehow perverted, misshapen, wronged. Swollen and sickly white. Pome cries out, tries to move away, but Surg has her in a firm grip.

"I need another bubble. You won't taste it. I will."

"But Machine." Pome can't stop gaping at it. It's like seeing an angel reduced to peddling flesh. "Is it...does it...the AI...?"

Surg catches her chin as slow whining, a travesty of Machine's song, begins to issue from the deformed mass. His eyes hold hers prisoner, hard, savage. "I found this in the industrial wastes. I've found them once or twice before, but this is the only one that survived. It hangs on and so I do the best I can for it. I rarely ask it to work, but you have questions and this is the only way we'll be able to answer them."

Tears spill down Pome's cheeks. The whining is so close to being song but so far away. It aches within her as if it's she who's broken. As if her voice is trying to sing and failing. It doesn't matter that it's an AI. This is wrong. As the whine runs down to silence and the bubble looses from a broken hole near the top of the mass, Surg lets go of her chin, says, "Save your pity; you'll need it for yourself soon enough. What they've done to you makes this Machine's suffering look like mercy." Then he leans down and catches the bubble on his tongue.

Purple eyes snap off, replaced by static, blank holes. A hiss of VR data. The muscles about his eyes twitch, staccato, as in REM sleep. Then he jerks. One hand flies to rest on Machine. Surg's head tilts, as if he listens to faraway voices. His mouth drops open on a soft exhalation of awe. For a moment, his face is clear, as soft as a child's. Then the hand on Machine twitches, convulses, lies still, and his expression shutters, closes down, bleak and grief stricken.

Haze stutters back to purple eyes then. He says only two words, his voice hoarse with unshed tears that are not for Pome. "Prelate Agastine."

Scope slumps against a tower of conjoined units. "Agastine?" His tone is dead, a ghost of itself.

Surg's mouth twitches downward. He says to Pome, "Given your death is defrag, I expected it to be a notable. But no matter who it was, there's no changing it. His death is now yours, and your life belongs to him."

"He wanted my eighty years," Pome says, still stuck on the shock of who it is that has her future, feeling thin, fragile, a touch unhinged.

"Not just your years," Surg tells her, "your death, too. It makes those years unassailable, unmarred. Clearly too big a prize to resist."

Pome stares at him, wretched. "How is it he could take them?"

Surg takes time pulling the needle from the back of her hand, his fingers sure and gentle. Speaks slow and even, as if he can make the words easier to hear somehow. "Priest created more than Machine. Word is, when he tested himself, his diagnosis was bad. Some degenerative disease, a slow killer. So he created something to fight it. Called it the bioscape virus." Surg reaches into his jacket, pulls out a vial, hands it to Pome. "It's data-intensive biotech. Reprograms cells."

Pome looks at the liquid in the vial. It glides up and down the vial as her hand moves. The liquid shimmers, millions of tiny glistening specks, trapped constellations, in thick, silvery solution. It radiates gentle heat. Her palm tingles with it. Feels like she holds a life in her hands, a thrumming heart.

"Can Pome use that?" Scope asks. The hope in his voice is a ragged edge.

Surg snorts. Takes back the vial. "No. It can do a lot, but it can't stop death." Surg tilts the vial, repockets it. "That's the problem, see; death is what notables like Agastine want to avoid. They can't, so they cheat it instead. Watch Machine records for people like Pome, people with a stock of years. Take them while they're sleeping, steal their blood. This"—he pats his pocket—"makes it all possible."

Pome can't take it in. It refuses to make sense. "How can that work? It's not the blood the future is tied to . . . it can't be. Why does no one put a stop to it?"

Surg gives Pome a crooked smile. There's no humor in it, just an acknowledgment of the breadth, the magnitude of his revelations. "Who's going to tell the Prelacy what it can and can't do, singer?" He rubs at the bead of blood on the back of her hand, turns it into a faint red smear. "After an exchange, there's a second reading. An infobubble is data. Once consumed, it binds with the bioscape data, creates a biofeedback loop, and integrates the new years into the body's cell memory. The new death uploads like a virus, slowly replacing the old."

"But how do they make donors do that?" asks Pome, face slack with confusion.

Surg laughs, darkly cynical. "In sleep, singer, force-fed the infobubble. That's where the damage occurs, the initial paradox. It's a brutal process, losing a future. Not every donor survives it." His fingers rise to Pome's hair, stroke the verdant curls. "Those that do wake up with a new death, changed, broken, and utterly unaware that everything they had has been taken from them."

"Like me." Pome feels hollow. All that remains in her is an echo of what was her self. Not even that. Just a memory. Vague and tremulous.

"Like you." Surg sighs. His hand leaves Pome's hair, wanders to the remains of the Machine in his care. The purple of his eyes dulls to a flicker. "I don't understand Machine. I've never seen an AI like it. When I connect to its soft drive I sense grief. Sorrow. This Machine is dying of a broken heart."

He lifts the shroud and replaces it over the wreckage of Machine, his face contorted with unspeakable emotion. "I'm no Priest. I can't mend it properly. I wish I could. And I wish I could help you, singer, but I can't. I won't try."

Scope steps forward, his face a helpless mask of rage. "Why?"

Surg looks up; those purple eyes sputter, fade out. Blank hollows regard Scope with emotionless cool. "It's a miracle she survived the first transfer. She'd never survive a second, and you can't volunteer your life to her; we all know how that will end. You can't change this. She's going to meet her end. Soon."

Scope doesn't look at him. He's staring at Pome; she stares back, her gaze too deep, too lost. "No," he says. Absolute certainty in the denial.

He reaches out, offers his hand to Pome. Surg steps forward, mouth open to speak, a look of tortured indecision on his face, but Scope shakes his head hard. Pulls Pome away. She follows him to the security roller, docile, reduced. They're halfway down the alley before they hear the rattle of the security roller, then Surg's voice behind them, calling out with such urgency it almost stops Pome in her tracks.

"You have to meet your death head-on, singer. Seven days. At Matin's square, eight after twelve, the Prelate's speech." He shouts louder as they reach the alley mouth. "Don't run from it. Don't die somewhere else. Machine told me. It spoke to me. Do you understand? Machine spoke to me. It *spoke*. For you, Pome. It never speaks. Do you understand?"

Scope ignores him, carries on walking. But Pome, curious, turns to look back. Surg's stuttering purple eyes flash in the gloom. There's urgency in them. Desperation. He lifts a hand as if reaching out to her, and she smiles, just a little. Just to show she's listened.

The look in Surg's eyes follows Pome all the way back to the Fly-

Stream. She can't stop thinking of all she's learned from the broken Machine, from Surgeon. It resonates through her. Shatters her beliefs one by one. Her understanding. Leaves her afloat, adrift. It is an odd way to face death. But is there any normal way to face it?

Pome pulls her arm from Scope's grasp. His hand falls back; he lifts it and stares at his empty palm as though bereft. But it is Pome who is bereft. A thief came in the night to take her life in her sleep. Machine was right about that at least. Her death has come in sleep, but she must face it in the waking. Perhaps even head-on, at Matin's square, in seven short days. Seven days. It's the merest fraction of eighty years. The magnitude of what she's lost staggers her.

She watches the vehicles flit through the FlyStream, thinks how she'll face the next seven days. Knowing your death is both horror and liberation. It doesn't matter what she does now; she won't die until eight after twelve in seven days' time. A bubble of laughter ripples up from her belly. She turns to Scope, grins.

"Race you," she shouts and tears off along the edge of the building. If all she's got are these seven days, she's going to live them. Wear them out. Wring them of each and every second they possess. Decide in that time whether death will come for her, or whether she will run to it, arms open, and surrender herself without fear.

Pome stands across from the Prelacy, at Matin's square. She wasn't sure if she'd come, there have been such extremes of fear and anger. But time and again Surg's voice has echoed after her. Followed her through this last week of hers, driven her to consider the unthinkable, facing her death head-on without hesitation, and she's gradually come to accept that this is her only option.

Scope's argued his voice raw, but why run from something that's bound to hit you? She doesn't see the point. Why not face it dead on, square up to it? There's more strength in acceptance than there is in denial. Scope stands beside her now, resigned to her choice and willing to support her. She couldn't love him more than at this very moment; it's not possible.

The Prelacy is a dark block on the night. Looks much like a

portal. Yawning. Vast. There are sky and stars abounding, the glittering scarf of Aleron's ribbon, then nothing. Just black. A huge square of it. Pome stops at distance, reluctant to continue. Heart in throat. It's not solid, that block of starless dark. Though it's only a silhouette upon the night, it appears hollow, endless. A black hole, swallowing stars. Fit to swallow her should she venture too close.

Two things drive her onward: the warm clasp of Scope's hand and the weight of her skull. The cutting edges of that origami of information shot through soft tissue. Pome knows there's nothing in her brain but the data. But pain feels real, as does weight. More burden than one mind can bear. Dazed notion crosses her thoughts that perhaps this is why, before Machine, no one knew their death. Enough to know that death is coming, without knowing how or when. Sometimes such knowledge is too much to hold.

Together they weave into the throng awaiting Prelate Agastine. If Pome stretches to tiptoes she can make out the lavish preparations in the light of Lumine trees on the steps. Swags and bunting, plush purple carpets across the threshold, down to the square. A dozen grim-featured guards flank the podium at the stair top. Despite his theft of her life, her years, the Prelate is taking no chances. Pome can't blame him. Fear is a great motivator.

It's what's drawn her here. But she's coming from the opposite side to Agastine. He's constructed fancy barricades of guards and stolen years against his fear; she's walked right into hers, refusing to be cowed. Accepted it. Might be a matter of choice. If Pome had the Prelate's power, his wealth, would she be here or at some exclusive surgery, stealing the life from another. She'd like to think it would change nothing, but she's unsure. That's a choice she didn't get to make.

They're mere rows from the front when the doors of the Prelacy swing wide. Regal and resplendent in his robes of office, the Prelate sweeps from the building. His swift, energetic steps swallow ground with arrogant purpose. Heavily lined skin hangs in folds from withered bones, yet he glows with stolen vitality, his fuel of stolen years. Hers. All eighty years of it. A ten-strong guard accompanies him.

Slender, deadly Verts, no more human than Machine. Their blank visages reflect the crowd like mirrors.

Pome strives on, taking no care now, moves ahead of Scope, untangling her hand from his; she needs to be at the front. But these last rows are penitents, disciples. They snarl at her, resentful to be moved, shove hard elbows out to hold her progress. She's reaching, struggling against a wall of bodies, when she sees him.

He walks at some distance behind the Prelate, a tall, hooded figure hemmed in by four Vert. Their formation is not protective—it's a forbidding square; the matte black solidity of their staves form a barrier, imprison him, remain active in an overt threat against escape. His face lifts a fraction. Soft blue light penetrates the shadows of the hood, washes over his features.

He's young but so burdened. It's in the set line of his mouth, the pallor on his cheeks, the dark hollows framing his eyes. Pome gazes at him, can't stop; he looks as troubled as she feels, and for a moment, she wants to reach out to him, tell him he's not alone. A reckless thought, because soon she will be dead and it will not be true.

Agastine begins to speak. His voice rings loud over the roar of the crowd, signals it to silence. The crowd surges forward in response. Pome redoubles her efforts to reach the front, grabbing clothes, limbs, but there's no give in the lines of penitents before her, too much pressure from bodies behind. She's about to give up, give in. Then, above the echoing cry of Agastine's words, she hears one of the guards roar at full volume.

"Stop! Hold her, she has a defrag. Move the Prelate. Move him!"

The Prelate's voice stops midsentence, the amplex crackles, cuts to silence. The crowd takes a breath. For several terrible seconds, Pome is unable to move as the press of bodies draws ever closer, strains forward, eager to witness the events taking place at the podium. Pome's heart leaps to frantic pounding. Here it is, her end, and she's not where she needs to be.

Straining through the gaps in bodies Pome sees a ragged, skeletal woman in the guards' clutches, her face a contorted, soundless scream. She's so thin, mere skin and bone, but she moves with such power the guards can barely hold her. Mouth stretched to impossible width, the woman wrenches her arms free, jackknifes, throws herself down to snatch up from the floor the innocuous oblong of a defrag gun.

A collective gasp rises from the crowd; a few isolated screams build to a hysterical cacophony. Bodies surge backward, pile into Pome's, toppling her. She shrieks, throws her arms up, eyes fixed on a tiny glimpse of blue among the heads above her. Shots break out and the crowd surges harder. Faster. Pome's breath explodes in hard puffs. Her legs piston at the ground, struggle for purchase, push up, forward. She whimpers, fingers scrabbling for purchase, lungs burning for oxygen.

"Not like this," she pleads.

Without warning the pressure eases. Still pushing forward, Pome catapults into the air, onto her hands and knees at the base of the stairs. The skeletal woman tears past her, buffeting her with wind. She's sobbing as she runs, defrag gun raised high. Blood seeps from wounds in her shoulders, legs, but she does not even so much as slow her pace.

The guards pound up behind her, surging around Pome's prone body. A volley of heavy cracks cut through the noise of the crowd. Pome covers her head with her arms, watches as the woman is thrown forward, screeching, a sound of unimaginable pain and fury. Her face smacks into the edge of a step. There's a wet crunching, a muffled grunt, and she's still. The guards split to two lines, spread out, and move toward the body. Slow, easy, weapons raised.

Pome rises to her knees, stares. Behind her the crowd noise forms a solid wall. Isolates her in the moment. Just her, the broken body on the steps, and the guards. It wasn't supposed to end like this. A terrible heaviness sits in her gut, as though all that weight from her head has moved downward. It's ominous, a foreboding, but she doesn't move. She can't.

The guards reach the body. Pome holds her breath as one reaches out a booted foot and rolls the body over. Teeth bared, coughing blood, the woman raises her arms, the gun. Pome watches the flat barrel sweep in her direction. There's a din of explosions as all the guards discharge their weapons at once. The emaciated, battered woman on the stairs jerks as if convulsing, arms flying up, down, hands curled tight about that gray oblong.

A deep thrum rips through the air, slices into Pome's head, a blade formed of vibrations. The sound it pulls from her is a retch, guttural, ugly. Scope cries out her name somewhere close, but it's muffled, as if heard underwater. And the knife slices deeper. Her head pulses fit to burst. The crowd noise blurs, joins the thrum, the increasingly panicked calls of Scope; they bind into one continuous note and she's singing it; it rips from her throat as loud as a scream.

Pome wants to stop, but her throat moves on its own authority. She raises her hands to shove them into her mouth. Catches sight of them through clouded eyes. Blood. So much blood. Where is it coming from? And the screaming, the thrumming, the notes so loud they fill her to her very edges. Push at her skin from the inside and she's tearing. Rupturing. Can't hold herself together. There's pain all over, fierce, unbearable cramps.

Scope's voice sounds through the tumult, right next to her. Such agony in it. "Pome. No." He's screaming almost as loud as the note. "Help her, please help her. No, no, don't take her away. *Don't take her away from me!*"

And she's moving, rising, floating along, can hear Scope's voice in the background, fading away. Hoarse, pleading, cracking apart. She tries to reach for him, but nothing works. Her body is no longer hers. Heat then. A blast so hot it burns her skin, and the endless note takes on a quality of hysteria. Over it, she hears someone speak. Their tone is lilting, fluid, as lyrical as song.

"Such a glorious voice. Even like this, the note is perfection. What have you done, Agastine? You didn't need to use her."

"Nonsense." The reply is harsh, swollen with conceit. "It's just another wastrel. What does something like that need eighty years for? Godless, wasting its gift on drunkards at filthy clubs. I have liberated those years, Priest. They serve me far better than her."

"It isn't right. Not with singers, never with singers. You could have waited. I'm close, Agastine, so close. You won't need more years when you have the key to mine. I promised you that." There's struggle in that response, as if more is longing to be expressed but cannot. It elicits no answer, only the fading reverberation of footsteps on carpet, stone. Then Priest speaks directly to Pome. "Easy, now. Easy. It'll be over soon."

A hand touches her hair. It should be excruciating, but it soothes her. Lifts some of the pain, the noise within. The weight of his presence appears at her side. Pome feels her body loosen; she falls toward that heavy presence. Into it. Pain slips further and further away from her. She can no longer hear the note, though the swell and ache in her throat tell her she's still singing.

Her dazed eyes flutter open. Focus on a hooded head, bent toward her as if in prayer. On that face, so troubled for one so young, so touched by sorrow. And at last she understands. Priest is as much a victim of his brilliance as she is. She cannot bear this; it's too much to know. Her eyes blur tears, veer away. Above them, Aleron's ribbon strikes through the darkness, a glorious burst of light and life.

She and Scope were to fly there one day, see other worlds, other races. It will never happen, but it wouldn't have anyway. She thinks of Jaim, the pain of her rejection. Feels at peace with it at last. It doesn't matter that she's no time left to fix it; what they had as children can never be lost. Not even death can take the past away. It is already lived. Stored forever in time. Perfect and unassailable.

All death steals is the future. Unlived. Unknown. Uncharted territory. Therefore, not worth the grieving. Distant now, as if on another galaxy, she hears Priest's voice murmur.

"Put her down; you're hurting her. She's in enough pain; have pity on her."

Pome doesn't feel the ground as they lower her to it. Her mind is lost in the stars, in memories. In Scope's eyes. Doesn't feel the impact on her small, fragile body as it splits, begins to defrag. The shatter of bones, the burst of soft tissues. The crack of her skull. Half-blind, sheathed in ice, she lies there, seeing the stars in her mind's eye. Waits for the end to come.

As she slips away by increments, warm breath caresses her ear. His voice, rich, as lulling as a melody, speaks to her once more.

"I would have waited for you," he says. "I would have waited eighty years." Then everything fades. And Pome is gone.

Pome awakes. Radiance surrounds her. Warmth. It envelops every inch. Drowsy, Pome goes to rub her eyes. But there are no hands, no arms. She blinks surprise and finds she has no eyes. Pome is everywhere and nowhere. Is she dead? Is this what death is? Then the most unbearable sensation. Too much all at once, as if every nerve is stroked and stimulated. And a voice.

"Sorry to touch. I know it's intolerable."

She recognizes the voice. Priest. He was there beside her as she lay singing that never-ending note, her body dismantling itself under defrag. Not dead, then. If not dead, then what? The touch leaves her and the relief is all encompassing. Pome sighs. Startles to hear the sound of it echo into the air. Swallows. Again that shock of finding no throat to swallow with. It's as if her body has vaporized. She tries to speak.

"Where am I? Where's my Scope?"

"This is my workshop. In my quarters at the Prelacy. Is Scope the man who was fighting? I'm so sorry. He was detained. He tried so hard to reach you."

Pome feels that as sharp as the pain of her death. Longs to be with Scope, to see him. But what is there left of her for him to recognize? She doesn't even know what she is, whether or not she's real.

"Am I alive?" Her voice sounds odd, too close and too far away all at once.

"In a way. You're Machine now," Priest tells her. "You've been on my list for this since you began singing. I never once imagined I'd have to do it without your consent."

Pome's thoughts dim, blur. She hears herself repeat as though a dullard. "List?"

"Only the soul of a singer can make a Machine," he says. "It's about where you go, what you see. I discovered by sheer accident... a woman I knew..." He falters. Continues softly. "I offer all singers on my list the option to live on like this."

Pome is bemused, too dazed to be furious. "Do they all accept?"

"No. Not all. But enough."

Pome sinks into silence, shudders to think how she has been used. Even in this rebirth she is being used. But it is better than a full stop. Pome's thoughts spin to the pitiable Machine in Surgeon's workshop. If she possessed a chest, wore a heart within it, she would be heartbroken. The thought of the singer inside that Machine, the loss of the voice, is beyond bearing. Pome has to ask him.

"I saw a Machine, before my death, one that couldn't sing anymore. Why was it so broken?"

She hears the ragged quality in Priest's breath in the silence that follows. He clears his throat, twice. But his voice still cracks when he speaks. "Reading altered deaths. It ruins them somehow. Eats away at them like rot."

Pome feels her entire self shrink to a ball of sheer misery. Even in this new life she could end broken; there is no end to the cruelty of the Prelacy. "It spoke," she tells him dully, "but only through a VR link-up. How do I speak as I could before?"

The silence is minute, loaded. "All Machines are the same to begin with. I have to preserve the vocal cords, use them in construction as part of a synthesizer. A singer is not a singer without their unique voice. For most Machines, silence is a meditation. You will understand it soon far better than I can explain it."

"My vocal cords?" Pome is stunned. If she were not right in the middle of it, she would laugh at how ludicrous, how impossible, this is.

"I had to work quickly to save them, to save you. We almost lost all of you. I wanted to give you a future, and this is the only one I could provide. It's one I'd always planned to offer you. I'm so sorry it had to be like this."

Pome recalls his words before the void consumed her. Thinks of the eighty years, the future she lost. Meaningless. She always had more than one future awaiting her. Better to receive one early, then, unexpectedly, than to lose both. Even if this future has its pitfalls, so did the one before. There is no difference; both are life and life is uncertain. Pome has a lot to thank that broken Machine for.

Even in its suffering, the loss of its song, it led her to the possibility of survival.

There is a stirring then. A displacement of air before, yet within, her.

"Feel that?" Priest asks.

"Yes, what is it?"

"My hand. Focus on it. Let your whole awareness bleed out until it hits resistance; then I want you to try and take a blood sample from me. You'll know how."

Pome tries to take a breath. Laughs as she recalls that there are no lungs to breathe with, even if she needed air. She stretches out, floods the space about her until she feels she can go no farther. It doesn't feel like confinement. She's never felt so vast, so powerful.

She feels the hand now. The shape of it, the density. The blood pumping through veins, capillaries. Texture of skin, the finest hair follicles. The lines of the palm, fingerprints even, each delicate whorl. Senses too, the needle, just the same. Her awareness is infinite, immeasurable. Yet she feels no fear. She touches the needle with her mind, pleased that it moves to her command. Guides it gently to a fingertip and pricks lightly.

Blood wells. She can taste it. It should be copper, salt, sickly, but instead it fills her senses to overload. Soars through her in a powerful flood, rich, dark, breathtaking. The curlicue of DNA, the vibrations of molecules, all joined together in wondrous harmony. A history reels out within her mind's eye, all Priest has ever been, will ever be; it is all there, and it is the most glorious music. It speaks into her, fills her soul.

Before it overwhelms her, she hears a soft sigh. Knows that it comes from her voice. Just as it does from the other voices in the Machines. Then she is plunged headlong into the beauty of the blood, and unable to prevent herself, she bursts into song.

Story by Ren Warom
Illustration by Claire Hummel

POISON

KC GREEN

CECILE

CECILE RISES FROM THE WATER, the little drops clinging to the curve of her hips and the swell of her breasts. Her dark hair is matted to her head, and she pushes it back off her shoulders. She looks just as good in a swimsuit as she does in anything else. Beautiful. Wonderful. I'd wonder why she was with me. Why she loved me at all—and it is love. It has to be. Then I remember what the machine said and smile. CECILE. Yes. It will be her. It should be her.

"Katherine?" she says and raises an eyebrow as she grabs the towel from the chair next to me. Her voice is heavily accented—French. The little hairs on my arms prick up every time she speaks. "Don't you want to swim?"

I look down at the boy shorts that are supposed to make me look every bit the curvy woman, but I'm still too skinny. "Do you want me to?"

She cups my chin in her hand, kissing me gently on the lips. "Only if you want, my love."

I shake my head and pick up my book.

Every man in the vicinity has his eyes on Cecile. She smiles, ties the sarong around her waist, and slips on oversized sunglasses before she sits back in the chair. A busboy hurries to her side as she raises a slender arm. "Wine?" she asks, and I nod, knowing anything she orders will be the best.

She rattles off her order to the busboy in French, and I understand only snippets of what she says. There's going to be food involved. There's always food involved. I wonder if that's how she'll kill me. Poison? It seems like her.

"Are you enjoying life in my home country?" she asks after the busboy rushes away.

"Of course. The beach is so different on this side of the Mediterranean."

She smiles and runs her fingers through my recently butchered hair. She said I'd look cute with it short, so I let her cut it one night before we came here. That was back in Cairo. She lifted the scissors in the dim overhead lights of our crowded apartment and I wondered then, like I always do, if this was going to be it. Was she going to slit my throat? Stab me in the heart? Would my hot blood stain her hands while she smiled her perfect smile, showing that tiny gap between her front teeth? No. She only cut my ill-maintained bob into a sassy pixie, blowing the hair off my neck and ears.

"It needs a trim soon," she says, and a little stab of excitement shoots through my stomach.

"Did you bring the scissors?"

She shakes her head. "*Non*. We'll have to buy a new pair while we're here. And no, it can't wait until we're back in Cairo; you'll have a mop on your head by then."

I laugh and nod. "You can do it whenever you want."

After a shower in our hotel room we dress for dinner. Cecile has friends in Nice. It's not a surprise. She has friends everywhere.

"The gold dress, love. It looks best with your hair," she says and slips on something red and backless. No underwear means no panty line. I'm not so brave.

I pull the gold drapey fabric over my head, and she zips it up without asking if I need help. Then she fixes my hair and points at the black heels. "You can borrow my black clutch."

"Does being fashionable come with being French?" I ask as she piles her loose curls into pins on her head.

"Perhaps," she says, a wicked grin on her lips as she dabs on red lipstick. It matches her dress. "Come, I'll make you up."

I stand obediently in front of her to get powdered and dabbed until I hardly recognize myself in the mirror. I'm not sure how she turns me from cute into whatever this is, but I'm not going to complain.

We get to the restaurant fashionably late.

Cecile kisses the cheeks of her old friends, a few hetero couples and a single man, and introduces me. "Katherine, my lover."

The heat rises to my cheeks, but I nod and smile. I should have studied French when I had the chance.

They all eye me like they wonder why she's with me. I can't blame them. It's hard to see from the outside looking in. I can hardly tell them she's the one. The one who's going to kill me someday.

We settle down for a meal of roasted fish drenched in butter and a number of other rich foods. I can hardly eat as I try to keep up with barely caught snippets of conversation. Cecile chats with the single man. He's handsome, for a guy, and eyes her like every other straight male in the world.

"How long have you known Cici?" one of the women asks in English.

"Five years," I say, and dab my mouth, careful to avoid smearing my lipstick. Cecile's lipstick is still perfect.

"Oh, where did you meet?"

I sip my wine and feel slightly light-headed. This is my third glass today. "Mumbai, actually. She was collecting for a museum, and I was a grad student working on an archeological dig outside of the city. She worked with us."

I can still taste the dust in my mouth from the time I first saw her wearing those high-waisted khaki pants, the crisp white oxford, and her dark hair in a braid down her back. I felt stupid and ugly just standing next her. When she introduced herself, I stared.

"Cecile?" I repeated. The name. I'd thought about that name my whole life. Since I was old enough to know what the machine told my parents the day I was born. Cecile was going to be how I died.

"*Oui,*" she said. "And you are?"

"Kathy—or Katherine." I don't even know why I told her that. I'd gone by Kathy since I was a kid, but she got a strange gleam in her eyes when she heard my name. I've been Katherine ever since.

After the party, Cecile kisses her friends again. The man—his name's Stephan—lets his lips linger on her cheek longer than the others. I almost giggle, if not from the wine then because I know her better than any of them. I know what she's capable of. What she'll do for love—for me.

When we get back to the hotel I fall into bed, but Cecile urges me into the bathroom and wipes all the makeup off our faces. "You were bored tonight, my love?" she asks as she hands me my toothbrush.

"Not bored. Your friends are very—"

"Snobby, you would call it?"

I brush my teeth, but I know my cheeks are pink, and it has nothing to do with the wine. She just smiles and pulls me to bed when we're done. She's warm and inviting.

My phone wakes me up the next morning. I look at the caller ID and walk out onto the balcony before I answer. Below, the water rolls in and out on the sandy beach. Cecile's still in bed, the blankets pushed down to her waist, showing off her pert breasts.

"Mom?" I say.

"Oh, Kathy! Finally! Where are you, dear?"

"Um, France, Mom."

"Oh, weren't you in Turkey last time?" I can see her sitting at the little kitchen table, her gray hair cut short, and a cup of tea going cold as she talks.

I lean against the balcony. "Istanbul for a while. We've been in Cairo for the last six months."

"Egypt, dear?"

"The very same," I say, and smile. She's never been farther west than Seattle.

"Oh, that sounds exciting. Did you know Ted is getting married? I'm not sure if he called you yet to let you know."

"No, I hadn't heard. It's Emily, right?"

"Yes, that's right. He wants you to come to the wedding. Do you think you could come back home for just a bit? I haven't seen you since you left for school; what's it been now?"

The familiar pit forms in my stomach. "About five years, Mom."

"Well, what do you say? I know you're busy, but I'd sure like to meet this friend of yours—"

"Lover, Mom. We're lovers."

She's quiet for a moment, like she always is when I tell her. "I know. I know. I was just trying to be discreet."

"I think it's best if you don't meet her, Mom." Best for all of us.

"Ted was really looking forward to—"

"I know. I'll see what I can do. Maybe I can come alone," I lie and bite my bottom lip, happy she can't see me. "I should go. International rates and all."

"Right. I love you, Kathy."

"Love you too, Mom."

I turn my phone off and climb back into bed next to Cecile. She reaches for me and half opens her eyes. "Why don't you want me to meet your family?" she asks, and runs a finger down my cheek.

I bury my face into her chest right over her heart, kissing it lightly, wondering when it will turn on me. A twinge of excitement runs through my body. I don't want them to catch her. I don't want her punished. Not for that. Not for loving me.

"I love you too much," I say.

Her hands caress the skin on my back, and her breath catches in her throat. "I love you too, Katherine."

Story by Hollan Lane
Illustration by Ramón Pérez

LA MORT D'UN ROTURIER

JULIETTE STOOD AGAINST THE PASTEL-PAINTED wall of the magnificent candlelit ballroom and watched disinterestedly as more than a hundred masked guests, mainly Parisians but with a few recently liberated Americans fresh from their French-funded revolution, each dressed in their finest clothes, danced and drank and gorged and indulged in any other *débauche* they could get away with in the flickering light of the chandeliers above, not to mention the numerous discreet shadowy corners they provided. Unfortunate servants all across Paris would be scrubbing unmentionable stains from the finery for days after this grand masquerade had ended. She was just deeply grateful that she wouldn't be one of them.

The windows of the ballroom were dark, midnight long since passed, though rain fell against the glass in a steady stream, and there were occasional distant rumbles of thunder that made Juliette shiver. Her costume was far less extravagant than those of the invited guests to this grand masquerade, of course, a simple dark blue masculine pageboy costume, her dark hair pinned up inside her cap. She wasn't there to be seen, not in the same way as these overweight nobles and other *bourgeoisie*. No, she was there for a far simpler function. The same function, she had to admit to herself with no small measure of reluctance, as the six drunken dwarves to her left juggling pigs' testicles tied with bright red ribbons while singing "Marlbrough S'en Va-T-En Guerre," and the raggedy stilt walkers who stalked the crowd, frightening delicate noblewomen by brushing spindly wooden claws across the backs of their corpulent necks.

She was an entertainment, a diversion, nothing more. She and Isaac. And clearly far less popular than the others, for obvious reasons. Those who partook in the... *demonstration* invariably walked away sucking their fingers and clutching a scrap of paper in their free hand, glancing time and time again at the writing there, working hard to look nonchalant and amused by the whole affair, but there was that disquiet in their eyes, a darkness that shadowed their mood.

Juliette smiled a little at that thought. You really shouldn't ask a question that you don't wish to know the answer to. They never learned.

"*Mademoiselle* Jaquet-Droz?" A light, effete voice spoke from beside her. She turned to face the speaker and recognized him immediately. Of course, she wasn't supposed to; the generous host of this masquerade made an ostentatious display of his anonymity, as he did of everything else in his profoundly entitled life. Nobody here knew who he was. *Everybody* here knew who he was. It was all part of the charade. The man was fat, of course, as were almost all the guests, and wore a flamboyant ball gown, his face half-covered by a deep purple mask. What flesh was exposed there was painted white, and his lips were stained red, as if he'd been eating mulberries. Juliette resisted the urge to look for his infamous wife, *la putain autrichienne.*

"*Oui, monsieur?*" Juliette responded as casually as she could manage. This man was her employer tonight. Her performance could mean considerable monies, or a swift exit to the shit-stained cobbled streets outside. The outcome was up to her. And Isaac, of course.

"You're not wearing a mask," the man pointed out, rather unnecessarily.

She smiled at him sweetly. "That remains to be seen. Do you wish to experience Isaac's wisdom?"

The man in the ball gown turned his attention to the incredible object that sat beside Juliette. A strange, crooked smile crept across his plump red lips. "*Ah, oui,*" he breathed.

Isaac was an automaton, his face and hands carved from delicate wax, sitting at a small mahogany writing desk. He was dressed from the waist up in the clothes of a peasant, rough-woven fabrics stitched together by hand. Below the waist he did not exist, his body merging with the desk and casings for the intricate machineries hidden within. On his shirt was a patch, sewed to his left breast, a coat of arms, two pure white crossed bones on a black background. One of his smooth hands held a quill, the feather dyed a brilliant red. The other hand rested palm down on the desk. His eyes were closed, his waxen face patient, implacable. Waiting.

"Incredible," the fat man in the gown said, his hungry eyes sliding across Isaac's mechanical form. He glanced back at Juliette. "It looks quite similar to *L'écrivain, n'est-ce pas?*"

Juliette nodded patiently. "The Writer was a superb piece of engineering, *monsieur,*" she agreed. "It could handwrite any twenty characters you chose, a marvel of intricate clockwork. It was, and still is, my father's finest creation." She smiled demurely. "Compared to my beautiful Isaac, though, it's a mere windup toy, a plaything for children."

He laughed at that, a surprisingly hearty laugh considering his reedy voice. His jowls vibrated with it. It made Juliette feel a little ill to see. "That's quite a claim, *mademoiselle.* We shall see." He walked in front of the automaton, examining it closely. On the desk, directly opposite the mechanical hand holding the quill, was an indentation, four fingers and a thumb. There were a few dark, wet spots near the groove for the index finger. "Place my hand here, *oui?*" he asked her.

"*Oui.*"

He turned his left-hand palm upward and placed it in the indentation.

Juliette walked around behind Isaac. "You understand how this works, *monsieur?*" she asked him.

The man grinned. "Like clockwork?"

She nodded. "*Exactement.* Isaac is named after Sir Isaac Newton, and with good cause."

There was a snort of derision from beneath the blue mask. "*Un anglais,*" he spat.

Juliette smiled. "Nobody is perfect, *monsieur.*" She looked down at the controls that jutted from Isaac's back through tiny holes in his shirt. "Newton showed us that the world, the entire universe, operates by a strict set of physical laws. These laws are consistent, and they are comprehensible, and, most important," she stressed, as she manipulated the automaton's delicate exposed gears with great care and practice, "they are *predictable*. As predictable as clockwork, in fact."

She placed one hand on Isaac's shoulder and pressed a metal button on his spine with the other. His eyes flicked open, and the man flinched at the sight of them. Juliette knew them all too well; they were the purest white, carved from ivory and shaped and polished for weeks until almost as clear as glass. "We are all automata, *monsieur*; you, myself, Isaac," she said. "Our bodies are mechanical creations, wound at birth, following our creator's will and purpose. And, as such, our inevitable conclusions are already written."

She pressed a second button, and with a faint whir, the automaton raised its quill into the air and moved it over the man's upturned hand on the desk. Juliette watched the fat man's eyes through the holes in his mask and saw that flicker of concern she'd seen so many times before there.

Then, in a single smooth motion, the point of the quill was plunged down into the fleshy pad of the man's index finger and out again. He released a yelp of pain and snatched his hand back, the finger going straight to his pouty painted mouth.

"Oh, *excusez-moi*," Juliette said, her expression disingenuous. "Didn't I mention that death is always written in blood? Your blood, to be precise?"

Isaac lifted the quill to its mouth, which opened, revealing a silvered tongue. The automaton pressed the point against this tongue three times, as if wetting it in preparation for writing, a crimson smear left on the shiny surface. Then its mouth closed again, and it lowered the quill to the desk, close to its other hand. That hand turned, revealing a small scrap of paper, and Isaac began to write upon it with the quill. In a matter of seconds it was done, and Juliette walked around to the side of Isaac and picked up the paper. She folded it in half without as much as glancing at it and offered it to the man with a small dramatic flourish.

"There you are, *monsieur*," she said. "Your future."

He hesitated only a moment before taking it, but longer before opening and reading the note. When he did, his eyes widened and he laughed. Then he looked at Juliette closely.

"You know, *mademoiselle*," he said, a nasty gleam in his eyes, "I know the Swiss clockmaker Pierre Jaquet-Droz quite well. I've enjoyed his company several times in court."

"Really?" she asked innocently. "You know my father?"

"I know Pierre Jaquet-Droz," he emphasized. "He is an old man. You seem terribly young to be his daughter," the man persisted.

She smiled at that. "I'm not as young as I look, *monsieur*."

He leaned toward her. "How does it work?" he asked her.

"I told you—"

"No," he interrupted. "How does it *really* work?"

She looked at him carefully, glanced around the room, the other guests still oblivious to the drama unfolding, each caught up in their own private scandals. Then she sighed.

"The primary mechanism is the movement of the right arm," she said in a defeated tone. "Getting the quill to jab the finger without actually injuring it, moving it to the right place to 'taste' the blood, then down to the paper...everything else is smoke and mirrors."

"I thought so!" The host of the grand masquerade, the man paying her wages, clapped his fat hands like a child, thrilled with his own cleverness. "It doesn't actually write, does it? The casing is far too small for such an intricate mechanism."

Juliette shook her head. "The message is prewritten in invisible ink, a substance sensitive to light. Once the left hand reveals the paper, the text turns red. The movement of the quill conceals this."

"An excellent trick," he declared, and grinned. "Never fear, *mademoiselle*, your secret is safe with me."

"*Merci, monsieur,*" she murmured, head bowed.

He looked at her again, still smiling. "I was wrong earlier, wasn't I? You *are* wearing a mask."

Juliette shrugged. "This is a masquerade, after all."

"Just one suggestion," the man said. "Something to improve your act."

"*Oui?*"

He crumpled the piece of paper in his hands. "Be a little more creative with your death predictions. Almost everyone here got the same message. And perhaps make them less obscure."

"I don't understand," Juliette said.

He snorted again. "All we got was a name, child. One I recognize, incidentally, a doctor I happened to engage some years back to help investigate Mesmer's claims of animal magnetism. I doubt that's a coincidence." He winked beneath his mask. "After all, if your precious Isaac had proven to be genuine, I was considering employing him again to look into it." He laughed, then tossed the scrap of paper to Juliette, who caught it out of pure reflex.

"See Jean-Luc as you leave," he ordered her. "He will see to your pay."

"Merci beaucoup, votre majesté."

"Hush now, child," he hissed, looking around with panicked eyes. "Mustn't spoil the mystery." He smiled again, took her bare hand, and bowed to kiss it. *"Au revoir,* Mademoiselle Jaquet-Droz, or whatever your name might be," he said, his fat painted lips unpleasantly warm and wet against her skin.

"Au revoir," she responded with a curtsy.

Then he released her and was gone, back to the masquerade, immediately surrounded by lackeys and sycophants. Juliette watched him go, waited until he was lost in the colorful whirlwind of fabric and flesh. Then she opened the crumpled piece of paper and read it. It made no sense to her, but regardless, it filled her with a terrible foreboding. She turned to the automaton. "You know what, *mon amour*?" she asked it. "I believe it's time we left Paris." She glanced out of the huge windows of the ballroom, at a flicker of lightning in the sky there. "There's a storm coming, I think."

She wheeled Isaac toward the exit with some haste, past the blithely dancing nobles, who ignored her as she went. Behind her, on the tiled floor, the scrap of paper lay open, a single word on it, written in a splash of bright-red royal blood.

Guillotin.

Story by Martin Livings
Illustration by Aaron Diaz

KRIS STRAUB

NOT APPLICABLE

I REMEMBER MASHED PAPER AND LEAVES clogging the storm drain and the sun glaring off the glass of the windows across the street, the windows black where the glass was gone. They had us lined up against the wall outside the store, and they moved down the line standing close and questioning us one by one. Jeremiah was two people ahead of me in the line, but I was careful not to look at him. I kept my eyes on the rotting leaves in the street and waited.

We never should have risked going out in the open, but we heard they had apples in at the store, and batteries. We needed the batteries most. The building where we were staying then had no power, and we'd been staying in the dark since the last batteries died. So Jeremiah and I set out, five minutes apart and on different routes, to see what we could pick up.

As soon as I came around the corner I saw the lineup and knew it was a trap. I thought about bolting, hurrying past or just turning around and getting out of sight, but one of them smiled and crooked his finger at me, beckoning me over. I went.

There were three of them in their black uniforms, no badges, no guns, no insignia except the little silver dagger pinned at the collar. These were not police, not army or even Immortals. They were Fulfillment Bureau men. Each of them carried a knife in a sheath. I remember thinking we could rush them, we outnumbered them, we could kill them and get away, but even as desperate as I was, I knew it was hopeless.

Two of them moved from person to person, questioning everyone with their faces close and their voices soft. The third hung back watching, holding a flat black box in his hand. When they got to Jeremiah I listened close, staring all the while at the delicate patterns of cracks in the concrete. I could hear the answers but not the questions. I heard him rattle off the name and date of birth on his forged papers. Then there was a question almost whispered, and he mumbled, "Gunshot."

One of them sucked in his breath, then said loudly, "This one needs to be careful." I glanced up and saw him pat Jeremiah on the cheek. "It's a dangerous life for you, isn't it? You're going to get yourself in a lot of trouble." He leaned in close enough to stare up Jeremiah's nose and whispered, "What are you going to do to deserve that gunshot, I wonder?"

Then he moved on to the woman next to me, and the other Bureau man came up to me. He had thinning hair, squinting eyes, and a wide mouth. He licked his lips and cocked his head to the side to question me. I gave him my fake name and my fake date of birth and when he asked my cause of death I told him the truth.

He lifted his eyebrows and jutted his head forward and said, "What was that?" When I repeated it he grabbed my arm and ripped the little card out of my hand to see for himself. Then his eyes bulged out and his lips peeled back from his teeth. He said, "Take a look at this," and held out the card.

The one who had questioned Jeremiah came over. He had a soft face and he held his mouth pursed like he was getting ready to whistle. When he read my death he looked me over, slowly and carefully. Then he smiled. "Well, now," he said, "that's a first." He giggled and looked at his colleagues. "That's a first, I say." They chuckled. He continued, "We'd better check this one." Before I could move, he had my arm in one hand and his knife in the other. He looked into my eyes as he made the cut, and I stared back into his.

He gestured to the third one, who came up and pressed a vial to the cut on my forearm to catch a drop of blood. Then he plugged the vial into his black box and waited. With a beep, the box spat out a slip of paper. The three of them huddled to read it, then smiled again. "This one's going to be with us for a long time. We're going to get to know each other real well, aren't we?" The one with the knife wiped the blade on my shirt and they moved on.

The person after me was shaking, pressed up against the cardboard-covered window behind him or he would have toppled over. When they asked his death he stammered out something. The one with the knife out raised his eyebrows and said, "Come again?"

The man goggled and gasped, "Not applicable!"

With his lips pressed tight, the Bureau man drew a long breath through his nose. "Death doesn't apply to you? Are you sure about that?" He lifted his knife to just below the man's eye and held out his other hand for the man's reading. He glanced at the printed card and flung it to the ground with disgust. The three agents moved on and the man next to me slumped back against the glass with his eyes closed and his skin pale.

Next in line was a woman wearing a red scarf. "Cancer," she said when they asked how she would die.

"Cancer? You've got to take care of yourself, make sure you get to the doctor for checkups. Have you been to the doctor recently?"

"Yes," she said, and she sounded confident. "Just last month."

"Good," said the one with the knife. "And did the doctor find anything wrong?"

"No."

"Good, that's good. You're safe for now, then." He laughed. "You just have to watch out for the sudden kind of cancer. Do you know about the sudden kind of cancer?" I closed my eyes.

There was a shriek, and when I looked again the woman in the scarf was in the street in front of us. The one with the small eyes had her hair in his fist. The one with the soft face was looking at me. When he caught my eye he said, "Watch this. And you too," he added with a gesture to the man next to me. "Watch what happens to people who think they're safe."

I watched. The one who did it seemed bored; he seemed to have his mind on other things. One quick flash of the knife and that was it. They left her in the street with her red scarf pooled around her head.

They bundled Jeremiah and me into the back of their van. The others they let go with a warning: "Don't think that NOT APPLI-CABLE keeps you safe."

They brought us to an old school surrounded by chain-link fences. The links were rusty, but the barbed wire that topped the fence was gleaming like new. The silent one with the handheld reader led us up to an empty classroom, closed the door, and walked away. We listened to his footsteps clicking down the hall. When they were gone I tried the door.

"Locked," I said, and rattled the knob. "From the outside." I didn't think they made them that way in schools.

Jeremiah asked, "Why do they have us here?" I turned to look at him. He was standing in the middle of the room and his face was sagging like a warm candle.

"The prisons are full." I stuck out my hand and introduced myself. It took him a second to remember we didn't know each other, but then he shook my hand and gave his fake name. After that he was more professional.

Still he seemed like a weight was pressing on him over the days we were there. We both knew we weren't likely ever to walk out of that schoolyard again, but he had his GUNSHOT to deal with. When they let us out in the yard we could see two of them pacing the roof, rifles in hand.

I had it easier, I guess. I knew they wanted to keep me around. So I walked the circuit of the yard all day, from the building to the flagpole flying the Speaker's red-and-black banner, then to the corner with the mailbox and back to the building. Every once in a while I saw a curtain move in a window of the apartment building across the street, but the streets themselves were empty.

There were dozens of us milling around, leaning against the walls and rocking back and forth on the swing sets, but for the most part we didn't speak. Everyone just looked up with frightened glances as they passed each other. I kept my mouth shut. The less I talked, the less I needed to keep my story straight. Anyone could have been working with them.

It was harder at night when they shut us up in the classroom again. We couldn't talk there either, but I could see Jeremiah sulking and sweating in the opposite corner. He was hardly eating the bread and beans they brought us, and every day he seemed to slump a little lower. I tried ignoring him and ignoring the cold that poured in through the gaps in the window sockets, just sitting there and hoping he would stop talking. But he kept asking questions. Once he tried asking me what was going to happen to us.

"They'll let us go eventually," I answered. "If they wanted to question us, they'd be doing it already." It was true that we rarely saw the Fulfillment Bureau. The guards on the roof and the ones who brought us our meals were rank-and-file Immortals. But every once in a while two or three Bureau men would swoop in with their black jumpsuits and silver pins. They would pluck someone off the playground at random and bundle them away. Once we saw the squad that brought us in. One of them gave me a wink, then slipped his arm around the shoulders of a trembling little man in a hat. They walked off. The man in the hat never came back. No one ever did.

I was walking with Jeremiah in the yard one cloudy day when we heard a sharp boom like nearby thunder and felt the ground shudder under our feet. He stopped suddenly. "What was that?"

I looked back at him. "Probably a car bomb," I answered. He frowned. I went on, "It didn't sound that close. We're fine."

But then there was a much louder explosion, much closer, and we barely stayed on our feet. People started running and shouting. The two men on the roof had stopped pacing and stood looking off in one direction. I could see smoke rising over the rooftops. A half dozen guards trotted out the front door and disappeared around the corner in the direction of the blast. I started looking around for shelter, and movement in one of the windows across the street caught my eye.

The curtain pulled back and I saw a familiar face staring back at me. He held up a hand with the palm flat down and pushed it down in a quick gesture.

I grabbed Jeremiah by the wrist and dragged him after me to the nearest shelter, a playground structure of tires propped together near the corner with the mailbox. I ducked behind it and pulled him down flat on the ground next to me. "What's going on?" he shouted, but before I could answer the air tore open with a crash that ripped the air from our lungs and sprawled us out gasping on the concrete.

I hauled myself up choking on the thick smoke that was suddenly blowing everywhere. The mailbox was gone and the fence links twisted back from a gaping hole. More white smoke kept pouring up from the broken ground. I shouted, "Run!" and bolted for the opening. Jeremiah was beside me, but then there was a lightning crack and he pitched forward. Gunshot. I saw him fall headlong into the death that was always waiting for him, and the curtains of white smoke pinched shut around me, and I ran.

Choking and sobbing, my eyes burned raw, I ran with no idea if I was heading away from the prison or back into the arms of the guards. A shadow appeared and grabbed me by the shoulders. I screamed and tried to twist away, but it said, "Let's go!" and I knew the voice. I followed it through the smoke and the shadows of buildings.

We stumbled along the alleyways, and the smoke seemed to trail after us for blocks and blocks, shutting out the air and muffling the far-off noise of guns firing and the high, lonely sound of a siren. We ran through the gloom of an underpass, ducked into a culvert, and popped out into the open air on the edge of a little stream through an industrial wasteland. All around us we could see banks of piled garbage and tufts of brown grass, and across the fields were factories and warehouses abandoned for generations.

Finally I could see his face clearly, and I started to say, "Mickey, what were you thinking?" but he pushed his hair out of his face and waved me forward.

"We have to hurry" was all he said, and we ran across the open ground. A cold rain started to fall, and we were drenched before we reached the nearest building. He pushed open a heavy metal door and led me onto the warehouse floor. The whole echoing space was empty except for the piles of litter in the corners and a van near a set of open hangar doors. Light fell in from all around, bright through the broken windows and yellow through the last panes of filmy glass. Mickey pointed to the van and said, "Our getaway vehicle."

We climbed in the back. Delia turned around in the front seat and gave me a sad smile. I started to cry. As we drove away, all I could do was sit with my head in my hands and the water dripping from my clothes to pool at my feet and ask them why they had come, why they hadn't run as soon as we went missing. We could have been questioned; we might have given them up. It was stupid and I loved them for it.

"But Jeremiah is dead," I said. "I saw it, they shot him." Mickey closed his eyes. No one said anything. I thought of something else. "Where did all the explosives come from?"

The driver cleared his throat and I looked at him more carefully, surprised to see he was no one I recognized, not one of our group. Just an ancient man with tanned skin and short white hair. "The weapons were my doing," he said, and he stuck one hand back over his bony shoulder and held it out for me. "I'm Victor."

I turned to Mickey. "Who is this guy?"

"This whole jailbreak was his idea." Mickey forced a laugh. "He's a mad scientist."

"And a spy," Delia added. "With guns."

I shook my head. "I don't get it. Where did you find him?"

"He found us," Mickey answered. "And he offered to help get you back."

"What are you saying? He showed up out of nowhere and told you to risk your lives on some rescue mission, and you just went along with it?" I was starting to panic. "Are you stupid? You do realize he's just taking us back to prison, right?" I was looking out the windows of the van to see if we could make it if we jumped, but we were on the freeway. We were going too fast and there were no other cars around.

With no real plan in mind, I made a lunge for the steering wheel. The van veered, but then Mickey grabbed me and hauled me back, and Delia climbed over the back of her seat to take me by the shoulders and say, "Trust us. Wait. Trust us. We trust him."

The old man said, "I think you'd better tell the whole story. From the beginning."

Mickey started. "When you didn't come back, we knew something was wrong. Like you said, they could have questioned you about us. So we left as soon as it was dark, we found another empty building, and we waited. We kept a watch on the old place to see if you came back, but there was nothing. Obviously. Then the Professor showed up at our door one day."

"What professor?" I asked.

"The mad scientist," Delia answered, and she jerked her head toward the driver.

"Right," said Mickey. "He showed up and said he knew who we were, he knew what we were trying to do, and he wanted to help."

"And it never occurred to you that he might be one of them? That he might be trying to get everyone out in the open so they could round you up?"

Delia nodded. "That's what I said. One quick blow with a blunt object and let's get the hell out of here was my advice."

"But he said we should look at his death first," Mickey continued. "It said PNEUMONIA. We double-checked it on the handheld machine. So that ruled out homicide."

I still wasn't convinced. "That's no reason to trust him."

Mickey leaned forward. "Here's the thing, though. When we looked at his reading, we saw the serial number. They count up from one, right? Maxwell and Joyce themselves had one and two. I never got tested until they passed the law, so mine has ten digits. The professor's is eight."

"Eight digits?"

"The number eight," said the old man. He smiled at me in the mirror. "I knew Maxwell back in the day. We used to work together, in fact."

"Work together on what?"

The Professor asked if I knew anything about the Cold War. I shrugged. It was before I was born. "Well," he continued, "back then, before you were born, our government and all its intelligence agencies were busy looking for any kind of advantage, any kind of weapon, against our enemies. The research took some, ah, imaginative directions. Mind control, telepathy, astrology, that sort of thing.

People such as Dr. Maxwell and myself ran experiments, caused a few casualties among our test subjects, and generally got nowhere."

"So you are a spy. You do work for them."

He shook his head. "I was. I did. I got out of that line of work a long time before any of you were born. Before the Speaker himself was born, as a matter of fact."

"That was sixty years ago," I objected.

"It was," he agreed, "and a date that changed history. Listen, do you know anything about the NOT APPLICABLE readings?"

"What is there to know? Almost everyone gets NA these days." I thought of Jeremiah and the woman in the scarf. "People with deaths generally don't last long."

"But in the early days everyone drew a death. There were no NAs at first."

"It's just an age thing. Old people always get deaths. The inventors were old men in lab coats, and they tested it on themselves first."

When the Professor smiled I could see his white teeth in the mirror. "We weren't old men at the time, you understand. But it's true that no one older than the Speaker ever got an NA. Everyone had deaths. That was always one of the great mysteries."

I quoted the billboards: "The Speaker brought an end to death."

"Which is nonsense, of course. Plenty of people have died since he took power."

"He's responsible for a lot of those deaths."

The Professor nodded and said, "Naturally. But it is a strange coincidence, don't you think? Billions of people have been tested, and nobody born before a certain moment draws NOT APPLICABLE. Do you know how much confusion those NAs caused at first? It's quite the riddle."

I glanced at Mickey. "We used to have long talks about it."

With a smile, Mickey said, "Because everyone dies."

"And the machines are always right," I finished.

The Professor went on. "Exactly! If the machines say death doesn't apply to you, then it doesn't. But death applies to everyone.

When the first few NAs appeared, most of us just wrote them off as some kind of occasional malfunction in the machines."

"Mickey used to think the machines made some people immortal."

But Mickey shook his head so that his hair fell back over his forehead. "I only speculated. Nobody knows how they make the predictions, right? So maybe they aren't predicting anything. Maybe they're causing these deaths. And if they could do that, maybe they could make exceptions. Exemptions. Anyways, I was just speculating."

"The Speaker used to think something like that himself," said the Professor. "This was still years and years ago, and he wasn't the Speaker yet, just an obnoxious politician with some strange ideas. But he started recruiting NAs to his cause. He had some ideas of an invincible army, I suppose."

I frowned at this. "I thought the Fulfillment Bureau used to round up NAs and try to kill them."

The Professor answered, "That was later, when there were too many of them for the Speaker to control. And I'm sure at some point it must have occurred to him that his army of immortals was going to outlive him. That was when they started putting them in villages. The Speaker got paranoid. As he tends to do."

"We used to say that every time the Speaker had a bad dream, a million people died." The rain was falling steadily now, and the wipers were snicking back and forth. We were back on city streets, bouncing over the splitting asphalt.

After a moment the Professor went on. "I wouldn't necessarily believe all the stories, though. The ones about NAs lined up in front of firing squads just to experiment, the guns misfiring every time. Remember who we're talking about. The Fulfillment Bureau are the specialists in creative death enforcement. They may be cruel—"

"They're monsters."

"But they play by the rules. They interpret deaths freely, but they always keep it literally true. I don't think they would touch someone without a death. They're believers, like the Speaker is. Believers don't experiment."

I thought about the ones who questioned us. "They let the NAs go. But they killed a woman with CANCER."

Delia said gently, "You know what that means. The one who killed her was born in July. They hire people for that reason alone. This is what happens when sadists discover the pun."

"At any rate," said the Professor, "everyone who ever drew NA is still alive today. They must be. And now the Bureau doesn't think twice about them. These days they're only interested in the handful of people left who still have deaths. Particularly the ones who aren't already terminally ill." He looked at me again in the mirror. "Such as yourself, as I understand." He waited, but I didn't say anything. He pulled the van into an alley between two buildings of grimy brick and stopped the engine. "So we have a start date for NAs, some sixty years ago. And the last people are dying as we speak, which suggests that we are quickly approaching an end date. That's how I finally figured it out. The NAs won't die, because they were never born."

"What are you talking about?"

The old man had his keys in one hand. The other was resting on the door handle. Grinning over his shoulder, he exclaimed, "Time travel!" Then he jumped out into the rain.

I looked at the other two. Delia rolled her eyes and said, "You'd better let him explain. He loves the drama."

We followed him down a flight of steps into a concrete-paved basement. There were no windows, but a buzzing dim light hung from the middle of the ceiling. "You have electricity here," I said. "That's good. I forgot to pick up the batteries." I got a sideways look from Delia and half a smile from Mickey.

The Professor had arranged himself at a seat at a card table, with the electric light throwing deep shadows on his face. He seemed eager to explain his theories, but I asked, "Where is everybody?" We were alone in the empty space.

Delia looked away. Mickey cleared his throat and said, "We always knew they were going to die fighting."

The old man was looking at me carefully. "We needed a diversion. They gave us a chance."

"They were the ones with the guns," I said slowly. "Your guns. Why? None of us ever used a gun. And you sent them to fight the Speaker's soldiers? Immortals and the Bureau." I couldn't look at any of them. "First Jeremiah. Now Paul, Lawrence, Kim. Everyone. You should have left me in there."

Leaning back in his chair, the old man said, "Well. When I found your friends here I was under the impression that you all wanted to fight. That you believed in the struggle."

I slumped into a chair, shaking my head and blinking. "What struggle? We're just the only ones left. We're orphans."

The Professor opened his mouth, but Mickey waved him quiet and reached across the table to touch my arm. "Listen. I know how bad it is. But we can fix it. Just hear what he has to say. He convinced Delia and me. That must mean something, right?" Delia had her arms folded across her chest. She didn't look convinced.

Still I listened as the Professor told his story. He and Maxwell had worked on time travel together. They thought they had something, but it never worked like they hoped. Then the money dried up and the two of them were out of a job. Maxwell applied some of their ideas to his work with Joyce and made a killing predicting people's deaths. Victor became a professor. But he kept coming back to time travel. Once he thought he had it figured out, he built a prototype on his own, but there was always some malfunction. So he gave it up and forgot about it for sixty years.

But he realized that the last deaths made up a kind of countdown. When everyone left had NA, *something* had to happen. Something had to intervene before anyone else met their fate. And we knew something happened not long after the Speaker was born, something that caused people to draw NOT APPLICABLE in the first place. "So," he finished, "why couldn't the beginning and the end happen in one moment? In one act. Go back in time, kill the Speaker before he gets started, and in the process replace this whole suffering world with a better one. But one where none of the NAs were ever born."

I looked at the other two and said, "You bought this?"

Mickey shook his head. "Of course not, not at first. It's impossible, right? What about the paradoxes? If none of us was ever born, then there was never anyone to go back, no one to kill the Speaker, no one to change the world in the first place. And if it is possible, why hasn't someone already done it? Why aren't there whole armies of assassins from the future hunting him? And why stop with the Speaker when we could erase every bad guy from history?"

"Kill the serpent in the garden," Delia added, "and none of the rest of it matters."

But the Professor waved his hands. "All reasonable concerns, but not relevant. No one else has tried this because no one else knows it's possible. I built the prototype in my free time, with spare parts and elbow grease. And I didn't go public with it. All I had was a time machine that didn't work. It wasn't something to brag about.

"As for going farther back, that really is impossible. The prototype has to exist at both ends. And it seems clear that the assassin, whoever it is, doesn't disappear along with everyone they leave behind. Once they're in the past, they're there to stay, and their actions are real. And permanent. It's the only way the whole thing fits together."

His voice grew quiet as he said, "That's why I needed to find someone with a death. Someone young and in good health. No sudden deaths, no violent deaths. Someone who is going to be around for a while. That will be our assassin."

I was staring at the wall behind him. The others were staring at me. "That's why you rescued me? My death."

"I'm told yours is unusually cryptic. Even for the machines."

"LAST," I said. "They were going to keep me around until the end, while they killed everyone else. I know they were."

Nodding, the Professor went on. "Of course it could be last of a group, but I think it means last of all. That's why I contacted your friends."

"How did you find them? How did you find out about me?"

"I did this for a living once, a lifetime ago. And I have old friends who made new friends. It doesn't matter. What matters is that you're here, and you have the chance to change the world."

We argued. I didn't give in without a fight. The Professor had a death, so why couldn't he do it himself? Or find someone else. I wasn't a killer. But Victor had all the answers. He couldn't go back because he was already there, in the past. Existing twice at the same time caused all kinds of logical problems, and he thought it was flat impossible. That was why the prototype never worked for him. Anyone else who was alive sixty years ago was out for the same reason. As for younger people, my friends who had died that day were among the last. In a matter of days the countdown would tick to zero and there would be no one left. There was no time to search for someone else.

Besides, he said, there was my own death to consider. I was in good health, I was safe now from the Fulfillment Bureau, and my reading suggested I wasn't going anywhere anytime soon. My death was in the future, and this world apparently didn't have a future. It had to be me.

Still I argued for a long time. Whoever reads this should know I didn't want to do it. If the Speaker had walked in on us while we sat at that table, I would have killed him gladly. Easily. And it isn't that I worried about killing someone who hadn't done anything yet, because I know what he would do. Has done. But when I kill him, Mickey and Delia and everyone I've ever known will vanish. They'll all be forgotten, and they deserve to be remembered.

I'm writing this so that someone might know why I eventually gave up arguing and agreed to do it. I'm writing because every word of this is treason and it feels like spitting in the Speaker's face. Mostly, though, I'm writing to remember everyone who deserves to be remembered. Mickey and Delia. Jeremiah and the woman in the red scarf. All of the victims, all of the orphans.

Late that night, after the arguments and the persuasion, I went to bed. I had my own room there, my own bed and my own light-bulb hanging from the ceiling. It was nicer than a lot of the places we've stayed. I was sitting there, staring up at the lightbulb and the paint chipping from the ceiling, when Mickey knocked on the door.

He had his reading in his hand, one of the new ones printed in the official passbooks with the seal pressed into the cover. "Can I come in?" I nodded. He sat on the edge of the bed and thumbed open the little book, but he didn't look at it or at me. He was staring at the wall.

After a moment, he said, "Do you know why I never wanted to get this?" He waved the passbook absently. "I felt like it took something from us. Like there was something we used to have. Free will, I guess. Maybe it's stupid, but I felt like fate was something the machines created, because knowing made it real. So I didn't want to know. I didn't want to make it real.

"But then they started pulling people off the street to check their readings, so I went in. I was all set to walk out again without ever looking, but I think they could tell. They gathered around, three of them, and read it out as soon as it printed. NOT APPLICABLE. And I felt like I dodged a bullet."

He looked at me for the first time, and then looked down at the book in his hand. "And now—" he started.

I think I know what he meant. It was bad enough to face your death. Never living was much worse. But I didn't say anything. I didn't know what to tell him.

Suddenly he smiled and he was Mickey again. He ran his hand through his hair and said, "I have a theory. All of the last sixty years is going to get cut off, right? It'll be like a closed loop, and you'll be outside it. So you'll be free again. What could the machines know about someone in another universe? That's probably why they were so vague about you. Maybe no one will ever invent a machine to predict deaths. It'll probably be impossible in the normal flow of time. So everyone will be free!" He was grinning.

I wasn't convinced, but I didn't argue. He seemed happy to have it figured out. We talked for a while about what it was like when we were younger, before everything. Then Mickey said, "You should get some sleep," and he left. I didn't sleep that night. I haven't really slept since.

We left the next night, making our way on foot through the darkest of the deserted streets. We held close to the shadows, afraid even though we knew we wouldn't fail. Billions of predictions depended on our success, and the machines were never wrong.

By the time the sky began to grow light, we were crossing a field of weeds and broken glass out in the suburbs. The Professor led the way, picking among the skeleton silhouettes of electrical transformers crowding against the dawn like dead trees. "We'll need a lot of power," he explained as we walked. "When we pull the switch, the lights are going to go out all over the neighborhood."

He stopped at the door of a tiny shed built of cinder blocks and corrugated tin. With a flourish, he pulled a ring of keys from his pocket and unlocked the door. When he pushed against it, the heavy steel door refused to shift, so he stood back frowning as Mickey kicked it open. Inside was nothing but the top of a flight of stairs leading down into darkness. The three of us held back on the highest steps until the Professor switched on a light overhead and closed the door behind us.

Underground was a whole set of rooms holding beds, worktables, ancient machinery, and the Professor's prototype. Mickey looked around and asked, "What is this place?"

Victor shrugged. "Something from the old days. No one was using it."

We have been here three days. We each have our own room again. The Professor has been bustling around, getting his prototype back in working order, but there's nothing for the rest of us to do. We asked.

So we've spent our time trying not to think about what's coming, talking a little, playing cards. One time we started speculating about the Speaker's death. He never made it public, but he must have been read. People like him care very much what happens to them. The only thing for certain is that he didn't draw NA. But we know how the machines love their mind games, so we guessed. MURDER, OVERDOSE, or AT HOME IN BED SURROUNDED BY FAMILY would all be technically true. Delia suggested FOR THE GREATER GOOD, which is also true, but I don't like it. It would only feed his self-righteousness.

I don't want it to comfort him. I want him to stay awake thinking of it, afraid just like his victims who lay awake waiting for the Bureau to knock on their door. He should suffer with the knowing;

it should be specific. It could name me, give him my picture and address. It wouldn't matter. Knowing ahead of time doesn't change the fact of death, as we've learned.

But all the philosophical discussions, the speculation, the games—they're just ways of taking our minds off the real thing. Sometimes it's okay; sometimes we laugh at the smallest things, just as if we weren't planning the end of the world. But the strain is there. I look at Delia and I see the sadness in her eyes, always.

Delia was just here. I was writing when she came in, sat on the bed, and stared at the wall just like Mickey had done. I pulled my knees up to my chest. She turned toward me and asked, "Do you remember the wedding?"

"Yes." She meant Mickey's.

"Remember the rain?"

I smiled. "I remember Mickey standing there, barefoot in the mud. He had his shoes in his hand and that stupid grin like he had no idea what came next." It was pouring, our clothes were all soaked through, the water was running down our faces. The day was so hot that the rain was warm on our skin, and it washed the sweat from our foreheads so we could taste the salt on our lips.

"We said to him, 'You're married now! Get used to it.'"

"Then we danced out in the rain. We jumped in the puddles. There was thunder, remember? But we didn't care, we just sang along."

"There were so many people there."

"Everyone was there."

We were quiet a moment. Then Delia took my hands in her hands. "Don't forget," she said. There were tears on her face and tears in her eyes. She leaned close and all I could see was her eyes and she was crying and she said, "Remember this."

Remember this:

Mickey on the day he got married, with the rain pouring down. That look he gets when he has a puzzle to solve. The way he's always pushing his hair off his face.

The woman in the red scarf. Remember her in the street with the scarf under her head. And Jeremiah. Remember what happened to them.

Delia. When we were kids we used to go swimming; we would run across the grass barefoot in a race to the water. She stood there shading her eyes with her hand, looking out over the lake like she was the first person ever to see it. Remember Delia. She is the last honest person, she says, and it's true. I am in love with her. I think she knows.

This is why I'm writing. Tomorrow it will all be over. I'll be the only one to remember them.

We don't know exactly when I'll arrive, but we know almost to the minute when I'll do it. When the world will change. I'll have a syringe; I'll have an address; I'll have these words and these memories.

I know perfectly well that I could be caught afterward and locked up. I don't care, as long as it's done. I'll deserve to be locked up. Mickey says I'll be setting the world free, but what does Mickey know? He pretends like he isn't terrified. Delia isn't as good at pretending. Neither am I.

All these years, people have been reading their own deaths without ever knowing what the machines were really telling us. If the Speaker had known, he would have destroyed them all. Because they were telling us how to beat him. They told us when it would happen; they told us who had to do the act; they even promised us success. And the machines are never wrong.

Sometime tomorrow, the last person will die. Then we'll pull the switch, the lights will go out, and the machines' last prediction will come true. NOT APPLICABLE. I'll have my whole life to think about that.

Story by Kyle Schoenfeld
Illustration by Chris Schweizer

SMUG

RYAN PEQUIN

PEACEFULLY

THERE'S A BEAR IN THE CLEARING, its muzzle deep in the torso of a zombie.

Ben stares at the scene from behind a mossy tree trunk. It's kind of like those nature documentaries his mom used to like, back when there was such a thing as nature documentaries. Like the bear's ripping bloody mouthfuls from some big fish it's just slapped out of a river, and Ben's got a front-row seat to the natural wonder that is the food chain.

Part of him is a little bit smug at this proof that, other evidence to the contrary, horde aren't necessarily at the top of that chain. Part of him's fascinated—and, weirdly, relieved—to see nature still capable of taking its course, in this day and age. Part of him's taking clinical notes about the damage to the zombie, because hell, bears are probably a great resource for tips on how to take down horde.

Part of him watches the bear's questing snout jostle the corpse's head to the side, floppy like a rag doll's, and has to swallow against rising bile and hysteria of the sort he hasn't felt in years.

Beside him, Louisa whistles low through her teeth. "Somebody needs to post a sign: do not feed the animals." She's smiling; he hears it in her voice. When he doesn't answer, she jabs him with her elbow, right in the kidney. "Hey. How does it die?"

The joke stopped being even remotely funny long ago, but the routine of it grounds him, replaces the hysteria with a distant kind of calm. He plays along automatically. "The soon-to-be-zombie bear?" He pretends to give the matter serious thought. "I'm gonna guess violently."

"You think?" she says. She gives him her handgun to hold and swings her shotgun off her shoulder. When she steps out from behind the tree, the bear looks up from its meal, right at her.

Her aim, as always, is good. The bear does not get up.

The echoes fade out, leaving the forest shocked into silence. The noise of Louisa's foot snapping a twig as she strides from their hiding place to stand above the corpses seems almost as loud as her gunfire. Ben follows slowly, staring at the bear. He's seen plenty of dead horde; the bear is different, something thoroughly wild and natural and *other*. He watches the stillness of its huge body, its dirty fur ruffling in the breeze.

Louisa's attention is on the gaping carcass of the zombie. "New rule," she says, reshouldering the shotgun and reclaiming her automatic from Ben. She doesn't holster the handgun, but then, she never does. "Anything with teeth gets shot on sight."

They leave the sun-dappled clearing and its musky, fresh-blood stink. The forest closes in around them, lush and serene, untouched by the chemical and radioactive wastage of the remains of civilization; it's more beautiful than any place Ben's seen in the seven years since the bombs. The longer they walk without incident, the more he thinks he could almost believe they're there because they want to be.

In fact, they're there because of Castor.

"The place you want to be," Castor said, conspiratorial blue eyes shining in the candlelight like the glass of the bottle dangling from his hand, "is up north."

They were sprawled across the furniture in Castor's suite—the penthouse of his compound, a tricked-out basement with one obvious entrance and one hidden exit and enough munitions and nonperishables to last a month—drinking home brew and eating meringues. It was obscenely decadent, by far not the best use of the two fresh eggs Castor had presented them, with a wink and a bow, when Ben and Louisa returned from a week of scavenging across the border. But Louisa had lit up at the sight of them, and she'd dug through Castor's private pantry until she found half a bag of white sugar, and Ben didn't want to *know* how she'd got hold of a lemon, but somehow she had, and this was how she wanted to use it. Faced with her near-childish glee as she arranged her ingredients in Castor's kitchen, he couldn't bring himself to suggest a simple scramble.

The meringues were delicious. Light, sweet, sinful zests on their tongues. A taste of another time.

Ben paused in the middle of sucking sugar off his fingers. "Okay, but if we get there and Santa's elves are all horde, I'm coming back to eat your brain."

Louisa snorted. Three fingers still wrapped around the neck of his bottle, Castor mimed shooting Ben in the head. "Not that far north. There's a place up by the bay that's been turned into a hell of a compound." He leaned forward in his torn-leather chair, amusement giving way to earnestness. "It's an honest-to-God village up there: self-sufficient, fortified. They've even got gardens. Friend of mine told me about it last week. Impeccable source," he added, because even higher than angels on sugar and booze, he saw the glance Ben sent Louisa and knew what it meant. "Wouldn't go spreading false hope. Especially not to me." He grinned, showing his gums. "Jeannie *likes* me."

As reassurances went, it was lacking: everybody liked Castor, either genuinely or out of necessity. The more concrete proof was whether he liked you. Ben measured the stretch of his smile, the softness around his eyes that had nothing to do with the indulgences diluting his bloodstream, and decided he could probably trust this woman with the world.

The world as it had been, anyway. When it was something worth entrusting.

Louisa picked up a meringue and stared at it as if searching out flaws. "And this haven of isolation is open to new members?"

"The right kind of new members." Castor's grin faded. His eyes slid from Louisa to fix on Ben. "They test you at the gate," he said evenly, "twice. First, for infection, and if you're infected, they shoot you. Then, if you're not gonna go peacefully…" He shrugged and leaned back again, deceptively casual. "Depends what else you have to offer." After a moment—and another pull from his bottle—he added, "Notice how, out of everybody under my roof tonight, I'm only telling you two."

Later, Louisa slipped unsteadily through the door to their room—at Castor's place, everyone was paired or grouped off, because everyone wanted to stay at Castor's and Castor only had so many rooms—and climbed into bed with Ben, curled up at his side with her arm wrapped across his belly. Hugging him like a little girl with a teddy bear. She smelled like sweat and liquor and lemon and Castor.

"What do you want to do?" she asked.

Ben curved his arm around her shoulder, settled his hand on her hip. The taste of meringues was long gone from his mouth. "You think we could make it?"

"Cas said he'd give us a truck. Driving 'til the gas runs out should get us into the middle of nowhere, and there's a lot fewer horde in the middle of nowhere. We could hike the rest."

"And if we make it?"

"Then whatever happens, happens," she said firmly, and shifted closer to him, tucking her head more comfortably on his shoulder. "We'll worry about it when we get there."

Ben noted the "when." "They'll have to take me," he said, just as firmly, because it was true. "And if they want me, they're taking you."

It was rare, these days, to meet someone who'd drawn "peacefully" from the predictor machine. The theory was that most of them had been killed quietly in their beds during the bombs or had since barricaded themselves in Greenland. Those still wandering the hellscape were sought after, tended to be treated like lucky talismans in the bunkers; before Ben stopped wearing his pendant—after he lost Joseph, the simple, clean-lined *P* his parents gave him when he turned sixteen had become much too heavy—he got used to warm welcomes and clingy hosts. Violents who assumed they would be at least marginally protected from most postapocalyptic dangers if they had a Peaceful with them.

Most of those Violents were dead now. Ben had watched far too many of them die.

Ever since he'd met her, Louisa had shortened it to Peace. "I spell it with an *i*, too," she'd told him once, fondly, out of nowhere. "My very own Piece."

Like I'm one of your weapons, he'd wanted to say, but hadn't.

Louisa was succumbing to whatever she'd drunk, her body listless and heavy against him. "You're sweet," she mumbled into his shirt. He could feel the hard *V* shape of her pendant trapped between them.

Six days later, their truck was stocked, their packs were full, and Castor kissed them both good-bye.

Their campfire seems little more than a flickering orange pinprick in a dark, empty world.

Ben's used to cities, to enclosed rooms and the knowledge that there are people thinking and acting and living—or, on bad days, frantic and fighting and dying—on the other side of every solid wall. Three nights into their wilderness trek, as every animal cry that echoes suddenly through the trees reminds him of the horde-eating bear, as open space presses insistently on him from all sides, he's still on edge.

Louisa, lying on her back on the other side of the fire with stars reflected in her eyes, looks more relaxed than he's ever seen her.

"This reminds me," she says to the sky, her voice a lilting, human sound in the forest's immense, inhuman quiet, "of when I was a kid. My aunt used to take us camping, me and my sister." A little smile plays at the corners of her mouth. "Just in her backyard when we were really small, but as we grew up, we did a bunch of the provincial parks. And when I was fifteen, we went portaging in Quebec."

Her openness surprises him. He's pretty certain he knows more about Louisa's life pre-apocalypse than anyone—except maybe Castor—but that's not saying much. She doesn't often talk about her past. Some people just don't, or can't, and Ben understands why; there are times, increasingly frequent, when he feels that disinclination too, the feeling that whatever he could talk about is so decisively gone, so thoroughly disconnected from who he is now, that to try to share it would be meaningless. Still, he and Louisa *talk*. She knows all about his family, and after Joseph's death, Ben had found himself sharing the most random stories with her: about the mandatory science class they'd shared in first-year university, which Ben had passed only because of Joseph's tutoring; about Joseph's near-giddy enjoyment of perpetual motion gadgets, regardless of their actual perpetuity; about how Joseph had teased Ben mercilessly for being nervous about meeting his parents.

And yet, Ben realizes, before this moment, he never knew Louisa had a sister.

He watches the firelight play, warm and friendly, on her face, and forgets his nighttime uneasiness in a fierce swell of affection. "Those sound like good memories."

Her tiny smile broadens for a moment into a flash of a grin. "Yeah." But then she catches herself: her body tenses, her lips press into a thin, dry line, and the shine in her eyes goes hard. Ben feels the end of her unguarded moment even before she speaks. "My aunt died in the bombs," she says, her voice flat and blunt, "and then my sister got infected. Her son had just turned two. He didn't have a chance."

Ben feels sick. And angry. And horrified and sorrowful, and he moves to go to her. "Louisa—"

But she's already turning away, curling up with her head on her pack and her back to the fire. "You take first watch," she says, and Ben sits back down, defeated.

He can always tell when Louisa's sleeping; she doesn't do it well, her rest always either too light or broken by nightmares.

That night, he watches her hold herself still for hours.

A few years after the bombs, a group somewhere across the border started broadcasting a TV signal. There wasn't a television industry anymore, of course, so all the group had to broadcast was whatever they could make.

Their show was called, creatively, *How Do They Die?!* Every episode was exactly the same.

It started with the hand-drawn title card, its uneven block letters and excited punctuation held in front of the camera by someone whose hand wasn't entirely steady, whose calloused thumb was visible along one side. When it fell away, it revealed the show's host, a burly man in filthy fatigues whose *V* was tattooed in solid black across most of his face. Luther, he announced himself, his voice booming out of his barrel chest; then, garrulous in his showmanship, he directed the camera's attention to his surroundings, a former newsroom now repurposed and nearly unidentifiable. To his right, an area fenced off with iron bars and barbed wire, full of snarling, ravening horde; to his left, a broad patch of bare floor and wall, both painted in thick spatters of dark brownish red. And behind him, presented with theatrical relish, a predictor machine.

His stage set, Luther, his wiry friend Lily, and a handful of nameless, brutally efficient assistants wrangled the captive horde from their cage one at a time, bound their mouths so they couldn't bite, held their grasping fingers to the predictor's needle, and made a clownish show of pretending they didn't know what would be printed on each and every ticker-tape result slip.

Everyone knew the result, every time. Luther, Lily, the assistants, everyone watching in the relative safety of their bunkers. The very first time Ben ever saw the show—three months after Joseph, standing against the back wall with Louisa sitting on his shoulders because everyone at Castor's wanted to watch and the common room had only so much floor space—he knew. Everyone knew; of course they did. Horde died violently.

Of course they did.

And when Lily made the inevitable pronouncement, Luther pushed the pronounced toward the bare, blood-drenched space and, accompanied by the cheers of the audience both in studio and at home, fulfilled the machine's prediction.

Violently.

Every episode, exactly the same.

Until it wasn't.

Ben didn't make a habit of watching the show. The only reason he caught it that day was because he'd sprained his ankle in a skirmish the day before; he was laid up, in a bad mood, and desperate for distraction from the pain in his leg. *How Do They Die?!* seemed like just the solution.

For the first twenty minutes or so, it was. Luther and Lily processed their batch of horde as they always did—with guns and machetes and wide, hard grins—and Ben let himself share in the buzzing current of retributive viciousness that hummed out from the TV's grainy picture, through the crowd of people watching with him. By the time the stocky horde-woman with blood-matted blond hair was wrestled out of the cage and dragged to the predictor, everyone was into the rhythm: tape over her mouth, assistants holding her legs, Luther's two hands pulling one of hers to the needle. Banter between Luther and Lily as the machine pricked and retracted, whirred and analyzed. The printing noise; Lily's little flourish as she snapped the slip free.

But instead of holding the slip aloft and crowing a victorious, "Violently!" Lily stared at it in silence while joy leached from her face.

Luther, distracted by trying to keep the horde-woman's arms pinioned behind her back, didn't notice right away; when he finally glanced up, it was with more annoyance than worry. "This bitch is making me tired, Lily, c'mon—"

"Peacefully." The first time Lily said it, it was little more than a shape of her mouth; her voice, hearty and ringing short minutes earlier, was barely audible. It slammed silence like a sledgehammer through Ben's crowd of spectators, and they heard her perfectly when she repeated, "It says 'peacefully.'"

"What?" Luther's eyes narrowed; he fought the woman's wrists close enough together that he could hold them one-handed and reached out to snatch the paper from Lily. "Let me see—"

But his hold on the woman wasn't as solid as it should have been. Before anyone could react, she *wrenched* her body, and Luther lost his grip. Her arms now free, the woman raised her hands to the tape over her mouth; the assistants grabbed at her, but their angles were wrong; she ripped off the tape with enough force to knock Luther off balance. The half second he stumbled was just long enough for her to catch his arm and drag it to her mouth and sink her teeth in all the way.

The stage drowned in panic. The assistants fell back, their fear of being bitten overriding whatever loyalty they might have had for their leader. Luther howled, his face twisting with pain and fury and terror, the sight of it broadcast live to his transfixed audience. Only Lily kept her senses: within seconds she was behind the horde-woman, raising her gun to the back of her head, pulling the trigger. And as the woman fell, Lily pressed the gun to Luther's temple and pulled the trigger again.

And then the feed cut out, and Ben was staring at static.

"She was supposed to die peacefully," he mused for the fourth time later that night, as Louisa helped him rewrap his ankle. His mind was stuck on the incident, circled it restlessly, replayed those few seconds—less than a minute, really—over and over and over. No one who'd seen it had been able to talk about anything else all evening.

"The machine was probably just wrong," Louisa said again, more of her attention seemingly on her work with his bandage than the conversation.

"But the machine isn't wrong. Ever. That's why it's the machine." Ben shifted uneasily, anxious to his fingertips, almost afraid to think too much about the other possibility. The one that people already acknowledged, at least a little, when they believed that Peacefuls could be blown to bits in their sleep. The one that meant that maybe—*maybe*—what he'd done for Joseph—

Louisa misjudged her angle as she pinned his bandage, jabbing him sharply. "Sorry," she said to his wince, and smoothed her hands over the hurt. Her palms were warm. "The machine predates the infection," she added, and she sounded eminently reasonable, as if the explanation was so self-evident it was scarcely worth her time to speak it. "I doubt it can read horde blood properly." And that, Ben could tell by the set of her jaw, answered that, so he didn't argue and didn't bring it up again.

But the look on the horde-woman's face in the second before she died stayed behind his eyes: her teeth deep in the meat of her meal, the taste of it flooding her tongue, the corners of her lips curved up. Her eyes closed, but smiling. In the second Lily had pulled the trigger, the woman had what she wanted out of life and was content.

At peace.

It's a relief when they join up with a road. After hiking for so long through the scrubby terrain of the lowlands, walking on hard-packed dirt feels amazingly easy, and they make better time than they have in days.

They know they're getting close when they find the pit.

The stench hits them first: woodsmoke, gasoline, and burning flesh wafting over them with the gentle summer breeze. It's nothing Ben hasn't smelled before, but never at such strength; he coughs unstoppably, the smell cloying, practically physical in his throat, and he and Louisa quicken their pace, stumbling, anxious to get upwind.

The pit itself is an irregular ditch dug a short distance from the road. Smoke billows sullenly from its depths, obscuring their view of its contents. They pass by without trying to see.

Less than twenty minutes later, a fence begins to rise out of the ground in the distance: chain link, at least fifteen feet high, with barbed wire stretched and coiled at the top. Behind it, a collection of low, sheet-sided buildings and long reaches of pavement; the place looks like an airstrip, or maybe the outer edge of what used to be a small town.

There are people walking inside the fence line. Ben knows when they've been spotted; he can hear shouting, emphatic but indistinct, and sees the patrollers start jogging toward the gate that bars the road.

Beside him, Louisa tucks her pendant under her shirt and holsters her gun.

By the time they get within easy speaking distance of the gate— really just a smaller, movable fence, built into the space between two of the girders anchoring the big, immovable one—a welcoming committee has gathered. Five people, armed to the teeth, watch them approach with wary eyes and tense shoulders. "You can stop there," one of them calls out, and they do.

Louisa holds up her empty hands. "We're Castor's friends," she says. "Louisa and Ben. Is Jeannie here?"

The people inside the fence exchange looks. A lean Aboriginal woman with her hair in a thick plait down her back raises her chin, her assessing gaze darting from Louisa to Ben and back again. "How is Castor?"

Louisa shrugs. "Alive, last we saw him."

"Well, then." Jeannie's mouth curves sharply. "Welcome to heaven," she says, gesturing at the dirty buildings and cracked pavement and all-encompassing cage. "Where the peaceful people go," she adds, with the same tone Castor uses when he's mocking his own cleverness. Then, almost an afterthought: "Weapons on the ground, then step forward one at a time for testing."

Ben goes first. A nebbishy, balding man wearing latex gloves pokes a plastic-wrapped swab through the chain link; Ben takes it, unwraps it, and swipes it inside his mouth before wrapping it again and handing it back. The man dunks the saliva-coated swab into a vial of clear liquid and stirs steadily for a full minute, and when the liquid remains clear, nods.

Beside the man, a middle-aged woman with short, curly hair pushes a trolley with a predictor machine on it right up to the fence. "You know how this goes," she says brusquely, and Ben sticks his index finger through the chain link and into the little alcove housing the machine's needle.

After the prick, as they wait for the machine to render its judgment, she gives him a Band-Aid through the fence. It's patterned, ridiculously, with monkeys.

"Peacefully," the woman reads from his slip, and it's like clouds parting: everyone on the other side of the fence smiles at him, mixing relief and acceptance. The change from the impersonal threat they'd projected moments before feels like whiplash.

Jeannie turns to reach for the lock on the gate. "Okay, Ben, come on in—"

But he takes a step backward. "Actually, I'm going to wait for my friend."

Jeannie glances back at him sharply before her expression goes carefully blank. "Your choice," she says, her tone neutral, and Ben wonders, his gut hollowing out, how much Castor told her about them.

Louisa doesn't seem to share his dread. But Ben's seen her mask any number of things with swaggering confidence; he decides to follow her lead and tries not to spoil her bluff with his worry.

She winks at the nebbish while swabbing her cheek and smiles sweetly as the predictor draws her blood.

"What did you get?" she asks him, peering at his hand after she's applied her own Band-Aid. "Monkeys? Sucker. Mine's dinosaurs."

On the other side of the fence, the machine spools out her slip. Ben meets Louisa's bright eyes, his mind racing with the arguments he's been formulating for days—all the things he can think of to tell these people about Louisa, about who she is and what she can do and why she should be allowed to stay.

Even if she is a Violent.

The curly-haired woman tears Louisa's result free and peers at it and reads, "Peacefully."

It was supposed to be a simple salvage.

Joseph, Castor's resident gearhead, had been grumbling about the list he was keeping of useful items they didn't have. When a patrol returned with news of an abandoned house that had belonged to a serious electronics hoarder—and, more important, that hadn't been ransacked by anyone else—a foraging crew was put together. Joseph, Ben, and a handful of death wishers set out one sunny morning with good spirits, lots of weapons, and a long shopping list.

Three hours later, with shouting and gunshots still echoing through the rest of the sprawling house, Ben turned his back on a room strewn with dead horde to kneel beside Joseph, who wasn't dying fast enough.

"Hey. Hey, Joseph, no—" He dropped his gun on the slick, gritty floor and put his hands on Joseph's shoulders, under his jaw, up into his sweaty, matted hair. Everywhere he could. "God, Joseph, I wish— You should've told me. I could've— If I'd known you were—" He ran out of words, choked off.

Countless times, Ben had seen people infected and had done what was necessary to end the process for them as mercifully as possible. That's just what you did, if you could, if you were any kind of good person. This time, he thought—as he looked at the ragged-crescent tears all over Joseph's body, smelled the blood and sour horde saliva soaking through his clothes, felt the way he twitched and shook under Ben's hands—this time should really, if there was any kind of god or balance or scrap of fairness left in the universe, be the last.

He made himself breathe and smiled at Joseph as much as he could. "You know," he said, because this was no time to be anything but honest, and because he knew Joseph would understand, "you Violents have this way of making me feel anything but peaceful."

Joseph's eyes rolled, showed white for long enough that Ben told himself to let him go and pick up his gun. But then they closed, and when they opened there was the brown again, warm and steady through the growing cloud of pain and infection. Focused on Ben like there was nothing else to look at in the world. "That's a—hell of an assumption to make," he said weakly, struggling for every handful of words. "Although—granted—the evidence is—strong." Ben's confusion must have showed on his face; after a second, Joseph huffed out a chuckle. "I don't know—which I am. Never got tested."

Ben stared. It seemed impossible. Everybody got tested. Before the bombs, it had been commonplace for parents to schedule predictor machine tests for their children; after, society's brush with violent mortality made survivors desperate to find out if they had something nicer to look forward to, or if they should resign themselves early to more of the same. He'd never asked Joseph whether he was slated to die peacefully or violently, and Joseph had never volunteered to tell him; Ben had always just assumed it was something that, for whatever reason, Joseph wanted to keep to himself.

But that wasn't it at all. He didn't know.

And if he didn't know, Ben thought, anything could be true.

He kissed Joseph. His mouth, close lipped and careful. His cheek, his temple, his eyelids. The tip of his nose. Light, precise, tender. And, gradually, Joseph's labored breathing eased; his shaking quieted until he barely trembled. And when Ben pulled away, there was the hint of a smile pulling at the corners of Joseph's mouth, and something like tranquillity on his tear- and grime- and sweat-streaked face.

And Ben picked up his gun and shot him once between the eyes.

The quiet afterward was painful. Ben stayed crouched next to Joseph's body as the absence rang in his ears, as it filled his head, as it crowded out everything until he thought nothing at all.

He reacted automatically to the sound of shuffling feet: Ben turned, raising his gun.

One of the death wishers stood just inside the door, a shotgun held casually at her side. She was a member of Castor's inner circle, Ben remembered dully, although not one of the more inspiring specimens. When Ben had met her that morning, he'd thought she was a kid, she was so small, her shoulder about level with his elbow, her ammunition belt and holster cinched as tight as they'd go and still hanging loose. But she'd survived the charnel house. There was a solidity to her, a steadiness despite the gore spattering her clothes, and the look in her eyes seemed as old as time. Ben realized she hadn't just arrived; she'd likely been there all along, watching, waiting for him to do what was necessary. Ready to do it for him if he couldn't.

The *V* hanging dully from a chain around her neck looked like she'd made it herself from scrap metal.

She cleared her throat. "Sorry."

Ben pushed himself to his feet, the stretch of his legs a distant relief after crouching for so long. He felt bone weary. When he turned back to Joseph, he saw the tiny smile still curving his lips, now bisected by the trail of blood wending slowly down from his forehead. "He looks peaceful, right?"

She made a disbelieving noise. "You shot him in the head while he was turning horde. You think that was *peaceful?*"

"I hope it was."

She didn't say anything else; the silence stretched, and Ben thought she'd left. But when he turned away, finally finished with looking, she was still standing in the doorway, in thoughtful study of the scattered horde. As Ben crossed the room toward her, picking his way through the corpses he and Joseph had made, she slid him a sideways, appraising glance.

"I'm Louisa," she said, as casual as anything, as if they weren't surrounded by contagious death, as if the floor under their boots wasn't sticky with unspeakable bodily fluids. "I'd just graduated culinary school. Before. I was gonna open my own bakery. You?"

He came to a stop beside her. She looked up at him frankly, seemingly unaware of the non sequitur that was her choice of conversation. "Ben. I was a music major." He almost left it at that, then remembered that, as of five minutes ago, no one else in the world knew what he'd wanted to be when he grew up. The knowledge hitched his breath in his throat; he forced himself to swallow it and added, roughly, "Opera singer."

Louisa's eyes shone, then crinkled merrily at the corners, and then she was grinning, her face split with mirth. "Oh my God," she said, gesturing dismissively at the carnage they'd wrought, the blood on their clothes, the fit of their weapons in their hands. "We're useless!" The laughter in her voice was so unexpected, so ridiculous, so *genuine* that Ben felt himself half smile in reflex; in response, the sharp edges of Louisa's humor softened. "I like Gilbert and Sullivan," she said.

His smile grew, somehow, an unstoppable counterweight to the heavy emptiness spreading through his chest. "I like cupcakes."

She reached out and took his hand, lacing her warm, damp fingers with his, thoroughly unself-conscious. She held his hand like she held her gun, comfortable and firm; Ben found himself returning her grip. Her wrist bumped against his pendant where it dangled, tarnished and blood speckled, from its leather tie. "Come on, Ben," she said, and turned her back on the room strewn with dead horde. "Let's see if anyone else is still alive."

"My mom died when I was thirteen," Louisa says. She sits on a creaking wooden chair at the tiny table in the kitchen of the shabby, four-room house that's now theirs.

Ben has just seen Jeannie out after a long evening of orientation and conversation. His smile has been an alien, uncomfortable thing on his face for hours; now, as he turns from the door, he lacks the energy even to frown.

It's the first time they've been alone since the road.

"You should have told me," he says.

She blinks up at him, slow and exhausted. In her hand is an apple from the orchard behind the house, small and green and so sour as to be inedible. "I'm telling you now."

Ben looks at the floor, traces the pattern of scuffed linoleum with his eyes. Shifts his weight, aching from the soles of his feet all the way up his legs, all the way through his back. Reaches up and digs his fingers painfully into the tight cords of his neck. Postpones the moment he agrees to listen.

They made it. They're *here*. It should feel like a triumph—and it does—but he can't share it with his best friend because he doesn't understand who she is anymore.

He's being petty, taking his time. Making her wonder, if only for a minute, whether he even wants to understand. He's being cruel.

When he finally sinks into the chair across from her, he looks for any sign of relief. The sigh she breathes and the way her grip slackens on the apple makes him feel slightly better.

"My mom died when I was thirteen," Louisa says.

She'd been sick for almost half Louisa's life.

When Louisa was seven, her mother had a partial mastectomy; a year later, they went back for the rest. After almost two years of everyone thinking they'd gotten it, she was in remission, she was fine—she woke up one morning and couldn't move her legs. The doctors found new tumors pressing against her spine and gave her eight months to live.

A year and a half later, Louisa's mother started having trouble speaking. The doctors measured the size of the tumor in her head and gave her, at the absolute most, three months.

A year after that, the cancer had metastasized to her lungs; she started getting pneumonia every time it rained, but by then the doctors—who had given up the futile game of managing her family's expectations with time limits—had her on so many drugs it was anyone's guess whether she even knew that she couldn't really breathe.

When it became clear, finally, that hospital care didn't matter at all, the doctors let her family take her home. Louisa remembers the endless presence of guests in her house, her mom's friends and distant relatives joining her at the sink after supper to help with the dishes, or stocking their fridge with strange groceries, or making repeated offers to Aunt Mae to do this or that necessary chore, to "take some of the load off." She remembers the way they all looked at her and Anne, as if their instincts were telling them to smother them in hugs and run away from them at the same time. She remembers everyone walking into her mom's room with brave smiles and walking out of it crying.

When Louisa's mother died, it was there, in her own home, in her own bed, warm and safe. She was surrounded by people who loved her, and so full of medication she couldn't feel any of the pain her body was in.

According to the predictor machine, she died a violent death.

"That was an awful thing the machine did, labeling my mom a Violent." Louisa puts down the apple and folds her hands neatly on the tabletop. Their composed position is at direct odds with her gun calluses and dirty, ragged fingernails. "It gave me hope."

Ben's tired. Maybe too tired to be having this conversation. His eyes are gritty, there's a trembling kind of ache in his stomach, and his brain's too slow at processing what Louisa's saying, but he thinks he'd rather die of exhaustion than stop her before he understands. "Hope for what?"

She smiles, small and shy, like a child admitting a much-valued secret. "Hope that my mom—my smart, strong, wonderful mom, who couldn't bake to save her life, who watched me roll out piecrusts like I was performing miracles, who'd been through *so much*—had been allowed a moment of peace at the very end. Hope that my aunt hadn't felt a thing. That she'd been having a nap when the bombs fell on her city, and died in her sleep, or that it had been so quick she didn't have time to be afraid or in pain. Hope that the machine could be wrong." Her smile ends. "Because after I killed my sister and cremated her body with what was left of my nephew, I needed it to be wrong. About me."

Louisa looks at him across the table, level and unashamed. Ben finds himself shaking his head and tries to pretend there's only one thing he's denying. The simplest thing. "It's not wrong, Lou. It never is. You're going to die peacefully."

"I know." She says it with love, as if she's comforting him. "I know. But I was done, Ben. After that—after everything—I was just... done. And with the world the way it was..." She watches him with such kindness. "How was I supposed to die peacefully?"

Her softness, her steadiness, her calm—it's too much, too jarring when he thinks about what she's *saying*. Ben casts about for anything else to look at; his gaze falls to her throat. The dull gleam of her *V* isn't there, and he realizes with a jolt that she's taken it off. The thought of her without it is shocking, even—somehow—obscene. He tries to picture her wearing a *P* instead. It's impossible. "You tried to make yourself a Violent."

"Nobody knew I wasn't. The way I acted, the things I did—the suicide runs I volunteered for—everybody just assumed I was." Her eyes shutter; her voice goes hard. "The luckiest goddamn Violent ever, because no matter how many times I walked into caving-in buildings and horde-infested slaughterhouses that killed the fuck out of everyone I was with, I always walked back out. I figured it out eventually: no matter what I did, it wasn't ever going to work, because of course the machine wasn't wrong. It's never wrong. My mom had been at war with her body for years; of course she died a violent death. And I wasn't going to die by walking willingly into death traps, because that wasn't me being peaceful. That was me wanting it too much."

There's fever heat buzzing through his head. His fingers are freezing. He wants to sleep and start over in the morning. Start over the way they should have the moment they walked through the gate. The moment they became, finally, safe.

Ben has never actively wanted to die. Not even on the worst days. Not even after Joseph, because after Joseph, there was Louisa. "Louisa..."

"I can't die violently, and I can't be at peace surrounded by Violents. But a place like this..." She turns her attention back to the apple, unfolds her hands, and picks it up again, squeezes it lightly. "It's different here. Out there, it's one or two Peacefuls in with a bunch of Violents; that's how everybody around you dies and dies and dies, and you do nothing but survive." She looks at him again, and there's sympathy in her eyes, and yes, Ben knows how that feels and wishes he didn't. "But here," she goes on, putting down the apple and reaching out, clasping her dry, steady hands around his shaking ones, "here, with lots of Peacefuls in one place—that's a centralized target. That's a bomb, or something painlessly toxic in the water supply, or, hell, a suicide pact." She smiles and looks so *happy*. "That's how we die."

Louisa sleeps easy that night, deep and still.

Ben watches, wide-eyed and anxious, 'til dawn.

Story by M.J. Leitch
Illustration by Tyson Hesse

OLD AGE

I T'S NOT EASY WATCHING HER LIKE THIS, her face bloated and yellowish from the last chemo treatment, disfigured to the point where her features only barely resemble his wife of five years. Her eyes are the same, though, somehow darker and deeper but hers. He watches her from the kitchen table, where she told him with a bright smile to sit and wait for his breakfast. She hasn't stepped into the kitchen in five weeks. He lets her cook this morning because he thinks it makes her feel alive and strong. But he winces when the knife slips from her hand while she's cutting the bread. The blade rattles on the tiles when she picks it up with a trembling hand, grabbing the counter with the other for support.

She's only thirty-three, he thinks.

She smiles sheepishly over her shoulder. He smiles back. She will be fine. The doctors say the treatment is going well, the tumor is shrinking, and after another treatment it should be gone altogether. He believes them, but his certainty doesn't stem from the doctors' skills.

They agreed not to do the test when the machines first came out years back. But then they didn't live in this cancer-infested uncertainty, he thinks, although he knows he's only trying to justify his actions. He slipped a vial of her blood taken for the lab tests and went downtown where there was a machine in an alley by the butcher's shop. When he got her prediction that said OLD AGE, he was so relieved and euphoric that he placed his finger in the slot too. His said HEART FAILURE. He never told her what he'd done.

"Here," she says as she puts a plate of greasy scrambled eggs in front of him. "Let's not worry about cholesterol today, eh?" Her face beams with hope.

"Let's not," he says, and smiles.

Story by Brigita Orel
Illustration by Braden Lamb

FURNACE

IN THE QUAD OUTSIDE THE ARCHAEOLOGY CENTER of Pnn-kiai, two students, male and female, were making love. They were probably doing it to reproduce; Mrrkli could smell their fertility hormones.

He sent the command to his olfactory cortex to tune out that distracting scent, though he chose not to turn down his sense of smell as a whole. When in unfamiliar surroundings, he preferred to run all his senses at full enhancement. The Pnn-kiai archeology center wasn't exactly unfamiliar, but he hadn't been here since he had completed work on the last discovery, the one that had defined his career.

Mrrkli wondered, as he passed the couple on his way into the building, whether they had a license for offspring or had gotten the necessary adjustments on the black market. His home country wasn't nearly as crowded as Pnn-kiai, but even there, people were engineered sterile from birth and were only rarely granted fertility devices. He found it hard to believe that reproduction would be permitted in a nation this overpopulated, but it seemed equally far-fetched that any couple would be stupid enough to conceive illegally in the middle of the quad like that.

He wondered if he should report it to Skeeiao when they met but decided against it. That wasn't her department, and she had much more important things on her mind.

And here she was, just inside the portal to the building; she had probably heard him coming all the way from her lab. Her enhanced

hearing was legendary, as much so as her archaeological instincts. She stood there welcoming him in, asking him about his trip, offering him food and drink that he declined. Her pale-skinned skull was oblong and shining, her hands and body slender, her feet large and thin like the flippers of some extinct sea animal.

She wore a thick necklace with a faceted black stone, and a brown and gold belt, and even a wide orange sash around her hips, actually going down far enough to cover her groin. Wearing any garment besides jewelry was a fashion statement only an archaeologist would make: a nod of respect to ancient civilizations that had needed clothing to protect themselves from the weather (or perhaps for some other reason … there had been traces of clothing found with remains of societies that seemed to have had no climatological need for it, so there must be more to that ancient tradition than modern people knew).

"I invited you because you're the one I trust most," she told him. "Also probably the only one who'll believe me. Also probably the only one anyone else will believe, if you write the news release."

She spoke in her native Pnn-kiai language, a tonal language with fewer clicks and more whistles and trills than Mrrkli was used to. Not that it mattered to him. Every archaeologist, even one like Mrrkli who hailed from the backwaters of Ksss, had enough linguistic implants to speak the languages of Pnn-kiai, Vinch, Evevev, and Sisithi, the four corners of the world as far as ancient ruins were concerned.

"I'll try to believe you," he promised, "though I'll need to examine it myself before I can let myself hope that it's really—"

"Oh, it is from the Vesk-chh civilization. I can tell you that without any doubt in the world." She made an amused face, with her four front teeth showing and the inner two rings of her irises dilated. In the Pnn-kiai language, the sentence she had just spoken was an aural palindrome: recorded and played backward, it would sound the same. Skeeiao had always been a lover of wordplay.

Mrrkli wondered what had passed for wordplay, or humor at all, in the civilizations that he and Skeeiao studied, the worlds of people from millions of years ago.

The two of them had worked together on the first discovery of artifacts from the Vesk-chh people—named for the coastline where their only known remains had been found—and although Mrrkli's name was more famous in connection with that discovery, Skeeiao had always had the greater ambition and curiosity. She might have done it; it might be true. Maybe, just maybe, today, the Vesk-chh treasure trove would finally contain more than just a fossilized skeleton, some weapons, and a data disk full of erotica. He would know soon enough.

And then they were in the lab, and it was there, black and cylindrical and half as tall as Mrrkli, standing on top of the half-circular white lab table, with a steady stream of nanites creeping out of it and swarming across the table's polished polymer. Skeeiao had used the nanites to restore the artifact, of course, crawling inside it in swarms and patching holes, rebuilding the spots where wires and circuits had crumbled apart, bridging the gaps in this piece of ancient history...

"It's a machine, isn't it?" Mrrkli said.

"Yes," Skeeiao replied, her voice soft. "A machine from the Vesk-chh civilization."

Mrrkli followed her eyes as they traced over the object's surface: the single small round hole, the horizontal slot below it, and the metal plaque above them both, embossed with symbols both foreign and familiar.

"You were right," he said. "It's the same language. It's Vesk-chh. You were right."

"So you have the machine working?" said Chiaiass, running his hands all over it without even asking. Skeeiao winced but couldn't tell him to leave it alone. Chiaiass was the highest financial adviser in Pnn-kiai, the one who granted the archaeological center its funding.

"Yes, sir," Skeeiao said. "It's working. At least, there's no reason it wouldn't be, although we're not sure yet what it does."

She took a breath. Mrrkli watched her. She was wearing clothing again today, an entire robe, blue and thickly quilted, although it was open in the front. She seemed anxious, as well she might. The two of them had just sent out the news release, and all the archaeologists and archaeology patrons of Pnn-kiai were full of questions, crowding to her door. But she shouldn't have to worry about Chiaiass—this was undoubtedly a discovery worthy of funding.

"See," she went on, "it had been preserved in some kind of vault, a lot like the one where we found the other Vesk-chh artifacts, and actually very close to the original site. A strong vault. Ruins of it were still around the find when we dug it up, and it may have protected the machine until as recently as last millennium. The machine itself—well, it's millions of years old, at least as old as the other artifacts, but it's amazingly well preserved. The nanites had enough of the original design to work with; they had no trouble filling the gaps."

She looked to Chiaiass for appreciation of her word joke—this time a mathematically interesting melody formed by the different tonal pitches of her words—but he showed no reaction. She cringed and went on.

"We were able to adapt its power cord to take energy from our own reactors. There's also a reservoir inside the machine, where we found traces of some black pigment, and we were able to synthesize enough to fill the reservoir. There's a—a roller of some kind, which seems intended to push out sheets of some thin material. Whatever that material was, it's long since rotted away, but we replaced it with small sheets of fabric. My hypothesis is that the machine somehow prints the pigment onto the fabric."

"And that." Chiaiass touched the embossed plaque on the machine. "What does that writing say? Is it writing?"

Skeeiao looked at Mrrkli—this was where they both had to explain. "It is writing," she began. "It's the same language as the Disk from our last find."

The Disk. Mrrkli trilled softly at the memory. After the first set of relics had been found, the two of them had spent months figuring out how to use lasers and computers to read the data contained in that flat, round silver object. Then they had spent years deciphering it. It had turned out to be a collection of erotic stories, and much of their meaning was still uncertain, since it was such a small sample (and the only known sample of that language, until now). A few illustrations had also been on the Disk, which had aided in the translation, but not enough to know everything.

"It says," Mrrkli began, and then he spelled out the message on the plaque, using the names that he and Skeeiao had made up for the symbols, back when they had first studied the language. The names were based on the symbols' appearance, nothing more. There was no knowing what the Vesk-chh had called them... or how, or even if, they had been pronounced aloud.

Then he translated into the Pnn-kiai language: "Find out how your DEATH will happen."

Chiaiass contracted all the rings of his irises. "And what is 'DEATH'? You just spelled it out again. Do you not know its meaning?"

Mrrkli closed his eyes and scanned through his mental database; the entire Disk had been downloaded into his mind long ago. "The collection of erotica on the Disk only mentions that word twice. In both cases it is preceded by words meaning 'the little.'"

"The little DEATH?" Chiaiass seemed mocking as he spelled it out, mispronouncing a few of the made-up symbol names. "In what contexts?"

Skeeiao spoke up. "In contexts that suggest that it's one of many terms the Vesk-chh used for the concept of... orgasm."

"Orgasm." Chiaiass tilted his large tapered head, staring at the machine as if his vision were so enhanced that he could see inside it and steal its secrets. "So, if a DEATH, little or otherwise, is an orgasm, then we can assume this machine is meant to predict how one's orgasm will happen. A virility idol of some sort? Or a computer to teach people of the Vesk-chh how they could find their greatest sexual satisfaction?"

"We still need to examine it further," Skeeiao said, "but—"

Chiaiass reached over to the machine again, and Skeeiao looked murderous. Mrrkli tensed. People nowadays might not be as fragile as the ancient people the two of them had studied, but anyone could still be killed, if there was a great enough destructive force to tear apart the body, and a skilled enough hacker to erase the personality backups. Skeeiao looked ready to do both to Chiaiass, but she held back, even as he touched her machine again, violated it, stuck his forefinger right into its little mysterious hole.

And winced, and pulled away, his finger dripping with the blood-and-nanite mixture that was supposed to stay inside his veins. "It cut me!" he cried, then stilled, as the rollers behind the slot began to move, pushing out one of the sheets of fabric. A word was printed on it in black pigment.

It read, ROCK.

"What does that mean?" Chiaiass said, shaking his finger as if that would speed up the nanite repair.

"When mentioned on the Disk," Mrrkli answered, "that word is always used in some construct like 'hard as a ROCK.' Usually referring to male arousal. But the Vesk-chh seem to have had a tendency toward exaggeration, so ROCK is probably not something of the exact same hardness as any part of their bodies. More likely, it's just the hardest thing they could think of."

"Vai-tilki?" offered Chiaiass.

Mrrkli lowered his eyes. Chiaiass was an idiot; the substance called vai-tilki had been invented within his own lifetime. Yet one must be polite to the chief financial adviser.

"Possibly," said Mrrkli, his eyes still downcast, "although I'm not sure if they were aware of vai-tilki."

Chiaiass stared at his hand, at the machine, at the word ROCK. "I've seen enough for today," he said.

After he left, Skeeiao and Mrrkli had a panic/rage attack together. Skeeiao ran around the room, alternately shouting curses about Chiaiass and shuddering in fear that the cut from the machine, or its printed word, had offended him, that she wouldn't be getting any more funding after all. Mrrkli was just shaky and uneasy, sitting in a corner too weak from anxiousness to move, although he couldn't figure out exactly why.

They didn't expect Chiaiass back again for a long time, but in fact he returned the next day. "A most extraordinary thing has happened," he said. His irises and pupils were fully expanded and his skin was flushed with emotion, and for once it did not seem to be a bad emotion.

"I went home yesterday, wondering how the machine had come to the conclusion that I could be brought to orgasm by—by vai-tilki, or some similarly hard substance. I thought of the machine's original makers, with their fully organic bodies and their primitive culture, and yet I realized that they are, after all, our ancestors; that somewhere inside you and me, traces of their instincts, their drives, their sexuality, must remain."

Skeeiao looked at him out of the corners of her eyes, giving most of her attention to her computer console. Mrrkli's eyes were cast down in respect, but he said nothing.

"And on a whim," Chiaiass went on, "simply on a whim, I synthesized a thin rod of vai-tilki, and asked my mate to touch me with it. She tapped it gently against my backside. And—it was the strangest thing—the sensation of being tapped by a substance so hard and strong—it aroused me. I asked her to slap me harder with it, and—well, I must say, I have more confidence in this machine's accuracy now than I had expected to have."

Skeeiao just stared at him. "So you want to stick your finger in the machine again?"

Chiaiass made a mild negative gesture, his hands pointing downward and his irises contracted. "Perhaps later, but now I have an offer that you both should find attractive. I would like to make this machine open to the public. Sex sells. I am sure it always has, even a million years ago; that was undoubtedly why the Vesk-chh put so much effort into building, and then protecting, this machine. It is a fount of money. People will come from all over the world to pay for its predictions. It will enrich you, and me, and the whole nation of Pnn-kiai."

"But we don't know what else it might print," Mrrkli objected. "Not all words in the Vesk-chh language have known meanings."

"It would be enough," insisted Chiaiass. "To touch a sexual relic of prehistory, to know that someone a million years ago had an idea of what your own blood might say of your sexual preferences—oh yes. Even if they could not understand what it told them, people would pay."

"It's a priceless artifact!" Skeeiao shouted. "Daily use would wear it out again."

"If your nanites could restore it after a million years, then they can continue restoring it," Chiaiass said. "And both of you will become richer than you could imagine."

It was viral. It was spreading through the population like a joke or a new game or a video: the ancient machine that could tell you how best to enliven your sex life. The line of people waiting to use it went on as far as Mrrkli and Skeeiao could see.

"Well, at least," said Mrrkli, as they worked late into the night, "at least we have money now."

"But we didn't agree to this," Skcciao said, slumped onto folded arms. "He never gave us a choice."

Mrrkli looked down. "But we have a choice now. Others will look after the machine. We can go, leave this place, do whatever we want."

"All I ever wanted was to learn and study," Skeeiao said.

"Then do that. Do as much of it as you like. You have enough money to fund yourself." Mrrkli sat close. Skeeiao looked vulnerable, wearing a scarf around her head and sashes around her breasts and groin beneath her open robe, as if clothing would protect her.

"Except I don't want to anymore," she said. "When anything I discover can be bought and sold and made into a sex toy for the masses, what's the point?"

They stayed in Pnn-kiai taking care of the machine because they didn't know what else to do.

The machine's fame spread all through the nation. People

claimed to have found their true sexual orientations through it, or their soul mates, or simply the greatest pleasure they had ever experienced. Memoirs and songs were written about it. It had fan clubs everywhere. Chiaiass had been right: sex might be a natural bodily function, as ordinary as eating and sleeping, but it held people's attention much, much more strongly. Lovers were seen everywhere, incorporating stranger and stranger objects into their lovemaking: fruits and vegetables, cleaning supplies, computers. Most of them even seemed to be enjoying themselves.

Mrrkli worked overtime translating the results for eager customers, or, sometimes, telling them he couldn't translate their results, that the words weren't mentioned on the Disk. It didn't matter. When a mysterious word was printed, it only added to the fascination. There were people offering all sorts of made-up possible meanings, and even people inventing new sex toys and naming them after the words the machine printed.

Even when meanings were clear, the machine was often wrong. A man whose slip said HEART complained when he was unable to become sexually excited through cardiovascular training, cardiopulmonary resuscitation, or even eating the hearts of animals. But for many, it was a self-fulfilling prophecy: just thinking that something could arouse you was enough to become aroused. It was the premise on which aphrodisiacs had worked throughout history, Skeeiao said, looking through notes from other archaeological studies. It was nonsense and it was useless, but it worked.

One day, the woman of the couple who had been trying to conceive in the quad came in to be tested. Mrrkli watched from the window in his office as she inched to the front of the line, shifting her weight from foot to foot as others received their slips ahead of her.

Her mate was at her side but seemed uninterested in having his own sexual fortune told. He stood by tolerantly as she put her finger in the machine's hole and squeaked at the sharpness when it drew blood.

The machine dispensed her slip, and after looking it over several times, she ran to Mrrkli's window, dragging her mate by his hand. He slid the window open. She shoved the paper in his face.

It read PREGNANCY.

Mrrkli translated it into the Pnn-kiai language for her. "The meaning is very clear," he added. "In the stories on the Disk, the characters mentioned it often. Usually as something to avoid, but it happened to a few of them anyway."

The woman looked at her mate, the inner rings of her irises expanding in amusement. "Silly machine," she said, and they ran off.

Mrrkli saw them making love in the quad again and again, several times in the next few days, reeking of fertility, apparently sure that making a baby would bring her the greatest orgasm of her life. Mrrkli didn't think it would, and he still didn't think she was licensed to have a baby, but he didn't care. Nothing mattered to him and Skeeiao anymore. The dark feeling that they had sold themselves for money hung over their heads, making it impossible to enjoy anything that their money bought.

And then it happened. The young woman succeeded in getting pregnant. And the black-market fertility device she'd been using malfunctioned, destroyed her womb, destroyed her body faster than her nanites could repair it. She crumbled to dust in days. And— poor careless kid, careless enough to conceive illegally in public, careless enough to buy such a risky device in the first place—she hadn't even backed up her personality in years. The person she had been at that moment was lost forever, killed.

Then the other stories started coming out. A man whose prediction said ADULTERY had started cheating on his monogamous partner and found it so exciting that he decided the machine was right. He kept on doing it until the jealous mate of his illicit lover poisoned his nanites and erased his backups. A woman who had gotten EXPLOSION actually decided to set one off in her bedroom, of all things. She meant it to be small, yes, but she used too much of the explosive and blew up herself and her home with all her backup drives.

Finally, for the first time, the government seemed to regret funding the machine. The leading council of Pnn-kiai ruled that the machine was dangerous, that it was using the irresistible promise of sex to lure people into putting their lives in jeopardy.

Even Chiaiass, the first person to use the machine, came out against it. Fans of the machine called him a traitor, and one day he was found crushed by a boulder on the route of his daily walk, with all his backups mysteriously missing.

The leading council struck back, arresting a large number of suspects, and that was the beginning of the end. Pnn-kiai fell into civil war. Freedom fighters, striving for the freedom to use the machine, and using that grievance as a platform for all their other grievances, fought bitter battles against the government and its allies.

The military built great hot ovens, ovens of execution, and threw rebels into them along with their backup drives, melting their bodies and minds into nothing. It was the surest way to kill people who were as strong as people were these days...and the more it was done, the less strong people seemed.

Mrrkli and Skeeiao were hunted, simply because they had discovered and restored the machine in the first place. They went into hiding in a deep vault built by their admirers. The machine sat inside with them, the one condition of their protection. Skeeiao had wanted to destroy it, but their fans had refused to build the vault and protect them unless they could protect the machine as well.

The two of them sat alone together for months, eating dry rations and staring at the machine. Skeeiao wore long cloaks with laced-up robes underneath them, boots on her feet, heavy caps on her head.

"Did you ever want to use the machine?" Mrrkli asked her one night. "Were you ever curious, what it might say about you?"

"No," Skeeiao said. "I think that was the only thing I've ever not been curious about."

"But I have, sometimes," Mrrkli admitted. "I never thought it was worth the trouble of waiting in the line, but I was a little bit curious."

"Well, you can use it now, if you want," Skeeiao said, huddling in her cloak. "It has one strip left in it, and enough pigment to print once."

Mrrkli stood up and went to the machine. What else was there to do? It was the only entertainment left to them, this relic of a million-year-old civilization, a civilization that he imagined teeming with machines and pornography—it would fit with the fact that one sample of each was all that remained of their language. Were the Vesk-chh really so different from his own people?

He put his finger in the hole, felt its bite. The last strip of fabric printed. It said FURNACE.

"What is that?" murmured Skeeiao, too listless to consult her mental database.

"The Disk mentioned it once," said Mrrkli. "It said, 'Her warmth was like a FURNACE, engulfing his whole body.'"

"So maybe it was a piece of clothing," Skeeiao suggested. "Something they put around their bodies to keep warm." The inner rings of her irises fluctuated weakly: she had made a tonal pun with the words "keep warm," but it wasn't a very clever one.

Mrrkli sat down, nursing his bleeding finger. The machine was worthless. Clothing did not arouse him.

But—maybe it wasn't so wrong. Clothing, in and of itself, directly, could never arouse him. But the only place he ever saw clothing was on Skeeiao, the one who had called him when she trusted no one else, the one who had always been beside him.

And now they were alone together in the world, with nothing but each other. He could see the need in her, the need for closeness in the face of despair, even though her body was wrapped up in layers and layers of fabric. At the center, inside the clothing, was the person he now realized could probably give him his most powerful orgasm, his greatest sexual satisfaction—for what else could be as sexually satisfying as love?

The machine might be right, after all.

He leaned close to her, and she leaned back, and together they began taking off her clothing.

Story by Erika Hammerschmidt
Illustration by Trudy Cooper

EDITORS' NOTE

THE IDEA OF THE MACHINE OF DEATH first appeared in an episode of *Dinosaur Comics*, written and published by Ryan North (who is also one of the editors of this book). Death predictions, of course, are an ancient storytelling trope. But this particular comic strip from December 5, 2005, is the first time that this particular method of predicting deaths was described—the machine, the blood test, the print-out predictions.

In October 2010, the first book based on this idea was published. It was an illustrated anthology of thirty-four stories called, simply, *Machine of Death: A Collection of Stories About People Who Know How They Will Die.* That book went on to be a #1 bestseller on Amazon, to sell more than 27,000 English-language copies in its first two years of publication, and to be translated into eight more languages.

Fast-forward to now, and you're holding in your hands the second book in the series, *This Is How You Die: Stories of the Inscrutable,*

Infallible, Inescapable Machine of Death. Far from being a retread of the first book, this is an expansion in every way. There are more words, more art, more diversity among the stories. We challenged the writers for the second book to take us places that the Machine of Death had never gone before, and they delivered.

Thinking back to the very first appearance of that *Dinosaur Comics* strip, and the first conversation that the three of us had about an anthology (with help and encouragement from many other fans of the comic), through soliciting stories from eager writers worldwide (twice!) and all the way up to now—it's incredible how far we've come. We couldn't have predicted any of this, but we hope the future holds many more surprises in store for us.

Thanks for being a part of this amazing journey!

LEARN MORE AT:

HACHETTEBOOKGROUP.COM

MACHINEOFDEATH.NET

ALSO, WE HAVE A GAME:

Machine of Death: The Game of Creative Assassination

MACHINE OF DEATH.NET/GCA

RYAN NORTH

The original Machine of Death Development Team poses with a prototype circuit board, prediction card, and diagnostic machine—nicknamed "Moddy."
Palo Alto, CA. August 1982

(L to R) Pat Finneman, Lisa Markowitz, Tim "Bomber" Michaels, Franklin Patterson, Rich Pardlo, and Brendan Darrow. Photo by Kevin McShane.

CONTRIBUTORS

Editors

MATTHEW BENNARDO is the writer of more than thirty-five published short stories. His work has appeared in markets such as *Asimov's Science Fiction, Lightspeed* magazine, *Strange Horizons, Beneath Ceaseless Skies,* and others. This anthology is the second he has edited. He lives in Cleveland, Ohio, but people anywhere can find him online at MBENNARDO.COM or on Twitter at @MBENNARDO.

DAVID MALKI ! is the author of the comic strip *Wondermark,* a gag strip created entirely from nineteenth century woodcuts and engravings, AKA *a collaboration with the dead.* In 2009, the *Wondermark* collection *Beards of Our Forefathers* was nominated for the Eisner Award—the highest honor in comics—for "Best Humor Publication." It's possible that this was a clerical error. He lives in Los Angeles with his wife, Nikki, a special-effects makeup artist. Read his comics at WONDERMARK.COM, or use the Internet website "Twitter" to find him at @MALKI.

RYAN NORTH is the author of *Dinosaur Comics,* which you can read at DINOSAURCOMICS.COM. He writes the bestselling *Adventure Time* comics published by BOOM! Studios, and his choose-your-own-path version of *Hamlet,* called *To Be or Not to Be,* recently became the most funded publishing project ever on Kickstarter. You can check that out at HAMLETBOOK.COM! He lives in Toronto with his rad wife and sweet dog.

Authors

KAREN STAY AHLSTROM has written dozens of English adaptations for manga, several volumes of which landed on national bestseller lists. She also had an epic poem published in *Leading Edge Science Fiction and Fantasy*, the magazine for which she also served as Fiction Director. While working at the magazine she met her husband, Peter Ahlstrom, as well as the writers Brandon Sanderson and Dan Wells, for whom she now serves as an alpha reader. Karen lives in Utah raising three daughters as future lepidopterists.

LIZ ARGALL grew up in Canberra, China, and Australia. Her first real job was at a women's refuge and her last normal job was managing a circus. She writes love letters to inanimate objects and creates the sporadic webcomic *Things Without Arms and Without Legs*. LIZARGALL.COM

REBECCA BLACK has taught English in Japan, studied linguistics in New York, and is currently in Maryland studying math, so that she may have the luxury of spending her life showing people how beautiful mathematics is. In her spare time she muses about the use of language, designs websites and then rarely updates them (MYRIADBALLOONS .NET/REBECCA), sings along to Japanese pop songs, reads fiction aimed at twelve-year-olds, and laments not having more time to paint or write.

'NATHAN BURGOINE lives in Ottawa with his husband, Daniel. His short fiction appears in *Fool for Love, I Do Two, Saints + Sinners 2011: New Fiction from the Festival, Men of the Mean Streets, Boys of Summer, The Touch of the Sea, Night Shadows,* and *Mortis Operandi*. His non-fiction appears in *I Like It Like That* and *5x5* literary magazine. His first novel, *Light*, is forthcoming from Bold Strokes Books. You can find him online at REDROOM.COM/MEMBER/NATHAN-BURGOINE.

DALISO CHAPONDA is a Malawian writer and stand-up comedian whose fiction has appeared in publications such as *Ellery Queen,*

Apex Magazine, and the first *Machine of Death* anthology. His last one-man show, "Laughrica," got him in trouble with the Malawian censorship board. He cowrote a radio play called "When the Laughter Stopped" inspired by these experiences. It will air on BBC Radio 4 in 2013. DALISO.COM

BILL CHERNEGA is best known for being John Chernega's brother, but he's also a picture editor, digital asset manager, screenwriter, programmer, and whatever other crazy thing he can think of doing. He lives with his amazing wife and two awesome kids in Los Angeles, and you can find out about his latest projects at BILLCHERNEGA.COM. His death prediction card simply reads, "Robot."

JOHN CHERNEGA is an English professor in southeastern Minnesota, where he lives with his awesome wife, Jenna, and their two amazing sons. John's first published work was "Almond" from the first volume of *Machine of Death.* His hobbies include singing, playing board games, and saving Christmas. CHERNEGA.COM

RYAN ESTRADA is an artist/adventurer who travels the world making comics, videos, and trouble. He is the author of the graphic novels *Aki Alliance, The Kind, Plagued,* and the short "Mystical Monkey" from *Flight: Volume 4.* He loves saying yes to random new experiences just in case he ever needs to write a story about them, so he knew that buying those illegal goods in that Mumbai black market and wandering through all those riots would pay off one day! RYANESTRADA.COM

TOM FRANCIS plays and writes about video games for a living at *PC Gamer,* and in his spare time he's making one called *Gunpoint.* He writes about that, entertainment, happiness, and plane seats on his blog, PENTADACT.COM.

ERIKA HAMMERSCHMIDT is the author of *Born on the Wrong Planet,* a memoir about autism, and *Kea's Flight,* a science fiction novel about parrots, robots, and embryos in space. She has a webcomic called *Abby and Norma* and lives in Minnesota with her husband, John. ERIKAHAMMERSCHMIDT.COM

ADA HOFFMANN's fiction has appeared in *Imaginarium 2012: The Best Canadian Speculative Writing.* She lives a nerdy, awkward life in southern Ontario and is currently taking a break in between different grad schools. She is online at ADA-HOFFMANN.LIVEJOURNAL.COM and on Twitter as @XASYMPTOTE.

CHANDLER KAIDEN is an Affiliate Member of the Horror Writers Association (HWA). Previous short fiction has appeared in the anthology *The Mothman Files,* as well as a number of small press magazines. He lives and works in the Midwest.

RHIANNON KELLY was not old enough to sign a legally binding contract when she sold her story to the *Machine of Death* people. She is now reveling in such adult rights and studying English at Cal Poly SLO. You can find her daily bite-sized pieces of writing at 55WORD STORIES.TUMBLR.COM.

HOLLAN LANE lives in Spokane, Washington, and writes stories and books for a living under various pen names. She writes weird flash fiction and short stories, epic YA space operas, and gay erotic romance—mixing genres how she sees fit. In her spare time, she collects vintage pins and dresses like she lives in the 1950s. THEVINTAGEUNICORN.BLOGSPOT.COM

M.J. LEITCH lives nocturnally in Ontario, Canada. She enjoys reading, writing, and engaging critically with TV shows that may or may not deserve such attention. She can be reached at MJ.LYNHURST @GMAIL.COM.

MARTIN LIVINGS is a West Australian writer who has had more than eighty short stories published in a variety of magazines and anthologies both locally and internationally. His first novel, *Carnies*, was published in Australia in 2006 by Hachette Livre, and his first collection of short fiction, *Living with the Dead*, was published by Dark Prints Press in 2012. MARTINLIVINGS.COM

MARLEIGH NORTON is a game design consultant currently residing in Boston. She occasionally gets tricked into writing things. Don't read this book, it will only encourage her. WEB.MIT.EDU/MARLEIGH

BRIGITA OREL has had her stories and poems published in *Rose & Thorn Journal, Cantaraville, Autumn Sky Poetry, Islet,* and other print and online magazines and collections. She was nominated for the Pushcart Prize and the Micro Award. She studied writing at Swinburne, Australia, and she lives and creates in Slovenia. BSOULFLOWERS.BLOGSPOT.COM

GEORGE PAGE III is a Texan who writes fiction, exports heavy equipment to Asia, and bounces at a nightclub. His short stories have appeared in a number of anthologies, and he wrote the business novel *Under the Gun*. He lives with three dogs and a turtle—all of whom are worthless with dictation and editing. More info can be found at TGAPGEORGE.COM.

SARAH PAVIS is a mechanical engineer and writer who wants to play board games with you. SARAHPAVIS.COM

D.L.E. ROGER is Ian Stoner. Ian earned his B.A. from St. John's College in 1999, and his Ph.D. in philosophy from the University of Minnesota in 2011. WWW.TC.UMN.EDU/~STONO235/

TOBY W. RUSH is a professor of music theory by day and an author by night, or at least whenever the kids are in bed and only after the dishes are done. He lives in Centerville, Ohio, where the drivers are friendly and the Wi-Fi is strong. By the time you are reading this, he hopes to have scraped something together worth discovering at TOBYRUSH.COM.

RICHARD SALTER is a British writer and editor living near Toronto, Canada. He has had more than twenty short stories published and has edited two short story anthologies, most recently the shared-world collection *World's Collider*, a mosaic novel about the end of the world. His debut horror novel, *The Patchwork House*, should be available to buy before the end of 2013. Check for updates at RICHARDSALTER.COM.

KYLE SCHOENFELD took a westbound train one day and ended up in Seattle, where he recently finished graduate school. This is his first published story, but you can follow future projects at KYLESCHOEN FELD.WORDPRESS.COM.

GORD SELLAR is a Canadian author and screenwriter who was born in Malawi and spent more than a decade working in South Korea. He attended Clarion West in 2006 and was a finalist for the John W. Campbell Award for Best New Writer in 2009. For more information on his writing, see his website at GORDSELLAR.COM.

GRACE SEYBOLD is a science fiction writer and poet. She lives in Montreal, where she spends her time working as a copy editor and waiting for her latent superpowers to manifest.

JOHN TAKIS is a part-time librarian and freelance writer, specializing in film music journalism. His short fiction has appeared in several volumes of *Star Trek: Strange New Worlds* and in the anthology *Professor Challenger: New Worlds, Lost Places*. JOHNTAKIS.COM

ED TURNER is a writer, RPG designer, and academic with a scholarly interest in games and the interaction between mechanics and narratives. He lives in the Seattle area with his wife and their hamster. THOUGHTCHECKGAMES.WORDPRESS.COM

REN WAROM is a writer of the strange, dark, and bizarre, residing in Middle England. Ren's stories are published here and there, and her novels are represented by the fabulous Jennifer Udden of the Donald Maass Literary Agency. RENWAROMSUMWELT.WORDPRESS.COM

Illustrators

NICK ABADZIS is a British cartoonist, writer, graphic novelist, and visual and editorial consultant of international renown. As an author, he has been honored with various awards including the prestigious Eisner for his graphic novel *Laika*. He lives and works in Brooklyn, NY. For more info, portfolios, and links, please visit NICKABADZIS.MY-EXPRESSIONS.COM.

GRAHAM ANNABLE is a Canadian cartoonist living in Portland, Oregon. When he's not busy creating new *Grickle* comics and animation, he spends his time working as a storyboard artist at Laika Entertainment. GRICKLE.COM

C.BILLADEAU is an illustrator working out of Chicago, variably spending her time freelancing her skills or drawing a graphic novel. Portfolio and prints of her work are available at BILLET-DEAUX.COM.

SAM BOSMA is an illustrator living and working out of a burrow in Baltimore, Maryland. He works largely on editorial and book illustrations and more specifically, the kind of illustrations with monsters and swords and stuff. SBOSMA.COM

TONY CLIFF is a contributor to the *Flight* series of comic anthologies, has been nominated for Shuster, Harvey, and Eisner awards, and is the author of *Delilah Dirk and the Turkish Lieutenant*, a light-hearted adventure tale available at delilahdirk.com. He owes his draftsmanship skills to a series of teachers who emphasized strong fundamentals, hard work, good manners, proper nutrition, and regular flossing. He internets at TONYCLIFF.COM.

SHARI CHANKHAMMA is a comic artist, illustrator, reluctant writer, and technology enthusiast. SHARII.COM

ANTHONY CLARK is a cartoonist and illustrator from Indiana. You can see more of his drawings at NEDROID.COM.

TRUDY COOPER, as a child, was annoyed that Betty's and Veronica's skirts didn't ride up when they bent over. She now illustrates the dirty webcomic *Oglaf.* OGLAF.COM

MIKE DAWSON's graphic novels include *Freddie & Me: A Coming-of-Age (Bohemian) Rhapsody* (Bloomsbury USA), *Ace-Face: The Mod with the Metal Arms* (AdHouse), and *Troop 142* (Secret Acres). He is also the cohost of the popular comics-related podcast, "The Ink Panthers Show!" His next book, *Angie Bongiolatti*, will be published by Secret Acres in late 2013. MIKEDAWSONCOMICS.COM

AARON DIAZ is an ex-professor and dread cartoonist. Creator of the science webcomic *Dresden Codak* and the art theory blog "Indistinguishable from Magic," he currently resides in Brooklyn. DRESDENCODAK.COM

ALEXANDRA "LEXXY" DOUGLASS is a freelance fantasy and sci-fi illustrator, working for clients all over the world from the comfort of her pajamas. In her free time, she plays video games and works on her pet project, *The Cloud Factory.* ALEXANDRA-DOUGLASS.COM

BECKY DREISTADT is a painter and comic artist living in Los Angeles. She mostly works with her partner Frank on the hand-painted webcomic *Tiny Kitten Teeth*, the vintage-style children's book series *Tigerbuttah*, and the 151-painting project Capture Creatures. Becky likes animals, old cartoons, and Bavarian folk art. BECKYDREISTADT.COM

ALICE DUKE is an illustrator and concept artist. She has also illustrated several comics for anthologies, including *The Graphic Canon* Volumes 1 & 2 (Seven Stories Press), *The Lovecraft Anthology* Volume 1 (Self Made Hero) and *Nelson* (Blank Slate Books). Find her online at ALICE-DUKE.COM.

MEREDITH GRAN is a freelance cartoonist, animator, and writer from Brooklyn, New York. She spends a lot of time taking pictures of her dog. OCTOPUSPIE.COM

KC GREEN is currently possibly on the East Coast drawing comics and stuff. He might, however, be on the West Coast still drawing a bunch, but possibly not as many, comics as he used to. Wherever he is, you can be sure he is second-guessing his every move. KCGREENDOTCOM.COM

DUSTIN HARBIN is a cartoonist and illustrator living in Charlotte, North Carolina. He has never died before. More information, comics, and even more information at DHARBIN.COM.

TYSON HESSE has a college degree in who cares from the school of whatever. He's animated characters on video games like *Skullgirls* and illustrated on comic books like *Bravest Warriors*. He has two comics of his own: *Boxer Hockey* and *Diesel*. The Machine has predicted he will die before he finishes either of them. BOXERHOCKEY.COM/TYSON

CLAIRE HUMMEL grew up in Los Angeles, went to school in Rhode Island, and ended up in Seattle, working as an associate production designer for Microsoft Studios. When she isn't drawing art for video games, she spends time with her two boa constrictors and tries not to think too much about what her Machine reading would be. Preferably not "SNAKES." SHOOMLAH.COM

INDIGO KELLEIGH is an illustrator living in Portland, Oregon. His latest projects and interests are tracked online at LUNARBISTRO.COM.

BRADEN LAMB is a Boston-based illustrator. He and his wife, Shelli, are the series artists for the *Adventure Time* and *Ice Age* comics, as well as some self-published comics that are less lucrative. BRADENLAMB.COM

LES MCCLAINE has worked as a librarian, a janitor, a record store clerk, and a Santa wrangler. He currently lives in Portland, Oregon, where he sits in a big room with his friends and draws cartoons all day. LESMCCLAINE.COM

CARLA SPEED MCNEIL is the author of the Eisner Award–winning science fiction series *Finder*. Her forthcoming book, recently serialized in *Dark Horse Presents*, is titled *Third World*. Her latest book, written by Sara Ryan, is called *Bad Houses* and will begin life as a webcomic any split second. Her websites: LIGHTSPEEDPRESS.COM and FINDERCOMICS.COM

KEVIN MCSHANE is a cartoonist, designer, actor, filmmaker, writer, photographer, and a dozen other things that won't impress you either. He can be found digitally at KEVINMCSHANE.ORG.

BEN MCSWEENEY is an illustrator, animator, and director on projects such as *The Way of Kings, PostHuman,* and *Darksiders II*. Find out more at INKTHINKER.NET.

CARLY MONARDO lives and draws in Brooklyn, New York, with her husband and their ridiculous dog. A graduate of the School of Visual Arts Animation Program, Carly has worked on projects as diverse as *Venture Bros.* and *Diana Vreeland: The Eye Has to Travel.* You can find more of her art at WHIRRINGBLENDER.COM.

DANICA NOVGORODOFF is a painter, comic book artist, writer, graphic designer and horse wrangler from Kentucky who currently lives in Brooklyn, New York. She has published three graphic novels: *A Late Freeze* (2006 winner of the Isotope Award), *Slow Storm* (2008, First Second Books), and *Refresh, Refresh* (included in Best American Comics 2011). Her fourth graphic novel, *The Undertaking of Lily Chen*, is forthcoming from First Second Books in 2014. DANICANOVGORODOFF.COM

EMILY PARTRIDGE is an illustrator/cartoonist from British Columbia, Canada. She is a cutie-pie. EMPARTRIDGE.COM

RYAN PEQUIN is a tiny man who lives in Canada and draws cartoons for a living somehow. If he had to choose a way to die, he would probably choose being carried off by an eagle and then eaten by its young. You can read his comics at THREEWORDPHRASE.COM if you want to do that.

RAMÓN PÉREZ is the multiple-award-winning cartoonist best known for his graphic novel adaptation of Jim Henson's *Tale of Sand* for Archaia Entertainment. Currently he's illustrating *Wolverine & the X-Men* for Marvel. Notable recent works also include *John Carter: The Gods of Mars, Captain America and the First Thirteen,* and *Deadpool Team-Up* for Marvel Comics, as well as his creator-owned endeavors *Butternutsquash* and *Kukuburi.* RAMONPEREZ.COM

MIKE PETERSON, aka Halcyon Snow, is suspiciously comfortable with nameless dread and gibbering horrors. Approach with caution. HALCYONSNOW.BLOGSPOT.COM

GREG RUTH is the Spectrum Award–winning artist and writer whose most recent projects include *Red Kite, Blue Kite* (with Ji-Li Jiang), *A Pirate's Guide to Recess* (with James Preller), *INDEH* (with Ethan Hawke) from Hyperion/ABC, and his latest creator-owned graphic novel from Scholastic/Graphix!, *The Lost Boy.* He lives in western Massachusetts with his wife and two boys. GREGTHINGS.COM

CHRIS SCHWEIZER is the cartoonist behind *The Crogan Adventures,* a historical fiction graphic novel series. He grew up in Kentucky and now lives with his wife and daughter outside of Atlanta, where he teaches comics at the Atlanta campus of the Savannah College of Art and Design. CROGANADVENTURES.BLOGSPOT.COM

KRIS STRAUB is the author of the comic strips *Chainsawsuit, Starslip,* and *Broodhollow.* He lives in Seattle, where he can be frequently seen on Penny Arcade TV. KRISSTRAUB.COM

LISSA TREIMAN was born in the city of Los Angeles and has never managed to leave it. After graduating CalArts with a degree in cartoons, she began working at Walt Disney Feature Animation in 2007. She's been storyboarding there ever since, contributing to films such as *Tangled* and *Wreck-it Ralph.* She loves dogs. All dogs. At the time of writing this, she still does not know how to ride a bicycle. LISSABT.BLOGSPOT.COM

LEELA WAGNER has made some choices that make it difficult to predict what her life will look like at the time of this volume's publication. She will certainly be in a time, in a place, drawing things and drinking tea. She would love to hear from you at LEELAWAGNER ART@GMAIL.COM.

DANA WULFEKOTTE is an animator and comic artist who lives with her two rabbits in Queens. She has worked on a variety of projects for clients like Nickelodeon, Fox, and PBS. In her spare time she makes ridiculous comics with Mike Cornnell, which you can read at LEADPAINTCOMICS.COM.

ACKNOWLEDGMENTS

This book wasn't going to happen. It wasn't even on the horizon, not even vaguely. We published one book about the Machine of Death in 2010, and that took us *years* to put together. When it was finally released, we dusted off our hands and said, "Finally, we're done."

But people *loved* the Machine. They loved the questions it rose, the stories it provoked unprompted into their imaginations, and the tantalizing possibilities it hinted at. So they—*you*, statistically— wanted to keep going. And we were overjoyed to jump in the driver's seat again.

So the first people we need to thank are the 1,705 writers from forty-six countries on seven continents who submitted stories for this book. We wish we could have published them all. (Well, most of them.) But we had to choose just a handful, and while it was a difficult task, we think we chose well. We also want to thank the 151 illustrators who submitted portfolios to us for consideration. It is your work that graces these pages.

Professionally, thanks are due to PJ Mark and his colleagues for tirelessly pushing this volume forward, and Ben Greenberg and his colleagues at Grand Central for taking things to the next level. When we retire to a globe-circling space-yacht we'll invite you both aboard.

The Machine of Death phenomenon owes a debt to the many people who have helped us do a variety of strange things over the past few years: Zachary Sigelko, Robynne Blume, Kris Straub, James Sutter, Michael Mohan, Brett Donnelly, and Chris Anderson are a few names among many. Thanks as well to Jenn, Katie, and Nikki, who have had to live with this thing now for as long as we have.

Finally, thank *you*. Thank you for reading our book. If it wasn't for you, we'd be off doing something else not half as fun. But instead, we did *this*, and we hope you like it as much as we do.